1831

D1286147

DREAM
BABY

DREAM
BABY

Bruce
McAllister

TOR

A TOM DOHERTY ASSOCIATES BOOK
NEW YORK

This is a work of fiction. All the characters and events portrayed in this book are fictitious, and any resemblance to real people or events is purely coincidental.

DREAM BABY

Copyright © 1989 by Bruce McAllister
All rights reserved, including the right to reproduce this book or portions thereof in any form.

A TOR BOOK
Published by Tom Doherty Associates, Inc.
49 West 24 Street
New York, NY 10010

First edition: October 1989
0 9 8 7 6 5 4 3 2 1

To Annie, Ben, Elizabeth, and Caroline

I feel I haven't said it, that there must be another story I've forgotten, one that could explain it.

— Jill Ann Mishkel, 24th Evacuation Hospital, Long Binh, 1970–71

To this day I'm trying to figure out why he died. You always remember one patient that struck you, and you remember forever and ever and you try to think why. Was it the way he looked, the way he spoke, did he look like somebody you knew, might have known years ago? He just hits something in you. For me, he will be the one.

— Kathleen Costello Cordova, 24th Evacuation Hospital, Long Binh, 1967–68

And you dream about those that you lost. You wonder if there wasn't something you could have done to save them.

— Archie "Joe" Biggers, 1984

It said on the death certificate "Da Nang." He was not killed at Da Nang. He was killed in the field. He was supposed to be in charge of the ammo dump and never leave base, but it was one of those days, I guess, that they needed men. He went out and was killed. He never came back.

When I received the letter, it said he was blown up in an ammunition dump. The night before, I had dreamt. I was carrying his daughter at the time, and I dreamt that he was killed. When I woke up and told my mother, she said, "Oh, it's your imagination. It's because you're pregnant. You're going to have a baby and you're dreaming all sorts of things." I said, "Nine o'clock, Mom. The doorbell's going to ring and it's going to be two officers." Well, at nine o'clock the doorbell rang and it was two officers. Three days later I had his daughter. She was late. She was supposed to be born on his birthday, but she was late.

 —Katherine Mary Cammarata, widow of Salvatore
 Peter "Sammy" Cammarata, 1984

The Army does not like the word "extermination" in connection with its spraying of the flocks with tergital, which strips the birds' protective oil, allowing them to die of exposure. A mimeographed report given out on request says that at Fort Campbell there was a pre-treatment population of about two million birds and the treatment resulted in a percentage reduction of 26%, mostly starlings, grackles, brown-headed cowbirds and redwinged blackbirds. The treatment was even more successful in Tennessee. There the pre-treatment population of three million was reduced by 83%.

 —*Los Angeles Times*, March 9, 1975

We're *all* niggers here.

 —Drill instructor, Parris Island, 1966

When I die, I know where I'm going to go. I'm not going to go to hell, and I'm not going to go to heaven. I'm going to Vietnam. J.L.'s going to be there, and Gallagher's going to be there, and Fats is going to be there, and Tennessee is going to be there, and the lieutenants too. A lot of the dudes I knew that died are going to be there. We'll be back walking down the old red dirt road and getting dusty and nasty and stuff, but we'll all be together.

—Stephen Gregory, 1965

Dream Baby, got me dreamin' sweet dreams
The whole day through
Dream Baby, got me dreamin' sweeet dreams
The night time too

—Cindy Walker, "Dream Baby (How Long Must I Dream)," 1962

Acknowledgments

I am indebted to the following authors and publishers for their willingness to allow quoted portions of their work to be used in this book. For story purposes these materials appear fictitiously in the files of John Bucannon; if these authors have kin here, however, it is Charles Narda, a man who listens, uses his profession as it was meant to be used and votes to end what another man began.

Text excerpt and graph from *True Americanism: Green Berets and War Resisters—A Study of Commitment*, by David Mark Mantell, copyright © 1974 Teachers College Press, Columbia University. All rights reserved.

Excerpts from *The War Trap*, by Bruce Bueno de Mesquita, copyright © 1981 Yale University Press. All rights reserved.

Excerpt from "Inequality and Insurgency: A Statistical Study of South Vietnam," by Edward J. Mitchell, in *World Politics*, April 1968, p. 424. Copyright © 1968 Princeton University Press. All rights reserved.

Excerpt from *Electromagnetic Theory*, by J. A. Stratton, copyright 1941 McGraw-Hill Book Co.

Excerpt from "Psychic Research and Modern Physics," by Russell Targ and Harold Puthoff, in *Psychic Exploration*, edited by Edgar

Mitchell, copyright © 1974 G. P. Putnam's Sons. All rights reserved.

Excerpt from *The ESP Experience: A Psychiatric Evaluation*, by Jan Ehrenwald, copyright © 1978 by Basic Books, Inc. All rights reserved.

Excerpt from *Mind Reach*, by Russell Targ and Harold Puthoff, copyright © 1977 Delacorte Press. All rights reserved.

Excerpts from "The Vietnam Era Prisoner of War: Precaptivity Personality and the Development of Psychiatric Illness," by Robert J. Ursano, in the *American Journal of Psychiatry* 138, no. 3, (March 1981), p. 317, copyright © 1981 The American Psychiatric Association. All rights reserved.

"MAC-SOG MIA to Date," pages 375–76, adapted from "Special Forces Personnel Missing in Action," in *Green Berets at War*, by Shelby Stanton, copyright © 1985. Published by Presidio Press, 31 Pamaron Way, Novato, CA 94949. All rights reserved.

I would like to thank the following individuals and publishers as well for their gracious permission to reprint material in these pages:

Excerpt from "The Testimony of Political Repression as a Therapeutic Instrument," by Ana Julia Cienfuegos and Cristina Monelli, in the *American Journal of Orthopsychiatry* 53, no. 1 (January 1983), pp. 48–49, copyright © 1983 The American Journal of Orthopsychiatry.

Jill Mishkel's epigraph, from *A Piece of My Heart*, by Keith Walker, copyright © 1986. Published by Presidio Press, 31 Pamaron Way, Novato, CA 94949. All rights reserved.

Kathleen Costello Cordova's and Stephen Gregory's epigraphs, from *The Vietnam Experience: A War Remembered*, by Stephen

Weiss, Clark Dougan, David Gulghum, Denis Kennedy and the editors of the Boston Publishing Company, copyright © 1986 Time-Life Books, Inc. All rights reserved.

Katherine Mary Cammarata's epigraph, from *Casualties*, by Heather Brandon, copyright © 1984 St. Martin's Press. All rights reserved.

Lyrics from "Dream Baby (How Long Must I Dream)," by Cindy Walker, copyright © 1962 Combine Music Corporation. All rights controlled and administered by SBK Blackwood Music, Inc. All rights reserved. International copyright secured.

Harold Crosby tape, page 27, from Haywood T. Kirkland's story; Dale Tuttle tape, page 27, from Charles Strong's story; and the Archie "Joe" Biggers epigraph, from *Bloods: An Oral History of the Vietnam War by Black Veterans*, by Wallace Terry, copyright © 1984 Random House, Inc. All rights reserved.

James Torres tape, page 28, from Robert Santos' story in *Everything We Had*, by Al Santoli, copyright © 1981 Random House, Inc. All rights reserved.

Lawrence Ballet tape, pages 188–90 inspired by Dan Pitzer's story in *To Bear Any Burden*, by Al Santoli, copyright © 1985 E. P. Dutton.

And finally, I would like to offer special thanks to D.A., R.J., R.K., B.M., J.M., J.P., J.S. and A.W., rare friends and invaluable consultants; and to the many veterans of a war in Southeast Asia who, by living so much of this book, gave it its very soul and shape.

PROLOGUE

TOP SECRET NOFORN

SIGNED CONTROL ACCESS #7769
CODEWORD: LITTLE BOY BLUE
OPERATION ORANGUTAN COMMAND FILES
(PERSONNEL)

SP4 Edward Lancaster, 728352100, 1st Battalion, 28th Infantry,
Tape 1 Transcript

Subject: Is there a mike I should talk into?

Interviewer: No, the machine will pick it up.

Subject: Okay. [Pause] My name is Edward Lancaster. I'm a combat medic and was originally with D Company, 1st Medical Battalion, 1st Infantry Division. After three months I was assigned to the 1/2 and 1/26. I'm now with the 1/28th Infantry Battalion. Is this what you want?

Interviewer: Yes, that's fine.

Subject: D Company's base camp was at Phuoc Vinh in War Zone X of III Corps. I was on night perimeter guard duty when it happened. The compound was up against the Viet ville there and the bunker I was assigned to was on an inside corner with concertina wire going in two directions. At the juncture there was a large corner post with lights set down low, flooding the perimeter. It was well after dark and I was the one up, my partners sacked out. I was scanning the perimeter when I saw a shape sitting on top of the post just above the lights. I wasn't sure if it was a rat or a bird or what. In a few seconds it began to hoot. At first I didn't understand that the hoot was actually a word. When I did, when I understood that it was actually a word and that the word was my name, I also understood that it was trying to warn me about a mortar attack. I can't describe it really. It said my name four times and I understood what it was trying to tell me. There was going to be a mortar attack and it would happen in ten minutes. I didn't try to explain it away, the way I usually would have: as fatigue, as my imagination. I *believed* it. I didn't even know there were owls in Vietnam, but I believed it. I notified the company command post on our PRC 25 that a mortar attack was imminent and when he asked me how I knew, I pretended I couldn't hear him. I told him where they would probably fall—I could see the quadrants, the four places, two by the machine gun emplacements, one by the CO and one by our bunker, and I told him. I got my partners up and told them to get under their cots and when the round hit by the bunker door, we got covered with dirt but that was it. The CP acted late but no one bought the farm. There were two or three shrapnel wounds and that was all. I've been waiting for the owl to return and have done some reading about it, sir. The Indians in our country believed in owls. But I don't think it was an owl. I believe it was a man, a very special man who was asking me to serve Him. When I've truly committed my life to Him, He will return for me. Whether it will be as an owl or a man or something else, I have no idea. But I'm doing my best to commit and I'm waiting for Him to return. Is this what you want, sir?

Interviewer: [Unintelligible]

Maj. Ely Billings, 453287906, 101st Airborne Division, Tape 2 Transcript

What you've got to understand, Colonel, is how many people over here have seen their own deaths. I don't mean in some general way. I mean the details, the firefights, the weapons, with witnesses. They can't stop it from happening, but they know beforehand that it's going to happen. I'm not talking about two or three, I'm talking about fifty or sixty. We just don't have the paperwork that shows it. The Army doesn't have that kind of paperwork. Even if you did, Colonel, what in the hell would you do with it?

PFC Lindsay McDonald, 564387690, 1st Armored Cavalry, Tape 1 Transcript

In the fall of '68 I was a senior in high school and I started having what you'd call vivid premonitions. From September of '68 to when I graduated I knew I was going to get hurt in Vietnam. I don't mean that the way it sounds. Everybody knew they were going to get hurt in Vietnam. I was 1-A and my lottery number was 1, but what I mean is that I knew I was going to lose my right hand. I'd tell people and they'd laugh. Joey Martinez would say, "You're going to have to learn to jerk off with your left hand, asshole." Nobody understood. I'd wake up in the middle of the night with this picture in my head and I couldn't forget it. I could see my hand lying on the ground like a crab, not moving. It should've been funny, but it wasn't. I didn't feel I was going to die, just that I'd lose my right hand. When I did, near Song Mao in October of '69, it didn't bother me. It didn't hurt that much and they got a tourniquet on it right away. I'd known it was going to happen, so it wasn't really a shock. Sometimes I think that's why I knew, so I wouldn't fall over and die from the shock of it. I was actually relieved. I'd been afraid for so long. I just hadn't seen how I was going to lose it, the kind of booby trap it was.

Sgt. Anthony Trevino, 786539045, 173d Airborne Brigade, Tape 2 Transcript (Priority)

I would sit by the paths and Charlie would go by me and I wouldn't even be there. It got to the point where I could sit for six or seven hours without moving and Charlie would almost step on me. I just wasn't there. In the SEALs they supposedly teach you how to look like a rock. I didn't think it was possible. Other things have happened. In Operation Junction City, last February, I left my body and saw the Chucks who'd pinned us down. I was able to lead my body to all of them—two M-60s and two spider holes— and take them out with either my M-16 or my Randall. It doesn't sound real, talking like this now. The guys saw me do it. They said it looked like an animal going through the jungle—they'd never seen anything like it. They didn't want to be around me afterward. I don't remember that part. I was still out of it. I did it again in April, when the 173d was in Binh Thuan Province and we were sweeping, looking for anything we could find. We were checking out this French hospital outside Phan Thiet and I see this Spec 5 walking toward a C-rat can in the yard. The can starts to glow. I don't know how else to say it except it starts to glow. I tell him not to touch it but he laughs. I tell him, Listen, motherfucker, you touch that can and you'll lose an arm. He doesn't know me, he's salty, he's supposed to know about these things. He's never seen Charlie wire an empty C-rat can, so he leans over to show me. Fuck you, buddy, he's thinking. He picks it up and boom, his arm flies off. It's booby-trapped, just like I was telling him. If they're booby-trapped, they glow. I can find the Chucks in a treeline be- cause they're glowing. Anything that threatens my body will glow. That's been the way it's been for four months. I could say they were like little suns or radioactivity, but it's not like that. When I tell people about it, I always put in Martians or black syphilis or vaginas with razor blades, that kind of thing, so they'll think: Hey, what excellent bullshit. I could listen to this all day. If you try to tell them, they don't believe it. *I* believe it. You would, too, if it kept you alive.

Col. John Fitzgerald, 897654390, 5th Special Forces (retired),
Tape 11 Transcript

I worked for ICEX, the forerunner of the Phoenix Program. There were about ten or twelve guys in the program I was in. I only knew three others and we worked all over Nam. One got killed in the summer of '67, one is a beat-up old bastard in worse shape than I'm in, and another of the guys is down in Central America. The VC called us *Moi con Dao*, Savage Knives. People who don't know much about the Rhade don't realize that they can and do use their knives. I'd heard about them in '60, when I was with White Star in Laos, and had become interested in them enough to learn their language. They were a lot like my father's people, the Tsalagi Cherokee.

It took three or four years for me to get straight with the world when I got out. Like I told you, Colonel, I had a blood clot in my left brain that left me paralyzed on my right side. I couldn't move my right eye for a long time and I had to learn how to speak all over again. The clot killed me. I mean, I went through a hell of a deal. It sounds strange but I don't have any other way of saying it: my life's being left my body, I could see it laying on the bathroom floor, and I hovered above the door before I moved outside the quarters where I was living then. I couldn't see the inside of the major's quarters next door, but I could see Ruth and the four kids just as plain as if the top of the roof was off the house. I could see Bragg, which I'd seen from the air many times, but not over my quarters in Hammond Hills. Then I came back to my body and started living again. I want to tell you, I thought I was going crazy. It bothered me for a long time. I wouldn't talk to anyone about it except Ruth.

I've been trying to track down the guys I worked with, but it's hard. Most of them are dead, or you just lose track of them. At my age you keep trying, but it's hard.

Staff Sgt. Gerrald Zuminski, 760983456, 3d Battalion, 1st Infantry, Tape 1 Transcript

When I lost my leg—what they call a traumatic amputation—I never lost consciousness. I triggered the mine and one ARVN was killed and another was badly wounded in the head. All of this happened after dark. While I was waiting to be medevacked I saw Grandfather Zuminski—who died in December of 1967—standing off to the right watching everything. He was dressed in the same bibbed overalls and the battered felt hat he always wore. It was dark. I couldn't see any of the other GIs but I could see my grandfather just a few feet away. He stayed with me until I was on the chopper that took me away. I haven't had any other experiences like that since then, no.

PO3 Daniel Klein, 497234094, SEAL Team One, Tape 1
Transcript

There are guys who can tell who's going to die by looking at them. Everyone thinks it's something in the eyes—you hear that all the time—but it isn't like that. People talk about a blankness in the face, a distance, like the guy is already gone, boarding pass and everything. It's a little like that, but it's not that either. It's not something you can photograph. You can't say, Hey, see that guy over there—Jesus, does he look like death warmed over. Maybe he's tired, maybe he's got malaria or dysentery. Maybe it's just the thousand-yard stare. That doesn't mean the guy's going to die. It's nothing you can describe. It's something you feel when they're standing next to you. They're just not there, the way you and I are, our bodies taking up space, weighing something.

You try it one day and you find out you can do it. It's like winning a lottery. It's the last thing you imagined you could do and bingo, you can do it. These are guys you know, so when they die, when you think maybe they're going to die and they *do*, you feel like shit. But you're also saying, "I can do it! Jesus, I can really do it!" Then one day someone in the bunker says, "If a guy can tell who's going to die by looking at him, he should be able to look in a mirror and tell himself whether *he's* going to die, right?" It's a joke, but in a couple of days you've got this little mirror and you carry it around everywhere. You'll kill anyone who takes that mirror. You look in it every day before a patrol, every night before H&I and then every five minutes when you're short, when you're down to weeks. You know it's not something you can *see*, but you go crazy, wanting to know.

Capt. Joseph O'Connell, 676909159, 3d Marines, Tape 1
Transcript

I'm the oldest captain in the Marine Corps. You don't want to talk to me. [Laughs] Vietnam's a sissy compared to what we saw in Korea. Nothing's happened here yet to match that. ESP—whatever you want to call it—is around any combat soldier, always, whether he knows it or not. One time my mother—she was in Tampa, Florida, at the time—woke me up in the middle of the night—I'm in Korea—and told me to find the chaplain and make a good confession because I was going to be hit that day. I was still a kid. If my mother comes to me in a dream, it's still my mother. I went ahead and did it and was hit. Several hours after I told the battalion priest how my mother wanted me to talk to him, we attacked. I was hit on the first assault, though not grievously, and got a five-day rest in the regimental aid station. I was platoon sergeant then, very young, and my platoon had no officer. I felt guilty about going down the hill with a minor puncture wound, junked my casualty tag and went back up to my rifle company. I won a Bronze Star several days later. That was 1950. We landed at Inchon in September and by December the 1st Marine Division was heavily engaged in the Chosin Reservoir with ten Chinese divisions of their 8th Route Army. The weather was terrible. It went down to minus 37 Fahrenheit and there were twenty-five-knot winds out of Manchuria. Out of the 15,000 men there, we suffered 7,700 casualties, most of it frostbite. We got credit for more than 45,000 enemy dead. Vietnam is nothing. [Laughs] My blessed mother hasn't had to wake me up even once here.

CPO Terrence Leverhoudt, 567783120, Mobile Riverine Base 8, Tape 1 Transcript

I'm at my machine gun on the LPD. We're at the mouth of the Bassac River, in the South China Sea, maybe two weeks after the monsoons start. The ship is really rolling in this storm. The wind's a demon, there are dark waves everywere. I'm thinking of my mother—she died when I was a year and a half old—and suddenly, all around me, the storm stops, the air is warm, there isn't any sound at all. She's *there*. I can feel her. She's there for a long time and then my watch replacement appears. It hasn't been hours. It's been seconds.

PFC Peter Takukani, 576892007, 2d Air Cavalry, Tape 1 Transcript

This was the first time it happened. This is the one that still makes me shake when I think about it. In this dream the VC have killed and wounded a bunch of marines. They've stripped them and doped up the dying wounded. They've wrapped them in barbed wire to make them controllable, and they're marching them forward, toward us. We've got to shoot the legs out from under our own guys. When they try to move, the barbed wire goes deeper. Even though they're dying and doped up, they can feel it. I get sick over it in the dream. I had the dream for two or three nights but I'd never heard of VC doing this, so I didn't really think about it. On March 15 we were at Dong Ngai and the VC march these guys out. The three guys I could see clearest were from the dream. We had to shoot them to stop them. I got sick but I didn't tell anyone about the dream. It happened again near Phu Bai, these four guys got mutilated and strung up and I didn't want to see them. I got sick that time, too, and the captain said he was going to court-martial me. I told him about the dream and he said he was going to give me a Section Eight. When I had the third dream and told him how it was going to happen and it did happen that way, he didn't say anything. I didn't see him again because he was transferred out. He didn't want to be with our company, he said. He said we were the worst group of soldiers he'd ever been with and he wasn't going to spend the war with us. I got wounded in the hip on August 30 and again on September 9 in the arm. I was expecting to go home, but I'm still here.

Chapter 1

TOP SECRET NOFORN

SIGNED CONTROL ACCESS #7769
CODEWORD: LITTLE BOY BLUE
Special Clearance: OPERATION ORANGUTAN EVAL

1st Lt. Mary Damico, 557783021, Army Nurse Corps,
Tape 1 Transcript

I don't know whether I was for or against the war when I went, Major. I don't think that matters now. I joined and became a nurse to help. Isn't that why everyone becomes a nurse? We're told it's a good thing, like being a teacher or a mother. When I was ten I had to watch my grandmother—my dad's mom—die of a heart attack in her bedroom, which was right beside mine, and I told myself then that it wasn't going to happen ever again. I wasn't going to stand around like that and feel helpless ever again. I was ten. I'll never forget it. What they don't tell you is that sometimes you *can't* help.

Our principal gets on the PA one day and tells us how all these boys across the country are going over there for us and getting killed or maimed. We're in home room and I'm sitting right behind Little Bobby Carter, the guy who's asked me to the Waimea Romance—this *very* important dance. The principal tells us that Tony Fischetti and this other boy are dead, killed in action,

Purple Hearts and everything. A lot of girls start crying. Kathy Rosenbaum is crying and Donna Renaldo, who went steady with Tony Fischetti in the tenth grade, is crying. I'm crying. We're all crying. When President Kennedy was killed in '63, we cried the same way.

I think about John F. Kennedy and I think about Tony Fischetti and all the other guys who are dying or getting hurt over there. How my brother Jerry and his friends and Little Bobby Carter and other guys I know could be over there tomorrow. I call the Army the next day and I tell them my grades are pretty good, that I want to go to nursing school and then to Nam. They say fine, they'll pay for it, but I'm obligated if they do. I say fine, it's what I want. I don't know if any other girls from Poly did it. I really didn't care. I just thought somebody ought to.

I went down and signed up—I was eighteen—and my dad got mad. He was a tool and die man at the Naval Shipyards and very Italian and very strict. He's sitting in the living room and he says I just want to be a whore or a lesbian, because that's what people will think if I go. The Perottos will think it. *Family* will think it. I've always been a sassy kid, so I say, "Is that what you and Mom think?" He almost hits me. Parents are like that. What other people think is more important than what *they* think, but you can't tell them that.

I thought my mother would say something. We were close. But she didn't. She didn't want me to go either.

I never saw a nurse in Nam who was a whore and I never met one where the other thing ever mattered. How could it matter? There were a few who were a little loose, who got drunk and went to too many parties, who did things like fall in love with married guys, the doctors, but that you could understand. Everyone drank. Everyone wanted someone who understood.

But that's how some people thought back in the States. If you went, you were a lesbian or a whore. Why else would you go?

I grew up in Long Beach, California, a sailor town. Sometimes I forget that. Sometimes I forget that I went to Catalina for the proms, wore my hair in a flip and liked miniskirts and black pumps. Sometimes I forget that for a long time I didn't like the Beatles. Sometimes all I can remember is the hospitals.

I spent three years at St. Mary's, this Catholic nursing school up in the Valley, and when we were through, I drove down to Fort Sam Houston for basic with these two other girls. We had a great time. We were cutting up, we were making trouble and laughing all the way. One of the girls was from Louisiana and the other was a California girl, too—she was the funny one. She'd be covered with blood in ER, where we were the permitees, and she'd tell a joke that was as dirty as any joke I ever heard from the guys at Poly. She'd get everybody laughing, even the patients, and you couldn't stop. You'd be covered with blood from a knife or gunshot case and you'd be laughing so hard you nearly wet your pants. We had a great ride to Texas because of her.

At Fort Sam we were treated like queens. There weren't many women there and it got a little out of hand. They'd show us how to use a rifle and then wouldn't let us shoot it. Fran, the girl from California, would get a broomstick and cut it down and bring it to the firing range. If you won't let me fire yours, I'm going to fire mine, she'd say, and she'd get down on the ground and aim it and make the sounds you make when you play war, the sounds boys always make. The sergeant would look at her like he'd never met anyone that crazy, like: you're the last person I'd want in charge of *my* precious bodily fluids. We all got broomsticks. They didn't know what to do with us. We didn't know we were getting ready for a war. We thought it was a joke, a game. They didn't know how to tell us what it was really like over there. They should've let us shoot the weapons. They should have gotten some bodies, some cadavers, and let us see what our bullets and grenades could do.

I was stationed at Walter Reed for a couple of months but I kept telling them I wanted to go to Nam. They said you can't, you're too young, and I said I'll be twenty-one when I get there, so let me go, for Christ's sake. I kept saying this and writing it on every piece of paper I could and finally they said: Okay. You want it—you can have it.

Fran and I asked for the same station and got it. Cam Ranh Bay had thirteen hundred beds and great beaches, we'd heard. We could be nurses who were really helping out there, and we could also be some round-eyed women having fun on some great beaches. That was our plan. That's all we knew. Sherry, the one from Louisiana, wanted Long Binh. Her boyfriend was there with the 11th Armored Cav and she was going to go to Long Binh if she had to hitch a ride on a tank to get there. We said something stupid like "Everything's fair in love and war, honey," and hugged her and never saw her again.

We got stationed at Cam Ranh Bay, at the 21st Evac, for a month, then the 8th Field General in Saigon, then back to the 21st. It didn't help to get moved around like that but we got moved. That kind of thing happened all the time. At the 21st we were put in this hootch. It was right by the hospital compound, and we had the Navy on one side of us and the Air Force on the other side. We could hear the mortars all night, and the next day we'd get to see what they'd done.

It began to get to me after about a week. That's all it took. It's always bad the first few days, when you see the bodies and don't know what to do—because stateside ER, even Walter Reed, didn't really prepare you—all these guys crying for their mothers or girlfriends or sisters and telling you how nice you look when they're cut to pieces. But you put your feelings on hold and you do your work. You tell yourself it can't *possibly* go on like this, that the rest of the week has got to get better, how you're going to be wearing a really clean white uniform again real soon. You tell each other it's got to end and you *make* yourself believe it. But it doesn't end.

The medevac choppers would land and the gurneys would come in. We were the ones who tried to keep them alive, and if they didn't die on us, we'd send them on.

When it finally happened, it wasn't like anything I'd ever experienced before. I've thought about it a lot since then. You give something like that a lot of thought afterward, trying to understand how it started. Did you, for example, ever dream what you were going to get for Christmas as a kid and you were right about it, even though it was a surprise, even though you had *no way* of knowing? Did you ever dream that your brother was going to get hurt, and how and when, when he used to get hurt in football? Things like that. I don't remember ever having dreams of that kind when I was a kid.

We'd be covered with blood and urine and everything else. We'd have a boy with no arms and no legs, or maybe his legs would be lying beside him on the gurney. We'd have guys with no faces. We'd have a guy with a perfect face, but nothing below the chest, just a sheet. He'd talk to you and while he was talking you'd look only at his face. You'd keep your eyes on that part of him until he died. I remember this guy named Paul. I'll never forget him. Talk to any nurse and there's a patient, a name, a face she can't forget.

We'd have stomachs you could hold in your hands. We'd have bodies you could fold in half, because the spines were cut in two, and the guys would still be alive. We'd have backbones so infected you could pull them out like a rope, and the guys were still breathing. We'd have skulls that were open, with things lying in them—dirt and leaves and pieces of metal—and these guys would be breathing, too. We had all of these things, Major.

We'd be slapping ringers and plasma into them and we'd be shouting: *Stay awake. Don't go to sleep. Hang on. We love you, baby.* We'd have suction pumps going to get the secretions and blood out of them. We'd do this all day, day in and day out.

You'd put them in bags if they didn't make it. You'd change dressings on stumps, and you had this deal with the corpsmen that every fourth day you'd clean the latrines for them if they'd change the dressings. They knew what it was like.

They'd bring in a boy with beautiful brown eyes and you'd just have a chance to look at him, to get the IVs in and cut-down done. He'd say, "Ma'am, am I all right?" and in forty seconds he'd be gone. He'd say, "Oh, no," and he'd be gone. His blood would pool on the gurney right through the packs. Some wounds are so bad you can't even plug them. The person just drains away.

You wanted to help but you couldn't. All you could do was watch.

One day I said, "I can't handle this, Fran." She said, "Sure you can, kid." I said the same thing the next day, and she said,

"It's getting better . . . all . . . the . . . time." She sang it like that Beatles song. I didn't want to keep saying it, to be a Nancy Bringdown, but it was what I was feeling. I'd say, "No, it's never going to get better," and she'd go ahead and try some raunchy joke just to get me to smile. It didn't bother her at first, hearing what I was saying, but by the second or third week she started turning away. She'd get mad and she'd turn away and she wouldn't listen. I couldn't understand this. I was feeling terrible and she knew it. I had to tell *someone*. Who else was I going to tell?

I stopped putting it in words. I'd be looking at her and she'd know what I was thinking. She'd still turn away because she *knew*. She'd say, "Amazing what a broomstick can do, isn't it?" Or she'd tell a joke, but not to me. It would be to someone else, a corpsman maybe, or another nurse. She wouldn't look at *me*. She could keep it together as long as she didn't have to look at me. I understand that now.

I start crying and I can't stop. That goes on for days. I wait until the shift is over and I'm back in my room, but sometimes, when it's heavy casualties, I can't wait and I go to one of the storerooms. I don't tell her what's happening, but she knows. She knows when I've been crying back at our hootches. One day she comes into the storeroom and finds me there and she gets mad. She tells me: "You think *you've* got problems, Mary. What about the rest of us—what about *me*?" I tell her it's *not* me, I'm not crying about *me*—it's what we're having to do, how the bodies never stop coming, they come and they never stop. It's not about *me*, I say, but I'm the one crying, so it sounds like I am. She doesn't say a thing. She storms out of the room and the next thing I know she's gotten a transfer to OR. I see her at night, back in the hootch, but we don't talk much and she avoids me. I know now what she was going through, how we were going through the same thing really, I just didn't know it then. I thought she was the strong one. I thought the only thing bothering her was my crying.

When the dreams started, I thought I was going crazy. It was about the fifth week and I couldn't sleep. I hadn't talked to anyone for weeks—to Fran or a nurse I'd gotten to know from Cleveland or the corpsmen or the head nurse. I'd had four guys code on me the day before and when I dreamed about them that night they all had Paul's face, just like always. They had different bodies, sure, but they had Paul's face—the smile, the dimple in the chin, the sunburn. All the dreams before that night had been like that. When I was awake, it was even worse. I'd close my eyes in post-op and think of trip wires. I'd think my bras and everything else had trip wires. I'd be on the john and hear a sound and think that someone was trip-wiring the latch so I'd lose my hands and face when I tried to leave. But the next night the dreams changed.

I started dreaming about wounds, different kinds, and the next day there'd be the wounds I'd dreamed about. I thought it was just luck, coincidence. I'd seen a lot of wounds by then. Everyone, all the nurses and corpsmen, were having nightmares. The doctors said they didn't, but they did. I'd dream about a sucking chest wound and a guy trying to scream, even though he couldn't, and the next day I'd have to patch a chest and listen to a guy try to scream. I didn't think much about it. I couldn't sleep. That was the important thing. I knew I was going to go crazy if I couldn't sleep.

I wrote letters to my parents at night. I made them the kind of letters I thought they would want to get. I wrote "Dear Mom and Dad," but they'd really be to my mom. All I could see when I was writing them was her face, so I knew they were really to her. I remember this one letter—I copied it over six or seven times, I guess. I wrote a letter every night for about a week and then I stopped.

Sometimes the dreams would have all the details. They'd bring in a guy that looked like someone had taken an ice pick to every part of his body. His arms and legs looked like frankfurters with holes punched in them. That's what shrapnel looks like. You puff up and the bleeding stops. We all knew he was going to die. You can't live through something like that. Your system won't take it. *He* knew he was going to die, but he wasn't making a sound. His face had little holes in it, around his cheeks, and it looked like a catcher's mitt. He had the most beautiful blue eyes, like glass. You know, like that dog, the weimar-something. I'd started shak-

ing because he was in one of my dreams—those holes and his face
and eyes. I'd shake for hours, but you couldn't tell anybody about
dreams like that.

The guy would die. There wasn't anything I could do.

I didn't understand it. I didn't see a reason for the dreams.
They just made it worse.

Photostat, Letter 4/12/71 (Intercept), 1st Lt. Mary Damico, 557783021, Command Files, Operation Orangutan, Tiger Cat, Vietnam

Dear Mom and Dad,

It's difficult to describe things here. I don't want to
tell you sad stories but that's about all there is. The guys
come in with every imaginable problem and we send
them on if they live and we never know how they do. I
guess a movie of it would show you exactly what it's like,
but that's one movie I wouldn't want any of you to have
to see. My social life? I get to a party now and then with
the other nurses and with the 18th Engineers, the unit
we've kind of adopted, but usually we're so tired we don't
even make it to the early parties. Yes, Dad, the guys here
are perfect gentlemen. You'd think we were their mothers or sisters or that God told them He'd slap their hands
if they touched us. The guys are barely out of high
school. But this isn't high school and everyone knows it.
We work together as a team, which makes a big difference. I'm learning a lot about medicine and about
people, as you can tell, and I know it will all help me in
whatever I do when I get back to the States (the guys call
it "The Land of the Big PX"—which should tell you
something about the war, Dad). Well, I guess I ought to
turn out the light and get some sleep. Don't worry about
me. I'm fine. Cam Ranh Bay is as safe as you can get—

we'll *never* give up these beautiful beaches. *Baci* and *abbracci* to everyone.

Love,
Mary

P.S. Tell Jerry not to do anything drastic about his love life until he gets his big sister's advice.

Chapter 2

It got so I didn't want to go to sleep because I didn't want to have the dreams. I didn't want to wake up and have to worry about them all day, wondering if they were going to happen. I didn't want to have to shake all day, wondering.

I'd have this dream about a kid, the name beginning with a *T*, with a bad head wound and a phone call, and the next day they'd wheel in some kid who'd lost a lot of skull and brain and scalp, and the underlying brain would be infected. The word would go around that his father, who was a full-bird colonel stationed in Okie, had called and the kid's mother and father would be coming to see him. We were all hoping he'd die before they got there, and he did.

I'd had a dream about him. His name was Tom. I'd even dreamed that we wanted him to die before his mom and dad got there, and he did, in the dream he did.

When he died I started screaming and this black corpsman who'd been around for a week or two took me by the arm and got me to the john. I'd gotten sick but he held me like my mom would have and all I could do was think what a mess I was, how could he hold me up when I was such a mess? I started crying and couldn't stop. I knew everyone thought I was crazy, but I couldn't stop.

After that things got worse. I couldn't talk to anyone about it. I'd see more than just a face or the wounds. I'd see where the guy lived, where his hometown was and who was going to cry for him if he died. I didn't understand it at first—I didn't even know it was happening. I'd just get pictures, like before, in the dream, and they'd bring this guy in the next day or the day after that, and if he could talk, I'd find out that what I'd seen was true. This guy would be dying and not saying a thing and I'd remember him from the dream and I'd say, "You look like a Georgia boy to me." If the morphine was working and he could talk, he'd say, "Who told you that, Lieutenant? All us brothers ain't from Georgia."

I'd make up something, like his voice or a good guess, and if I'd seen other things in the dream—like his girl or wife or mother—I'd tell him about those, too. He wouldn't ask how I knew because it didn't matter. How could it matter? He knew he was dying. They always know. I'd talk to him like I'd known him my whole life and he'd be gone in an hour, or by morning.

I would get a letter from my parents. My mother would write it and sign it for both of them. The letter would sound just like the ones I'd sent them and I'd put it in a drawer but I wouldn't read it again. The letters from Jerry were different. He would joke, but he would ask questions, too. He wanted to know what it was really like.

I had this dream about a commando type, dressed in tiger cammies, nobody saying a thing about him in the compound—spook stuff, ICEX, MAC-SOG, something like that—and I could see his girlfriend in Australia. She had hair just like mine and her eyes were a little like mine and she loved him. She was going out with another guy that night, but she loved him, I could tell. In the dream they brought him into ER with the bottom half of him blown away. I know he's coming. I know there's nothing I can do about it. I go to a bar with this doctor who's married, who's got two kids, and I get drunk. If I get drunk enough, I tell myself, the doctor will get disgusted with me and leave me. If I get drunk, I won't have to see the guy when they bring him in. If I get drunk enough, I won't even remember that I dreamed about him when they bring him in.

The next morning, first thing, they wheeled this guy in and it was the dream all over again. I could barely stand up I was so sick, but it was him. He was blown apart from the waist down. He was delirious and trying to talk but his jaw wouldn't work. He had his shirt still on—I'm not sure why—and we had to cut it off. I was the one who got him and everyone knew he wasn't going to make it. As soon as I saw him I started shaking. I didn't want to see him, I didn't want to look at him. You really don't know what it's like, seeing someone like that and knowing. I didn't want him to die. I never wanted any of them to die.

I said, "Your girl in Australia loves you—she really does." He looked at me and his eyes had that look you get when morphine isn't enough. I could tell he thought I looked like her. He could see my hair and he thought I looked like her.

He grabbed my arm and his jaw started slipping and I knew what he wanted me to do. I always knew. I told him about her long black hair and the beaches in Australia and what the people were like there and what there was to do.

He thought I was going to stop talking, so he kept squeezing my arm. I told him what he and his girlfriend had done on a beach outside Melbourne, their favorite beach, and what they'd had to drink that night.

And then—this was the first time I'd done it with anyone—I told him what I'd do for him if I was his girlfriend and we were back in Australia. I said, "I'd wash you real good in the shower. I'd turn the lights down low and I'd put on some nice music. Then, if you were a little slow, I'd help you."

It was what his girlfriend always did, I knew that. It wasn't hard to say.

I kept talking, he kept holding my arm and then he coded on me. They always did. I had a couple of minutes or hours and then they always coded on me, just like in the dreams.

I got good at it. The pictures got better and I could tell them what they wanted to hear and that made it easier. It wasn't just faces and burns and stumps, it was things about them. I'd tell them what their girlfriends and wives would do if they were here. Sometimes it was sexual, sometimes it wasn't. Sometimes I'd just ruffle their hair with my hand and tell them what Colorado looked like in summer, or what the last Doors concert they'd been to was like, or what you could do after dark in Newark.

I started crying in the big room one day, in front of everyone, and this corpsman takes me by the arm and the next thing I know I'm sitting on the john and he's got a needle in his hand, a two percent solution of morphine. He doesn't want to see me hurting so much. I tell him no. You weren't supposed to do that kind of thing. Junkies on the Pike back home did it—everyone at Poly knew that—but not doctors or medics or nurses. It wasn't right, I knew. I shouldn't need to.

I start crying two days later, too—in the same room—and this doctor, this surgeon from Texas, takes me by the arm and pulls me into the hallway. He's got this look on his face, this look of disgust, and he says, "I'd send you home tomorrow morning, Lieutenant, if we didn't need your hands. Do you understand what I'm saying?" I nod. I keep nodding. I'm trying not to cry. "But I also have," he says to me, "no intention of putting my staff through one of your little displays again. Do you understand me, Lieutenant?" He's writing out a prescription. He's handing it to me with that same look on his face and saying, "Fill this, Lieutenant, and come back when you're ready to work."

I go ahead. I fill it. It's a two percent solution, too. I use a needle. I put it in my arm—the way he would want me to. I'm shaking, but I do it, and when I do, I know why they both wanted me to. It helps. It lets me do what I need to do.

Later I get it from the corpsman instead. I just tell him to put more morphine in the order, and he does. He knows what I'm doing, and he knows why.

After that I try places on my body where it won't show as much. He would want me to do that, too, I know.

There's this guy I want to tell you about. Steve—his name was Steve.

I come in one morning to the big ER room shaking so hard I can't hold what they give me and thinking I should've gotten a needle already, and there's this guy sitting over by a curtain. He's in cammies, his head's wrapped and he's sitting up real straight. I can barely stand up but here's this guy looking like he's hurting, so I say, "You want to lie down?"

He turns slowly to look at me and I don't believe it. I know this guy, this lieutenant, from a dream. I can see brown water, like a muddy river, and uniforms up on a low ridge, looking down. I can see a body lying in the mud below them, jerking and jerking in the reddish mud.

Here's this guy sitting in a chair in front of me unattended, like he could walk away any second, but I've had a dream about him, so I know he's going to die on a riverbank somewhere.

He says he's okay, he's just here to see a buddy. But I'm not listening. I know everything about him. I know about his girlfriend and where he's from and how his mom and dad didn't raise him, his aunt and uncle did, but all I can think about is, he's going to die. I don't know when, but he's going to die and I can't do a thing about it. I'm thinking about the supply room and needles and how it wouldn't take much to get all of this over with forever.

I say, "Kathy misses you, Steve. She wishes you could go to the Branding Iron in Merced tonight, because that band you like is playing. She's done something to her apartment and she wants to show it to you."

He looks at me for a long time and his eyes aren't like the others. I don't want to look back at him. I can see him anyway—in the dream. He's real young. He's got a nice body, good shoulders, and he's got curly blond hair under those clean bandages. He's got eyelashes like a girl, and I see him laughing. He laughs every chance he gets, I know.

Very quietly he says, "What's your name?" and I look down. The name tag is gone. I don't know where it is.

I guess I tell him, because he says, "Can you tell me what she looks like, Mary?"

Everything's wrong. The guy doesn't sound like he's going to die. He's as alive as anyone, though he's jerking, jerking in the mud.

I say something like "She's tall." I say, "She's got blond hair," but I can barely think. He keeps staring at me and I keep looking away. I'm trying to remember.

Very gently he says, "What are her eyes like, Mary?"

I don't know. I'm shaking so hard I can barely talk, I can barely remember the dream.

Suddenly I'm talking. "They're green. She wears a lot of mascara, but she's got dark eyebrows, so she isn't really a blonde, is she?"

He laughs and I jump. "No, you're right, she isn't," he says, and he's smiling. He takes my hand in his. I'm shaking badly but I let him, like I do the others. I don't say a word. His hand is just like Jerry's, I tell myself.

I'm holding it in. I'm scared to death that he's going to die and I'm going to lose him like the others. I'm cold-turkeying and I'm letting him hold my hand because he's going to die.

He squeezes my hand like we've known each other a long time and he says, "Do you do this for all of them?"

I don't say a thing.

Real quietly he says, "A lot of guys die on you, don't they, Mary?"

I can't help it. I start crying. I want to tell him. I want to tell someone, so I do. I tell him everything I can and he listens, he squeezes my hand and he listens.

When I'm finished he doesn't say something stupid, he doesn't walk away. He doesn't code on me. He starts to tell me a story and I don't understand it at first.

There's this G-2 reconnaissance over the border, he says, from Cam Lo, base camp, across The Trace, where the trees are dead and there's a crater every ten feet, then across the Ben Hai like a silver ribbon below us in the night. The insertion's smooth and I'm at point, I'm always at point, he says. We're out of the highlands by first light, into the little delta where Uncle Ho's trail heads west. We're humping across paddy dikes like grunts and we hit this treeline. This is a black op, Little People stuff, nobody's supposed to know we're here, but somebody knows. All of a sudden the goddamn trees are full of Charlies. The whole world turns blue—just for me, I mean, it turns blue—and everything starts moving real slowly. I can see the first AK rounds coming at me and I step aside nicely, just like that, like I always do. Three indigs and the RTO go down and I can't do a damn thing about it. I can't do a thing.

The world always turns blue like that when he needs it to, he says. That's why they make him point every goddamn time, why they keep using him on special ops to take out infrastructure or on long-range recon for intel. Because the world turns blue. And how he's been called in twice to talk about what he's going to do after this war and how they want him to be a killer, he says. The records will say he died in this war and they'll give him a new identity. He doesn't have family, they say. He'll be one of their killers wherever they need him. Because everything turns blue. I don't believe what I'm hearing. It's like a movie, like that *Manchurian Candidate* thing, and I don't believe it. They don't care about how he does it, he says. They never do. It can be the world turning blue or voices in your head or some grabass feeling in your gut, or, if you want, it can be God or the Devil or Little Green Martians— it doesn't matter to them what you believe. As long as it works, as long as you keep coming back from missions, that's all they care about. He told them no, but they keep on asking. Sometimes he thinks they'll kill Cathy just so he won't have anything to come back to in the States. They do that kind of thing, he says. I can't believe it.

So everything's turning blue, he says, and I'm floating up out of my body over this rice paddy twenty klicks from the DMZ, these goddamn snipers are darker blue, and when I come back down I'm moving through this nice blue world and I know where they are, and I get every goddamn one of them in their trees. I get every one of them.

It doesn't matter, he says. There's this light-weapons sergeant, a guy they called the Dogman, who's crazy and barks like a dog and makes everyone laugh even if they're bleeding, even if their guts are hanging out. He scares the VC when he barks. He humps his share and the men love him.

When the world turns blue, the Dogman's in cover, everything's fine, but then he rubbernecks, the son of a bitch rubbernecks for the closest gook—he doesn't have to, he just doesn't—and he takes a round high. I don't see the back of his head go, so I think he's still alive. I go for him where he's hanging half out of the treeline, half in a canal full of stinking rice water. I try to get his body out of the line of fire, but they're good, they're NVA specials, and the zip puts the next round right in under my arm. I'm holding the Dogman and the round goes in right under my arm, a fucking heart shot. I can feel it come in, I can feel the wind. It's for me. Everything goes slow and blue and I jerk just a little—I don't even know I'm doing it—and the round slides right in past me and into him. They never get *me*.

I can always save myself, he says—his name is Steve and he isn't smiling now—but I can't save others. What's it worth? What's it worth if *you* stay alive and everyone you care about is dead? Even if you get what *they* want.

I know what he means. I know now why he's sitting on a chair nearly crying, I know where the body is, which curtain it's behind, how close it's been all this time, and how muddy.

Nobody likes to die alone, Steve says. Just like he said it in the dream.

In a little while I say, "There was a river?"

He doesn't understand. He says, "Yes, the Ben Hai."

I say, "No, I mean, was there a river near you when it happened?"

He says, "When they hit us?"

"Yes," I say.

"No, not there," he says.

"But there was a river somewhere," I say. "You went across a river somewhere, right?"

"Yes." He says it quietly and neither of us is shaking anymore.

This is what the dreams do, I'm thinking. They tell the truth even when they lie. There was a river, but they'd passed it, Mary. It wasn't *Steve* by the riverbank, it was a man he knew. Steve was the one I was going to meet, so I'd dreamed about them both. I dreamed about Steve, because I was going to meet him—even though he wasn't the one who died.

He stays, and we talk. We talk about the dreams and his blue world, and we talk about what we're going to do when we get out of this place and back to the Big PX, all the fun we're going to have. He starts to tell me about other guys he knows, guys just like him that the head honchos are interested in, but then he stops. I see he's looking past me. I turn around.

There's this guy in civvies at the end of the hallway, just standing there, looking at us. He nods at me and then he nods at Steve and Steve says, "I got to go."

Real quickly I say, "See you at nineteen-hundred, Lieutenant."

He's looking at the guy down the hallway. "Yeah, sure," he says.

When I get off, he's there. I haven't thought about a needle all day and it shows. We get a bite to eat and talk some more, and that's that. My new hootchmate—the one from Cleveland—says I can have it for a couple of hours if I want it, but I'm a mess. I'm shaking so bad I can't even think about having a good time with this guy. He looks at me like he knows, and says his head hurts and that we ought to get some sleep.

He gives me a hug. That's all.

The same guy in civvies is waiting for him and they walk away together down a street we call Abbey Lane.

The next day he's gone. I tell myself maybe he was standing down for a couple of days and had to get back, but that doesn't help. I know lots of guys who traveled around in-country AWOL without getting into trouble. What could they do to you? Send you to Nam?

I thought maybe he'd call in a couple of days, or write. Later I thought maybe he'd gotten killed, maybe let himself get killed. I really didn't know what to think, but I thought about him a lot.

Ten days later I get transferred. I don't even get orders cut, I don't even get in-country travel paper. No one will tell me a thing—the head nurse, the CO, nobody. I go to MacIntyre, the hospital director, and he says he really can't talk about it, they've asked him not to. "Just do what they want you to do," he says.

I get scared because I think they're shipping me back to the

States because of the needles or the dreams—they've found out about the dreams—and I'm going to be in some VA hospital the rest of my life. That's what I'm thinking.

All they'll tell me is that I'm supposed to be at the strip at 0600 hours tomorrow, fatigues and no ID.

I get a needle that night and barely make it.

Transcripts, Command Files (Personnel), Operation Orangutan, Tiger Cat, Vietnam

SP4 Harold Crosby, 576336754, 25th Infantry Division, Tape 1

When I was twelve years old something very strange happened to me, which has always been with me, even today. I was sitting there on the stoop and it seemed like I had this great vision. I saw two things. I saw myself on this wall, just as clear as day. I mean just *clear*. I saw myself in a war. Then I saw myself in prison for five years. The number was right there. Five. You know what happened after that. You've talked to The Man.

SP4 Dale Tuttle, 590913437, Americal Division, Tape 1

Before I went to Vietnam I had three dreams that showed me places there. When we were assigned to this one area, it was just like in the first dream. I felt like I had been there before, but I didn't place much value on it. But when I saw the second place, it dawned on me that this was like the second dream. There was supposed to be a foxhole about fifteen feet to the left of me and a little tin can sitting in it. At the LZ I was at I walked straight to the place where the foxhole was supposed to be. It was there. The can was too. The third dream said I was going to be crossing a rice paddy and was going to get shot in the chest with a wound I would never recover from. One of my buddies was holding me in his arms and saying I would be all right until the medevac came in. But I didn't make it. The first and second dreams had come true. That was when I knew I wasn't going back to the bush.

Lt. James Torres, 735985039, 101st Airborne Division, Tape 1

I told the guy's squad leader that morning, "Tell him to stay behind with the gear and the chopper will bring him forward later." But he wanted to go out. To this day I still think you can tell ahead of time when someone's going to die. Whether they know it or not, I'm convinced that I can tell. It's not something deliberate. Kind of a blankness comes over their face. It's not like they're already dead. It's like a distance and a softness to their features.

Staff Sgt. Richard Mello, 483305678, 1st Battalion, 27th Infantry, Tape 1

First Platoon got to be known for drawing fire. Not just that, but also for getting through, not losing any men. Guys would come up to us and say, "Hey, how do I get into your outfit? I want to see some action, kill some gooks." We'd say, "No, you don't. You want to stay alive. You want to kill some gooks, but you also want to stay alive." If we didn't like the guy we would make sure he didn't get into the platoon. We weren't losing any guys, so that wasn't hard to do. We didn't have many openings. We didn't talk about it. I don't know why we had so much contact and didn't lose anybody. We never really talked about it.

Chapter 3

Special Clearance: OPERATION ORANGUTAN EVAL

1st Lt. Mary Damico, 557783021, Army Nurse Corps, Tape 7
Transcript

This Huey comes in real fast and low and I get sand in my eyes from the rotorwash. A guy with a clipboard about twenty yards away signals me and I get on. There's no one there to say goodbye and I never see the 21st again.

The Huey's empty except for these two pilots who never turn around and this doorgunner who's hanging outside and this other guy who's sitting back with me on the canvas. I think maybe he's the one who's going to explain things, but he just stares for a while and doesn't say a thing. He's a sergeant, a Ranger, I think. He's been here a long time.

It's supposed to be dangerous to fly at night in Indian Country, I know, but we fly at night. We stop twice and I know we're in Indian Country. This one guy gets off, another guy gets on, and then two more. They seem to know each other and they start laughing. They try to get me to talk. One guy says, "You a Donut Dolly?" and the other guy says, "Hell, no, asshole, she's Army, can't you tell? She's got the thousand-yards." The third guys says to me, "Don't mind him, ma'am. They don't raise 'em right in Mississippi." They're trying to be nice but I don't want in.

I don't want to sleep either. But my head's tipped back against the steel and I keep waking up, trying to remember whether I've dreamed about people dying, but I can't. I fall asleep once for a long time and when I wake up I can remember people dying, but I can't see their faces.

I wake up once and there's an automatic weapon firing somewhere below us and maybe, unless I'm dreaming, the slick gets hit once or twice. Another time I wake up and the three guys are talking quietly, real serious, but I'm hurting from no needle and I don't even listen.

When the air changes I wake up. It's first light and cool and we're coming in on this big clearing, everything misty and beautiful. It's triple-canopy jungle I've never seen before and I know we're so far from Cam Ranh Bay or Saigon it doesn't matter. I don't see anything that looks like a compound, just this clearing, like a staging area. There are a lot of guys walking around, a lot of machinery, but it doesn't look like regular Army. It looks like something you hear about but aren't supposed to see, and I'm shaking like a baby.

When we hit the LZ the three guys don't even know I exist and I barely get out of the Huey on my own. I can't see because of the wash and suddenly this Green Beanie medic I've never seen before—this sergeant—has me by the arm and he's taking me somewhere. I tell myself I'm not going back to the Big PX, I'm not going to some VA hospital for the rest of my life, that this is the guy I'm going to be assigned to—they need a nurse out here or something.

I'm not thinking straight. Special Forces medics don't have nurses.

I'm looking around me and I don't believe what I'm seeing. There's bunkers and M-60 emplacements and Montagnard guards on the perimeter and all this beautiful red earth. There's every kind of jungle fatigue and cammie you can think of—stripes and spots and black pajamas like Charlie wears and everything else. I see Special Forces enlisted everywhere and I know this isn't some little A-camp. I see a dozen guys in real clean fatigues who don't walk like soldiers walk. I see a Special Forces major and he's arguing with one of them.

The captain who's got me by the arm isn't saying a thing. He takes me to this little bunker that's got mosquito netting and a big canvas flap over the front and he puts me inside. It's got a cot. He tells me to lie down and I do. He says, "The CO wants you to get some sleep, Lieutenant. Someone will be by with something in a little while." The way he says it I *know* he knows about the needles.

I don't know how long I'm in the bunker before someone comes, but I'm in lousy shape. This guy in civvies give me something to take with a little paper cup and I go ahead and do it. I'm not going to fight it the shape I'm in. I dream, and keep dreaming, and in some of the dreams someone comes by with a cup of water and I take more pills. I can't wake up. All I can do is sleep but I'm not really sleeping and I'm having these dreams that aren't really dreams. Once or twice I hear myself screaming, it hurts so much, and then I dream about a little paper cup and more pills.

When I come out of it I'm not shaking. I know it's not supposed to be this quick, that what they gave me isn't what people are getting in programs in the States, and I get scared again. Who are these guys?

I sit in the little bunker all day eating ham-and-motherfuckers from C-rat cans and I tell myself that Steve had something to do with this. I'm scared but it's nice not to be shaking. It's nice not to be thinking about needles all the time.

The next morning I hear all this noise and I realize we're leaving, the whole camp is leaving. I can hear this noise like a hundred slicks outside and I get up and look through the flap. I've never seen so many choppers. They've got Chinooks and Hueys and Cobras and Loaches and a Skycrane for the SeaBee machines and they're dusting off and dropping in and dusting off again. I've never seen anything like it. I keep looking for Steve. I keep trying to remember the dreams I had while I was out all those days, but I can't.

Finally the Green Beanie medic comes back. He doesn't say a word. He just takes me to the LZ and we wait until a slick drops in. All these tiger stripes pile in with us but no one says a thing.

No one's joking. I don't understand it. We aren't being hit, we're just moving, but no one's joking.

We set up in a highlands valley northwest of where we'd been, where the jungle is thicker but it's not triple canopy. There's this same beautiful mist and I wonder if we're in some other country, Laos or Cambodia.

They have my bunker dug in about an hour and I'm in it about thirty minutes before this guy appears. I've been looking for Steve, wondering why I haven't seen him, and feeling pretty good about myself. It's nice not to be shaking, to get the monkey off my back, and I'm ready to thank *somebody*.

This guy opens the flap. He stands there for a moment and there's something familiar about him. He's about thirty and he's in real clean fatigues. He's got MD written all over him—but the kind that never gets any blood on him. I think of VA hospitals, psychiatric wards, and I get scared again.

"How are you feeling, Lieutenant?"

"Fine," I say, but I'm not smiling. I know this guy from the dreams—the little paper cups, the pills—and I don't like what I'm feeling.

"Glad to hear it. Remarkable drug, isn't it, Lieutenant?"

I nod. Nothing he says surprises me.

"Someone wants to see you, Lieutenant."

I get up, dreading it. I know he's not talking about Steve.

They've got all the bunkers dug and he takes me to what has to be the CP. There isn't a guy inside who isn't in real clean fatigues. There are three or four guys who have the same look this guy has—MDs that don't ever get their hands dirty—and intel types pointing at maps and pushing things around on a couple of sand-table mock-ups. There's this one guy with his back turned and everyone else keeps checking in with him.

He's tall. He's got a full head of hair but it isn't going gray. He doesn't even have to turn around and I know.

It's the guy in civvies at the end of the hallway at the 21st, the guy that walked away with Steve that night.

He turns around and I don't give him eye contact. He looks at me, smiles and starts over. There are two guys trailing him and he's got that smile that's supposed to be charming.

"How are you feeling, Lieutenant?" he says.

"Everybody keeps asking me that," I say, and wonder why I'm being so brave.

"That's because we're interested in you, Lieutenant," he says. He's got this jungle outfit on with gorgeous creases and some canvas jungle boots that breathe nicely. He looks like an ad from a catalogue, but I know he's no joke, he's no strac lifer. He's wearing this stuff because he *likes* it, that's all. He could wear anything he wanted to because he's not really military, but he's the CO of this operation, which means he's fighting a war I don't know a thing about.

He tells me he's got some things to straighten out first, but that if I'll go back to my little bunker he'll be there in an hour. He asks me if I want anything to eat. When I say sure, he tells the MD type to get me something from the mess.

I go back. I wait. When he comes, he's got a file in his hand and there are two guys with him. One's a young guy who grins and has a cold six-pack of Coke in his hands. I can tell they're cold because the bottles are sweating. I can't believe it. We're out here in the middle of nowhere, we're probably not even supposed to be here, and they're bringing me cold Coke.

The other guy is older. He's tall and skinny and wearing fatigues and he looks sick. He's thin, the way people get when they're sick for a long time—you know, the veins showing. He stares at me for a second and then looks away. He cocks his head, like he's listening. He's a captain—the patch on his collar says that—but I don't catch a name. He stays outside. He doesn't say a word out there.

The young guy leaves but the older skinny guy doesn't. I can see his shadow through the flap and I'm starting to wonder why he's here at all—he's not a guard, he's not saying a thing—and then the CO sits down on the opposite end of my cot and says, "Would you like one, Lieutenant?"

I say, "Yes, sir," and he pops the top with a church key. He doesn't take one himself and suddenly I wish I hadn't said yes. I'm thinking of old movies where Jap officers offer their prisoners a cigarette so they'll owe them one. There's not even any place to put the bottle down, so I hold it between my hands.

"I'm not sure where to begin, Lieutenant," he says, "but let me assure you you're here because you belong here." He says it real gently, but it gives me a funny feeling. "You're an officer and you've been in-country for some time. I don't need to tell you we're a very special kind of operation here. What I do need to tell you is that you're one of three hundred we've identified so far in this war. Do you understand?"

I say, "No, sir."

"I think you do, but you're not sure, right? You've accepted the difference—your gift, your curse, your talent, whatever you'd like to call it—but you can't as easily accept the fact that so many others might have the same thing, am I right, Mary—may I call you 'Mary'?"

I don't like the way he says it, but I tell him yes.

"We've identified three hundred like you, Mary. That's what I'm saying."

I stare at him, not knowing whether to believe him or not. I hear the thin guy outside cough. I remember a man my father knew who coughed just like that. He'd survived some terrible march in World War II. He still coughed that way.

"I'm only sorry, Mary, that you came to our attention so late. Being alone with a gift like yours isn't easy, I'm sure, and finding a community of those who share it—the same gift, the same 'curse'—is essential if the problems that sometimes accompany it are to be worked out successfully, am I correct?"

"Yes, sir."

"We might have lost you, Mary, if Lieutenant Balsam hadn't found you. He almost didn't make the trip that day, for reasons that will become obvious later. If he hadn't met you, Mary, I'm afraid your hospital would have sent you back to the States for drug abuse if not for what they perceived as your increasingly dysfunctional neurosis. Does this surprise you?"

I tell him it doesn't.

"I didn't think so. You're a smart girl, Mary."

The voice is gentle, and it's also not.

He waits and I don't know why.

I say, "Thank you for whatever it was that—"

"No need to thank us, Mary. Were that particular drug—that blocker—available back home right now, it wouldn't seem like such a gift now, would it?"

He's right. He's the kind who's always right and I don't like the feeling.

"Anyway, thanks," I say. I'm wondering where Steve is.

After a moment he says:

"You're probably wondering where Lieutenant Balsam is, Mary."

I don't bother to nod this time.

"He'll be back in a few days. We have a policy here of not discussing missions—even in the ranks—and as commanding officer I like to set a good example. You can understand that, I'm sure." He smiles again and for the first time I see the crow's-feet around his eyes, and how straight his teeth are, and how there are little capillaries broken on his cheeks.

He looks at the Coke in my hand and smiles. Then he opens the file he has. "If we were doing this the right way, Mary, we'd be in a nice air-conditioned building back in The World and we'd be going over all of this together, but we're not exactly in a position to do that, are we?

"I don't know how much you've gathered about your gift, Mary, but people who study such things have their own way of talking. They would call yours a 'probable TPC hybrid with traumatic neurosis, dissociative features.'" He smiles. "That's not as bad as it sounds. It's quite normal, in fact. The human psyche always responds to special gifts like yours, and neurosis is simply a mechanism for doing that. We wouldn't be human if it weren't, would we?"

"No, we wouldn't."

He's smiling at me and I know what he wants me to feel. I feel like a little girl sitting on a chair, being good, listening and liking it, and that's what he wants.

"Those same people, Mary, would call your dreams 'spontaneous anecdotal material,' and your talent a 'REM-state precognition.' They're not very helpful words. They're the words of people who've never experienced it themselves. Only you, Mary, know what it really feels like. Am I right?"

I remember liking how that felt—*only you*. I needed to feel that. He knew I needed to.

"Not all three hundred, of course, are dreamers like you. Some are what those same people would call 'kinetic phenomena generators.' Some are 'tactility-triggered remoters' or 'OBE clears.' Some leave their bodies in a firefight and acquire information that could not be acquired in ordinary ways, and that's how we know their talent is authentic. Others see auras when their comrades are about to die, and if they can get those auras to disappear, their friends will indeed live. Others experience only a vague visceral sensation, a 'gut' feeling which tells them where mines and trip wires are. They know, for example, when a crossbow trap will fire and are able, despite all odds, to knock away those arrows before they're hurt. Still others receive pictures, like waking dreams, of what will happen in the next minute, the next hour, the next day in combat.

"With very few exceptions, Mary, none of these individuals experienced anything like this as civilians. These episodes are the consequences of combat, of the metabolic and psychological anomalies that life-and-death conditions seem to generate."

He looks at me and his voice changes now, as if on cue. He wants me to feel what he is feeling and I do. I do. I can't look away from him and I know this is why he is the CO.

"It is almost impossible to reproduce them in a laboratory, Mary, and so these remarkable talents remain mere anecdotes, events that happen once or twice in a lifetime—to a brother, a mother, a friend, a fellow soldier in war. A boy is killed on Kwajalein in 1944. That same night his mother dreams of his death. She has never before dreamed such a dream, and the dream is too accurate to be mere coincidence. He dies. She never has a dream like it again. A reporter for a major newspaper looks out the terminal window at the Boeing 707 he is about to board. He has flown a hundred times before, enjoys travel and has no reason to be anxious today. But as he looks through the window, the plane explodes before his very eyes. He can hear the sound ringing in his ears and the sirens rising in the distance; he can feel the heat of the ignited fuel on his face. He blinks. The jet is as it was before—no fire, no sirens, no explosion. He is shaking—he has never experienced anything like this in his life. He does not board the plane, and the next day he hears how its fuel tanks exploded, on the ground, in another city, killing ninety. The man does not have a vision like that again. He enjoys air travel in the months and years ahead and dies of cardiac arrest on a tennis court twenty years later. You can see the difficulty we have, Mary."

"Yes," I say quietly, moved by what he has said.

"But our difficulty does not mean that your dreams are any less real, Mary. It does not mean that what you and the three hundred like you in this theater of war are experiencing isn't real."

"Yes," I say.

He gets up.

"I am going to have one of my colleagues interview you, if that's all right. He will ask you questions about your dreams and he will record what you say. The tapes will remain in my care, so there isn't any need to worry, Mary."

I nod.

"I hope that you will view your stay here as deserved R&R, and as a chance to make contact with others who understand what it is like. For paperwork's sake, I've assigned you to Golf Team. You met three of its members on your flight in, I believe. You may write to your parents as long as you make reference to a medevac unit in Pleiku rather than to our actual operation here. Is that clear?"

He smiles as a friend would and makes his voice as gentle as he can. "I'm going to leave the rest of the Coke. And a church key. Do I have your permission?" He grins. It's a joke, I realize. I'm supposed to smile. When I do, he smiles back and I know he knows everything, he knows himself, he knows me, what I think of him, what I've been thinking every minute he's been here. He's *that* kind of doctor, and he's good.

His name is Bucannon.

*   *   *

Subject: I was still dreaming about the muddy river then. I was dreaming about it every two or three nights, just the river, and didn't know what it meant.

Interviewer: Couldn't you see where it was heading, Lieutenant?

Subject: That's not fair. I was dreaming about a river, but there wasn't any *body* lying there. There was just the river. How could I possibly have known what it meant?

Memo 1/13/62, Joint Chiefs of Staff to the Secretary of Defense. Copy to the President (covering) 1/27/62

3. *Military Considerations*

b. Possible eventualities: Of equal importance to the immediate losses are the eventualities which could follow the loss of the Southeast Asian mainland. All of the Indonesian archipelago would come under the domination and control of the USSR and would become a communist base posing a threat against Australia and New Zealand. The Sino-Soviet bloc would have control of the eastern access to the Indian Ocean. The Philippines and Japan could be pressured to assume at best a neutralist role, thus eliminating two of our major bases in the Western Pacific. Our lines of defense would then be pulled north to Korea, Okinawa and Taiwan, resulting in the subsequent overtaking of our lines of communications in a limited war. India's ability to remain neutral would be jeopardized and, as the bloc meets success, its concurrent stepped-up activities to move into and control Africa could be expected. . . .

Memo 4/25/71, Deputy Director of Plans to Deputy Director of Operations, Internal

I don't see the problem. The Man wants Le Duan and Pham Van Dong at the bargaining table more than he wants Cronkite off his back, so it's got to be a JCS call.

Wheeler's interests are an end to the bombing (with *honor*) and a last dig at Henry. If we can shut Hanoi down once and for all with anything resembling an act of God—*and* do it below JCS or NSC level (that's our promise—remind them)—everybody gets a denial and still walks away with a piece of the pie. Remind them also that the Company's rain dance may make that river nice and high and that pretty rice bowl awfully wet but Mother Nature's been doing the same thing for years and the dikes are still standing. If there's a problem, Dave, it's with SACSA. Find out who, why and what they want to see it our way. If it's Waller or Childress at SOD, do same. If there's a problem in Room 52 or (God forbid) the E Ring, get Finney and play good cop/bad cop—or ask LaMora. I'm not yet ready to think the good doctor was wrong about their willingness to cut us loose with this one.

Chapter 4

The man that came was one of the other MD types from the tent. He asked and I answered. The question that took the longest was, "What were your dreams like? Be as specific as possible about both the dream content and its relationship to reality—that is, how accurate was the dream as a predictor of what happened? Describe how the dreams and their relationship to reality (that is, their accuracy) affected you both psychologically and physically (for example, sleeplessness, nightmares, inability to concentrate, anxiety, depression, uncontrollable rages, suicidal thoughts, drug abuse)."

It took us six hours and six tapes.

We finished after dark.

I did what I was supposed to do. I hung around Golf Team. There were six guys, this lieutenant named Pagano, who was in charge, and this older demo sergeant named Christabel, who was their "talent." He was, I found out, an "OBE clairvoyant with EEG anomalies," which meant that in a firefight he could leave his body just like Steve could. He could leave his body, look back at himself—that's what it felt like—and see how everyone else was doing and maybe, just maybe, save someone's ass. They were a good team. The sergeant had a drinking problem, they said, but who didn't? If anyone was worried, it wasn't about any drinking problem. They loved this sergeant and it really showed. He was forty years old. He was like somebody's father.

We talked about Saigon and what you could get on the black

market. We talked about missions, even though we weren't supposed to. The three guys from the slick even got me to talk about the dreams, I was feeling that good, and when I heard they were going out on another mission at 0300 hours the next day, without the sergeant—some little mission they didn't need him on, someone said—I didn't think anything about it. I didn't know it was because he wouldn't go out.

I liked him and I think he liked me. I never thought it was because he was afraid.

I woke up in my bunker that night screaming because two of the guys from the slick were dead. I saw them dying out in the jungle, I saw how they died, and suddenly I knew what it was all about, why Bucannon wanted me there.

He came by the bunker at first light. I was still crying. He knelt down beside me and put his hand on my forehead. He made his voice gentle. He said, "What was your dream about, Mary?"

I wouldn't tell him. "You've got to call them back," I said.

"I can't, Mary," he said. "We've lost contact."

He was lying, I found out later. He could have called them back—no one was dead yet—but I didn't know that then. He had sent them out without a "talent," to see what would happen, but I didn't know that then. So I went ahead and told him about the two I'd dreamed about, the one from Mississippi and the one with good manners. He took notes. I was a mess, crying and sweaty, and he pushed the hair away from my forehead and said he would do what he could.

I didn't want him to touch me, but I didn't stop him.

I didn't leave the bunker for a long time.

No one told me the two guys were dead. No one had to. It was the right kind of dream, just like before. But this time I'd *known* them. I'd met them. I'd laughed with them in the daylight and when they died I wasn't there, it wasn't on some gurney in a room somewhere. It was different.

It was starting up again, I knew.

I didn't get out of the cot until noon. I was thinking about needles, that was all.

* * *

He comes by again at about 1900 hours, just walks in and says, "Why don't you have some dinner, Mary? You must be hungry."

I go to the mess they've thrown together in a big tent. I think the guys are going to know about the screaming, but all they do is look at me like I'm the only woman in the camp, that's all, and that's okay. They haven't seen a round-eyed woman in a long time and I don't mind.

Then I see Steve. He's sitting with three other guys and I get this feeling he doesn't want to see me, that if he did he'd have come looking for me already, that I should turn around and leave. But one of the guys is saying something to him and Steve is turning and I know I'm wrong. He's been waiting for me. He's wearing cammies and they're dirty—he hasn't been back long—and I can tell by the way he gets up and comes toward me that he really does want to see me.

We go outside and stand where no one can hear us. He says, "Jesus, I'm sorry." I'm not sure what he means.

"Are you okay?" I say, but he doesn't answer.

He's saying, "I wasn't the one who told him about the dreams, Mary, I swear it. All I did was ask for a couple hours' layover to see you, but he doesn't like that—he doesn't like 'variables.' When he gets me back to camp, he has you checked out. The hospital says something about dreams and how crazy you're acting, and he puts it together. He's smart, Mary. He's *real* smart—"

I tell him to shut up, it isn't his fault, that I'd rather be here than back in the States in some VA program or ward. But he's not listening. "He's got you here for a reason, Mary. He's got all of us here for a reason and if I hadn't asked for those hours he wouldn't know you existed—"

I get mad. I tell him I don't want to hear any more about it, it isn't his fault.

"Okay," he says finally. "Okay." He gives me a smile because he knows I need it. "Want to meet the guys on the team?" he says. "We just got extracted—"

I say sure. We go back in. He gets me some food and then introduces me. They're dirty and tired but they're not complaining. They're still too high off the mission to eat and won't crash for another couple of hours yet. There's an SF medic with the team, and two Navy SEALs because there's a brown-water aspect to the mission, and a guy named Moburg, a marine sniper out of Quantico. Steve's their TL and all I can think about is how young he is. They're all so young.

It turns out Moburg's a talent, too, but it's "anticipatory subliminal"—it only helps him target his hits and doesn't help anyone else much. But he's damn good because of it.

The guys give me food from their trays and for the first time today I'm feeling hungry. I'm eating with guys that are real and alive and I'm really hungry.

Then I notice Steve isn't talking. He's got that same look on his face and I turn around.

Bucannon is looking at us. The tall, skinny captain is with him, a few feet back, watching *me*. Bucannon's smiling, and I get a chill down my spine like cold water because I *know*—all of a sudden I *know*—why I'm sitting here, and who wants it this way and why.

I get up fast. Steve doesn't understand. He says something and I don't answer him, I don't even hear him. I keep going. He's behind me and he wants to know if I'm feeling okay, but I don't want to look back at him, I don't want to look at any of the guys with him, because that's what Bucannon wants.

He's going to send them out again, I tell myself. They just got back, they're tired, and he's going to send them out again—so I can dream about them.

I'm not going to go to sleep, I tell myself. I walk the perimeter until they tell me I can't do that anymore, it's too dangerous. Steve follows me and I start screaming at him, but I'm not making any sense. He watches me for a while and then someone comes to get him, and I know he's being told to take his team out again. I ask for some Benzedrine from the Green Beanie medic who brings me aspirin when I want it, but he says he can't, that word has come down that he can't. I try writing a letter to my parents—I haven't done that in a long time—but it's 0400 hours and I'm going crazy trying to stay awake because I haven't had more than four hours' sleep for a couple of nights and my body temperature is dropping on the diurnal.

I ask for some beer and they get it for me. I ask for some scotch. They give it to me and I think I've won. I never go to sleep on booze, but Bucannon doesn't know that. I'll stay awake and I won't dream.

But it knocks me out like a light, and I have a dream. One of the guys at the table, one of the SEALs, is floating down a river. The blood is like a woman's hair streaming out from his head. I don't dream about Steve, just about this SEAL who's floating down a river. It's early in the mission. Somehow I know that.

I don't wake up screaming, because of what they put in the booze. I remember it as soon as I wake up, when I can't do a thing about it.

Bucannon comes in at first light. He doesn't say, "If you don't help us, you're going back to Saigon or back to the States with a Section Eight." Instead he comes in and kneels down beside me like some goddamn priest and says, "I know this is painful, Mary, but I'm sure you can understand."

I say, "Get the hell out of here, motherfucker."

It's like he doesn't hear me. He says, "It would help us to know the details of any dream you had last night, Mary."

"You'll let him die anyway," I say.

"I'm sorry, Mary," he says, "but he's already dead. We've received word on one confirmed KIA in Echo Team. All we're interested in is the details of the dream and an approximate time, Mary." He hesitates. "I think he would want you to help us. I think he would want to feel that his death meant something, don't you, Mary?"

He stands up.

"I'm going to leave some paper and writing utensils for you. I can understand what you're going through, more than you might imagine, Mary, and I believe that if you give it some thought—if you think about men like Steve and what your dreams could mean to them—you will do it, you will write down the details of your dream last night."

I scream something at him. When he's gone I cry for a while. Then I go ahead and write down what he wants. I don't know what else to do.

Bucannon has food brought to my bunker but I don't eat it. I throw it against the bunker wall and I scream some more. Christabel tries to visit me, but they won't let him in. He stands outside in his dirty T-shirt, with his potbelly, like some drunk, and says, "I've got to see her, sir." He pokes his head around them and gives me a smile and says, "Hello, Lieutenant," but they tell him to get back to his bunker or they'll grease his ass. He peeks around and says, "Good night." I can hear a beer or two in him, that's all. He isn't drunk, I tell myself. I can see his red face, his white teeth, even in the darkness.

I ask for the Green Beanie medic and he comes. I ask him where Steve is. Is he back yet? He says he can't tell me. I ask him to send a message to Steve for me. He says he can't do that. I tell him he's a straight-leg ass-kisser and ought to have his jump wings shoved, but this doesn't faze him at all. Any other place, I say, you'd be what you were supposed to be—Special Forces and a good medic—but Bucannon's got you by the balls, doesn't he? He doesn't say a thing.

I stay awake all that night. I ask for coffee and I get it. I bum more coffee off two guys on the perimeter and drink that, too. I can't believe he's letting me have it. Steve's team is going to be back soon, I tell myself—they're a hunter-killer team, not a LURP—and if I don't sleep, I can't dream.

I do it again the next night and it's easier. I can't believe it's this easy. I keep moving around. I get coffee and I find this sentry who likes to play poker and we play all night. I tell him I'm a talent and will know if someone's trying to come through the wire on us, sapper or whatever, so we can play cards and not worry. He's pure fucking-new-guy and he believes me.

Steve'll be back tomorrow, I tell myself. I'm starting to see things and I'm not thinking clearly, but I'm not going to crash. I'm not going to crash until Steve is back. I'm not going to dream about Steve.

At about 0700 the next day we get mortared. The slicks inside the perimeter start revving up, the Skycrane starts hooking its cats and Rome plows and the whole camp starts to dust off. I hear radios, more slicks and Skycranes being called in. If the NVA had a battalion, they'd be overrunning us, I tell myself, so it's got to be a lot less—company, platoon—and they're just harassing us, but the word has come down from someone that we're going to move.

Mortars are whistling in and someone to one side of me says, "Incoming—fuck it!" Then I hear this other sound. It's like flies but real loud. It's like this weird whispering. It's a goddamn fléchette round, I realize, spraying stuff, and I don't understand. I can hear it, but it's like a memory, a flashback. Everybody's running around me and I'm just standing there and someone's screaming. It's me screaming. I've got fléchettes all through me—my chest, my face, I'm torn to pieces. I'm dying. But I'm running toward the slick, the one that's right over there, and I'm running, but I'm not. I'm on the ground. I'm on the jungle floor with these fléchettes in me and I've got a name, a nickname, "Kicker," and I'm thinking of a town in Wyoming, near the Montana border, where everybody rides pickup trucks with shotgun racks and waves to everybody else. I grew up there, there's a rodeo every spring with a country fair and I'm thinking about a girl with braids, I'm thinking how I'm going to die here in the middle of this jungle, how we're on some recondo that no one gives a shit about, how Charlie doesn't have fléchette rounds, and how Bucannon never makes mistakes.

I'm running and screaming and when I get to the slick the Green Beanie medic grabs me, two other guys grab me and haul me in. I look up. It's Bucannon's slick. He's on the radio. I'm lying on a pile of files right beside him and we're up over the jungle now, we're taking the camp somewhere else, where it can start up all over again.

I look up at Bucannon. The skinny captain is with him. I

think they're going to turn any minute and say to me, "Which ones, Mary? Which ones died from the fléchettes?" They don't. I look down and see that someone's put some paper and pencils beside me on the floor. I can't stand it. I start crying.

Photostat, Draft Conference Paper, Command Files (Bucannon), Operation Orangutan, Tiger Cat, Vietnam

A "Survival Readiness" Model for Psi
John W. Bucannon
Division of Psychiatry
Johns Hopkins University Medical Center

Leaning heavily on psychoanalytic models, Ehrenwald (1969) has proposed—and most of us have accepted—early mother-child symbiosis as the evolutionary source and model of GESP. In light of certain GESP phenomena, even entire modalities, which would appear inconsistent with this model, I would like to propose yet another—one which circumscribes and subsumes not only the Ehrenwald model but all psi phenomena and modalities except for PK, which remains problematic. This model, which for lack of a better term I call "survival readiness," is as primal in evolutionary terms as Dr. Ehrenwald's and as a consequence equally "need-intensive" in its psychodynamic behavior.

Part 1

The Nondirectional, Nonlocational Function

As Karmen and Johnson (1968) have shown, the five universal exosenses comprise an articulated sensory system designed, through increasing degrees of locationality and directionality, to carry a threatened vertebrate from initial sensory alarm to "fight-flight" readiness and, if necessary, to physical contact with the threat. Extending this model, GESP, depending on both modality and temporal-spatial dislocation of the threat, may be seen as an *alerting, focusing* and *substituting* "pre-sense," that is, a "sixth sense" which (1) through initial alarm readies the universal-exosense system for threat-responsive behavior, (2) helps "focus" one or more of the five universal senses during that behavior, or (3) during that behavior substitutes for one of the five conventional exosenses. In this model, GESP, the least directional and locational of the system's senses, assumes its role as that sense which over evolutionary time has operated through naturally achieved ASCs to raise the organism— whether as individual, member of a mother-child dyad or member of Belstein's "altruistic group"—to *survival readiness.*

While the telepathic dreams of patients in therapy may appear inconsistent with this model, when viewed as resolutions of the ego threat posed by events within the patient-doctor relationship (termination of therapy, excessive transference, even cure) they can be seen to function in one or more of the three "pre-sense" roles. A therapy room is, after all, no different from a jungle; whether it is the psyche or the physical body that is at threat, self-protective behavior through the universal-exosense system of defense is fundamental, and the "arming" of that system inevitable. . . .

Chapter 5

I sleep maybe for twenty minutes there on the floor and have two dreams. Two other guys died out there somewhere with fléchettes in them. Two more guys on Steve's team died and I didn't even meet them.

I look up. Bucannon's smiling at me. The captain is standing right behind him, leaning on the steel, his head cocked, listening.

"It happened, didn't it, Mary?" Bucannon says gently. "It happened in the daylight this time, didn't it?"

At the new camp I stayed awake another night, but it was hard and it didn't make any difference. It just made it worse. It happened three more times the next day and all sorts of guys saw me. I knew someone would tell Steve. I knew Steve's team was still out there—Echo hadn't come in when the rocketing started— but that he was okay. I'm lying on the ground screaming and cry-ing with shrapnel going through me, my legs are gone, my left eyeball is hanging out on my cheek and there are pieces of me all over the guy next to me, but I'm not Steve and that's all that matters.

The third time, an AK round goes through my neck so I can't even scream. I fall down and can't get up. Someone kneels down next to me and I think it's Bucannon and I try to hit him. I'm trying to scream even though I can't, but it's not Bucannon, it's one of the guys who were sitting with Steve in the mess. They're back, they're back, I think to myself, but I'm trying to tell this guy that I'm dying, that there's this medic somewhere out there under a beautiful banyan tree who's trying to pull me through, but I'm not going to make it, I'm going to die on him, and he's going to remember it his whole life, wake up in the night crying years later and his wife won't understand why.

I want to say, "Tell Steve I've got to get out of here," but I can't. My throat's gone. I'm going out under some banyan tree thirty klicks away in the middle of Laos, where we're not supposed to be, and I can't say a thing.

This guy who shared his ham-and-motherfuckers with me in the mess, this guy is looking down on me and I think, Oh my God, I'm going to dream about him some night, some day, I'm going to dream about him and because I do, he's going to die.

He doesn't say a thing.

He's the one that comes to get me in my hootch two days later when they try to bust me out.

They give me something pretty strong. By the time they come I'm getting the waking dreams, sure, but I'm not screaming anymore. I'm here but I'm not. I'm all these other places, too, I'm walking into an Arc Light, B-52 bombers, my ears are bleeding, I'm the closest man when a big Chinese claymore goes off, my arm's hanging by a string, I'm dying in all these other places and I don't even know I've taken their pills. I'm like a doll when Steve and this guy and three others come and the guards let them in. I'm smiling like an idiot and I'm saying, "Thank you very much"—something sweet some USO type would say—and I've got someone holding me up so I don't fall on my face. "Is Steve coming?" I say. "Is our drunk sergeant coming?" I say. "Thank you very much," I say.

There's this Jolly Green Giant out in front of us. It's dawn and everything's beautiful and this chopper is gorgeous. It's Air Force. It's crazy. There are these guys I've never seen before. They've got black berets and they're neat and clean, and they're not Army. I think, Air Commandos! I'm giggling. They're Air Force. They're dandies. They're going to save the day like John Wayne at Iwo Jima. I feel a bullet go through my arm, then another through my leg, and the back of my head blows off, but I don't scream. I just feel the feelings, the ones you feel right before you die, but I don't scream. The Air Force is going to save me. That's funny. I tell myself how Steve had friends in the Air Commandos and how they took him around once in-country for a whole damn week, AWOL, yeah, but maybe it isn't true, maybe I'm dreaming it. I'm still giggling. I'm still saying, "Thank you very much."

We're out maybe fifty klicks and I don't know where we're heading. I don't care. Even if I cared I wouldn't know how far "safe" was. "Is Sergeant Christabel here?" I say. Someone says, "Not this trip, honey." I hear Steve's voice in the cockpit and a bunch of guys are laughing, so I think *safe*. They've busted me out because Steve cares and now we're *safe*. I'm still saying thanks and some guy is answering, "You're welcome, honey," and people are laughing, and that feels good. If they're all laughing, no one got hurt, I'm telling myself. If they're all laughing, we're safe. Thank you. Thank you very much.

Then something happens in the cockpit. I can't hear with all the wind. Someone says "Shit." Someone says "Cobra." Someone else says "Jesus-Christ-what-the-hell." I look out the roaring doorway and I see two black gunships. They're like nothing I've ever seen before. No one's laughing. I'm saying "Thank you very much" but no one's laughing.

I find out later there was one behind us, one in front and one above us. They were beautiful. They reared up like snakes when they hit you. They had M-134 Miniguns that could put a round on every square centimeter of a football field in seconds. They had fifty-two white phosphorus rockets apiece, I'm told, and wire-guided TOW missiles. They had laser designators and forward-looking infrared sensors. They were nightblack, no insignias of any kind. They were model AH-IG-X and they didn't belong to any regular branch of the military then. You wouldn't see them until the end of the war.

I remember thinking that there were only two of us with talent on the slick, so why couldn't he let us go? Why couldn't he just let us go?

I tried to think of all the things he could do to us, but he didn't do a thing. He didn't have to.

I didn't see Steve for a long time. I went ahead and tried to sleep at night because it was better that way. If I was going to have the dreams, it was better that way. It didn't make me so crazy. I wasn't like a doll someone had to hold up.

I went ahead and wrote the dreams down in a little notebook Bucannon gave me, and I talked to him. I showed him I really wanted to understand, how I wanted to help, because it was a lot easier on everybody that way. He didn't act surprised, and I didn't think he would. He'd always known. Maybe he hadn't known about the guys in the black berets, but he'd known that Steve would try. He'd known I'd stay awake. He'd known the dreams would move to daylight from "interrupted REM-state sleep" if I stayed awake. And he'd known he'd get us back.

We talked about how my dreams were changing, how I was having them much earlier than "events in real time." The same thing had been happening back at Cam Ranh Bay probably, he said, but I hadn't known it. The talent was getting stronger, he said, though I couldn't control it yet. I didn't need the "focal stimulus" anymore, he said. The "physical correlative." I didn't need to meet the people who were going to die to dream about them.

"When are we going to try it?" I finally said.

He knew what I meant. He said we didn't want to rush into it, how acting prematurely was worse than not understanding, how the "fixity of the future" was something no one yet understood, and we didn't want to take a chance of stopping the dreams by trying to tamper with the future.

"It won't stop the dreams," I said. "Even if we keep a death from happening, Colonel, it won't stop the dreams."

He never listened. He wanted them to die. He wanted to take notes on how they died and how my dreams matched their dying, and he wasn't going to call anyone back until he was ready.

"This isn't really war, Mary," he told me one day. "This is a kind of science and it has its own rules. You'll have to trust me, Mary."

He pushed the hair out of my eyes, because I was crying. The skinny captain wasn't there. He hadn't been around for a long time.

Bucannon wanted to touch me. I know that now.

I tried to get a message out. I tried to figure out who I'd dreamed about. I'd wake up in the middle of the night and try to talk to anybody I could and figure it out. I'd say, "Do you know a guy who's got red hair and is from Alabama?" I'd say, "Do you know this little black RTO who's *short* and can't listen to anyone except Sam Cooke?" Sometimes it would take too long. Sometimes I'd never find out who it was, but if I did, I'd try to get a message to him. Sometimes he'd already gone out and I'd still try to get someone to send him a message—but that just wasn't done.

I found out later Bucannon got them all. People said yeah, sure, they'd see that the message got to the guy, but Bucannon always got them. He told people to say yes when I asked. He knew. He *always* knew.

But I didn't have a dream about Steve, and that was the important thing.

When I finally dreamed that Steve died, that it took more guys in khaki uniforms than you'd think possible—with more weapons than you'd think they'd ever need, and in a river valley awfully far away—it was the dream I knew. I knew it from the 21st Evac and I knew it from my bunker. It was Steve in the mud, not the Dogman. It had been Steve all along. I just hadn't known it. I didn't tell Bucannon. I didn't tell him how Steve was jerking, jerking in the mud on a riverbank up North, doing his best to dodge the rounds with every single muscle in his body, even though there were too many of them—too many uniforms looking down at him, the river rushing by, his body jerking and jerking even though it wasn't alive anymore.

I cried for a while and then I stopped. I wanted to feel something but I couldn't.

I didn't ask for pills or booze and I didn't stay awake the next

two nights scared about dreaming it again. There was something I
needed to do.

I didn't know how long I had. I didn't know whether Steve's
team—the one in the dream—had already gone out or not. I
didn't know a thing, but I kept thinking about what Bucannon had
said, the "fixity," how maybe the future couldn't be changed, how
even if Bucannon hadn't intercepted those messages something
else would have kept the future the way it was, and those guys
would have died anyway.

I found the Green Beanie medic who'd taken me to my
bunker that first day. I sat down with him in the mess. One of
Bucannon's types was watching us, but I sat down anyway. I said,
"Has Steve Balsam been sent out yet?" He said, "I'm not supposed
to say. You know that, Lieutenant."

"Yes, Sergeant, I do. I also know that because you took me to
my little bunker that day I will probably dream about your death
before it happens, if it's going to happen here. I also know that if I
tell the people running this project about that dream, they won't
do a thing about it—even though they know how accurate my
dreams are, like they know how accurate Steve Balsam is, and
Bingham and Clipper and all the others, but they never do a thing
about it." I waited. He was listening now.

"I'm in a position, Sergeant, to let someone know when I
have a dream about them. Do you understand me?"

He didn't blink. "Yes," he said.

I asked him again. "Has Lieutenant Balsam been sent out
yet?"

"No," he said.

"Do you know anything about the mission he is about to go
on?"

He didn't want to answer, but after a moment he went ahead
and said, "The dikes."

"I don't understand."

He didn't want to have to explain it either. It made him mad
to have to. He looked at the MD type by the door and then he
looked back at me.

"You can take out the Red Dikes with a one-K nuclear device, Lieutenant. Everyone knows that. If you do it, Hanoi drowns and the North is down for the duration of the war. Balsam's team is a five-man night insertion from Laos with special DOD ordnance from a carrier at Yankee Station. All five are talents. Am I making sense, Lieutenant?"

I didn't say a thing. I just looked at him.

Finally I said, "It's a suicide mission, isn't it? The device won't even be real. It's one of Bucannon's ideas—he wants to see how they perform, that's all, that's all it ever is. They'll never use a nuclear device in Southeast Asia, Sergeant, and you know that as well as I do."

"You never know, Lieutenant," he said.

"No. Sometimes you do." I said it slowly, so he would understand.

He looked away, uncomfortable.

"When is the team leaving?"

He didn't answer. The MD type looked like he was going to walk over to us.

"Sergeant?"

"Thirty-eight hours. That's what they're saying."

I leaned over. I said, "You know the shape I was in when I got here, Sergeant. I need it again. I need enough of it to get me through a week of this place or I'm not going to make it and you're never going to know what you need to know to get out of here alive. You know where to get it, Sergeant. I'll need it tonight."

As I walked by the MD type at the door, I wondered how *he* was going to die, how long it was going to take, who would do it and *when.*

Photostat, Letter 4/28/71 (Intercept), Jerry Damico to 1st Lt. Mary Damico, 557783021, Command Files, Operation Orangutan, Tiger Cat, Vietnam

Hey Proud Mary!

Here's a snapshot of Dickie taken with Dad's new Polaroid. Dickie says he still wants you to marry him, but I told him fat chance—that you don't date kids.

Is it getting to you just a little? You can tell your brother. If you ever want to try a call on that military channel, just let me know. Guys call their girlfriends here all the time.

Wish I were there to carry all those bedpans around for you. (Hey, I may be getting there sooner than you think. Bobby and Hank are 1-A and I'm waiting. Save some of that beach for me!!!)

Love ya,

Jerry

Chapter 6

I did it the only way I knew how.

I started screaming at first light and when Bucannon came to my bunker, I was crying. I told him I'd had a dream about him. I told him I'd dreamed that his own men, guys in cammies and all of them talents, had killed him, they'd killed him because he wasn't using a nurse's dreams to keep their friends alive, because he had my dreams but wasn't doing anything with them, and all their friends were dying.

I looked in his eyes and I told him how scared I was because they killed her, too, they killed the nurse who was helping him.

I told him how big the .45-caliber holes looked in his fatigues, how someone put a round in his mouth—just one shot—and how the back of his head came apart. I told him how they got him dusted off as soon as they could and got him on a suction pump and IV as soon as he hit Saigon, but it just wasn't enough, how he choked to death on his own fluids.

He didn't believe me.

"Was Lieutenant Balsam there?" he asked.

I said no, he wasn't, trying not to cry. I didn't know why, but he wasn't, I said.

His eyes changed. He was looking at me now.

He said, "When do you think this will happen, Mary?"

I said I didn't know—not for a couple of days, but I couldn't be sure, how could I be sure? It felt like three, maybe four days, but I couldn't be sure. I was crying again.

He believed me now.

He knew it would never happen if Steve was here—but if Steve was gone, if the men waited until Steve was gone?

Steve would be gone in two days and there was no way this nurse, scared and crying, could know that.

He moved me to his bunker and had someone hang canvas to make a hootch for me inside his. He doubled the guards and changed the guards and doubled them again, but I knew he didn't think it was going to happen until Steve left.

I cried that night. He came to my hootch. He said, "Don't be frightened, Mary. No one's going to hurt you. No one's going to hurt anyone."

He looked at me and I thought: He isn't sure. He hasn't tried to stop a dream from coming true—even though I've asked him to—and he doesn't know whether he can or not.

I told him I wanted him to hold me, someone to hold me. I told him I wanted him to touch my forehead the way he had, to push my hair back the way he had.

He looked at me like he didn't understand, but then he did.

I told him I wanted someone to make love to me tonight, because it hadn't happened in so long, not with Steve, not with anyone. He said he understood. He said that if he'd only known, he could have made things easier on me.

He was quiet. He made sure the flaps of my little hootch were tight and he undressed in the dark. I held his hand just like I'd held the hands of the others, back at the 21st. I made his hand *feel* like theirs.

Even in the dark I could see how pale he was, like a dream. He seemed to glow in the dark even though there wasn't any light. I took off my clothes, too. I told him I wanted to do something special for him. He said fine, but we couldn't make much noise. I said there wouldn't be any noise. I told him to lie down on his stomach on the cot. I sounded excited. I even laughed. I told him it was called "around the world" and I liked it best with the man on his stomach. He did what I told him and I kneeled down and lay over him.

I raised the needle with the overdose, wondering how long I

would have to hold it in, whether I'd be able to aim well enough in the darkness, whether I'd be strong enough to hold him down.

A voice in the darkness said, "She's going to do it *now*, sir."

I screamed. I should have brought it down anyway, I should have jammed it in his eye, in his neck, anywhere, but I didn't. The voice was right there in the darkness with us, on the other side of the canvas, and I could feel something touching my eyes. It made me want to scream. I don't know how else to say it. It was like something touching my neck and my eyes.

Bucannon found my wrist in the dark and took the needle from me. He took it as if I were a kid, as if he'd known all along that he was going to take it, and that it wouldn't be hard.

I didn't fight him. I could feel someone else in the darkness with us, so I didn't bother fighting. I should have, I know that now.

I heard a cough. The feeling on my neck, in my eyes, came again and then stopped.

Chapter 7

Bucannon's holding my wrist in the darkness. The light goes on. I look away. I don't want to look at him, I don't want to see him naked, his arm next to mine. I don't want whoever is with us to see us like this either.

Bucannon gets up. He lets go of my hand and I can hear the rustling of clothes, the metal of a belt buckle. He puts his pants on and then his shirt. I don't watch him, but I know he's doing it—I can hear him doing it. Then he stands waiting for me to get dressed. I keep thinking of the needle, wondering where it is, where it went. I keep thinking the cough is going to come again and I'm going to scream when it does.

I don't know whether Bucannon watched me while I got dressed. I didn't look at him, so I don't know. When I'm finished, he takes me by the wrist again and we go past the canvas flap into the light.

The other person is there. I've never heard him speak, I've never seen him this close, but I know him. He's standing by the steps and he's not wearing cammies now. He's not wearing night-black on his face. He's not dressed for war at all. The OD fatigues with captain tracks on the collar are baggy on him, he's so thin. The bones of his face show, the skin is translucent, the adipose tissue all gone—the way it is when someone's been sick for a long time. I'm telling myself once again that he must've been sick for a long time.

The light is from a lamp on the dirt wall. He doesn't like it.

He's turned his face away from it as if it hurt, as if whatever's made him so thin has also given him photophobia. He's going to look at me, I tell myself. He's going to turn his face until all of it's in the light and he's going to look at me. I'm the reason he's here, aren't I? I'm the one he was supposed to watch all this time, aren't I? I want to see his eyes.

But he doesn't turn. He keeps his stare to one side, away from the light and into the darkness of the other wall. It's as if I'm not here at all, as if no one is, just him and what he's thinking—what he's hearing, what he's seeing in the dark.

I look for infrared goggles, a starlight scope, anything he could've used to see me. He's got a Browning automatic on his belt, but everyone's got that. There isn't any hardware near him, on the floor, on the wall, nothing. I turn around. Even with the lamp on, the little canvas hootch Bucannon made for me is full of shadows. *No one* could have seen that needle in my hand, I know.

When we go past the captain, Bucannon doesn't say a word. We brush against him, it's that tight, and the thin captain still doesn't look at us. We move up the steps and when we reach the top, I start feeling the feeling again—on my neck, inside my eyes. I tell myself he's right behind me—*someone* is. I pull against Bucannon and I turn.

He isn't there. No one is. I hear a cough and see a shadow moving by the lamp at the bottom of the stairs, and the feeling goes away again.

When we reach my bunker Bucannon doesn't let go. He holds my hand in his and like a disappointed father, like a father who's expected something better from his kid, says very quietly, "What were you thinking of, Mary? Did you really imagine that by killing me you could stop your dreams, that you could keep Steve and others here safe forever?" He's looking at me and I can't look back. He wants me to feel the shame and I do. "If they weren't here, Mary," he says to me, "they would be somewhere else in this theater of war. They'd be dying somewhere, Mary—with or without me. They would be dying with or without you, too, Mary. That's what war is." He stops. I can hear his breathing. I can smell his breath, the toothpaste smell. His voice gets gentle, as it always does. "I'm not angry with you, but I *am* disappointed, Mary. I'm not going to report this to Saigon—I don't see any reason to—but in return I hope you'll do something for me. I hope you'll get a good night's sleep. I hope you'll think about what nearly happened tonight." He stops. "Will you *please* do that?" He stops again. "We'll be receiving incoming tonight, Mary, and if you'd like something to help you get that good night's sleep, just ask for it. Either Major DuRall or Major Miller can get it for you."

He's not holding my wrist anymore and I don't remember nodding. I do remember saying, "Who is he, Colonel? Who is that guy?"

He knows which one I mean, but he doesn't answer. He isn't holding my wrist anymore, so I go down into the bunker, into the dark, and when I find the cot with my knees, I lie down and try to sleep.

One of the MD types comes to my bunker at 0900. The thin captain is with him but he stays outside again and doesn't say a thing. I'm going to scream if he comes inside, I tell myself. I'm going to scream and not stop screaming, I know—so he doesn't.

I haven't slept with all the mortars. I haven't dreamed about Steve, I haven't dreamed about anyone, and I'm not sure why. They're out there dying. I *know* this. They never stop dying, Mary. I've cried a lot—old dreams, Bucannon holding my hand, the voice in the darkness saying, "She's going to do it now, sir." I didn't want to cry, but I did, and I don't want these guys to see me crying now. I'm not going to cry in front of them ever again, I'm telling myself.

I'm thinking: *Why did you even try? You didn't have a dream. You knew it wasn't going to happen, but you went ahead and tried.*

I get up off the cot. It smells. *I* smell. I don't want this guy standing over me like this. I don't want him standing over me like this, smelling the smell.

He just stands there in his pressed utilities and says:

"The colonel has made some changes in Lieutenant Balsam's upcoming mission and feels certain you'll see the wisdom of those changes. In light of what happened last night, Lieutenant, the colonel feels you should begin spending more time with your peers, and he suspects you won't have any objections to this. Can I tell him he's right?" The man's smiling. We're sharing a little joke. *You can trust me. I can trust you,* he's saying. It's Bucannon talking. It's *pure* Bucannon.

The guy goes on. "Colonel Bucannon wants me to stress again, Lieutenant, that he is *not* angry, that he does indeed understand what you're going through, that 'projection'—something which all people experience—is a natural mechanism. He believes, however—and he's confident you'll agree, Lieutenant— that it will be much healthier for all concerned if you and he spend less time together."

He stops. He waits, wanting to hear my gratitude, wanting to be able to report it. When I don't say a word, he says:

"The colonel has also asked me to tell you that you will be working with Captain Kelly, whom you met last night. Captain Kelly will be your team leader, Lieutenant Balsam your assistant TL. The colonel has chosen each team member carefully, and hopes that you will keep that in mind."

He's crazy, I tell myself. I've tried to kill the man and he sends me someone to talk like this, this nicely, as if nothing has happened. No, I don't like the thin captain—I don't even like thinking about him—but if it means spending more time with Steve, why not? *You're right, Colonel. I see the wisdom. I have no objections.*

I'm starting to smile. I'm getting giddy. I'm starting to feel what it's like to *win.*

The guy is still talking: "The colonel has had some medication flown in from the States for you, Lieutenant. I will be the one dispensing it. I hope you'll feel free to ask any questions you may have about it. The drug is a T-lobe inhibitor, an ASC-suppressant which, you'll be happy to hear, should help keep your gift from interfering with your performance." He sees my smile and thinks he understands. *I've got a smile to report. I've got gratitude.*

"Take one every twelve hours on an empty stomach. If you experience any nausea or dizziness, let me know."

I take the pill while he stands there. I don't care what it is.

I'm supposed to believe that Bucannon wants to help, that he wants to give me something to stop the dreams? I don't care. I've won. The guy is leaving. He's saying something to the skinny man, to this Captain Kelly, and they're both leaving.

I'm grinning like an idiot. I'm as giddy as a prom queen. I'm telling myself: *You've done it, Mary. You didn't kill a man but you've stopped the dream from coming true.* If Bucannon has changed the mission, Steve can't die on it, can he? Steve can't die by the riverbank, jerking and jerking in the mud. He can't die on a mission *you're* on because you weren't in the dream dying with him, right? You're not lying on the riverbank with him, anywhere near it, the uniforms looking down on you, the river, the mud, all of it rushing by. You're not in that dream because Steve's not going on that mission anymore, you're all going somewhere else, and he's not going to die. It makes sense. It all makes sense, doesn't it?

I want to tell Steve. I want to feel how good it feels to tell someone, to make *them* feel it and by feeling it keep it alive. I haven't felt this good in a long, long time, Colonel. Thank you. *You've done it,* I'm telling myself. *You didn't kill Bucannon*—no one *can kill Bucannon*—*but you've stopped it, haven't you? You stopped the dream from coming true.*

Christabel comes down the bunker steps at 1200 hours. They let him through. I can't believe it. I want to hug and kiss him but I remember how I smell, how the whole bunker smells. I'm not going to hug him until we get outside, then I'm going to do it. I'm going to kiss him like we're not wearing uniforms and make his face even redder and laugh while I do it. I'm going to tell him about Steve and the dream—he doesn't know about it—and how Bucannon has changed the mission, Steve's mission, how I'm in on it now, because, get this, Bucannon thinks it'll be good for me.

I'm smiling. I'm going to make this big man, this ex-marine and Special Forces demo sergeant who doesn't smile anymore, smile too.

"I'm supposed to take you to lunch, Lieutenant," he says. I smell the old beer breath and I love it. We *both* smell bad, Sarge.

He won't mind. I give him a kiss and he hugs me back, but it's slow, it's weak. He's barely smiling and I can't get him to say it— the way he used to say it, the way his team always expected him to: "Ain't this a glorious day? Ain't this a day to let Uncle Ho's chillens know we love 'em?"

I say, "Sounds like a glorious day to me, Sergeant," teasing, trying to get him out. How about a smile, Sarge? I'm thinking: *How much has he had today?* I'm thinking: *Why does Bucannon let him sit there, in the bunker and do it?* I'm thinking: *Why did Bucannon send him to take me to lunch? Does it matter?*

I know why he sits in the bunker and so does he. I remember someone saying: *What is it worth, this talent, if you can't save others? What is it worth if you stay alive while others die?* Maybe it was Steve, maybe it wasn't. It doesn't matter.

I know he has a wife in Virginia, a girl in high school, that he drinks, that he's always been a drinker, but now it's even more. That he doesn't want the guys on his team to die anymore. He thinks he should be able to say this, but when he does, it feels wrong—like an excuse. It should be simple, the words for it: *I can't go out with them again, sir. If I do, I'll lose another one. And if not this time, then the next, sir.* The words should be easy, just like dreaming. But they're not. The drinking is a lot easier.

I know that he's an OBE, like Steve, that he can leave his body just like Steve can, float over a paddy or a highland LZ, see things he shouldn't be able to see and keep himself—just himself—alive.

No one ever said the gift was for others.

I know why he wasn't on that chopper with us. It's a terrible thing to be afraid, Colonel.

Like an idiot I say it again, "Sounds like a glorious day, Sarge."

He doesn't say a thing and I know something's wrong. We're walking across the compound and he should be saying, "You've got to watch the canned peaches and the canned angel food cake, Lieutenant. Charlie can't stand beautiful round-eyed women and he'll find a way to get a little krait snake into your peaches or a praying-buddha spider into your cake and it'll bite you on that pretty little lip of yours and all we'll have is a bunch of old mamasans to look at for the rest of this war. If you'll forgive the insubordination, ma'am." This is what he should be saying, and I would be laughing. It would be good for me, right, Colonel? "This pill is good shit," I want to say.

He says: "You ever fired an AK, Lieutenant?"

He won't look at me.

"Have you ever fired an AK-47, Lieutenant?"

I tell him no, all I've fired is a .45. I want to tell him about the M-14 at Fort Sam—the one they wouldn't let any of us fire— but I'm thinking: *Tell him now. Tell him what you tried to do last night, Mary, how Steve won't be going out on that mission, how you won't have to dream about it ever again. It'll make him smile, Mary. It'll make whatever's driving him crazy go away.*

But I don't.

He's looking at me now and I can see he *knows*. He knows all about last night. He knows more about it than I do, and he's not smiling.

"Why do I need to know how to fire an AK-47, Sergeant?" I hold my breath, waiting. He looks away again.

"The CO says I've got to find an AK for you and get you some range practice, ma'am. That's all I know."

He's lying. He looks at me again, then away. He knows I know he's lying. *They all lie—even the good ones, Mary*, I tell myself. "The colonel says he'd also like you to get some Makarov practice over the next couple of days. A Makarov is a nine-milli-meter—"

"I know what a Makarov is, Sergeant," I say, lying. I'm getting angry. I can't keep the happiness alive. He's killing it. He's not even trying.

He wants me to forgive him for what he's doing, but I won't.

He doesn't say a thing. We're almost to the mess and because he won't look at me, won't see what's in my eyes, I can't make him feel what he doesn't want to feel, right? That's the game, isn't it?

"Have you seen Steve?" I ask.

He doesn't want to, but he says: "The last time I saw him,

Lieutenant, was two days ago. He was on a chopper to Vientiane."
He says it again: "That's all I know."

It's the same lie.

Vientiane is Laos, I remind myself. Political capital, so everyone's there—the Chinese, the Russians, the Thai, the North Vietnamese, the French, the Americans, everyone who's *anyone*. It's
neutral territory, I remember, and everything under the sun, every
operation imaginable, is run through it. I know this—everyone in
this war knows it—but I don't understand what it means. I'm supposed to be with Steve—and he's in Laos?

"No, it isn't," I tell him.

He knows what I'm saying.

We're inside, in line. We don't say a thing until we're eating
and the silence is so loud we can hear each other chew.

"I don't know why Steve is going to Laos, Mary," he says at
last, with an old man's sigh. "I don't know *anything*. I don't like
what I see, what I hear, but that doesn't mean I really know what's
going on. All I know, Mary, is that I'm supposed to get you familiar with an AK and a Makarov, that I'm supposed to put you on
some WIAs, have a medic watch you and see how you do, and
that's that. I don't *know* why Steve is in Vientiane. I don't really
know why I'm supposed to have you do these things, Mary."

"But you can *imagine*," I tell him. I say it the same way I said
it to the Green Beanie medic three days ago—in the same tent.

I think he's going to say something like "I'm sorry, I really
am," or "Getting you proficient on a Soviet assault rifle, Lieutenant, is probably the most important thing I could do for you right
now—however you look at it." But he doesn't. He looks away at
the cammies and the weapons rattling at the tables around us and
doesn't say a thing.

"I tried to kill Bucannon," I tell him.

"I know that, Lieutenant."

"Bucannon says he isn't angry about it," I tell him.

I wait, but nothing comes.

"I'm supposed to work with this captain by the name of Kelly,
Sergeant. I'm supposed to be spending time with Steve on this

captain's team. Steve won't be going on that Red Dikes mission after all, right, Sergeant?"

He looks up at last and there's a little fleck of yellow in his right eye, in the blue there, like a sadness, something you can't hide. Then he says:

"There's something you need to understand. Bucannon is *never* angry. Even when he is, he isn't. That isn't his way. There are only *reasons* and *methods* in his world, Lieutenant. If a man dies on a mission, that isn't a *loss*, it's something to be learned from. Another *reason*, another *method* that gets fine-tuned." He's looking into my eyes and I feel this chill. He wants to change the way things are, I know. He wants to make them different for me—for *all* of us—but he can't. There's a little smile now, but it's got other feelings in it and I know suddenly why he wasn't on the chopper that day. *You knew. You knew we wouldn't get away, didn't you?*

He's saying: "If a man can save himself, Lieutenant, but not others—if he's got to stand by and watch the men in his charge perish—that isn't really any reason for sadness or regret, is it? That is simply something *to be learned from*. Even if a woman—a nurse—tries to kill you in the dark, any anger you might feel—any fear—is nothing in the face of what you can learn by keeping her, by seeing what she will do. . . ."

I feel the chill again. He's looking at me. He's telling me something important, something I really need to understand. And he's not going to look away until I do.

Copy, Cable 7/5/71, DDO to Col. John W. Bucannon, CCN, MAC-SOG, Saigon

It's a go. You've got until 11/20. After that we lose control.

Chapter 8

He gets an AK from the guy named Clipper and we go to the southeast corner of the camp, outside the concertina and fu-gas and claymores. The plows have taken the jungle back about a hundred meters, but the jungle's still there, looking at us. I don't have to ask him. He knows what I'm thinking.

"We've got an M-60 tower behind us, Lieutenant," he says, "and a listening post half a klick in front. If you don't shoot at our listening post, Lieutenant, they won't shoot at you." He's smiling. He wants me to laugh. He wants us both to laugh—even if we have to fake it—but I'm standing there stiff as a board.

"Charlie won't shoot, Lieutenant. He knows we wouldn't come out like this just for range practice. He knows we wouldn't be out here like this if we weren't trying to draw his fire. So that one of our day patrols can hit him from behind, right? Charlie's not *dumb*."

He points at the treeline, at a bulldozer stump, and says, "Try that hardwood," slams a magazine into the AK and hands it to me. It's heavy. An M-16 is light, a toy for kids like me, but this thing is *heavy*.

"It's a good weapon, Lieutenant," he says. "The M-16 jams. And every cherry uses up his ammo in five seconds on full auto with it. I wouldn't touch an M-16 if you paid me by the round, Lieutenant." He's waiting for me to smile and I do. "One of these is worth $2,500 on the straight-leg black market in Saigon. Get a case of these packed in jelly back to the U.S. and you'd be able to retire for life, get yourself a man, have all the babies you want."

That's not what I want to hear, but it's the sergeant talking again and I leave it alone. I don't say, "You ever hear of bra burning, Sarge?" I don't say, "What are babies?" or "We're not going to make it back, are we, Sergeant?" I leave it alone. I'm glad to have him back.

He starts to put cotton in my ears, to protect them, but the cotton pops out. He tries it again and then says, "Fuck it," like, who cares, cotton isn't going to keep us alive. He says, "Go ahead, Lieutenant. Single shot."

I move the selector and fire. The kick isn't *that* bad.

"You're going to get the listening post, Lieutenant. Left leg back and keep the barrel down. Use your left hand."

I try again and my thumb gets caught in the trigger guard and I think I've lost it, I can't do it. "Help," I say, trying to pull it out, and he laughs. This time it *is* funny. Maybe it's the pill. Maybe it isn't. I fire again, watching my thumb and my chin.

"Now give me a burst, Lieutenant," he says, and I start to spray.

"Five shots!" he shouts, but I'm spraying, the thing is arcing into the jungle on full auto, ripping into vines and low canopy everywhere. The jungle is coming apart.

When I finally get it stopped, he's saying something, but I can't hear it. The silence is so loud I can't hear a damn thing. There's this incredible smell and I think the jungle is on fire. It's cordite, I tell myself. A *jungle can't burn*. He says it again and my ears start working.

"Didn't you hear me, Lieutenant? Only fucking-new-guys *spray*."

I try again.

"Not by your head!" he shouts, and I drop it to chest level, give him another burst of five. It hurts, and the stump a hundred yards out spits wood.

He says: "Lieutenant Balsam would kill me if I let anything happen to that face of yours, ma'am. You ought to know that."

"How about my chest?" I say, and he laughs.

He likes Steve as much as he likes you, I tell myself. It feels good and I give him another burst, feeling good.

"Charlie doesn't stand still. If you stand still, Lieutenant, he'll shoot you. The trick is to shoot from the hip. You run, you dive, you twist, you crawl, you fall, you get up—you do all of these things and while you're doing them you *shoot*. You do *not* shoot standing still unless you're on an ambush, Lieutenant. Is that clear?"

I nod. I nod like some really eager kid.

We move toward the treeline and I get stiff again. The jungle is like this big green face, this green skin you can't see a thing through. You see two feet into it, that's all, and you know *they're watching*. They're standing about two steps into the foliage, you know, maybe three, and they're *watching*. He slaps me on the back and I almost scream. "If it feels that cold, Lieutenant, why aren't you doing something about it?" I don't know what he means. "Are you just going to keep walking toward it, let them track you and cap you when they're good and ready?" All of a sudden my heart is hammering like the bass on a stereo. "What do you *want* to do, Lieutenant?" I open my mouth and nothing comes out. He's got his arm around my shoulder and he's pulling me close. He's scaring me, he's pulling so hard. "That's right— you want to *run*." Suddenly he shouts, "Then why, Lieutenant, aren't you *running*?" He's screaming so loud now I'm pulling away, I've got to, it's hurting my ears, he's scaring the shit out of me. But I can't. He's holding on to me, I'm trying to get away— my AK in one hand, his hand in my other—but I can't. "The only difference, Lieutenant, between what you *want* to do and what you *should* do is direction. You want to run *away*, but you can't. You've got to run *toward* them, just as if you truly loved them. You are safer running toward them like some crazy woman than you are running from them. Do you understand this? If you do, you'll live. If you don't, you'll die."

I'm shaking like a leaf. My heart is pounding like crazy, I've never been so scared in my life, this man screaming in my ear, holding me, keeping me here in *their* sights, so they can kill me when they're good and ready—

"So *do* it, Lieutenant. *Run.* You want to hug them and they don't want you to. If you're hugging them, Lieutenant, if you're holding them like a lover, they can't shoot you, can they?" He lets go, lets go of my hand at last and I'm tearing away, stumbling backward.

"*Toward them*, Lieutenant! They're in the jungle, in the tree-line. They're going to shoot you if you don't hug them first!"

I'm running. I can hear the bullets, I'm sure. I can feel them moving past me, smacking into the fresh-plowed earth, just missing my legs, my arms, my skull. I'm running and I've got this gun in my hand and I don't know what to do with it.

When I stop, it's at the treeline, the edge of the jungle covered by dirt, by the plows, and I know I can't stop. I turn around and run back, I run back through the bullets, across the plowed earth, to Christabel, who says: "*Now* do it with your weapon, Mary. The more of them you kill, the fewer of their scrawny stinking bodies you'll have to hug."

I do it with my weapon, zigzagging, my heart bellowing like a little elephant, *bossa nova* style, five-shot bursts into the treeline, where I know they are—the darker the spot the more I *know* they're there—muzzle flashes against the darkness (thank you), another five-shot burst, and another. It's *not* a dream. It doesn't feel like one. The pill is working, I tell myself. It's working. The major was right—it can't be a dream now. *It's just fear.*

I find the rhythm. I run with it. I run back, turning and shooting, and when I'm back to Christabel, I hand him the weapon and I say, "Your turn, Sergeant." Then I lean over and throw up.

"It's not something you *think* about, is it, Lieutenant?" He's trying to be serious, because it *is*. He doesn't want to laugh, because I've given it my best and if that isn't enough, then I'm going to die. "You start with how it *feels*—the fear, the urge to run—and then you turn it into something else, something that feels a little like *love*. . . . Am I right?" He stops. Class is over. He's going to make me laugh now, I know it. I've done good, I'm one of the boys now, even though my bra has rubbed me raw, and he's proud of me. "You know how many of those sonsabitches I've had to kill, Lieutenant, just so I wouldn't have to kiss 'em?"

I want to laugh, but it isn't really funny. I want to lie down and die. I'm drooling like a rabid dog and every muscle is doing a lactic-acid burn. I haven't felt this bad since basic, not even then, because the adrenaline wasn't like this—the fear wasn't.

"I should make you do this in your sleep, Lieutenant. I should come by your bunker in the night and shoot at your cot, to see if you can do it, which direction you'll run and whether you'll remember to take your goddamn weapon with you. That weapon, Lieutenant, is what makes you a *man*. I should shoot your ham-and-motherfuckers out of your hands at dinner-time and see if you'll run toward me like some crazy woman who wants my body but knows she's got to kill me first—or I'll never let her have her way with me. Do I *really* need to do this, Lieutenant?"

I'm leaning over, hands on my knees. I shake my head: *No, you don't, Sergeant. I don't think I'm going to forget.*

I don't hear the shout, but he does. He looks around. I try to look around. This guy in fatigues is waving at us from the nearest M-60 tower and he shouts again. Christabel takes me by the arm. "Tricky Dick's calling," he says. I laugh, start to lose it again and let him guide me home.

We pass through the gate and three or four guys nod at us, grinning.

The guy from the tower is there and Christabel takes off with him, leaving me standing. I lean over again to catch my breath and am happy, very happy, that I'm not going to throw up in front of them. *Women do more than cry and throw up*, I want to say. *Women do more than cry and scream and throw up or say inane things, you assholes.*

I stand up straight. I give the world a light-bulb smile, you know the kind, and I start walking back to the gate. When no one stops me, I start walking faster, out the gate, past the concertina and fu-gas and claymores. I start to trot, to zigzag, twist and shout and when I'm back to the spot, I start practicing again. I'm grinning like a fool. *Women do more than cry or throw up, Colonel.*

You're changing, Mary, a voice says quietly. *You're talking just like them.*

Hell, yes, I tell it.

I spray the treeline and watch the vines and branches fall, the jungle come apart. Go ahead, I say, shoot at me. Go ahead, let me know where you are so I can have my mad minute, so I can find you and hug you to bits. They're the people who killed Paul, the one I'll never forget. They're the people who filled the beds at the 21st and the 8th with guys who died on you, Mary. Now it's payback time.

I spray the ground fifty meters out. It's like a hose with water that somehow hurts you, I tell myself. It's like a weed cutter, a trimmer, a pruner of bad people. I'm smiling.

Then I see a body, what it would be like to hit a body with that hose, and I look away. I stop firing. You're not doing that, I tell myself. You're not hitting a body. *They're the guys who killed Paul. They killed Tony Fischetti and all the others—all the ones in your dreams.* I'm shooting at leaves and red earth. I'm in the shooting arcade at Disneyland, that's all. I'm shooting quail or ducks in Iowa. *And even if you weren't, they're the ones who did it, Mary. Thank God you were never asked to treat one of them at the 21st. Thank God you never had a chance to let one of them die.*

I think of something I've heard, the tunnels of Cu Chi, the little hospitals under the ground, miles of tunnels, how there's a VC doctor who does brain surgery with a household drill there, how his wife died of her own wounds, how the little lamps glow in the damp earth and half of the amputations die of shock, though the others do live. I see a body and I don't know whose it is. *Does it matter?* this voice says. *Does it really matter?*

No, I tell it, and I stop shooting.

I walk back to the gate, where the guys look at me like I'm crazy (*Would you go out there by the treeline like that, James? Hell, no, man. She must be* dinky-dau). I'm thinking of Fran on the ground with her broomstick, but it's not the same. They should've made us shoot at cadavers, I know. They should've shown us what *our* bullets can do.

The medication's working, I know. The major was right. It makes life easier because I know where I am, I'm not somewhere else, bleeding and dying somewhere else. If you take the pills, Mary, you won't dream. You'll be able to smile. If you don't dream, you'll be able—what did he say?—to *perform*. You'll be able to carry a weapon and, check this, *perform*. You'll be able to *smile* and *perform*.

I stop walking. I don't move. I try to get a dream to come. I try to feel like I'm somewhere else, bleeding, watching my arm hang by a piece of skin, the artery shooting up from my thigh like a Roman candle, anything at all, anything to bring them all *closer* to me—so I can *feel* it—but I can't. I can't make the feeling come at all.

Did the major say: *It's proven effective in laboratories in the U.S. . . . ?* Did he say: *. . . in tests you'll never hear about. . . ?* Did he say: *. . . like this one, Lieutenant. . . ?*

I find them by the mess tent—Christabel, the guy who shouted from the tower and another guy I can't really see because he's in the shadows by the tent pole. Christabel turns as if one of them has said, "Here she is," and he looks at me. I can't see his face either—he's too far away—but he looks at me for a long time. Then he starts walking toward me.

I squint. I think it's my imagination. I think it's the sunlight, the angle of the light, washing his face out like that. As he gets closer, I step sideways to change it, but it doesn't change. He looks pale. He looks ill.

I look at the other two again. I *know* I don't know the guy who shouted at us, some kid in cammies. But the other one . . . I squint again, looking at the guy in the shadows. The way he's leaning against the post, not moving, standing there with his head at an odd angle, I know who it is.

A voice says: *You lost Bucannon, Mary, but you've got this guy now. You've got him forever, Mary.*

I don't know why, but I start shaking.

He doesn't move. He doesn't come out to the sunlight to talk to us, to make a gesture. He doesn't do a thing. He stands in the shade of the mess tent in his baggy fatigues, watching us. The private is in the sunlight, ready to do what his captain—this skinny quiet captain—wants him to do.

I close my eyes. *Am I going to feel it? Am I going to feel him touch me again—eyes and neck and skull?*

I don't feel a thing. I hear Christabel's boots, that's all.

"Are we finished, Sarge?" I say, opening them.

"No," he says quietly, not looking at me. He swallows hard, takes a deep breath. He has an esophageal ulcer, I remember. It's painful. Is that what's bothering him?

"What's next?" I say. I'm trying to be cheerful, but I keep looking at the figure in the shadows, at the private standing in the sunlight, both of them waiting.

He's supposed to tell you something, Mary.

Yes, I know.

And he does:

"We need to take a little chopper ride, Mary," Christabel says. There's no feeling to the voice. It's flat. It's dead.

I fire a burst into the air but Christabel hardly moves. I barely know I've done it. Guys pop out of bunkers, emplacements, out from under tents, weapons snapping up for a moment, and then it dies down. *That woman just fired an AK by the mess tent, sir. Yes, I know, Simmons.*

A sergeant like Christabel should be chewing me out. You don't fire a weapon like that, a Russian weapon used by the VC and NVA and recognizable by its sound, in the middle of a camp. This isn't *Gunsmoke*, this isn't Dodge City on a Friday night, Mary. But he doesn't say a thing. He's looking at the treeline and I see his throat move.

I start to ask him how his ulcer is, if he's taking care of it, but I know that isn't it at all.

We start walking toward the airstrip and when I look back, the figure by the tent post is gone. *He really likes the dark, doesn't he,* I tell myself.

I feel something on my neck and I spin around, ready to scream, ready to shoot again.

It's Christabel. He doesn't pull away—he doesn't even seem to notice. He's got his hand on my neck, the way a coach does, the way you see it on TV, during a game, a little massage for one of the guys. The barrel of the AK is in his face, but he doesn't seem to notice. He puts his arm around my shoulder and I let him. We walk like that for a while.

"You're a fast learner, Lieutenant," he says, but that's not what he wants to say.

"*Who is he?*" I say.

We walk another hundred yards and he says, "You don't want to know, Lieutenant. You really don't."

Or I *think* he says it. Maybe he says something else entirely. I get a whiff of his breath and the beer's gone. It's my father's breath now, my uncle's, some old man's breath, his arm around me— and I know how badly he wishes the beer wasn't gone.

Photostat, Letter 7/24/71 (Intercept), Command Files, Operation Orangutan, *Tiger Cat*, Vietnam

Dear Mom, Dad and Jerry,

Life is full of surprises. I've been assigned to a small evacuation unit in the highlands, but I can't tell you where. (The CO says I can tell you we're near Pleiku, but that won't help you much. By American standards *everything* in Vietnam is close—by helicopter anyway.) The work here is very different from the 21st, as you might imagine. I'm really more of a medic. We do what we can with the limited resources we have and then chopper the wounded out to a *real* hospital as fast as possible. Sometimes the chopper barely touches down and we treat the wounded and then send it on its way.

There's other news, but Jerry has to promise not to hum "Here comes the bride." I've met a young man by the name of Steve (no "oo-lah-lahs" either, Jerry). I can't tell you his last name or what he does, because he's Special Forces, but if you'll read Robin Moore's book *The Green Berets*, you'll get a pretty good idea. How I met him is one of those coincidences you always hear about in war. A friend of Steve's was seriously wounded (on one of those missions I can't tell you about) and his CO let him accompany this friend to the 21st, where I ran into him in a hallway, of all places. His friend had just died (this happens), Steve was upset and we had our first long talk right there in the hallway. We both needed it, believe me. How did I end up at a highlands camp that will have to remain nameless? A number of us at the 21st had been asking for field assignments and Steve's camp needed a triage nurse. Steve talked to his CO, I talked to mine and here I am. It's hard to believe, I know, but you don't hear me complaining. Steve's a perfect gentleman and exactly what you'd approve of, Mom—good-looking but not conceited, smart but not smart-alecky. And Jerry, he's a Green Bay fan! Boss! Bitchin'! I worry about him—you worry about all of the guys you meet here, because they're out on missions a lot—but he's better trained than ninety percent of the soldiers in this war and if anyone is going to make it through without a scratch, it'll be him. (Read the training section of the Robin Moore book, Dad. You'll see what I mean.)

We've been hearing about how more and more Americans are against the war, and, to be honest, it's a little demoralizing. You wouldn't believe the looks on the GIs' faces when they hear their country isn't behind them anymore, how they're risking their lives, and their friends are dying, for a country that isn't backing them. The war may be wrong, Mom and Dad, but there are some things that *are* right about it. There are MEDCAP projects, orphanage projects, Vietnamese wards in our military hospitals, agricultural projects—efforts that really *are* helping the Vietnamese people stand on their own two feet, even if some of the missions our soldiers

are on are a little controversial. There's a lot of courage
and caring in this war, too, and that's something we
nurses get to see. Please tell the Perottos and anyone else
you have a chance to talk to that the war may be wrong,
but that's not something the soldiers need to hear right
now.

If I don't write for a while, you'll know why. Every
day you don't hear from me, just tell yourselves I'm
thinking about you with more love than you can imagine. Please tell the Perottos, the McLellands, Uncle Carl
and Zia Puppa I'm thinking about them, too—even if I
don't write often.

With lovin' spoonfuls,
Mary

P.S. The snapshot is great, Jerry. I've shown it to everyone. Please send more.

Photostat, Letter 7/1/71 (Intercept), Staff Sgt. George Christabel,
980774852, to Dorothy Christabel, Command Files, Operation
Orangutan, Tiger Cat, Vietnam

Dear Dot,

I've thought a lot about your letter over the past
weeks. You seem to be having a hard time understanding
why a man might extend his tour in a war that's so important to his country and to a free world. I'm a professional soldier and you knew that when you married me.
We're living in times of war and that's when professional
soldiers are called upon. I really don't think I'm forsaking
homelife any more than the other 15,000 professional
soldiers—many of them married, with kids—in this war
are. I *know* Kristy misses her father. I miss her, too. I
hope you don't feel you have to make a decision about
any of this until we can really talk it over and know what
the other person is feeling. You will find this hard to

believe, I know, but I love you as much as I did twenty years ago. I also respect your feelings and don't want to hurt you, even if it seems like I do. Letters have never been the best place for me to say what I'm thinking and right now there are things I need to get a little clearer in my own head—about myself and about this war—before I can really say them to you. I truly believe you will be happy to hear them.

All my love,
The Bell

P.S. Please tell Kristy that I love her and will be writing to her very soon.

Chapter 9

1st Lt. Mary Damico, 557783021, Army Nurse Corps, Tape 21
Transcript

Subject: I could have killed someone with it, sure. I could have killed Christabel or any of the guys at the strip. I could have shot up the Huey that was there. I could have gotten a few rounds off and done some damage before anyone could've stopped me. But I didn't see a reason. If I'd shot someone, someone would then have shot *me*, so there had to be a reason. I didn't see one.

Interviewer: [unintelligible]

Subject: That's true. I could've gone back and killed Bucannon or the captain, or at least tried. I remember thinking about it, too, and saying to myself: Christabel will stop you, *someone* will, and all you'll do is fail again. But that wasn't the main reason. I wasn't dreaming about Steve anymore—because of the pill. I wasn't dreaming about the mission I was about to go on, about anyone on that mission, or any other mission, so I didn't really have a reason to kill Bucannon. That's how it *felt* anyway. It doesn't make sense, I know. [Laughs] Now I can see all sorts of reasons to have killed them both.

Interviewer: Can we go back to the training?

Subject: Sure. [Pause] When we reached the strip, they had this Huey waiting for us and a squad of Montagnards were sitting in it. They were Rhade or Jarai or Muong, one of those groups—I don't know which. I'd never been this close to Montagnards in my life.

They didn't look like Vietnamese—they looked like Australian aborigines, maybe a mix between American Indians and Australian aborigines. I remember Steve once saying they were great little people, they fought like tigers, they were loyal and the Green Beanies loved them. Steve had a brass bracelet some Montagnard headman had given him and so did Christabel and some of the others. It meant they were brothers, they were accepted—the Yards loved them. The Vietnamese hated Montagnards, Steve said. They hated their guts and it was mutual. This had been going on for something like two thousand years. I remember thinking, trying to remember, about this rebellion somewhere up in the highlands, Jarai or Rhade against ARVN, a lot of little Vietnamese heads about to be cut off with machetes until some Green Beanies stopped it. Too bad, Bothwell had said. He was a Green Beanie lieutenant Christabel knew. He said: I'd live with those Yards if this war were over. I'd marry the headman's daughter—he tells me she's waiting for me—and I'd live here with them and be their white God and, Jesus, I'd never have to see Phillie again.

When Bothwell said it, no one looked at him funny. He was saying what a lot of guys thought and there were two Beanies working with Air America in Laos who'd done just that. The Yards they went to live with were Yeh or Hmong, not Rhade, but it was the same. These two guys were never coming back. Like Huck, I said. Bothwell looked at me funny. She means Huck Finn, Steve said, but nobody laughed. [Pause] You *do* have to wonder how many of JFK's Peace Corps warriors in their little green berets just aren't going to go home when this war's over, don't you? [Laughs] MACV must be praying for hundreds.
Interviewer: [unintelligible]
Subject: Right. Sorry. [Pause] There was a Huey waiting for us and a squad of Montagnards sitting in it. [Pause] The Montagnards were just sitting in it. . . .

The Yards were little, even littler than the Vietnamese, and they didn't move the same way. They had on these tops that looked like black Arrow shirts, with nothing below except jockey shorts, this jungle version of jockey shorts. They had carbines and

M-16s and there was a Vietnamese guy, an ARVN, in this pressed
uniform, but he wasn't talking to them. He wasn't going to unless
he absolutely had to, I knew. They're *moi*, Steve once said.
They're fucking animals to the Vietnamese and it's the same way
up North. The Golden Triangle is this gorgeous intersection of
three countries where the fields of opium poppies look like a fairy
tale and the Hmong tribesmen grow it on the hilltops and the
ethnic Tai broker it, sometimes with the help of old Kuomintang
bandits, and the poor hard-core communists, the North Vietnamese, can't control it at all. *They* hate the Yards, too. It isn't
going to change for a long, long time, someone said, and it wasn't
Steve. It was a guy named Bingham, this old Green Beanie sergeant who'd been in Laos twice before Vietnam ever got started.
Uncle Ho couldn't stop it, he said. No one can. The Yards will
fight for us if we pay them because they hate the lowland Vietnamese, and they'll fight for the NVA in Laos or Cambodia or old-
time Champa, against us—against ARVN—because killing ethnic
Vietnamese is wonderful to them no matter which side the body is
on, and, and, hell, if there's a little kip thrown in, that's just gravy.
Ethnic Vietnamese have been fucking with their mountains, with
their homeland, for two thousand years. Right, Lieutenant? And
Bothwell says: Right, your honor—I just wish I could stay here
and live with them after the war. You're going dingo, Lieutenant,
Bingham says. You've got Rhade titties in your eyes. You don't
care if you smell like fried manioc root 'cuz you'll have someone
to do your wash forever, you'll get to hear brass bracelets tinkling
on her pretty little arms every morning and you'll get to die from a
heart attack on top of her some night. We're losing you, Lieutenant. We're losing him, men. Get this man a *Playboy*—right now!

So we're standing by the Huey. There's a Yard, this barrel-
chested Yard, in charge of the other Yards. He's their leader and
he's grinning with teeth missing and this baseball cap on his head.
He snaps his hand up and salutes Christabel and says, *"Mon capi-
taine."* This is how they talk to the ARVN—who shouldn't really
be here, because Bucannon never uses ARVN, I know. They all
talk French. They're doing it now and I'm thinking: Did that guy
with the baseball cap—he's forty or fifty, he's got to be—fight *with*

or *against* the French? Was he Viet Minh or was he fighting with
the French? Then I think: Who cares? People have been fucking
with his mountains for two thousand years. The Yards and the
ARVN in his very pressed uniform are babbling away in French
and I do a count. There are seven Yards, the pressed ARVN,
Christabel and me, and two Americans in cammies who're holding something smaller than an M-16—those submachine guns
they call Swedish Ks—in their laps. I've got my AK on safety and
we pile in. It's crowded, the rotors aren't moving yet and suddenly
I'm worried about how I smell, all these bodies together like this,
what people will think. I'm a woman, after all. Then I get a whiff
of everyone else. Someone smells like rancid fish sauce, *nuoc
mam*, someone else smells like incense, someone like meat smoke,
and *everyone* like old gym socks, jungle rot, gun oil, sweat. I can't
even remember what I smell like. Even with my period, even
without Tampax for a whole week, no one would know the difference here.

The Yards are staring at me, the first round-eyed woman
they've ever seen, and I don't know what I'm supposed to do.
("Don't touch their kids on the top of the head," the pamphlets
say. "Don't show them the soles of your feet. Don't wear shorts.
Don't laugh loudly. Don't be a *woman*.") The Americans aren't
looking at me and I tell myself Christabel's given them the word—
leave her alone—or maybe they're just being nice. *Everyone* wants
to look at a round-eyed woman. Maybe everyone even wants to
touch her, too—Vietnamese, Montagnards, Americans, all of
them. But I don't care. I've got this Russian assault rifle taken from
a dead man out in the jungle somewhere and I'm wearing cammies like real men wear and I must look ridiculous. Everyone gets
to look. Everyone gets to touch. Go ahead, guys, and I'll shoot
you in the pecker.

The rotors are whumping now and suddenly I don't care
about smells. There aren't any doors on the Huey and the rotorwash whips everything out, the cool sweet air in, and there isn't a
smell that's human anymore. I wonder if I'm going to fall out the
door when we bank, whether anyone will save me—this crazy
woman with the AK—and I wonder where we're going. I'm not

dreaming—I don't feel rounds going through me—so I'm ready to laugh. But no one else is, so I don't.

You can feel the ice between the Yards and the ARVN, who's sitting stiff as a board, like he knows he's sitting in garbage and how he's going to smell afterward. The Yards are grinning at me, the ARVN is giving me a smile, too, but they *won't* look at each other. The Americans are holding on to their spook weapons like G-men, pretending there isn't really an ARVN in the chopper— because MAC-SOG *never* uses ARVN. And Christabel's still looking out the door. *Jesus Christ*, a voice is saying. *We could be blown out of the sky, and all this misery would disappear from the earth forever.*

It's just a voice—it's not a dream—and we finally drop down on this little village with perfect little rice paddies on either side of it. It's a Vietnamese village, a lowlands village, and there are Americans and Montagnards already there cleaning up. There's been a sweep—you can tell—and it's cleanup time. I've never seen it, but I've sure heard. You hear an awful lot.

I can see this pile in the middle of the path that runs between the huts and I really don't know what it is. We're dropping in and I think it's clothes or belongings, the villagers' belongings, because we're moving the villagers out—to deny the village to the VC. Isn't that how it goes? Isn't that what we're doing these days— moving the villagers out? I don't see any villagers, so we must be moving them out.

There's another Huey on the ground already, rotors turning, ready to go if it needs to. We drop in right behind it.

Christabel says something to the ARVN officer, who stares back at him, then we hit and we all jump out. I drop the AK as I do, Christabel picks it up without swearing—without even looking at me—and I take it back with a thank-you that's lost in the noise. We're jogging toward the pile of whatever it is—anything to get away from the Huey. All it would take, Colonel, is a LAW or an RPG or an M-79 round from the treeline and up you'd go with the Huey. Who knows who's watching? Who can ever possibly know?

We run and the ARVN is talking French to the head of the Yards. The Yard keeps grinning under his baseball cap, flashing two or three betel-nut-black teeth and little earrings, and you know what kind of grin it is. He turns to a couple of his own men and says something in Rhade, or whatever, and they laugh. The ARVN isn't laughing. He isn't even smiling and you know why. All this time we're running toward the pile.

Two of the Yards from the first Huey are dragging something from out of the huts. I stop jogging. I stop moving at all.

It's a body.

They're dragging it toward the pile and all of a sudden it's very clear. This voice says: *How could you not have known, Mary? How could you have thought it was* clothes? Someone slaps me hard on the back, grabs my arm, and I'm having to run again, though I don't want to, toward the pile.

The bodies are in loose black pants, loose white pants. They're in loose shirts and blouses with perfect little patterns on them—all from the same material, big pieces of fabric dyed and laid out in the sun somewhere, the way I'd always heard it's done. They're in conical hats, almost but not quite like the ones in that movie *The Good Earth.* They've got woven rice baskets with them, and all of them are wearing clothes.

The Vietnamese are small. There are a lot of small bodies in that pile and I think to myself: The children are somewhere else. *Yards* don't hate children. *Americans* don't hate children. They've herded them up somewhere and the kids are standing there—wherever it is—and crying. You just can't hear them over all this goddamn noise.

No, Major, I didn't go over and check. I can only say what I saw, and what I thought.

Someone had set fire to two of the huts—just two. I didn't know why then. The Hueys were close enough that the wash was fanning the fires, the fires were blowing back and up into the jungle like a woman's bright red hair. I could see Christabel talking to a guy with a Zippo lighter. The guy was nodding—"Sure, Sure"—but I couldn't really hear them over the noise.

We're down to a walk but we're still moving toward the pile

and I'm thinking: *Why are you doing this, Mary? Why do you have this weapon in your hand? Why are you here at all?*

I try to get Christabel to look at me, but he won't. He's pale, he still looks sick. The closer we get to the pile, the more he won't look at me. I want to say, "Why are we walking toward those bodies, Sergeant Christabel?" But I know—with all this noise— he'd just pretend he didn't hear me.

The Yards with the body have stopped, though they haven't let go of the arms. The head Yard, the one with the baseball cap, says something. Two of the Yards from our Huey have grabbed the arms of another body in the pile, and are dragging it away. A Yard I don't know has grabbed the legs of a third body and is pulling it down the path, too, toward one of the huts, one of the huts that isn't burning.

I watch one body go to one hut and the other two bodies go to another hut and then out of the corner of my eye I see something move. I turn. These two Yards have a fourth body in loose black pants out of the pile and they're tying it to a tree, wire under its arms to hold the chest up, wire around its throat to hold the head up, its legs spread wide.

I watch another body get dragged from the pile and I don't like how everyone is looking at me now. How some of the Yards are laughing, looking at me. I hear someone lock and load, and I turn. There's this Montagnard about fifty feet from the body on the tree. He's chambered a round in his rifle, this really old rifle, and he's aiming it at the tree.

The head Yard snaps something at him and the Yard lowers his rifle, but laughs. Everyone's looking at *me* now.

The ARVN officer comes up to Christabel and says something. Christabel starts toward me, eyes on the ground, and when he gets to me and finally looks up, the words don't come easy. "The CO wants you to get a little more practice, Lieutenant. He says the practice needs to be as realistic as possible or it won't benefit you—it won't really help you in what you'll be doing. He says you need to trust him and that if you do you'll see the wisdom of it. . . ."

It sounds like a tape recorder. It doesn't sound like Christabel's voice at all. "I'm sorry," he says, and the voice is different now.

I look around. They're all waiting. The Yards have stepped back from the tree where they've wired the body. Its head is hanging down, its legs are out akimbo, like the Straw Man in Oz. The Yards that have dragged other bodies to the huts are standing around now, too, and everybody's waiting.

"It won't," Christabel says—his voice now—"be worth anything if you don't do it *quickly*, Lieutenant." He's barely able to say it. It's making him sick to have to, I know. "You won't have time in a real firefight to stare at the enemy and *think* about it, Lieutenant." He stops. He can't do it. "Just get it over with," he says.

"No," I say. "I'm not going to."

"I don't like this any more than you do," he says slowly, and it's the dead voice again. The dead man in him.

"Nope," I say.

"They're *dead*, Mary," the voice says. "They can't feel a thing. You're not mutilating them for the *hell of it*. You're shooting them because that's what they're going to look like when you have to do it yourself. Their faces will be the same, Mary."

I'm staring at him and I'm feeling dizzy.

"He's not giving you much time to get ready, Lieutenant. A little range practice, a few dead bodies—that's it." It's Christabel saying it but it's a voice floating somewhere else, too, and it makes me dizzy. "He doesn't *care* if you're ready—the way soldiers need to be ready. He's interested in other things, Mary. You know that now." Christabel's voice is far away. He's saying things about being ready, about there not being much time, about what Bucannon is interested in, and I'm very dizzy. "You know what I'm saying," his voice is saying.

"I'm sorry, Mary," the voice says again.

And then everything is clear. The pill is working, so it's not a dream, I know. But it *is* a dream—the red earth, the river and the mud and I can't get away, jerking from the rounds even though I've got this beautiful blue gift that should be keeping me alive

even while others are dying. I'm lying in the mud on a riverbank. . . . It's not a dream, no, it's a *memory* of a dream, Major,
and I'm dizzy because I *know*, because Christabel's guessed it,
too—I *know* he has—because Steve is still going North, and *I'm*
going with him, we're all going with the skinny captain North, to
the riverbank, to the red red earth, to those uniforms and mud I've
dreamed about—where we're all going to die. *The colonel has
made changes in the mission, Lieutenant.* Wasn't that what the
major said?

I know, I tell him now. *I'm one of them, Major.*

"You're a nurse," the distant voice is saying. "You've seen
worse things than this, Mary."

I'm on my knees in the village and I've got a wood stock and a
cold metal barrel in my hands. I'm about to be sick and the voice,
closer now, is saying:

"You've got to do it. We can't leave until you do, Mary.
Those are his orders."

I'm thinking of Bucannon, how he lied, how the fathers always lie, how I've got to try it again, with *this* weapon, because if I
don't, if Bucannon lives, Steve and all of us are going to die—

"Please, Mary," the voice is saying.

I go ahead and do it, so I'll know how. So I'll be able to do it
to Bucannon, if I can—or if I can't, so I'll be able to do it to the
ones on the riverbank, by the red red water, who are trying to kill
us all.

I go ahead and do it. For Christabel, and for Steve.

I don't do the body wired to the tree. I save him until last. I
stand in the doorway of the nearest hut and shoot the body they've
propped up inside. For a second it's wearing a blue uniform—the
whole world is blue—and I am trying to stay alive, to keep the
others alive, even though I can't, even though the uniforms stretch
forever, the river rushing beside us, the mud as blue as it will ever
be. But then the blue disappears and it's just a body jerking, jerking on the earth of a hut, sliding down walls made of reeds.

I stand behind the next hut, wondering if I can hit a body

blind just by spraying. I spray—and on the other side three Yards jump out of the way.

"*Don't*," the voice shouts. "Not that way. Stand in the doorway."

I was wrong. There are two bodies in this hut and one was laid out low. I'd never have gotten him. I shoot them both. I tell myself they're wearing uniforms, NVA strac, and that by shooting them I will keep Steve and maybe even a few others alive. I use five-shot bursts, just like Christabel taught me, and the thudding of the rounds is what I'll always remember. It doesn't work. In the dream, the blue dream, Steve is still dying.

I know now that the huts that aren't burning are the ones with bodies. I go where there isn't smoke or fire and I use my five-shot bursts. I try to be as light on my feet as I can, as fast as I can, so that Christabel will be proud.

I remember pulling the AK around and aiming it at the Yards. I remember wondering what it would be like to shoot them. I don't remember wanting them to die, only wondering what the rounds would do to their bodies.

You're a nurse, Mary, a voice is saying.

Christabel knocks the rifle away, gets the barrel back toward the doorway, and I go ahead and spray the inside of the hut. I do it on full auto, as if to say: *Fuck you, Bell Man. I'm rockin' and rollin'. There it is—there it fucking is.* I hit the bodies, every one of them. I tear the walls to pieces, spraying.

I remember standing about thirty yards from the tree with the body wired to it and putting the AK on selective fire and shooting the body in the stomach. As I did it, I fixed it up. I remembered what it was like to fix gut wounds, intestines you can hold in your hands, and I fixed it up. I shot him in the head and remembered what it was like to debride, to put the tubes in, pick the bone fragments out, and so I fixed him up. I shot him in the chest—because he was going to kill Steve, that was why—and I remembered the sucking chest wounds at the 21st and I took a cigarette wrapper from the ground and plugged the hole and fixed him up. He *lived*. He actually lived, because I fixed him up.

I shot him and fixed him up and then went ahead and let him

die. He wasn't breathing, so I went ahead and let him die. He was
going to kill at least one of us, I knew, so I shot him. But this time
I didn't save him. I let him die.

I remember the ARVN officer standing beside me—I didn't
know how he got there. When I looked at him, he smiled, as if to
say, "You're doing well, your aim is better," but then he stopped. I
think he saw something in my face—that's what it felt like, like he
saw something in my face—and so he stopped, and because he
did, I liked him better. I'm holding the AK, the magazine is empty
(amazing what a broomstick can do, Fran) and I have this feeling I
was wrong, that this officer wasn't sitting in the Huey the way I
thought he was, that he isn't what I thought he was at all, that he
doesn't hate the Yards and that I'm going to get to know him
awfully well.

I remember thinking how none of the bodies they'd given me
were children—I *knew* they weren't—and how there was probably
someone somewhere I should thank for it.

I don't remember the trip back to camp. I don't remember
cleaning the pieces of bone and skin off my shoulders in the Huey,
and knocking Christabel's hand away, which he said I did. I don't
remember kneeling down in one of the huts and putting my arms
around one of the bodies and hugging it, which he said I also did.

I remember Christabel taking the AK from me when we got
off the Huey, knowing that someone had told him to. *He knows
what I'd like to do.*

I remember thinking: *They're getting you ready for something,
Mary.* I remember thinking: *They've got a reason for all of this.*

Chapter 10

PFC John Tull, 455639237, 82d Airborne Division, Tape 1
Transcript

My name's John W. Tull, but they call me "J.W." On the night of August 29 we leave this C-123 and when we hit we move out of a small field to our checkpoint. We're dug in and safe. I'm in the fire team, which has the point. I can feel the others around me even if I can't see or hear them. That's the way it always is. About ten or fifteen minutes later I start feeling this movement outside—outside the grunts on our team, I mean. I don't hear anything but I turn—to the left—because I can feel something moving out there. There's no sound, no lights, but I can *feel* a body. A couple of seconds pass and the feeling gets stronger. I keep turning to my left, because that's where it is. All of a sudden this voice says: *You're a dead man.* It's what he's thinking. He's out there and I'm here and we know what the other is thinking. I pull my weapon up and fire three rounds and I get him. They go out in a little while and they find him where I killed him, without him firing, without any light.

PFC Harold Woodley, 309573120, 2d Brigade, 25th Infantry
Division, Tape 1 Transcript

It happened only once and I don't know if it's what you're looking for. It was a dream. I was on patrol with Private First Class

James Burrows and a couple of other guys. We'd taken fire that morning near the Parrot's Beak and had radioed back for instructions. We were told the 4023d NVA Battalion was in the area and we'd probably made contact with their point. We weren't supposed to hang around and take on the whole 4023d, so we headed back. On the way we stopped at this little village and checked it out, like always. We looked for stores of rice or too many pots cooking for the number of people in the huts—that kind of thing. We started getting a bad feeling. You hear what's happened to other guys and you know it can happen to you. There weren't enough people in the village. That was one thing. There weren't any draft-age males and that always makes you suspicious. So our sergeant grabbed an old man and shook him a little and said "VC! VC!" and of course the old man shook his head and said, "No VC! No VC!" Right then we started taking fire from one of the huts, so we returned the fire. Private First Class Moffet fired a couple of 40mm grenades and the hut blew up and this figure came out running. It was a kid. A teenager. He was burning and he still had the M-16 in his hands. We just stared. Private First Class James Burrows had lost two buddies at Lai Khe two days before and he wasn't in very good shape. We all knew that. He walked over to the kid and we knew what was going to happen. The M-16 came from a dead American. The VC get their weapons that way or on the black market, and this kid, out in the middle of nowhere, had an M-16. He was the one who'd been shooting at us. Burrows walked over to the kid and stood there and watched him roll around on the ground. The Willy Peter was still in him and he was screaming.

Willy Peter gets into your skin and burns down to the bone. You've got to take it out surgically or it'll go all the way to the bone. Burrows got down on one knee and took his own M-16 and shot the kid in the head. It was what any of us would have done. The kid was going to die anyway, he was VC, and he had that rifle. Maybe if he hadn't been VC we'd have done it out of mercy, because he was going to die anyway, but that wasn't the reason now.

At first this kind of thing surprises you. You want to think you're a good person—that's how you were raised—someone who doesn't kill civilians or shoot women or shoot anyone who isn't a soldier in a uniform, a clear situation like COMBAT, like a movie or a television show, I mean. At first you tell yourself you can't really blame a kid who was raised to think like a VC, to hate and kill Americans, or one who'd better shoot at you or the VC will hurt his family—but then you see so much of it you get tired of watching guys you know and like die, you get angry and finally you start doing it yourself. After that you can't go back, so you just keep on doing it.

It happens inside. It's not you anymore, because you've done something you never could have done before. The world where you never could have done it is a very long way away. It's not *your* world anymore. That world, the one you were raised in, wouldn't want to even know you now, wouldn't want to even know what you're doing.

In fact, you don't have a world anymore. This one certainly isn't yours. How can you go from a world like that one, where kids and women are to be cherished and protected, to one like this? If you didn't change, that would be different, but you do change. You change so that you can do the things you couldn't have done before. At first you say to yourself: How can *God* let this happen? How can *God* let a world like this exist? How can He let both of these worlds exist together? Then you start saying: How can I go back? How can I go back and be the same ever again, God? How can I go back without understanding what's happening here, what's happening to *me*?

Private First Class Burrows shot the kid in the head the way any of us would have, and afterward he stayed on his knees. He looked around at the huts that weren't burning and he kept his hands where they were, palms down on his thighs, like he was resting. He looked neat and calm, I remember that. We watched him for a little while, trying to figure out what he was doing, and then finally we had to go get him. I was one of the guys who did it, so I saw his face. He just wasn't there.

He wouldn't get up. We had to pick him up and help him walk to the slick.

When we got back to the base camp I didn't think much

about it. I knew he wasn't doing well, but you see guys like that all the time—and they pull out of it. He wasn't saying anything at all. He was staying off by himself. We went to sleep for a couple of hours. That's when I had the dream. Seeing his face back at the ville had something to do with it, I'm sure. In the dream Burrows stood in front of me and said, "I'm not going back, Woodley. I'm not going home." I tried to reason with him—in the dream, I mean. I told him he was short, that he had only a few weeks left. He said I couldn't make him go back, *nobody* could, and that he had a reason for staying. If he went, he said, he'd leave himself here. That's how he put it. If he left, he wouldn't know what he was, what it all meant, why it was happening, how we could all change so much. He said he couldn't go until he understood it all.

I told him—in the dream—that I knew exactly what he was saying, but that he had to go home, that he couldn't stay.

He said, "That isn't home, Woodley."

I was crying when I woke up and I didn't want anyone to hear it. I didn't really know why I was crying. I didn't know Burrows all that well. Other guys knew him better. I didn't know why I was dreaming about him when there were so many other things I could have been dreaming about.

I remember where he was standing in the dream. We were in a living room somewhere. There was a purple couch and a little table, and a bird in a cage over by a kitchen door. It was someone's living room somewhere. He was saying, "I'm not going home, Woodley," but there he was—in the middle of someone's living room—back in The World. It didn't make any sense.

A week later they medevacked him out. They took him away in a chopper. He hadn't talked to anyone for three or four days and we knew they were going to have to pull him out. The CO kept warning him, but we all knew. He would sit with his palms down on his thighs like he was resting and thinking. He would do that even with the CO screaming at him. It was dangerous for everybody to have him like that, the CO kept saying. The CO was an asshole but he was right. You can't have someone in the bush who isn't operational, who's going to get people killed.

I wrote to his parents. I don't know why. I'd heard he was

back in the States, in a VA hospital, so I decided to write them. We exchanged a couple of letters, not really talking about James but about other things. We did that for about six months. At the end of the letters they would always say, "James is doing fine. We see him often and he says to say hello." Then I got the picture, the photograph. He'd come home. They'd brought him home and there he was standing in the middle of the living room, his mother and father on either side of him. There was that purple couch and that little table. There was that cage with the bird in it, back in a corner by a doorway. I still have that picture.

It wasn't a physical survival thing, the dream. It didn't keep me alive. But it was important in other ways, I think. You get closer to people over here than you get anywhere else. Things happen to you here that just don't happen back there. When you go back, you lose it, you lose something in you that's important. I think that's what he was trying to say. You leave a part of yourself over here and you're never the same again.

I saw him when I went back between tours. He isn't really there. He's still here. That's what I'm trying to say.

Capt. Herman Malik, 956703457, 1st Cavalry Division, Tape 1 Transcript

I've said it before, Colonel. There's something going on out there that we take for granted, that we don't do enough with. I'm close to my men—you know that. Maybe it's been there all along, but that's not the point. We should be doing more with it. I have a tape where one of our best men, a very stable guy who comes back from every LURP we send him on, says—I've got it here. He says: "There are guys, Captain, who can do things with time. You can see them do it right in the middle of an action. I mean, they're two or three steps ahead of where they should be, where their minds should be. If you saw it, you'd understand. You see them take a step for no reason at all, and then three, maybe four seconds later, you see why, because that's when the grenade lands, that's when the M-60 opens up. Either a guy can do this or he can't, but when he can, he's a god. Everyone wants to be with him. They volunteer for LURPs just to be with him."

I've got the actual tape back at the post. The guy made it freely. He doesn't want to say he's one of them, but he is—I have evidence he is.

I had a conversation with him on the radio during a hot insertion and he was doing it then. He probably didn't even know it. He'd say something and it would be—whatever he was talking about would be two or three minutes away. Is this making any sense? He'd describe something, but it wouldn't have happened yet. We stayed on the line for ten minutes and he kept doing it. They'd pulled back to a crater, under heavy fire, he said. They were using their claymores and he said: "The first chopper's down." I didn't catch it at first. He said the first chopper was down, but the chopper *wasn't* down. Not yet. Three minutes later I could hear it hit. He said their claymores were gone but I could still hear the damn things blowing. He said NVA regulars were rushing them when the claymores were gone, and that's exactly what happened—but not until the claymores were gone, which they weren't yet. He wanted an air strike, he said. He said, "Our radio's gone." I'm talking to this guy on the radio, for Christ's sake, and he tells me an RPG has taken out his radio and he needs air support. Jesus.

He made the tape for me so I'd be ready, Colonel, so I'd believe him when the time came. He wanted me to be ready to call in air before the radio blew, so I'd believe what I was hearing. I don't think he really knew what he was doing. Those ten minutes we were on the radio I don't think he really knew. He was just trying to function, to keep his men and himself alive.

If you'd like to talk to him, I'm sure he'd be willing.

Can I tell him you're interested?

SFC Joseph Parmentier, 897191833, 4th Infantry Division, Tape 1 Transcript

My experiences really aren't that much. No ghosts or mind-reading or anything like that. Just some flashes. My CO tells me

I'm the most illogical son of a bitch he's ever met. He tells me I'm nuts, but I'm usually right and he calls it illogical because it doesn't follow procedures. I'll get a feeling that the camp will be hit. Sure enough, human wave that night. I have to be at the camp, on the site, but when I'm there I get the flash. I'm an operations NCO and can move around at will, which means I work for the CO, first sergeant and CSM. The first time I got wounded was pretty strange . . . a rocket attack I saw coming. I was on the run and saw it in the air coming toward me. I stopped, of course, when it exploded in front of me. When I saw the flash, my mother saw the flash back home. I should have said that before. Sometimes my mother knows when things happen to me. I've got the letters if you'd like to see them. She saw the flash back home and knew I'd been hit. I got her letter saying it the same day I sent mine.

The second time I was wounded I made it to ROC Toipir. I called home and before I could get a word out that I was on R&R she asked if it hurt and why was I in a hotel room if I was hurt. I was in a bed in the hotel and had taken some shrapnel back in Tay Ninh. We hadn't reported my leg and back wounds yet because I was to leave on R&R the next day.

My dad had some things like this happen to him in the Battle of the Bulge. My mom used to tell him in her letters where he was and where he was going. She saw him when he had frostbite in the hospital, and she wrote to tell him he'd be okay. She was right.

1st Lt. Glenn Bothwell, 3345668497, Command and Control North, MAC-SOG, Tape 1 Transcript

The guys you should be talking to are dead. You think the guys who've had these experiences and lived are the ones you should talk to, but you're wrong. You just don't hear about the others. They're gone. I remember a Montagnard, a Jarai, we used to call Virgin. He was twenty-three years old. One day right before we went out on patrol, I saw this look in his eye. He was my sergeant, my liaison, because he spoke some English, and I'd been on twelve or thirteen patrols with him, half of them with heavy contact. I'd never seen that look. I didn't have any idea what it meant. I thought maybe his liver was acting up again, or that he was worried about his wife, who was pregnant. He had that look the entire patrol. He just wasn't there. If you want to know the truth, I think he was already gone and he knew it. He didn't make it back from that patrol. He was the one guy we lost in an ambush that we managed to trip early. I think he knew. That was five years ago, sir. My first tour. I've known ten or twelve guys who saw their own deaths. You see a lot of that in operations like ours. Half of your friends are dead. You'll hear them talking about it. Sometimes they'll laugh, sometimes they'll shit in their pants the way anyone would, and then they'll go out and die exactly the way they knew they would. It's very eerie, sir.

You don't hear about it because everyone wants to forget it. It's bad luck. It might rub off on you. You might start seeing your own death. It's an actual statistic, but you don't hear about it. I could tell you about these ten or twelve guys, sure, but even I— even I don't want to get into it. The feeling is, you talk about it, you start to *believe* it, and then it'll happen to you.

Those are the guys you should be interviewing, Major. Not the guys that are living, like me.

Capt. Roger Hoskins, 908172455, 5th Special Forces, Tape 1 Transcript

I had a good friend who shouldn't have gone back to Nam, but did. He had a beautiful wife and this beautiful little girl. I said to him, "Why are you going back?" He wanted to be a teacher. He said, "I've got to go. They need us over there. You know that." He'd gone to college, he was from a good family, he knew what it was all about. He didn't believe in the way we were fighting it, but he went anyway. He loved this country. He loved it more than a lot of guys do. When he was killed, I dreamed that he went home, that he was with his wife and this beautiful little girl and the war was over. It was a beautiful dream, the kind that's so beautiful it's sad and you wake up crying. I'd been wounded in the same action but I didn't know he was dead. I was bandaged up and you know the kinds of dreams you have on morphine. They're strange. This one was different. In it he went back to America, to his wife and little kid, and the war was over. He said, "I don't have to go away anymore, honey." She was crying and hugging him and saying, "I'm so, so happy, Roger." That's what she said. Roger. His name was Howard but she called him "Roger," which is my name. "I don't have to go away anymore," he kept saying. He didn't seem to be bothered by the name at all.

When I got back—three months later—I went to see them in Tucson. I'd written her a short letter, nothing much. I went to see them because I'd always heard that a woman likes to know how her husband died, whether he said anything about her, what his last words were, things like that. I didn't know whether I was going to lie—to try to make her feel better—or whether I was going to tell her the truth: that I didn't know what he'd said because I really wasn't with him when he died.

We didn't really talk about him the first time. We said the things you're supposed to say, like "I'm sorry. I really am." "How's the war going?" "I know Howard valued your friendship." And "Thank you, Captain, for coming by." I came back again and after a while we started to talk about him—really talk about him. The little girl would come into the room and ask me questions, too, and I would do my best to answer them. I would do things with them, too—movies, the park—when I was in town. But mainly we started to talk.

I still see them. I'm under some pressure to go back, because the team I was on was pretty rare, because over-the-fence teams like ours don't usually have the mission success we had. We developed some pretty good snatch techniques, some deniable things no one else seems to be able to use. With Nixon doing his thing, with the negotiations, we're needed now, I gather. But I just can't do it. If I go, I'll start dreaming the dream again. As long as I'm here, *he's* here, and the dream has come true. The war is over as long as I'm here with them. Maybe I'm the one who should have died. I think that sometimes. Maybe that's what the dream really means. I don't know. I do know that as long as I'm here with them, the dream has come true.

She knows, I think. She seems happy. The little girl seems happy.

There's no way in the world I'm going back, sir.

HM2 Frederick Luther, 453698081, Military Provincial Hospital Assistance Team N-2, Tape 1 Transcript

I read somewhere that when you leave your body there's a cord. The first two times it happened I wasn't looking for any cord. I saw this silver river below me and I didn't think a thing about it. The next time, I saw the river was attached to me, like a leash, that I couldn't go any farther than it would let me. I didn't see much that time. I kept looking at the silver river, the silver leash, that wouldn't let me go any farther. . . .

Chapter 11

They give me something so I'll sleep, and I do. I get a good night's sleep. In the morning the pill man, the major who likes to report things, wakes me up with another one. "You're going to need one of these today," he says, putting it in my hand with a little cup of water. I don't ask him why. I'm thinking: *How many times have I done this? How many times am I going to do it again?* He stands there waiting and I pop it in. I make throat motions. I say, "See? You may now report to your superiors that I have taken my pill." I wave goodbye as he leaves and then I spit it out. It's wet, it's coming apart, but I think I can save it. I put it in the envelope with the others.

When they think the pill's working, they assign me to the medevac tent—just like Christabel said, just like I wrote my parents. I'm a *medic* now. It's triage and ER, nothing else. There's a team that's back from the Tonle Sap in Cambodia with two guys in very bad shape. I work on them. There's a battalion surgeon working, too, and he acts glad to see me. He's got three corpsmen helping him, but no nurse. There are other MDs in the camp, but they're Bucannon's. They don't touch things like this, the surgeon's been told. He doesn't understand what the hell is going on here, but he's glad to see me. He says, "We've got pulmonary edema here, Lieutenant."

I nod. I'm trying to say, "I'll help you all I can but you don't really know what's really going on here, do you—you don't really know why they've got me helping you like this, do you?"—but we've got this heart we're trying to save and the doctor's thirty, thirty-two, blond and serious. His eyes are wide open like someone has just slapped him. He's trying to be what a doctor's supposed to be in a place like this, and I know just by looking at him that he's on loan, that he doesn't know a thing about dreams or bodies or paddies that turn blue so you can kill other people. He's wondering why *I'm* here, an ER nurse, a round-eyed woman out here in the bush. He's telling himself she must be on loan, too, something's been worked out. Something important's happening at this camp or the CO here wouldn't have such incredible pull, am I right?

He's worked on two other teams this morning, he tells me, cutting and tying. Both of them ambushes. He doesn't know why they've got a surgeon out here when they don't have the facilities he needs. Unless it's some paper snafu. What other reason could there be? You don't put a surgeon out here like this. (You don't put a nurse out here either, Major.) He's a major and he shouldn't be talking to me like this, and wouldn't be, but we're both in the same situation and hell, I'm a woman—so he's safe. He's supposed to do his job and he can't do it here. He wants me to know that. I don't say, *Bucannon always has a reason, Major.* I don't even try.

"I've never seen anything like it," he's saying, and he doesn't mean the wound, the round he's trying to find while we both keep clamping off the bleeders that keep blinding him with blood. "I've never seen two groups of men chewed up like that," he says.

I know why. *There's always a reason.*

The teams didn't have talents with them, did they, Colonel? Neither of them had a talent, because you didn't *want* them to— like the ones who died by the banyan tree. Even a little talent, like Lancaster's or Shaffer's, might have been enough to save them, but you didn't want that. There was something else you needed to learn, and you couldn't learn it by having them live, could you, Colonel?

He can learn just as much if you die, Mary, Christabel had said.

I'm touching our patient, who's lying on the cot. I'm watch-

ing the drip and hoping and then, all of a sudden, I start screaming. I can't see the guy's face. He hasn't said a thing to me. But it
doesn't matter. I'm touching him—feeling his arm tremble on the
table—and I'm screaming again.

It hits me like a train. I'm on the ground. I'm on the ground
making a sound and the doctor has no idea what's happening. Did
she faint? Did she cut herself? Did she get shot and I just didn't
hear it? Is she a junkie? He's shouting at the medics and trying to
understand. There's a voice shouting somewhere.

*There's a darkness. I'm falling to it. All the way to the base
camp on the dustoff I was sure, I was really sure, Mom, that I was
going to make it. When I saw the base camp and felt us flare up—
stomach coming up through my chest—I was sure then, too, because I knew we had a surgeon, and he'd be able to do it, he'd be
able to do what medics can't do. But I'm sliding, Mom, I'm sliding
into the dark and I'm not sure anymore. I'm two weeks short,
Mom—I've got fourteen more boxes to mark on that calendar you
sent—and I ought to make it, anyone this short ought to make it,
but I don't think I'm going to, Mom. I'm sliding, I'm sliding into
the darkness. . . .*

We're losing him! I scream. Two of the corpsmen are holding
me up, walking me back toward my bunker. The surgeon is shouting—he's mad, he's mad that the only nurse they give him here
just fell down screaming like some fucking junkie. I want to say:
He's dying on you, Major. He was dying on the dustoff that
brought him here—because Bucannon has something he needs to
learn—and even you, a battalion surgeon, aren't going to be able
to keep him alive.

Even though he thought you would.

The major is pounding on the chest, the chest that's like a
sponge—it's so full. He's not listening, Major. *He's going.* I'm still
going with him, Major—but the major's not listening. Who am I
to tell him, this nurse who's fallen to the ground moaning, covered with dirt, escorted to her bunker by two corpsmen—who am
I to tell him who's dying and who isn't? *That's what's going on
here, Major. That's what's really going on.*

I try to tell the corpsmen all of this but they don't really understand. They're supposed to help me to my bunker, get me away from this surgeon who's on loan—that's all they know, that's all they want to know. They don't tell majors which patients are going to die just on the word of some screaming nurse who's as *dinky-dau* as all the other talents here—who drink, shoot up, cry, scream and you really don't know why the CO keeps any of them, do you, except that he's *dinky-dau*, too.

I can't breathe. Every breath I take hurts. My lungs are gone. The pleural membrane sticks to itself like jellied gasoline. I breathe. I try, and can't. The fluids won't let me. The ribs won't open. The heart just won't beat.

"You didn't take your pill, did you?" the pill man says, standing over me in the bunker. They put it in my mouth this time and they use their fingers. One of them says: "I'm going to push it down, Lieutenant. If you bite me, I'll hit you—it's that simple." I don't bite. I let them push it down with their fat, salty fingers and when I gag, it doesn't matter. It's not important. Getting my breath—getting my heart to start beating again in this darkness—is what's important. Do you understand?

When the pill's finally working, they let me out again. I go to the tent. I help the surgeon. He looks at me and I don't say a thing. "We lost him," he says, like it's my fault. *You motherfucker,* I want to tell him. *You arrogant son of a bitch. You don't know a damn thing.* But I go ahead. I help him. I help him with two gut wounds and a tibial amp. I think of Fran and her jokes—the ones about amps. I help him because the pill's working and I don't know these two guys whose stomachs we're working on. I don't know the guy whose leg we're taking off because the bone is shattered and after a month of osteo, of gangrene, we'd have to take it off anyway, wouldn't we? This way (we tell ourselves) we can stop the bleeding, right? This way we won't be risking a *life.* I don't know these two guys we're working on—I don't remember a thing about them from a dream—so I go ahead. I help the surgeon with them.

When the traffic slows, Christabel appears. He takes me to the range, but we don't stay. We take a couple of rounds of rifle fire from the treeline and he says, "Not today, Lieutenant." He hasn't heard about the screaming. He hasn't heard about the nightmare nurse who falls on the ground like a junkie. He's been in his bunker, of course. He's been drinking what they give him.

We go to his bunker and he hands me something. I look at the cover. It's a little Russian phrase book.

"I don't know a word of Russian, Lieutenant," he says quietly. "You're going to have to do this by yourself."

I look at him as if to say, *I could use the company, Sergeant*, but he doesn't utter a word. I want the company—and he doesn't.

"Any chance I can take the AK, Sarge, learn to strip it maybe?"

"No, Lieutenant."

He knows I won't clean it. He knows what I'll do with it. If it were anyone else standing there, I'd say, "Hey, I've got an idea. Why don't *you* kill him, Sergeant? You're the salty demo man. There must be all sorts of hi- and lo-boom ways to kill that sucker."

I can smell the whiskey—that's what they're letting him have—and I don't say it. He doesn't want to be a killer anymore. I know that. He doesn't want to kill anymore. He doesn't even want to be where people are killing—where they're dying. Why does it have to be any more complicated than this? Why can't Bucannon just leave him alone?

I take this little phrase book from him and I leave.

I get a carbine from one of the Yard perimeter guards, but before I can head toward the command post, two Green Beanies take it back. They're nice about it, but they take it.

I ask this fucking-new-guy for his .45 but he looks at me like I've got some disease, and keeps on walking.

I work on the little phrase book. We're heading North, of course. I knew that. We all did. Nancy Drew has her clues. The Chinese are on the North's shitlist, so it's *Russians* now. The place is crawling with Russians, all of them being very, very helpful. We're going to need AKs and Makarovs and we're going to need to know a little Russian.

Isn't that the plan, Colonel?

I learn *Ya khotel bee pozavtrakat* from the book. *I would like breakfast.* And *Gde doroga iz goroda? Where is the road out of town?* I go back to the first page, turn it over and read: "Copyright 1954 by The Defense Language Institute of Monterey, California." That makes sense. We were very excited about Russia in '54, weren't we? I work on *Na bortoo yest oobornaya?* and *Dobroye ootro* and *Dobry den* and *Vasha familiya* and then I hit the rack.

I dream something but it isn't very clear. It doesn't make me scream in the dark either, because the pill's still working. I sleep for an hour and when I get up, I go out looking for a pisstube. I reach down for my zipper and then I remember I'm not Steve, that women just don't do it this way, that it isn't the dream anymore.

This Green Beanie sergeant, this light-weapons MOS, comes for me. He's got two nice scars on this gorgeous face—this movie star's face. He's got my AK and he's got a Makarov, too, but you can tell it's just business. He doesn't know why he's supposed to be teaching a split-tailed nurse how to use Soviet firearms and he'd really rather be doing something else anyway.

"Where's Sergeant Christabel?" I say.

"He's indisposed."

I wait but don't even get a "ma'am."

We walk to the treeline and this time there's no incoming of any kind. The harassment is on the east side of camp today and we stand there like two kids on a date, sniffing the air, taking in the scene. The jungle's a wonder, like some crazy hat Carmen Miranda would wear, and the last of the mist is spiraling off into the sun.

I try it. I see if I can get away with it. I say, "I do appreciate your bringing me out here, Sergeant MacAvoy, but I'd rather practice by myself if Christabel can't be present. Is that all right with you?"

His eyes get narrow. No woman's ever told him no, I realize. *She would rather be* alone? he's thinking. But he says, "Lieutenant . . . Sergeant Christabel is the one who asked me to bring you out here. If you have a problem with this, take it up with him. He's in his bunker, I'm sure."

He hands both weapons over to me so fast I almost drop them. I start shaking as soon as I touch them. It's his chance to be free and he's taking it. He doesn't know what I want to do.

He walks one way and I walk the other, thinking: How could they be so stupid? I can feel the AK in one hand and the automatic in the other. I keep walking toward Christabel's bunker and when Troy Donahue is out of sight, I do a fast 180. I go to the CP first, thinking I'm going to see guns trained on me, thinking I'm going to hear bootsteps behind me and voices, like a bad movie, saying, "I'm sorry, Lieutenant, but we have orders to take you in."

No one stops me, not even the guard at the flap. There's an MD type inside, as always, and a captain in tiger stripes, too, and they turn around.

"Yes, Lieutenant," the MD says pleasantly. He's in charge. He's the XO, I realize, and all of a sudden I understand it. I know the answer before I ask it.

"Where's Bucannon?"

The MD looks at me without the slightest change of expression on his face and says: "In Vientiane. Why?"

I think of killing *him* instead and wonder whether I've dreamed of his death—but just don't remember it. How many guys have I dreamed about and just don't remember. *We remember but a fraction of our dreams, Mary, Bucannon said once. We remember only the ones near waking. The others we've forgotten. They're somewhere, sleeping. . . .*

If I killed them both as they stood there, my AK spraying, would I remember—days or months or years from now—that I'd dreamed their deaths, but like so many others, forgotten them?

I go away.

I go to Christabel's bunker and find him sitting on his cot, drunk.

I say, "Bucannon's in Laos."

He nods. He doesn't want to talk. He doesn't want to talk to *me.*

"What's happening?" I say.

After a while he says: "You know."

He's right. I do. I've got an AK. I've got a little Russian

phrase book. I'm heading to Vientiane with them, aren't I? It's a little party—Bucannon, Steve, me, a few good friends we just don't happen to know yet.

"He didn't lie to you . . . really," Christabel says, slurred, a little shot glass in his hand. It would be funny if we were somewhere else, a bar in Long Beach, fake IDs and a big dirty man like this with a pretty little shot glass in his hand, telling me how Bucannon *really* hasn't lied.

"After all, you're going to get to be with Steve, right?" he says, the slur getting worse. "Like Bucannon said. You and Steve are going to get to be together for a while. That's what he said, didn't he?" The voice changes. The slur's there but there's a problem with the words, a choking. He's saying, "Oh, God." He's saying: "I'm sorry, Kristy. I am."

He's so drunk he doesn't know who I am.

"Sergeant, will you please help me get ready for this trip? Will you please help me get a little more practice on these weapons? I need it badly and I'd rather that you be the one to show me."

He looks up. He's making a clown mouth, like he's holding it in.

"I'm sorry," he says at last, and then he begins to cry. He's breaking down and crying and I know he hasn't been on a mission in a long time, because Bucannon hasn't made him go, because there's even something to be learned from a man so full of fear, so afraid of losing one more of his men, that he won't even go out—even when he's got a gift that would keep *him* alive.

Christabel knows where we're going, and why. He has to.

We don't have a chance, do we, Sarge? Even a talent like Steve and a nurse who dreams the deaths of others don't really have a chance where we're going. You don't want to face it. You don't want to hear, a month from now, a year, that they've lost us, that we're lost forever, and in the night, when you're alone, feel you could have done something to stop it.

I can understand that, Sergeant.

"I won't tell Kristy if you don't," I say. It's cruel and as soon as I say it, I'm sorry.

I go out to the treeline and wait for rounds to come. When they don't, I shoot three magazines at nothing and come back. He's asleep. The bunker smells even worse now. I know that smell as well as he does.

I go over and put my hand on his forehead. It's sticky and cool and covered with freckles, the kind you get when you're older. I think of my father sleeping on the couch in our family room, and I tell myself: *If he's drunk, he can't die, can he? If he's here in the camp, drunk and sleeping, how can he die?* But it's not true. A mortar, RPG, LAW, M-79 grenade can come right through the corrugated metal of this damn bunker and kill him like a heart attack back home. *He* knows this. He's probably telling himself he wouldn't mind it either. All that whiskey and his talent might not even work, might not keep him alive when the round came through the roof. But he wouldn't mind. The only reason he'd ever mind is a dark-haired girl in junior high school in Richmond, Virginia, and sometimes, when he's had enough to drink, he forgets her, too, and then there isn't any reason left at all.

This isn't a dream I'm dreaming. It's just a picture in my head—nothing very important—because the pill is still working.

Photostat, Book Chapter, Green Berets and War Resisters—A Study of Commitment, *by David Mark Mantell, Command Files (Bucannon),* Operation Orangutan, *Tiger Cat, Vietnam*
Green Berets: Childhood and Family Life
Case 213

Interviewer: Did your parents get along well?
Subject: Oh, yes, they, uh, they've been married more than twenty-two years now and, apart from quarrels and arguments, I only remember one time that—that my Dad slapped my mother. Just one time, I guess if I were to, well, I was a young kid then. I didn't really know the circumstances but if I could see that again—maybe— maybe she asked for it, I don't know. Maybe. You know how women get now and then. They start rattling off at the mouth and you're just at the point where you can't

take any more and then you quiet them down. I mean, naturally it's not proper but, uh, and who's to know what a—a—a person who has a lot on his mind, well, what the reflex will be when something like that blows— makes them blow their top, you know.

Interviewer: Were you there at the time he slapped her?

Subject: Oh, yeah. . . .

Interviewer: And what did your mother do, do you re-member?

Subject: She cried a little bit. That was all.

Chapter 12

In the morning he's gone. There's a young sergeant I've never seen before who says he's his new bunker mate, who says the old guy's around somewhere—all I've got to do is look—but I don't believe it. Did they send him out? Did they send him out in that condition—just to see what would happen? Or is he hiding from me?

I don't remember a dream, but that doesn't mean a thing.

There's a patrol I'm supposed to go on, this Special Forces type tells me, and I know I'm not going to see Christabel until it's over—and maybe not even then. I know this even without a dream.

There are eight of us in all. We meet outside the command post and no one comes out to say a thing. No XO, no MD, not even the skinny captain who likes the dark. The Vietnamese officer, the one from yesterday, is the only one I know and he's wearing cammo now. He's got these very precise manners, this very courteous expression on his face, and it all looks ridiculous with his leopard spots, blousy fatigues tucked into combat boots and a handgun on his hip. There are five Special Forces types wearing tiger suits, too, while I'm just wearing olive drab. But what's really got my attention is this black kid—this young black soldier who can't possibly be *eighteen*—and his dog. He's wearing OD just like me. The dog's a German shepherd—very dark, the color you're supposed to use. Neither of them is making a sound.

One of the Special Forces types does the introductions.

The Vietnamese officer—his name is Van Bach—shakes my hand and smiles. I smile back. He's anywhere from twenty-five to thirty-five (you never can tell with these people, Jerry)—and I get this feeling that he's not *really* a soldier, that he really shouldn't be here, that he isn't really one of them.

I don't catch the names of the other tiger suits, but it doesn't matter. The guy introducing is Romaine, a Green Beanie lieutenant on loan from an A-camp near Pleime. The black kid is Corporal Cooper. His dog's a scout, not a sentry. When Cooper talks, it's soft—it's not very black at all—but he's so quiet maybe I'm just hearing it. He looks like he knows even less about this than I do. The others, except for Lieutenant Bach, don't seem to care.

The corporal gets down next to his dog and stays there, looking up—both of them looking up—at the lieutenant from Pleime, who's telling us when we're going out, the route, how many VC are supposed to be waiting for us at the foot of this little karst mountain, everything else. He squats there with his dog like an indig, just waiting.

The lieutenant from Pleime finally looks down at him and says, "Oh, yeah. We've got a K-nine with us on this patrol. His name is Crusoe and he's a scout dog. He's seen a lot of action with the 42d Scout Dog Platoon, right, Corporal?"

"Yes, sir," the corporal says, louder now, and the voice *is* black. It's not Deep South, it's not Detroit, but it's black.

"Crusoe's handler is Corporal Wallace Cooper," the lieutenant announces, grinning. "His handler's seen a lot of action, too, right?"

The corporal doesn't want all this attention. He looks down at the ground and says something that has another "sir" in it. He's leaning a little against the dog. The dog is leaning against him.

"They tell me," the lieutenant keeps on, "that this K-nine team is pretty special, that we can expect some real point magic from them. How about it, Corporal?"

The black kid still won't look up. The lieutenant isn't doing this out of kindness and the kid knows it, and he won't look up. It isn't fear, I know. He doesn't want to show the man what's in his eyes. He's smoothing the hair at the dog's throat with his hand and it's the dog who's watching the lieutenant, who's watching us all—all eyes and ears. It's pretty crazy.

No one bothers to ask why we've got a K-nine with us. *Point magic*, that's what the lieutenant said. You hear things—how the Army and the Marine Corps use them, but only sometimes, how the VC are scared shitless of them, how they've learned to wash themselves with American soap so the dogs can't smell them, how the handlers are moved from one unit to the next and keep pretty much to themselves—but I'm still wondering why. *Is it just for point work?* I want to ask them. *Is it for something more? We can expect something pretty special from you, right, Corporal?*

The corporal's still squatting with his dog, his very dark dog, and he's not even holding its harness. The lieutenant from Pleime says:

"Lieutenant Damico, you're squad medic. You'll need to assemble your own medpack from supply, but we've got a T-12 unit for you to start with, if that helps. This will be an overnighter. You can expect to see some action."

He's not sure why a nurse is on this patrol either, but he goes over to a stack of weapons, pulls two sets of cammies off the top, checks the sizes and tosses one to the corporal and one to me. Then he pulls an AK from the pile and hands it to the corporal, too. The corporal stands up at last. "Ever shot one of these, Cooper?"

"No, sir," the corporal says. The dog watches. He watches the lieutenant. He watches the weapon, which the corporal isn't sure he wants to take.

"An M-16 maybe?" The lieutenant isn't happy.

"Yes, sir."

"Glad to hear it," the lieutenant says, "but an M-16 isn't an AK." He pushes the AK at the kid again, saying: "Her name's 'Anna Karenina,' Corporal. Get to know her *real* well."

The corporal takes the rifle slowly. The dog's still watching. The corporal doesn't know why he's supposed to take it, but he does.

He's going with us, a voice says all of a sudden. *He's going North with us. Anyone with an AK, Mary, is going with us.*

I turn around and there's one other AK.

The Vietnamese lieutenant is holding it. I never saw him take it, but he's got it now and he's saying to the lieutenant from Pleime: "I will help him with it, Lieutenant, if you wish me to."

His English is *very* good. The words are right, the accent isn't any pidgin bar-girl's. *Like you,* a voice says, *he really shouldn't be here, Mary. He shouldn't be going . . . but he is.*

"You've got three hours to do it in, *Trung Uy,*" the guy from Pleime says to him.

Lieutenant Bach's looking at me again, smiling again, as if to say he'll help me, too . . . if I'd like him to.

The corporal is kneeling on the ground again with his dog—his AK propped on its stock—and I know I've never seen a human being and an animal sit like that, side by side, neither of them making a sound. The corporal isn't talking baby talk to it the way your Aunt Pupa would. He isn't saying, "Come on, Crusoe, let's go sniff out some Little People for our good buddies here." He isn't saying, "Come on, doggie, let's go get some gook meat." He's not petting him, he's not ruffling the fur on his neck like some dog food commercial, he isn't doing anything at all except stroking his neck quietly with his palm, with the pink palm of his hand. The dog isn't whining. It isn't jumping around like some poodle. It's just leaning against him, and you have the feeling that if either one of them was wounded, if either was lying by a stream some-where in the mud, the red red mud, no one else able to help them, they'd hold each other forever—the kid would hold the dog, the dog would let him, and they'd do it without a single sound until one or the other couldn't do it anymore.

I get a chill and look away.

The Special Forces types are leaving to pack. Lieutenant Bach's looking at me again. He gives me the same delicate smile and says, "*Vee zachem prishlee na rekoo?*"

I feel like an idiot. I have no idea what he's saying, but it's got to be Russian, right? It's a phrase I should know—it's something I'm *really* going to need—and I don't know it.

They're so small, I'm thinking. Their features are like birds, their voices are like birds—just like people say.

I shake my head and shrug but he keeps smiling. He doesn't want me to misunderstand him. He says, "I am sorry, Lieutenant. That phrase is not in our booklet. In fact, Lieutenant, it is a phrase we cannot afford to use where we are going. It means, 'Would you like to join us?'"

It's a joke of some kind, but I don't get it. He knows too much, this little man—he knows so much about where we're going, what we're going to be doing, that a Russian phrase like this can be a joke? I go ahead. I smile—a joke, sure, if you say so, Mr. Bach. I say, "Thank you, Lieutenant, but I'd probably better get started on the medical supplies."

"Yes. Of course," he says. He turns to the corporal, who's holding the damn rifle the same way I did the first time. He doesn't want to leave his dog. That's obvious. He's supposed to go out and get some practice on this goddamn weapon and he doesn't—he really doesn't—want to leave his dog. But he knows he can't take the animal with him either. Every Chuck in the jungle would give his index fingers for a shot at that dog.

All of a sudden I see it. I know what it means, what Bucannon's doing, who the dog and the corporal really are. I walk over to the corporal and my legs are a little shaky. I kneel down beside him, and I'm still shaking. The Vietnamese lieutenant watches.

The corporal looks at me. He's wondering who I am, who the hell this honky white lieutenant is—

"Are you a talent?" I say.

"Ma'am?"

"You're a talent and Bucannon's interested in you, right?"

He doesn't say a thing. He's looking down at the ground again, the way he did with the lieutenant from Pleime. He doesn't want to show me what's in his eyes. I don't want to see it. I'm doing the same thing that lieutenant did and I'm sorry, Corporal, but I've got to know. I look at him and I swear he's even younger than I am—nineteen at the most. He's got this baby face. He's got this baby face you always lose in the end.

"How long have you been here, Corporal—at this camp?"

He looks at me. *You're white,* the eyes say. He blinks and finally he says:

"About a week, ma'am."

"Have they asked you questions? Have they made tapes of you?"

He waits a little while, keeps looking at me and says: "Yes, ma'am." He's got to say *ma'am* because *sir* would be crazy.

I keep looking at him, too. I look at his dog and it's *there*—it's in the way they're sitting together, touching that way, without making a sound.

"It's your animal, isn't it?" I ask him. "It's something to do with your animal, right?"

The look on his face gets worse. It's *Jesus Christ*. He never thought he'd have to talk about it, but he *has*—hour after hour on that big-reel tape recorder, question after question, telling them— with a bunch of words, the only words he can find—things that just can't be said with words. It scares him, sure. *How did they find out?* he wonders. He never told *anyone*. It isn't the kind of thing you *tell* in a white man's army. Someone saw the two of them together, heard witnesses to an incident and *guessed*—was that it? What else could it have been? And now here's this white girl, this nurse who wants to know about it, who thinks she's got a right—

"Mine are dreams," I tell him, and I wait.

When he doesn't understand, I say: "I dream about people dying before they do, Corporal."

He stares at me. The eyes are a little different. The dog moves once, but settles down again. Finally he gives me a nod, like he does understand, like it's registering, but what can he really say? *There it is. That's the Nam, Lieutenant.*

"If you want, Corporal Cooper," I tell him, "I'll keep your dog for you while you go with Lieutenant Bach. If he'll put up with me, I mean."

The corporal is looking at me and he's looking younger all the time. He's got the face of a little black cherub in the corner of some map. The kind you could just hug.

He's not a cherub, Mary.

I know.

He doesn't want *you to hug him.*

I know. . . .

"Thank you, ma'am. I'd appreciate that," he says at last, gets up, doesn't say a thing to the dog—just makes a signal with his hands and his foot—and the dog sits back down again, looking at me. *Stay with her*, the hands said. And the dog is doing it.

I stand up, too, and he hands me the leash. "That's it?" I say. "He won't take my arm off if I pull on it?"

"No, he'll stick by you."

I turn around and the ARVN lieutenant's still there. He's not one of us. He's going North with us, yes, but he's not a talent, I know that now. He doesn't know about dreams or blue paddies or anything else like that. He's our walking dictionary, our interpreter. That's all. Because we're going to need one.

"Watch the left arc," I tell the kid. "It's a killer."

He nods. He even smiles. The Vietnamese lieutenant smiles, too, and they walk away together. When they're gone, the dog looks up at me, jaws open, tongue out in the heat—longer than any real tongue should be. The leash hangs between us. I give it a little tug and up the dog gets. I pull a little harder and the dog takes a step when I take a step.

I head for the supply tent and the dog walks with me. I keep thinking he'll act special, he'll start to talk like Mister Ed, bark and save someone like Lassie, do *something*, but he just comes along like a dog—big and friendly.

When I have what I need, I go back to the CP, slip the leash under a sandbag and start packing. What the hell am I going to do if someone gets hurt? I'm no combat medic, Colonel, I'm an evac triage nurse. That's a *major* difference. I can see one of the Special Forces types, the ARVN lieutenant himself dying out there by their little karst mountain, waiting for me to save him—when I can't. It's not a dream, Colonel. It's just fear. Do you know the feeling?

I'm starting to cry. I don't want to—there's no point—but I do. *There's a dog watching*, I tell myself. *There's a dog watching you.*

I laugh out loud and the dog looks away. I turn, too, to look where it's looking, but there's no one there. I listen *hard*. I don't

hear a thing. I look at the dog. It's just a dog, a German shepherd—you know, Nazi movies and Rin Tin Tin, overbreeding and
hip dysplasia, the most popular dog in California after cockers and
boxers. *That* kind of dog, I tell myself. *Maybe you were wrong,
Mary. Maybe it isn't special. Maybe Bucannon just likes dogs.*

No one came by to give me a pill before we left and it didn't
take me long to figure out why.

They did give me a little manual to read. You know which
one, Major.

U.S. Army FM 30-574-73, Section 73-02

Move as Member of a Patrol

Standards:
Move as a member of a patrol in accordance with guid-
ance given in the performance measures so that you:

1. Are not easily seen or heard during movement.

2. Properly demonstrate the techniques of using rally
   points, crossing danger areas, and passing up the
   count.

3. Remain appropriately alert and sensitive to enemy
   presence at all times.

Performance Measures:
   1. Stealth: As a member of a patrol, it is extremely
important that you be able to move across the terrain
unseen and unheard both day and night. Use the following techniques to help maximize stealth on a patrol:
   a. Camouflage and conceal yourself as discussed in
task number 051-202-10001. . . .

Chapter 13

We head out at 0100 and we've got everything tied down and blackened with matt-black tape, hand grenades taped so the pins won't get pulled by branches, canteens and dog tags so they won't make music, ammo magazines in pairs for easy switching. I'm carrying (1) the AK, (2) six banana clips, (3) a twenty-pound med-pack full of tricks and (4) six full canteens. That's all they make me carry and I thank them. After ten klicks the twenty-pound pack is going to weigh fifty, honey, and that's enough. One of the three Special Forces types is our RTO, radio on his back, the little antenna sticking up so the guys in black pajamas out there will know where to shoot. The lieutenant from Pleime, the one who likes to do introductions, is our team leader for this little outing, and there's no ARVN counterpart. He doesn't even *look* at Bach. They're both lieutenants, but he doesn't even look, and I know why. The Vietnamese lieutenant is on loan, TDY to a MAC-SOG operation like the rest of us, and Bucannon's SFers are running the show.

Bach's carrying an overnight pack, a weapon and ammo just like everyone else. Two of the SFers are carrying claymores and grenades and enough magazines for a small war. The third, a big guy who looks like Hoss—that big brother on *Bonanza*—has the squad weapon, an M-60, cartridge belts slung over him like some bandito. Corporal Cooper has his dog, his rucksack, his weapon, his magazines, a grenade or two and some special dog food made by Gaines-Burger in a belt around his waist. There are still only three AKs on the team and I have this sinking feeling that the corporal and I are the only two *talents* in the group—that we're no safer than that.

We're walking through the night single file—with maybe six feet between us—nearly touching, following each other by the sound, and I know it's not a mission, it's just a patrol, but that *someone* wants to know how well we can do—at night—the three of us. *What it's like up North at night, Colonel?* I want to ask. *Should we take a sweater?* I want to say. Whether he hears about it in Laos or back at camp, when he returns, he'll want to know exactly how we did. He's just that way, Corporal. *So much to learn and so little time. If we die, you'll have to find someone else to go North, John.*

I'm wondering how good the corporal is. He's young, but that shouldn't matter with a talent, should it? They've put him at point. He's the scout dog handler, so he needs to be at point, even if that's the worst spot there is—worse than RTO with his Prick-25 radio and little antenna, worse than the man in front of the RTO, the one-zero, the officer, a real catch. Point is where we do need our talent.

I close my eyes. I try to see it—who's going to get hurt, if anyone is—but I don't see a thing. I close my eyes so tight I see fosgenes, all those pretty colors of pressure, red balls of fire, black capillaries in the eye, the colors turning into pictures I really don't want to see. I see fire and water and red earth, fading. I see bodies blackened by something—and it's a memory. A memory of a dream. One that's sleeping.

I bump into someone in the dark and the body swears. "Keep your spread," a voice says.

Vines grab and I pull free. Everything gets thicker. I'm falling behind and know it. *Shit.* I stop to untangle, get slammed by the body behind me, hear a "Jesus H. Christ" and then Bach, in a whisper, says something to someone.

He's next to me now, the Vietnamese lieutenant, and we start moving again. He stays there, right in front of me, where I can touch his pack in the dark—to make sure he's there. I'm wondering why we're not on a *path*, in darkness like this, but I know why.

You can booby-trap paths. You can't booby-trap the entire jungle, right?

I keep thinking my eyes are closed and they're not. It's that dark, I'm holding my breath and when first light comes, I start breathing again. My right foot is numb, the other is screaming, my shoulders are being cut into thirds by hot wires, someone has put their rock collection in my pack, but at least I'm *breathing* again.

The dog will bark if anything's wrong, I tell myself. But that's stupid. Scout dogs don't bark. They give some kind of signal, to someone, without a sound. Even when they die with bullets through their rib cages, on riverbanks somewhere, they don't make a sound.

But in the *dark*? How do they do it in the dark, Mary?

At first light, we leave the jungle and take a path at last. Lieutenant Bach is still there, just ahead of me, and we're all staying ten meters apart, snaking down the path so that a mine or an ambush, if it gets us, won't get us all. They've buried me in the middle—away from the ends, where people tend to die fairly frequently. They've buried me with Bach and I don't see the corporal, I *never* see the corporal at point. I try to imagine what it's like to be inside that dog's head, smelling what he's smelling—more than wet earth, more than the hot wet air, than rotting leaves, the things *we* smell—*hearing* more than the boots, the breaking of twigs, the frustrated yanking of vines and the chaffing of cloth. But I *can't*. I really can't imagine.

The thorns go right through the cammies. In the open, the elephant grass cuts your goddamn hands. It's hotter than you ever thought it could be, like some attic in the summer where it somehow rains, a hothouse you'll never break out of. You can't breathe and you keep thinking of leeches—you can't stop thinking of leeches. You're too high here for them, you hope—highland jungles, highland pampas—but you keep thinking how they'll drop to your neck, wriggle in under your blouse, to your chest, and you'll never feel a thing. They'll just be there, their little heads buried in you, and you won't find them until you take your clothes off, looking at yourself in a mirror.

You're going to get wet, the lieutenant from Pleime said. The monsoons are getting their asses in gear and you're all going to get very wet. It isn't going to get cooler out there, Damico, it's just going to get wetter, and if you try to keep your candy-assed ladylike body *dry*, you'll go crazy. This isn't a LURP, Damico. You're not going to be out long enough for your clothes to rot off your pretty little body, so stop worrying. Get wet and forget it. Try thinking about leeches instead.

I hear something jangling and I have no idea what it is. It keeps on jangling and I stop and the guy behind me, the one with the M-60—who doesn't *really* look like Hoss—nearly runs over me. He grabs at my belt, under the medpack where I can't see them, and does something with the canteens. He gives me a big brother smile—like, you should be nursing in a nice white hospital in Japan, honey, away from this shit, you should be home watching a movie with your boyfriend, you should be watching television in a nice white house in a nice suburb, not humping the boonies with us, but we'll do our best to protect you, like big brothers should—and then he drops back to his position. I want to shoot him. I want to use the AK on him and I don't even know why.

The AK is like the biggest crowbar you've ever held and the rocks in the medpack have turned into those big fishing weights they use on the surf at Redondo. It's unbelievable. I think: *Maybe he's right.* Maybe I shouldn't be here. I get my period once a month, I cry easily, I can't do pull-ups. I can't even tote water. All I can do is dream about people dying, and maybe that's not enough. Maybe Bucannon isn't going to learn a damn thing from me because I'm going to keel over, I'm going to die right here on this little patrol and he'll have to find someone else to go North for him—some other nurse, some other dreamer. I'm going to be so tired when we're finally hit that I'm not going to be able to raise the AK, that's what'll happen. I'm just going to lie there on the ground and say, "Shoot me, please. I'm a *woman*. I shouldn't really be here."

You're not thinking clearly, Mary.

I know.

Everything's spinning. I don't push myself like this in Long Beach and I'm wondering why. I'm wondering how all those little women carry so much on their poles, how the men put five hundred pounds of rice or ordnance or bandages on their rickety bicycles and push them fifteen hundred miles down the Ho Chi Minh Trail, then turn around and push them all the way back again. How the women fight as mean as the men do, how they've got just as much piss and vinegar, every one of them a screaming commando bitch, a Florence Nightingale with a tommy gun, saving lives, taking lives, how it's got to be *me—my* goddamned body, these candy-assed civilian bones, Miss Clairol hair, Tampax and Zest—not *women in general*, right, Fran? How can it be *women in general* when *they've* got their lovers and sisters and daughters living and breathing and winning this war in those dark, humid tunnels like that?

I stumble. I must be stumbling because I'm picking myself up. *It's thinking a certain way*, I tell myself, *until the body is what the mind thinks it is. That's all, Mary.* I could be like them, Fran. I could, but I've been on a couch in my parents' living room watching television, eating hamburgers, way too long. I've been someone's daughter in Long Beach, California, way too long. I'm sweating. My muscles are on fire. I don't care if the VC capture me, what they do to me, I'm too tired to take another step. I need a couch. Everyone else is doing fine, of course. The *men* are doing fine.

We stop suddenly and my heart starts doing the Mashed Potato. I can see the corporal through the leaves. He's holding his hand up. He's making another signal and then another, without a sound. I'm panting like a dog. I'm panting so loud I wouldn't even be able to hear it if we started taking fire. I can't *see* the dog. The jungle's too thick. I can't even see the corporal now because I've taken a step, I'm getting ready to run—what else is there to do?

Lieutenant Bach comes back and stands right beside me. He

doesn't take my arm the way an American man would. He just smiles and whispers, "They find booby trap."

I listen and don't hear a thing. Nothing blows. No one screams. I close my eyes and pray just a little. *Hail, Mary. Pater et filius sunt.* . . . I haven't prayed in a long time. *Please God, don't let anyone get hurt so I have to fix them up. I* know *what booby traps can do. I do.* I've cleaned out pungi wounds with peroxide, pumped broad-spectrum antibiotics into white and black arms for tetanus. I've tied off arteries, used pneumatic tourniquets when they lost their toes or feet and the foot's still there, the gray bone sticking out of the boot. I've stood and stared at shrapnel like big pieces of pepper on someone's chest, on a face, sunk deep in the bone, unable to do a thing about it, except dig. I don't want to have to do that here, God. I don't want to use the few tricks in this pack and wish I had more. *I shouldn't* have *to do it, God.*

I haven't dreamed about these guys, any of them, but that doesn't mean a thing, of course. I don't dream about *little things,* like foot-long puncture wounds, missing toes, a leg without a foot, little black holes that don't even ooze blood. *Little things* like someone screaming, like someone losing an eye, a jaw, a nose. *Little things* like boys who can't think anymore because they've lost too much brain tissue. *Little things* like boys who breathe but don't know they're alive. I only dream about big things—

Like death.

I don't hear a thing. I don't hear a dog whining or scratching for a flea. I don't hear people whispering. I don't hear a booby trap explode and voices shouting *"Bac si!"* or "Band-aid!" or "Medic!" We start moving again.

The corporal and the dog aren't there when we reach the spot and there's nothing to mark it. I'm thinking: *Jesus, aren't they going to tell us where it is, like maybe warn us?* But they've taken it, I know—they've removed it somewhere without setting the damn thing, they've "denied" it to the enemy, they've saved the next patrol. How nice. *You're not thinking very clearly.*

I know.

It doesn't take a corporal or German shepherd with talent to do that—find a booby trap. Any dog nose with the right training can.

Show me what you've got, Corporal Cooper, and maybe I won't worry about either of us anymore.

We stop again. More hand signals, and I think Lieutenant Bach is going to drop back, tell me what's happening, but he doesn't. He moves up quickly to two SFers and makes hand signals to them. Everyone's moving faster now, quietly but quickly, and I can feel the adrenaline shoot through my chest. We're flying.

Someone touches me from behind and I nearly scream. I turn around and Hoss whispers, "Stay *down,* ma'am."

Down? I look at the AK in my hand and I understand. It's been a joke all along. The shit's going to hit the fan and they don't even want me to use this weapon. They want me *down,* out of the way, where any woman should be.

Hoss grabs me by the sleeve and pulls me off the path. I see everyone disappearing. They don't go far but they disappear. They're there—and then they're not. Cammies—base green with sunlight and shadow markings, the disruptive design—are a wonder.

Hoss takes me far from the path, up the slope, and points to this big depression in the jungle floor. There are shadows there. I don't want to go. He looks at me hard and it's big brother again, getting mad. For your own good, sis. So I do it. I step toward the shadows. The others are staying by the path, watching it, holding their breaths. I'm the last one down. *You're a helluva lot safer back here,* I'm telling myself. *You're a helluva lot safer in these shadows, sis.*

I lie down. Something moves beside me and I nearly scream again. It's hairy and big and for a split second I think of *phi,* those animal spirits these people believe in. The nurse gets killed by a "feather tiger" in the middle of this war because the spirits are angry at America—something like that. Or if not *phi,* then a *real* tiger, a *real* wolf, a bear, whatever they have in these jungles that they don't teach you about at Fort Sam.

But it's just Crusoe. The corporal is on the other side of him, too, lying in the depression the same way I am. I take a breath.

I look at the corporal and he looks at me and I think: *Laugh at me and die, sucker.* But he's not laughing. He's not even smiling and I wish he was. He's looking at the path, where something's going to happen, even though neither of us—black kid or round-eyed nurse—is a part of it. He's the scout dog handler. He's got a valuable animal to protect, they've told him, and she—this split-tail *nurse*—certainly can't shoot worth chili, guys.

The dog is warm. It stays against me. It's watching the path, too, head cocked like that old RCA dog, like it can hear Hanoi Hannah jabbering on a VC radio out there somewhere, singing Petula Clark's Favorite Hits. It's that kind of war, you know.

I can't see *anyone* out there and for a second I think they've gone and left us. I feel little wings beating in my throat. It's the adrenaline, I think. It's just palpitations. You don't have a *real* bird in your throat, Mary. They haven't really left you. What do you think camouflage is for?

Someone screams, "Fire!"—or I think they do—and all those rifles I can't see anymore open up all at once. I drop the AK beside me and cover my ears. I want to scream from the noise. Grenades blow—that's got to be what they are, but how would a round-eyed nurse know what grenades sound like, right? I hear screaming—and it's not me, it's someone out there with a bullet or two in him and there's nothing else for him to do but scream. I close my eyes. I don't *care* what I see. I'm already seeing someone screaming. I keep my hands where they are, I keep thinking the dog is going to start shaking beside me, too, start whimpering in fear, just like me. I'm afraid he's going to get up and bolt, he's going to howl like a wolf, do something hysterical, just like me. He doesn't. He stays warm against me. He doesn't move an inch. I pull my hands away from my ears and start listening to the incredible *sound*.

Hollywood just doesn't *know*, Major. There's smoke rising and leaves being chewed up and branches flying, and it's all happening in *your* ears. In *your* head. It's like getting tumbled in a

wave that's too big for you when you're a kid. It's like God's hand
lying on your heart. He won't let up and He's screaming. You're
on the ground. The ground is shaking, too, just like you are—the
grenades, rockets, whatever they are, landing right beside you,
blowing the leaves and vines and earth right at you, like a big dog
digging in your face. It makes you crazy. You're shaking. The dog
is shaking. It's the ground really, but the ground is everything. *We
who live on the earth*, a voice is saying, *shake when it shakes.* I
think of Arc Light, B-52s, the 750-pounders that turn the air white
from the shock waves, that leak blood from your ears if you're
within a klick, that leave giant craters to fill with gorgeous rain-
water at sunset. The napalm that sucks the air away, leaving you
nothing to breathe. The "daisy cutters" that remove whole forests,
because that's what they're made for—if not for killing things. If
these little things—these little M-33 grenades, these little rockets
we're throwing at each other—can make the world rock 'n' roll
like this, Fran, what must *it* be like: Rolling Thunder. The black
pajamas trapped in the miles of soft tunnels, growing older each
day, eating and sleeping in little rooms until the earth rises up like
a roller coaster at Belmont Park and buries them forever.

I'm shaking and it isn't the earth here. I'm against that warm
hairy body and it's the only thing in the world that feels good. I
can't breathe. The vacuum has stolen the air—I can't breathe at
all—the earth is rolling, blood is pouring from my nose—maybe
it's a dream, maybe it isn't—maybe I'm here, maybe not. It
doesn't matter. I'm shaking, I'm shaking any way you want me to,
Colonel, and there's this dog, this damn Rin Tin Tin lying beside
me, those freckles on Rusty's face, just like Huck Finn's, like the
red-haired kids who get all the jobs at Disneyland, like the dogs—
the collies, the shepherds, the golden retrievers, all of them, who
risk their lives for all the heroes in all those old movies, all those
dogs who are going to save you because the nurse can't—because
her dreams can't *really* save you—because she can't even save a
dog.

Chapter 14

I don't know how long it lasts but suddenly it's not a mad minute anymore, it's just a couple of rounds, like an engine running down. The silence is thick, like cotton, but you can think. You can hear someone you once knew start to think again.

The dog doesn't move. The corporal doesn't move. *Is it over?* I want to ask someone.

Guys start standing up now—SFers, Hoss, Bach. The jungle shifts and our guys stand up. It's over, yes. They want to see what they've got, lobsters in the traps of Coronado Island, rabbits in the steel jaws near Slater's Fork, a twelve-point buck in the Rockies, a 200-kilogram white catfish netted in the Mekong, whatever they're thinking, whatever these guys have done that boys and men do with their fathers, uncles, brothers and buddies in all those hometowns, all those villes, back home. They're going to check what they caught. They're going to find out how *good* they were.

Crusoe is panting, but he moves, too. I'm against him, so I feel him do it. I feel him get up and I turn. He's looking at me. It's the weirdest feeling. This dog's looking down at me and I'm looking up. *What are you thinking, Rin Tin Tin? Did Rusty get his twelve-point buck today?*

When it finally happens, I don't hear a thing. I don't *see* a thing but the dog snaps its head around and I go ahead—I look where it's looking and I still don't see it. The jungle behind us is a painting, great globs of green paint on a canvas, great slashes of shadow. In the corner of my eye I see the corporal reach for his AK. Adrenaline shoots like bird shot through my chest and everything starts to *slow*. I haven't seen a signal of any kind pass between the two of them—man and dog—but the corporal is reaching for his AK—a weapon he doesn't even like—and the dog is staring up the slope behind us, frozen. I think: *We are about to be in a world of hurt*. I grab for my weapon, too, but it's slow, like one of those dreams where your legs don't work. It's right there in my hand—I just can't feel it. The corporal's mouth, his white teeth, the baby cheeks, all of it opens up slowly and he uses those things he really doesn't like to use, because there's nothing else to use now. He uses words: "VC *flanking!*" he screams. My own AK is up at last. His is, too. He's looking where Crusoe is looking.

He knows what the dog knows, a voice says, and all of a sudden I understand it.

For a moment I'm in a square—you know, a *plaza*, the kind you see in Europe or South America. There's a face on a big screen behind me, time has slowed down, the air, the whole world is blue. There are jeeps with guns that somehow spit blue beams of light, and students—kids who look like students—are dying. It's real, but it's also not. It hasn't happened yet. It *will* happen, but it hasn't happened yet. It ends like a movie on an old projector, flickering to a stop. It's the jungle again, everything faster, the corporal firing his AK, our guys by the path turning toward us, turning to watch the flanking unit of little black pajamas stream out of the jungle, down the slope toward us—and I know, I know that if I stick my head up I'm going to buy the farm once and for all, either with *their* weapons or *ours*—one or the other, doesn't matter which. *You're supposed to die up North with Steve*, I tell myself. *You're not supposed to die down here shot by some American you've walked all night with or some little man who's running down a slope at you, some filthy guy who smells like Marlboros, or fish sauce, or both—so there's no way in the world you're going to get to your feet, Mary, or your knees, and shoot your goddamn gun, is that clear?*

Cooper fires. The dog lies back down. The guys by the path can't shoot without hitting us and I'm watching the enemy again—the nine or ten of them coming down the slope in a movement we called "hard lightning," the same fucking charge we learned in basic, popping up, dropping down, popping up again from the jungle floor like puppets, like Howdy Doody, like Princess Summer-Fall-Winter-Spring and Clarabelle. I lift the AK and it's the dead-weight crowbar again. I'm shaking, but it's not grenades or rockets—it's not Arc Light now. I'm thinking: *You want a needle—is that it? Would that make it all okay, Mary?* No. I don't. I don't want one and I know it's not the same anyway. *This isn't the 21st or the 8th, where they* die *on you and you can't do a damn thing.*

Here you can—

Here you can do unto others—

—before they do unto you.

I hear them crashing through on either side of me, heading toward the path, toward the rest of the team, thinking they've got them trapped—ambushing the ambushers—and isn't that what flanking is all about? We all learn the same things, don't we? Some of us just learn it a little better.

They don't know we're here, I know. They haven't seen the three of us lying in these shadows, in this depression. They haven't seen us at all. The dog's laid out like he's sleeping, no profile, another shadow on the jungle floor—the kind the skinny captain would just *love.* I'm lying right beside him and Cooper's on the other side—in shadow, too. They're both *dark. They don't see* any *of us, do they?*

The guys by the path are doing it at last, laying down fire and praying that the three of us right here in the middle don't get nailed in the cross fire. *Fields of fire. Killing zones. Cross fire.* Words that can kill you. Cooper isn't shooting either. He knows he can't get up.

I blink. I blink again. There's a guy running down the slope right at me. I keep blinking at him. I want him to *go away.* He stops six feet away and blinks back at me. He's little, he's wearing black—just like he's supposed to. His face is in shadow, I tell myself. It's as dark as it is because he's in shadow. But I'm wrong. It's his *skin* that's so dark. I realize. He's Cambodian, I realize—he's got Khmer blood in him—coarse black hair, skin that black GIs like, a face that's not even oriental. He's got an AK just like mine and he stands there for a second looking at the dog, a dog that isn't moving, looking at a big American in cammies who looks strangely like a woman, looking at a soldier who's as dark as his own people, and it feels just like a crazy dream to him. I *know* it does. It feels just like a crazy dream, Major.

When he sees what I've got in *my* hands, how I'm lifting the AK at last, he brings his own weapon up, too—and his technique is a lot better. He holds the stock correctly, barrel out—like he's showing me how. But he's late.

I spray him. I spray him like all the bodies in that village I remember. The rounds stitch his chest, throw him left, away from me, back between two little trees, where he falls. I hold the AK tight as it keeps spraying, arcing left, and the dog just lies there watching, while the corporal keeps firing, too. When I'm through, I throw it away like it's burned my hands.

I'm screaming now, because I can—because it's over.

I'm on my back looking up at a jungle canopy that isn't so strange. I've known jungles like this in the South, Camau and the U Minh forest, rich with Khmer blood like my mother's, the hamlets where my family lives, wife, brother, mangrove swamps on the coast, Hoa Hao zealots deep in the dark peninsula, the little boats—a honeymoon, yes—to sun-bleached Vung Tau, where I married her, all the Tets I have spent with her, showing her the people of my mother's blood. I'm lying here under this canopy that isn't so very different because Heaven wills it, because it is indeed the Will of Heaven. My father died like this, I know, in 1954—a Viet Minh. I'm dying three days after his birthday—Year of the Dog—four monkeys, four tigers ago. I hurt. I do. It's the Will of Heaven. It is the will of Cuoc Cach Mang, the many-headed struggle of the people—the body but one. I would if I could kneel at the shrine of my family, ignore the *phi*, tell my mother and father how *different* this war is—a war with dogs larger than any we have seen before, too big to be eaten—with Africans paler than any the long-nosed *français* brought with them—and big, round-eyed women holding weapons just like ours, using them as our own women would. We were never told about these things, *Dai uy*. I would if I could kneel with my wife and child and I would say: "If this is what the new war is, what it has become, we may all come to you soon, Mother and Father. Your land will pass unto those who should not have it. Your hedgerow will be destroyed. Your paddies will lie unplanted. Your spirits will be forgotten and we will be helpless to stop it. There will be a reign of a hundred years, you will be forgotten, Mother and Father, but in the end, as we know, you will have it back, as always, invader after invader, ruler after ruler, Buddha and Heaven be blessed. This I promise, for I am your loving son."

I am lying on the leaves. A large dog lies beside me. I cannot get up. I try, and cannot. *For I am your loving son.*

The African is saying something to me, but I cannot see him. I see high shadows and a bamboo hedgerow, your little shrine, Mother and Father, where I kneel. I hear other voices and they mix, like blood, with his. It is another language he speaks, pleading with me. It does no good. I do not speak his tongue.

When it is quiet except for the voices in their language, they try to pick me up. They ask me questions. They do not want to touch me, because I am a woman. I am a medic, *bac si*. I am the one who is supposed to help *them*. What happens, *Dai uy*, when the medic himself is wounded? That is what I would ask them.

I listen for Tranh, but he isn't weeping anymore. Nguyen Pau and his Hue arrogance, his imperial accent, isn't there either. I saw him die, but I did not hear him. Brothers and sisters in this struggle, we do not make a sound. We are fish in the sea of the people, soundless. There weren't enough of us, I know that now. The lieutenant who said "Try!" is dead. I saw him fall and the Americans, as we know, do terrible things to our wounded—they cut off penises and place them in the mouths of the dead, to keep them from Heaven. The Americans are looking for blood on me. It is here on my chest—*I* can see it and they cannot. They are blind, Father. They see what they wish to see. *Cau duoc—voc thay.* They think I'm all right, when I am really dying. They can't even see *this.* They can't even see that I am dead already and that it doesn't matter what they cut from me now, Father.

I am kneeling at a shrine—a little shrine, Mother. I am kneeling there forever.

Chapter 15

Letter, Lloyd Moore to 1st Lt. Stephen Balsam, 505628831,
Command Files (Personnel) Operation Orangutan, *Tiger Cat,*
Vietnam

Dear Lieutenant Balsam,

My name is Lloyd Moore. I live in a small town called Brown Mills, located in the central part of Ohio. I am seventeen years old and a senior at Brown Mills High School. In June of 1970 I will be leaving for the United States Army. I will first be issued clothing, medical checkups, haircut, etc. at Fort Jackson, S.C. I will then go to Fort Benning, Ga., for basic training, then Advanced Infantry Training and finally airborne training. The representatives from the Army told me I would then probably go home on leave before entering my final phase of training: Special Forces training at Fort Bragg, N.C. After four months of Special Forces training, and if I successfully complete it, I will then be stationed at Fort Bragg with the 3d or 7th Special Forces Group.

My reason for this letter is to find out more about what I should expect in my experiences with the Special Forces. First, I would like to ask you about your own experiences in the elite Green Berets. I saw your picture in our paper and hope to be a light-weapons specialist, too. What training is there after the first four months for someone planning to be a light-weapons specialist? Also, how would you compare the jungles you've fought in with the forests we have in Ohio? Is the training as tough as everybody claims? I have been running five miles a day as often as time will permit, which has been an average of about four or five days a week. I have also been doing 30 chin-ups/pull-ups a night along with 105 push-ups and 105 sit-ups. I am going to keep this up until I leave for the Army. Do you think this is enough?

Photostat, Book Chapter, The War Trap, by Bruce Bueno de Mesquita, Command Files (Bucannon), Operation Orangutan, Tiger Cat, Vietnam

The Expected Utility Theory

Having delineated the assumptions of the theory, we may turn our attention to the theoretical form of the expected-utility model hypothesized to discriminate between those who might expect to gain from war and those who would rationally expect to suffer a net loss if they initiated it. The size of the expected gain or loss depends on (a) the relative strengths of the attacker and the defender; (b) the value the attacker places on changing the defender's policies, relative to the possible changes in policies the attacker may be forced to accept if it loses; and (c) the relative strengths and interests of all other states that might intervene.

Expected Utility from a Bilateral War

. . . Nation i's expected utility from a *bilateral war* with j. $[E(U_i)_b]$ can be calculated as:

$$E(U_i)_b = [P_i(U_{ii} - U_{ij}) + (1 - P_i)(U_{ij} - U_{ii})]_{t_0} + P_{i_{t_0}}[\Delta(U_{ii} - U_{ij})]_{t_0 \to t_n} + (1 - P_i)_{t_0} [\Delta(U_{ij} - U_{ii})]_{t_0 \to t_n} \quad (1)$$

where

$U_{ii} = i$'s preferred view of the world. $U_{ii} = 1$ by definition.
$U_{ij} = i$'s utility for j's policies, U_{ij} can vary between 1 and
-1.
$(U_{ii} - U_{ij})_{t_0} = i$'s perception of what might be gained by
succeeding in a bilateral conflict with j in which i can
then impose new policies on j. This term reflects i's current evaluation of the difference between the policies
that i currently desires j to hold and i's perception of j's
current policies (hence it is evaluated at time t_0). Thus
the greater the perceived similarity between the policies i
desires for j and j's current policies (i.e., $U_{ij} \rightarrow U_{ii}$), the
less utility i expects to derive from altering j's policies.

Photostat, Journal Article, Command Files (Bucannon),
Operation Orangutan, *Tiger Cat*, Vietnam

**Inequality and Insurgency:
A Statistical Study of South Vietnam**
by Edward J. Mitchell

We conceive of the government's control as depending upon a small number of important factors and a
large number of minor influences. The latter, since they
are of negligible individual importance and are difficult
to measure, are considered here collectively and regarded
as merely introducing a random error into the relationship between control and the important factors. For-
mally, we are working with an equation relating a
control variable to a number of explanatory variables and
a random variable. For simplicity the equation is assumed to be linear; that is, it may be written in the form

$$C = b_0 + b_1 X_1 + b_2 X_2 + \ldots + b_n X_n + e,$$

where C, control, depends upon n explanatory variables,
X_1 through X_n, and e represents the random error . . .

* * *

Photostat, Memorandum 6/3/71, Col. Charles S. Narda to Col. John W. Bucannon, Command Files (Bucannon), Operation Orangutan, *Tiger Cat, Vietnam*

I would recommend assessing the patient in the more obvious areas: (1) psychosocial history with an emphasis on early family relationships and postadolescent relationships with significant others; (2) significant stressors in the history of her coping resources; and (3) the usual formative psychological assessment, including MMPI, Rorschach and TAT.

I would of course anticipate that while her MMPI would be marginally valid, she would show a distinct pattern of elevations on scales 2, 3, 4 and 8. Such a pattern would, I suspect, reflect extensive use of repression and denial as psychological defense mechanisms only temporarily successful in helping her address significant levels of anxiety. Such a pattern would also occur, I'm afraid, at a tremendous cost to her in psychic energy, producing (1) fatigue and depression psychologically and (2) withdrawal and isolation socially.

From the brief information you've given me on her psychosocial history, I would indeed anticipate a problem with rescue fantasies involving her patients and, in turn, with an overidentification with those patients in order to meet her own deficits in ego functioning. I would go further, however, and predict as well that the cumulative effect of (1) her continual involvement with the personality characteristics and needs of her patients and other peers and (2) her inability to separate those characteristics and needs from her own will be a steady deterioration of her personality structure.

Before saying any more, I would want more information on her past and current relationships. For example, before her experiences in Vietnam, did she have female friends she confided in? How close was and is she now to family members? Did she and does she draw on available resources? After returning from Vietnam, she may very well withdraw from friends and family. I would want to have at least some sense of how they will respond to her during this period and how they will react initially. I would like to know more about her relationship with the brother. Is that relationship a source of actual social support? Are they in frequent contact? Is it a relationship that could be developed to help her cope now and later?

Photostats, Excerpts, Command Files (Bucannon), Operation Orangutan, *Tiger Cat*, Vietnam

STRATTON: "(t-r/v) leads to an advanced time, implying that the field can be observed before it has been generated by the source. The familiar chain of cause and effect is thus reversed and this alternative solution might be discarded as logically inconceivable. However, the application of logical causality principles offers very insecure footing in matters such as these, and we will do better to restrict the theory to retarded action, solely on the grounds that this solution alone conforms to the present physical data."

TARG AND PUTHOFF: "The hypothesis presented here is that significant events create a perturbation in the space-time in which they occur, and this disturbance propagates forward and, to some small degree, backward in time. Since precognitive phenomena are very rare, this disturbance must fade rapidly in the $-t$ direction. The wave traveling in the $+t$ direction is associated with causality as usually experienced."

EHRENWALD: "The patient's telepathic dreams expressed her desire to move into a new apartment whose existence she could not have been aware of by means of ordinary cognition. Her dreams spelled out positive transference on the therapist as father surrogate. Mrs. D's dream, highlighting her identification with the therapist, is a variation on the same dynamic. Dreams of this order, including the telepathic element woven into the manifest dream content, are essentially need-determined."

TARG AND PUTHOFF: "In these experiments we attached the EEG lead of interest to the scalp at the midline of the head. When the significance of hemispheric specialization became apparent, we carried out three further experimental runs, this time with separate monitoring of left and right hemispheres. Each of these bilateral experiments consisted of twenty 15-second trials: ten no-flash trials and ten 16-flash-per-second trials randomly intermixed. The arousal response indicated by a reduction in alpha activity occurred for the flash cases as in the previous experiments, but they occurred only in the right hemisphere (with average alpha reduction 16 percent in the right, 2 percent in the left). This tends to support the hypothesis that paranormal functioning may involve right-hemispheric specialization, but the sample was too small to provide confirmation."

Letter, Dr. Michael Collins to Col. John W.
Bucannon, Command Files (Bucannon), **Operation**
Orangutan, *Tiger Cat,* **Vietnam**

309 Ravenswood Court
Falls Church, Virginia

Col. John W. Bucannon
DOD Box 7573
APO New York 09058

Dear John:

I suspect you're right. The spontaneous crisis-state psi you're seeing, if it's to be differentiated, *must* be operating out of either (1) fatigue-, injury-, or other stress-induced ASCs across personalities, or (2) the same extroversion and consequent trust of ASC perceptions we keep seeing under lab conditions. What I'd *love* to know is whether investigator faith or group interpersonals can play weighted-factor roles and also whether preconditioning "threat" can be manipulated. You can't tell me you're not wondering the same thing. Any ideas?

The good news is, Joan loves Falls Church, and the kids are adjusting fine. All of their classmates have "Property of U.S. Government" pens, they tell me, so they're feeling right at home. They also tell me they're going to cause a scene if you don't come by for dinner on your next swing through. How about it? Joan's threatening, too.

All best,
Mike

P.S. The Catalina should be ready by summer. Any chance?

Chapter 16

"Can you walk, Lieutenant?" a voice says.

I'm crying. I'm a woman now, crying, and I'm trying to stop. My legs are attached to my throat, to the cords that make the sounds, and when I cry, my legs won't work. I don't want to cry here, like this, with all these guys, but I can't stop.

"Conroy, hold her up till we're clear."

We're trying to get away. We've got to get away because a flanking unit that size could mean battalion point, that's what it's got to mean. Intel was wrong, someone says, and we're going to get our asses in a sling if we hang around here.

It wasn't, I try to tell them. It wasn't a battalion point. I *know.* I was with them. I'm trying to walk, I'm trying to tell them, and the guy holding me up smells like jungle, smells like my brother after a game. I'm getting used to it, I tell myself. The AK is light, the medpack is light. I don't even feel them. I *must* be getting used to it.

"It *wasn't,*" I say, but no one's listening. "You got one, Lieutenant," the guy beside me is saying, grinning, a sparkle in his eye, trying to make it feel better. A twelve-point buck, he's saying. "You get a six-pack of Coors when we get back, Lieutenant. That's what we do with cherries." I want him to say instead: *By killing that dark-skinned man, Lieutenant, you saved one of us—someone who might have died tomorrow, the next day, even on a bed at Cam Ranh Bay.* But he doesn't. He doesn't know what I need to hear. "They don't go to Heaven if a woman kills them," he's saying, and someone behind us laughs. It's a joke and I don't get it—I never do. I look again at the guy who's helping me. He's huge. It's Hoss. He's got so much gear on him it looks like he's carrying a body. (We don't take their bodies—we don't steal their bodies—do we, *Dai uy?*)

Then I see it—what he's really carrying. It's my stuff—AK, medpack, the rest. I'm not carrying anything at all. I'm barely carrying myself.

The African and his dog are somewhere else. The Vietnamese lieutenant is somewhere else, too. I start to fall to my knees, to kneel by a shrine somewhere, but the American—the big American—who feels a little like a brother—keeps pulling me up.

It's changing, Mary, Bucannon would say if he were here. *What began in your wards at Cam Ranh Bay will go wherever you go, Mary. Your hospitals will no longer have walls. The patients will no longer be just yours. You will dream of the deaths of the men on your team and you will dream of the deaths of men you help kill. They are the same. As we know.*

Two of the guys are wounded, but I don't touch them. No one asks me to. They're walking-wounded, someone else does the dressing and no one even asks me. *I'm* walking. I'm able to walk back to camp and that's what matters. The thin captain who likes the dark is waiting for us there in the sun, squinting, impatient. I knew he'd be. Bucannon goes to Vientiane and the captain stays. To help us get ready. To see how well we do on a little patrol.

Someone holds up a Chinese claymore, a big ugly thing, and I know it's the one we almost tripped. Someone else says something about the wounded, the ambushed ambushers, and I keep walking toward my bunker. The captain's looking at me—I can feel it in my eyes and neck—but I just keep walking. I don't have the AK. I don't have the Makarov. I don't have a thing I can use on him.

I guess that's true, Major. They knew I was changing. They *wanted* me to change. They wanted to see how far it would go, but they didn't want me to see it. They were like that. Both of them.

I could've stayed with Cooper or Bach, sure. I could've stayed and talked to either one of them and tried to find out more about the mission, but instead I just kept walking. I was thinking about Steve. I was thinking about him a lot. I was thinking: *Hey, you're going to be with him soon, Mary.*

I didn't stop walking.

I have a dream that night, but I don't know what kind. It's a dream about a one-armed man who wants to go home, who shouldn't be in this war at all, but is. His world is strange. It's full of halos. Angels are about to come down to him. Cooper's there with him, too, a halo on *his* head—a halo on Crusoe's head—and everyone is waiting for the angels to come down. There's this singing, this beautiful singing. The one-armed man, Cooper, the dog, even *me*—I'm in the dream, too—we're all dying—that's what the halos mean. But the angels are *singing*—which means they're coming down. It's okay. We're flying now—*we're* the angels now and we're flying over a big red river. We can see the whole world now, because we're dead, because we're *free at last*. It's that kind of dream, Major. The kind you have when you're a kid and you have it for years and years and when you're older wish you could dream it just one more time.

It isn't real, I tell myself. It's not *that* kind of dream, Mary. You don't use one-armed men in *war*.

I wake up to this voice and I'm somewhere else. It's a high voice—a man's, a woman's—and I'm in Saigon somewhere.

"Lieutenant Damico," it says gently, far away. But it's wrong. I'm *not* a nurse. I'm not a woman now.

I'm not in this war anymore and it takes me a long time to wake up. The voice says *everything's fine*, no one's shooting anymore, you don't need to be afraid. It says *Hom nay anh co den di choi voi me con im khong?* I know what that means. *Anh van yeu,* I tell it.

The voice calls again—a woman's now, and I, a man. She's standing outside, I know. She won't come in. She stays, in all courtesy, outside the little house, waiting for me to invite her in.

Bong hoa xinh dep cua anh. Her voice is beautiful. Why she must wait for an invitation I do not know. That is part of the mystery she is. . . .

"Just a moment, *Im Than Yeu,*" I tell her, and I'm not sure where I am. It's dark, like my room near the Saigon River. I'm dreaming of *ao dais* like her mother's, *ao dais* like Kieu's, five long dynasties ago. She shouldn't be here, I tell myself. A student should not come to her professor's house, no matter how much she loves him—*Kim Van Kieu.* She will be in trouble with her family and her friends. She will lose her position in life. I do not wish disgrace to befall her—to see her unhappy. I want her to be what she is, yet not to suffer for it. I want us both to be what we are—together—but only after the patience required by life. After a reading of the wind.

It's a voice whose beauty I will never forget, a face I will never forget.

It's the bunker again—the smells of it—and a man's high voice now. *Nguoi chong tre.*

"Lieutenant Damico," he says again, out in the humid sunshine—too shy to come in.

I pull my boots on, throw on a little perfume from the PX bottle, try not to laugh (what will he think of me, my suitor in the sunshine, my professor by the little pond near the Saigon River?) and stumble up the stairs.

It's Bach, of course, and the pictures go away, the beauty goes away, to begin its waiting. *Does this mean he will die, Mary? That because you have dreamed of him in the daylight, he will die?*

"Have you dined, Lieutenant Damico?" he asks, and his voice is as high as a woman's. "If you have not, Lieutenant, may I escort you? After our meal, perhaps you will join me for a Russian lesson."

I smile. I can't help it. I'm next to him now and the perfume hits him hard, he winces without wanting to, does his best not to show it, and I giggle behind a cupped hand. *Was it him?* the voice says. *Was it him, hearing his lover's voice near the Saigon River? Was it a year ago, or a thousand? Whose dream was it, Mary?*

Who will die—who has already *died because you dreamed the dream?*

"You're going with us, aren't you?" I tell him while we walk. I offer him a stick of Juicy Fruit and he takes it, not wanting it, but thanking me anyway. (*Do not pat the heads of their children. Do not show the soles of your feet. Do not defoliate their trees. Do not offer them what they must, by courtesy, take, Mary.*)

"Yes, Lieutenant. And I look forward to traveling with you. However, we have many phrases to learn first."

He's telling me nothing. They've asked him not to, or he's doing it on his own, out of kindness. *She's a woman,* he's said to himself. *She will die with the rest of us in the North and it would be an unkindness to tell her this.*

"Are all men from Saigon so gracious?" I ask.

"Only to women who are gracious enough to believe it," he answers.

It's from a book, a movie—courteous Orientals and skulking Shanghai bandits. People of Darkness. People of Light.

"Is that a line?" I ask.

He doesn't understand but the smile remains. (A smile is the least we can give others, *Im Than Yeu.*) Then it clicks and he laughs and says: "Yes. A *line.* It is a *line.* Please, Lieutenant," he says, "give me a line."

So I say: "*You* say, 'Only to women who are gracious enough to think so.' And *I* say, 'How long have you been using that line, Lieutenant?'"

It takes him a while, and he works hard at it. It's what he loves—working hard with words. When he gets it at last, he laughs again. "Of course! *Your* line needs *my* line. That is good, Lieutenant." He says something about women, about their voices, how men see them, how waiting can feel like losing—or I *think* he does. I may be the one who says it, remembering a little house by the river and saying it.

Chapter 17

We eat. We go back to my bunker and I get him down the stairs with many pleas. "Should we not stay in the sun?" he says like a good boy on his first date. "No," I say. "I don't want to go home with a sunburn." It doesn't take him long this time and he laughs, comes down, and we begin with *Pochemoo s sobakoi?* We learn *Poshlee?* and *Tvoi rang?* and *Moi rang nee imeyet znacheniya*. When Cooper appears at the top of the steps with his dog, looking for us—because someone's told him to—Bach says quickly: "Come down, Corporal, please. We have room for many more dogs down here."

It's a joke, so I laugh, but I have no idea what he means. *You find whatever you can and you laugh. It's good for you, Mary. It's good for you, too, Colonel.* When I hear it—when I hear us laughing, not knowing what we're laughing about—I see a little pond and wonder what it means.

Is it Bach's? Is it the pond he takes her to? Did he take her there once upon a time? Or was it someone else—a thousand years ago?

"Do you know what Americans mean by 'a dog'?" I ask him.

He says no, and when I explain it, he feels awful. He apologizes. He apologizes profusely. He's as white as a sheet in his shame and Cooper is grinning and I'm doing my best not to laugh.

"Do you know what 'teasing' is?" I say.

"Yes," he says. "I believe so."

"I have just teased you," I tell him.

148 • Bruce McAllister

"I am very happy to hear that, Lieutenant."

We're working on *Mee roosskiye, vezyom ris* and *Vashee dokoomenty?* when all of a sudden Cooper and Crusoe turn around. Crusoe should be turning first, but he doesn't. They do it together.

I haven't heard a thing. The lieutenant hasn't either, but we look where Cooper and the dog are looking and we see boots starting down the stairs. *Now* we hear them.

When the whole body appears, Bach gets up and stands at attention. Cooper does, too. The dog stays seated beside him. I don't get up.

The thin captain—baggy fatigues and deep-set eyes—stands looking at me. When I still don't get up, he says:

"Could you at least stand while I'm standing, Lieutenant?"

It's the same voice, the one from the darkness that night, hoarse, like someone trying to catch his breath. I take my time. I say, "Yes, sir," and then, real slowly, I get up.

"You're excused, Lieutenant Bach," he says. The ARVN lieutenant hesitates, looks at me and finally leaves, glancing back once from the stairs.

I hear a whimper from the floor, by Cooper's jungle boots, and then feel something on my neck. I move my hand without thinking, and there's nothing there. The whimper comes again and I know dogs like this aren't supposed to make sounds—not *any* kind. In a jungle you just don't make sounds.

He's never met someone like the captain, has he, Mary?

Cooper says something to the dog and then says, "Sorry, sir." But his voice is different, like he's lying, like he's not sorry at all, because he knows damn well what the dog just felt in its skull— knows it as well as I do.

The captain stares at the dog. The dog stirs, starts to make another sound, squirms a little and doesn't. It's doing its best. It really is. Then the captain says:

"I've been told your animal is EOD-trained, Corporal."

"Yes, sir."

"All generations of plastic, RC series, black powder?"

"Yes, sir."

The captain covers a cough with his fist and looks at them both.

"Is this your first animal, Corporal?" He doesn't have to ask, but he does.

He's *listened*. He already *knows*.

"No, sir," Cooper says, and stops. He wants to say more. He starts to: "He's the best animal I've had an opportunity to work with, sir. I mean. . . ."

"Yes, Corporal?"

Cooper doesn't want to say it anymore—not to this man—so he says instead: "He's a good animal."

"I hope so, Corporal. We're depending on you both."

Cooper wants to say he loves the goddamn dog. I know he does. He's a kid, like the rest of us, and this is really what he wants to say. He wants to say there's something special going on between them—he knows that better than anyone does—something even more special than Lassie and Timmy, than Rin Tin Tin and Rusty—real boy-and-his-dog magic somehow. But you just don't say things like that to an officer, a white one. A *dog is an instrument, a valuable one, Corporal,* the officer would say. *If you love it, if you love it the way you love your rifle, boy—not because it's alive and its heart is pumping and it's sitting warm beside you, but because it's a finely tuned instrument—it will keep you alive—like cold steel.* That's what a white officer would say. That's what a man like this, who can make your eyes and neck and skull crawl by looking at you, while he *listens* to you, would say. *Even if in the end, Corporal, we do have to destroy that fine instrument rather than let you take it home.*

Cooper starts to ask a question. He never asks many—I know he doesn't—but his heart's hammering now, the question's driving him crazy, and he's *got* to.

The captain beats him to it: "You'll be briefed on mission details when that's absolutely necessary, Corporal. Ops information disseminates in phases, Corporal, as you should know."

"Yes, sir," Cooper says, and we both think it's over—that this is really all the captain wants.

But he doesn't leave. In that same voice, like someone trying to catch his breath, he starts talking again:

"Corporal, on this mission you will have your Markham Process scout dog trained in multiple functions, with four months of experience under your handling, and you will also have what we have listed in our O&P files as your special 'gift.' You will use both of these resources to keep yourself, your K-nine responsibility and your fellow team members on this mission alive. You will, in turn, use both to help your team achieve its mission objective. Your own role will be made clear to you as tactical phasing dictates. Because you're an Afro-American and the team will be operating under a cover inconsistent with your obvious ethnic inheritance, you will not be able to risk the same high profile as other members of your team. Nevertheless you will have the same responsibilities as far as team support and mission objective are concerned. Is that clear?"

I don't hear the kid say, "Yes, sir," but I guess he has. The captain is turning to me and saying:

"Lieutenant Damico, on this mission you will have the medical experience you have acquired in-country as well as your formal stateside training, and you will have, as well, what we have listed in our O&P files as your *own* special 'gift.' You will use both to help you carry out your individual and team mission responsibilities. While the three SERE-qualified members of the team have been cross-trained as medics, you will be the official team medic. Is *that* clear?"

This is the man, a voice says, *who stopped you from killing Bucannon, who knew you were lifting that needle in the inky darkness.*

It's starting again. The eyes, the neck, the skin. I don't give him an answer. I want him to have to *listen* for it.

You asshole—you kissass with the heart of a butt-reamed Saigonese whore. What shit are you handing us? What number one doo-mommie bullshit are you handing us? You know what kind of mission this is going to be.

He jerks but says nothing. The dog doesn't whimper. *I'm* the one he's touching now.

"Yes, sir," I say finally, thinking instead: *No, sir. No fucking way, sir.*

He's looking at me with those eyelids down, hooded, like he's sleepy. I can barely see the eyes, they're so deep-set. *Were they always like that, Mary? Can eyes become like that?* He brings a fist to his mouth again and coughs. He *heard* me, sure. He *knows* what I'm thinking. *You knew he did a long time ago, Mary.*

Yes, I did.

He says to me suddenly: "What might seem justifiable action under personal stress at a base camp, Lieutenant, could very well mean the end of an entire team out in the field. Do you know what I am saying?"

Of course I do. He means the needle. How I tried.

"Of course," I say. But *I'll try again,* I tell him. *I'll try it with either of you, Captain—just give me another chance.*

It's stronger than it's ever been now. It's in my skull, down my back, the cervical vertebrae, the trapezius and plexus. He's holding me tight, like a lover, probing. I want to scream. *What do we have down in our O&P files for you, Captain? Do we have a man? Do we have a soul? Do we have thorazine, 300 milligrams per dose? Do we have someone who should have died in the Hanoi Hilton, at Hao Lo, in the Black Hole, but who somehow—somehow lived? Do we have someone who wants, very badly, to go back, to end it all at last? Do we have the living dead, Captain? Is that what we have?*

He hears every word. But what can he say?

"We will be leaving the day after tomorrow for the first staging area," he says, and the awful embrace—the fingers, the hands of it—fade. The voice changes because he's through now. "If you would like to have our team interpreter return, I'll tell him. You have at most a week to learn the phrases you'll need."

When he's gone, Cooper looks at me and doesn't have to ask.

"He was referring, Corporal, to my attempt, a few days ago, to kill our CO."

He just looks at me, waiting.

"Really," I say.

The eyes change a little. I know what that means, and it feels good.

"He's recommending, Corporal," I tell him, "that I don't try—when we're out there in the middle of nowhere—to kill him, too. That it might not be good for morale if I do." I pause and grin. "I'm a real maniac."

He grins back.

Why a black kid? I'm wondering. *Why take a chance on his skin? Why not a white kid and his dog?*

Because of their talent, Mary.

Is that all? Are you sure that's all?

Cooper's still grinning. He's shaking his head, like *Amazing—just amazing.*

And then our young professor of languages comes back down the stairs.

It's raining the day we leave, and I know it's going to be raining for a long, long time. We're heading North, where it never stops raining. That's part of the plan, isn't it? It's *got* to be. It's October, middle of the winter monsoons, white ginger fog in all the highland valleys—a good time to sneak around—though we're probably going to drown. I say this to Cooper, who's walking closer to me today, and he laughs. He thinks I'm funny. Killing the CO and drowning in the North. I'm this hilarious white girl and that's okay, that's not a lick, everything's okay.

I try to find Christabel. Cooper comes with me, which is nice. The sergeant is someplace else—that's all they'll say. He knows I'm looking for him—it's the day we're leaving—and he's not around. He doesn't want to see me. He doesn't want me to say, "We're going to drown up there, Sergeant." And really, that's okay. But he also doesn't want me to hug and kiss him for old time's sake—and that hurts.

I stand in front of the same young sergeant in the bunker and I say to him, "Well, Sergeant, when you see the old fart, please give him a hug and kiss for me, will you?"

Cooper grins but I don't.

The young sergeant doesn't know what the hell I'm talking

about. Who *is* this woman, who *is* this black corporal who's standing there grinning beside her with a dog—a dog that looks like it's
grinning, too? Who *are* these people? He knows there are crazy
people here—he's *seen* them. They're SEALs and LURPs and
MAC-SOG types, real death-wish weirdos, and he wants to know
what he did to deserve this, TDY and one month short, what in
God's name do they want him for? Who *are* these people?

"Hey, sure, Lieutenant," he says.

"On the lips, Sergeant. Even if he's drunk. And on the chest,
on his big hairy chest, right between the nipples. Is that clear,
Sergeant?"

We've got a killer dog and two AKs and this sergeant doesn't
know *how* crazy we are, who we'd be willing to frag. So he says:

"Of course, ma'am. By all means."

As we walk away, Cooper shakes his head, saying, "What a
rush."

I look. He's grinning again. It's the first thing like it I've ever
heard from him. I'm flattered.

"I'm flattered," I tell him.

"No big thang," he says, twanging it out. He wants *me* to
laugh. He's flirting. It's cute, so I do.

I take a chance. In my best Mae West voice I say to him: "If
you mean it, honey, sing me a song."

He thinks for a moment, and then sings me a line about "my
sister Mary Lou."

His voice is terrible. He knows it.

"You've got a great voice, Corporal," I tell him, and this
cracks him up, too. He loves it. It's Mickey Rooney and Judy
Garland in wartime. This isn't the kid in the bunker with the
captain staring at him, dog whimpering when it shouldn't be, hating so much to use *words* to an officer's face. This isn't even the
black boy you dream about, Colonel, the *boy*, the one who feels
comfortable around *just folk*, the one who'd rather be in a
meadow or a forest or a downtown parking lot running with his
dog, singin' the blues, happy as the day is long. This is the other
one, Colonel. The one you don't know.

Ain't it wonderful, a voice sings. *Zip-a-dee-doo-dah*, it sings.

Come on, Corporal, let's put on a play.

It's funny and it's sweet. We're having fun like two kids, like Huck—if Huck were a girl—and Nigger Jim on a raft going nowhere, liking it, though it ain't gonna last. *I can't keep you alive, Wallace Cooper. Don't you think I can.*

That's the truth, the voice sings.

Zip-a-dee-ay. . . .

I want to hug him. I really do.

"It doesn't bother you," I say to him. "The name, I mean."

He doesn't know what the hell I'm talking about.

"It doesn't bother you to be Crusoe's 'Man Friday'?" I say.

There's this silence. He's looking at me. He still doesn't understand, and then: "Oh." Then a little more: "You've got it wrong, Lieutenant. *They* choose the tattoo number for the dog's left ear, but the handler gets to choose the name. The handler always gets to choose the name."

"You're a regular Dick Gregory," I tell him, laughing. "Lassie would've been pretty funny, too."

He doesn't laugh. He doesn't make a sound. I think: *Oh, God, what have I done?*

Real quietly he says: "It's a good book, Lieutenant. It really is. They're buddies. They help each other through a lot."

"That's right, Corporal," I say quickly. "They do. They really do."

Letter 10/7/71, Corporal Wallace R. Cooper to Mrs. Jared A. Cooper, Command Files (Personnel), Operation Orangutan, Tiger Cat, Vietnam

Dear Momma,

I have not been able to find the exact kind of bowl you want. I will keep looking but I may not have a chance to for a while. If I cannot find it in Saigon or Da Nang I will try in Bangkok and Tokyo on my way home. Please tell Daddy that the dog I am working with now is the best animal I have ever worked with. We have also been chosen for some special work that I am not allowed to talk about.

I have applied to the commanding officer of the platoon to adopt this dog so that it will not be killed with the other dogs when our platoon leaves. But I have been told that this is not possible. It is upsetting to know what is going to happen when I leave.

I am happy to tell you that this should be the last time they send me into the field before I DEROS. They are not supposed to send you out into the field when you are less than thirty days short and as you know I am now thirty-five days short.

I think of you both all the time and know that you are praying for me every day. I will do my best to find that bowl.

> Your loving son,
> Wallace Ridley

Chapter 18

We don't look Russian. We're dressed in cammies without names on the shirts, without our dog tags on us, without anything else to ID us—a black kid, a thin white guy almost tall enough for basketball, a woman with California written all over her face. I'm saying *Chto vee zdes delayete?* and Cooper is saying *Ya zdes po deloo* back, and you can hear Long Beach in my *aw*'s and the South in all his vowels. Bach's smiling and nodding like some grade school teacher and doesn't look at all Russian. The dog, of course, looks German.

They do it anyway. They put us in a long-range Green Hornet with our gear—precious medpack, special dog food made especially for scout dogs, finest firearms our friends in the Soviet Union can supply—and we leave the goddamn camp. We're heading off to die *somewhere*, but at least it won't be the goddamn camp. As we get on, the MD gives me a pill but doesn't use his fingers, so I get to save it. *They know,* a voice says. *They always know.*

The captain's sitting up front on a fold-down cot, not saying a thing. This isn't some experiment for him, like it is for Bucannon, I tell myself. This is the real thing. He *wants* us to make it. He *wants* us to get there in one piece even if we do a little dying after that.

I move up, trying not to fall, and sit on the bench beside him. The rotors are like thunder.

"I have dreams, Captain," I shout.

"I know," he shouts back, and I jump. I can't believe he's answered.

We're three thousand feet up, wind howling through the doorway, through every crack, the big Sikorsky engines drumming. Even if I scream, can he hear me?

"Lieutenant Balsam and I are going to die up there, Captain," I scream.

The words are the wrong kind for screaming. *Lieutenant* is too long. *Balsam* isn't a word. He won't understand—unless he *wants* to.

"We're going North," I scream.

He's not looking at me. He's not mouthing a single word. *He doesn't need to hear the words, Mary. He can hear you without them.*

"We're going to visit some *very* big dikes, Captain!" I shout.

He still doesn't say a thing, but he's looking at me now and I know he knows. One way or another, he *knows*.

"Lieutenant Balsam and I," I shout again, taking a big deep breath, fighting the wind for it, "are going to die by those dikes, Captain!"

He knows. . . .

I don't want to, but I put my face right up to his, my mouth by his ear, and I scream:

"There are going to be too many NVA soldiers even for Lieutenant Balsam, Captain. He's going to die on the red red mud by those dikes. *I'm* going to die on the mud with him. *You're* probably going to die there, too." I'm taking breaths. I'm giving it to him word by word, breath by breath. I'm shouting and his face is so close I'm shivering. "Maybe Bucannon will get what he wants out of this, Captain, but *you* won't. You won't have a team left."

He grabs me by the shoulder and I go ahead and let him. He puts his mouth by *my* ear—I can't stand it, but I let him—and he shouts: "You dreamed all of this, Lieutenant?"

"Yes!" I shout back.

"Just like you dreamed your friends were going to kill Bucannon?"

I don't understand—and then I do. *He thinks you're lying*, a voice says.

I look at him hard. I think at him: *It's the truth, mother-fucker. All you've got to do is* listen. *Just* listen.

I wait but don't feel a thing. I keep waiting, and nothing happens. *He isn't listening, Mary. He isn't trying to find it. . . .*

I see what that means and a chill goes through me like something chattering in the night: *He already* knows. *He's listened, he knows what you've dreamed. And it just doesn't matter.*

Bucannon found his perfect one-zero, didn't he—his perfect team leader, a man who's had the training, wants to go and doesn't give a flying fuck whether he dies or not, right?

What happened to you up there, Captain? I want to ask him—and I do: *What did they do to you up there?*

You were supposed to die, weren't you? You wanted to—and they wouldn't let you. Red Dikes and the drowning of Hanoi, bodies lying on the red red mud—one way or another, you'll get to die, am I right?

What did you find in the darkness there, Captain? In the rooms where they kept you? In the manacles and dollops of rice and scuttling rats and the spreading fungus on your skin? Did you find what I found on hospital beds, by those beautiful beaches? Did you find one day that you could hear *them—that if you listened hard enough, you could* hear *them even when they didn't use words?*

Was there someone there who helped *you—more than anyone else—who helped you learn to* listen—

By bringing you pain. . . ?

I feel hands all over me, under my breasts, between my legs, on my throat so hard and heavy I can't believe they're not *real*.

He's heard me. He's angry. I'm right—I've guessed it—and it's driving him crazy.

Motherfucker! I shout, jaws closed, and he jerks, jerks hard. The hands are inside me, pulling at me—my stomach folding in on itself, my intestines crawling. *Motherfucking son of a bitch!* I scream. He jerks again, eyes closed, and I stand up, step back, nearly fall. His eyes open slowly, hooded. He starts to get up, but the chopper banks and he sits down hard—we *both* sit down hard—looking at each other. We stare. Neither of us says a thing.

I crawl back to sit by Cooper, who turns and grins at me. He's ready to hear something funny—*anything*—but I don't give him a thing.

That's okay. He'll wait. He's got his dog and a nurse who likes him and he's just glad to get away from that jive-ass camp. Even Laos sounds okay.

Bucannon is picking us carefully, but this isn't the whole team, I know. Steve is somewhere, and there have got to be others. A split-A team is six, Bingham said. A joint ARVN-MACV team is seven or eight, I think. Cooper's a scout and demo sniffer who needs to keep a low profile where we're going. Bach is our language man, interpreter, so his accent had better be northern. The captain's our one-zero, leading. He's *been* there. Steve is the one-one but hasn't. I'm the medic, though I shouldn't be. *What does it mean?* We're heading toward the Red Dikes—that's what it means and you know it. We're going to blow them. Maybe Kelly is a demo specialist, but maybe not. Steve sure isn't. We've got a dog that can sniff out ordnance but no one really to detonate it. There have *got* to be more guys.

When you blow the Red Dikes, what do you need, Colonel? You need brown-water navigation. You're sailing down the Red River, getting in or out—and you may be setting whatever you've got under water. Where's the riverine guy, the Navy SEAL, the scuba-trained Beanie who's demo-qualified? Is Kelly? Steve isn't. You need commo, too, you always need commo. Where's the RTO? We're not going in without commo.

I've learned a lot, I realize. I've learned an awful lot for a nurse.

You've put the wrong people together for it, Colonel. You must *want* us to fail—is that it? Flooding capitals, drowning civilians, ending a war so easily—this is stuff for the Oval Office, mahogany desks, coats and ties. They don't *want* you to pull it off—do they? If they did, if they really did, they'd have let you bomb the shit out of Hanoi and Laos and Cambodia from the very beginning—bomb them back to the stone age. They'd have let you send little teams of oriental Americans, little faces with epicanthic folds who learned their Vietnamese at the Defense Language Institute of Monterey, who look more like *them*—let you send them North to Hanoi to kill Ho and Le Duan, Giap and Pham Van Dong, Truong Chinh and Nguyen Thanh, *all* of them, and end the war *that way*—by nailing their heroes and scaring them half to death. They'd have let you move *all* the people in the South into one big hamlet, surrounded by concertina, bare earth and bodies—and give everyone a polygraph test and kill the ones that failed it. They'd have let you poison the rice in the Red River Delta with a slow-acting propylfluorophosphate dust, or the rice on the docks with botulin toxin—and call it Operation Quaker Oats. They'd have let you win by now, Colonel, if they'd really wanted you to.

You don't really *want* us to make it, do you?

I'm not going to scream this at the captain, over the thunder of the rotors, my breath right in his ear. I don't have anything to write it on. I can't mail it to Bucannon with a kiss. All I can do is *think* it and hope it makes the captain jerk and jerk like a body lying somewhere.

If I killed him right now—if I killed the captain right now—if I shot him through the larynx with my own AK, it would end it. I might have to shoot more than one round and scream as I did it. The round that missed might hit the pilot, his co, the engine, the Jesus nut, and if it did, we'd all go down. Steve would live, yes, but the rest of us would go down.

Isn't that better, Mary—stopping it before it begins?

I look down at the AK. There's no magazine.

I knew that. Bach has them. I *knew* that. The captain told him to take them—I remember him saying it. I remember it being done. I was laughing with Cooper but I remember it being done.

You're right, the captain's thinking. I turn and see it in his eyes. *If you try to kill me*, he's thinking, *the black boy and the ARVN lieutenant, who isn't a talent, who doesn't understand any of this, may die. If you try to grab a sidearm from the ARVN lieutenant, he'll fight you, not understanding. If you ask him for a clip, it'll take too long. I'll know in advance, because you'll think it, and I'll stop you. If you try to throw me from the open door like a VC suspect, I'll be stronger than you and you'll go out instead— we'll both go out—or I'll simply put you back on the floor like a doll with the others. If you try anything before the last stage of this mission begins, Lieutenant, I'll know it beforehand—because you'll think it. I'll know. By trying at all, you'll hurt us all. You'll undermine the confidence of everyone and by doing so, make your dreams—the ones I know you've had—come true. By trying, you'll make our deaths—the ones you have indeed seen in your dreams— come true on the red red mud of the dikes, by the rushing river, where we're going, whether you, Lieutenant, intend on joining us or not.*

They had the Hornet at the farthest corner of the airstrip, where no one was going to see it, where no one was going to say, "Hey, look at those AKs, man, look at all that sanitized gear, that spade, that dog, that woman, that gook—must be some outrageous op they're going on. Wonder who they're going to waste."

It took us three hours at three thousand feet, rain clouds and winds, to get to Vientiane (everything's close by air in Southeast Asia, Mom and Dad) and we did the same thing there. We came in at Wattay, northeast of the main airport. We sat in the hot plane till dark and then this major, very strac, comes and gets us. We were still carrying our AKs. It was like lifting weights and I knew that's what somebody wanted—a little practice carrying those rifles. We walked by the major in the dark, the lights of Lutmee in the distance, Pathet Lao mortars karumping out there somewhere, and I said in my sweetest voice, "Doesn't he *ever* salute?" Cooper cracked a smile. I couldn't go wrong. I was on a roll. Jack Parr said that once: "I'm on a roll," and the audience laughed *again.*

They put us in an old Mercedes and took us downtown. We were looking out the windows of this old car, like Nazis in an old film—the dog was *perfect*—and I knew, just knew, why they didn't have us in civvies, when it should have been easier that way. I turned to the ARVN lieutenant and I said: "Ever visited this fine city before, Lieutenant?"

"No," he said. And then he said, "It is *very* different, I think."

I didn't think so. How different could it be? It looked like Saigon, Nha Trang, all the rest. It looked like the Nam. I asked him what he meant and he said: "The people of Laos—they are, how do you say it?—they are like your happy-go-lucky American slaves."

I stopped breathing. What did he mean? What was Cooper thinking now?

It turned out that he had seen that same movie, the Disney one, Br'er Rabbit with all the happy slaves. He'd seen it in a cultural briefing in Saigon, held by MACV for promising ARVN officers who, if they behaved themselves, would get to work with the Americans. He said it modestly. He said he enjoyed the movie, especially the relationship between the old Negro and the little boy.

Like those slaves, he meant. The ones in the movie, poor but happy—except when the Pathet Lao and Thai and Khmer Rouge and the North Vietnamese come to visit. "We Vietnamese are too serious," he said.

Cooper didn't say: *They were never that way, Lieutenant Bach. They were never happy singin' the blues. Maybe the little white boy and Uncle Remus really had something—maybe things like that really did happen back then because sometimes people are all you have, but the rest is bullshit, Lieutenant—dumbass honky bullshit.*

He could've but he didn't.

It took about twenty minutes to get where we were going. We went through shantytowns on stilts, Buddhist wats that might or might not have been open and miles of dust that the rains just couldn't seem to keep down. In the city, we went through flickering neon lights, past shops that were closed, past the last cyclos heading home for the night, and it felt a little like Saigon, a little like Tijuana, but calmer than both of those. I found out later we'd driven down Pang Kham Road, the main drag that followed the Mekong, that we'd gone past the American Embassy without even knowing it, and the Chinese Embassy, and the British Embassy, too. There was even a Pathet Lao Embassy three or four blocks to the north of us at one point, but no one said it. It was a crazy city, but quiet. Everyone was there, and no one was fighting. It was like a peaceful daydream—everyone civil, everyone polite, embassy after embassy, while a war went on somewhere else.

If I'd known the American Embassy was there, would I have jumped out, tried to run? I don't know, Major. I really don't know.

It was a house we finally stopped at. Just a house. A French colonial thing with shuttered windows and a nice porch and an iron fence in front of it with a little iron gate—just like Da Lat or Vung Tau—and perfectly pruned little trees inside the fence, and this ancient Mercedes pulled up in front with us in it, like it wasn't supposed to draw any attention, and it didn't. No one was out on the streets at that hour. And besides, there were cars just like it parked everywhere.

We waited for a hand signal, the kind I was sure we were going to learn, but instead someone said, "We're here," and we all got out. We were wearing our cammies. We looked like little John Waynes skulking around—and that's what they wanted, I knew. If we slipped away into the night, they'd be able to find us easily. We'd stand out like Bozo with red hair. No one wore *war* clothes in Vientiane.

"Cammies like ours sure would be noticed in a city like this one, wouldn't they, Captain Kelly?" I said.

He didn't look around. He was the one we were walking behind and he didn't look around.

I knew Cooper wasn't going to laugh. All of a sudden he was serious, like he was thinking of other things, like he could see what was coming our way.

I remember Vientiane, Major. I think about it a lot. It was a little like Tijuana, I guess—pretty run-down, I mean—and a little like Saigon, all those French colonial houses, the bougainvilleas, the flame trees. It was lazy and peaceful and beautiful even in the middle of the war, even with the mortars in the distance. I'd like to go back someday. I really would. I know I can't right now, but someday I'd like to go back.

I remember the lights on Pang Kham Road. I remember how Cooper's face looked in all those lights, how all of their faces looked that night, and I'd like to go back again.

Chapter 19

There's a man in the house—no, two—and they're dressed the same, loud short-sleeved shirts like tourists in Hawaii, sweat stains down their backs, in their armpits. One of them isn't as serious as the other and when he says, "Welcome to Howard Johnson's," the captain gives him a look and the guy doesn't say another word. I'm wondering what he felt when he got that look— did he *feel* it? Or did he just see a tall Green Beanie staring at him and later he'll say to his serious friend, "We can't trust these guys, Smith. We need to *use* them, but we don't have to trust them. They're *cowboys*. They're all a bunch of fucking cowboys."

The two guys wearing Arthur Godfrey shirts show us to our rooms and suddenly I'm thinking of the nurses' dorm back at St. Mary's, dorm mother, curfew, the rest. I go ahead and say it. I say: "May we have male visitors in our rooms after ten, sir?" I say this to the one who's shown me mine, hoping for a laugh, but Cooper's walking down the hall, Crusoe beside him, heading to his own room, and there's no one to laugh at it.

"Anytime," he says. He's the funny one, but I don't like the feeling I get.

This guy in an orange shirt with big hibiscuses on it is standing in my room longer than he needs to be and I'm tired, I just want to lie down. He says, "If I can get you anything, Lieutenant, *do* let me know." He stands there like he's waiting for a tip and I'm thinking: *Just because I'm wearing cammies, I'm an easy lay? Is that written down somewhere? Like: 3. Women who wear camou-*

flage utilities, particularly jungle patterns in stripes or spots, have round heels, i.e., go down easy. How many women in cammies have you *had*, sir? I'd like to, but I don't like men. You know, we're all one or the other—whores or dykes—and I just happen to be the other. "What's your name?" I say, and he grins. "Harry," he says. "Well, well," I say. "Harry and Mary."

I step up to him, confidential-like, and I say: "Any chance, Harry, you could get me some pencillin? Us split-tails don't get jungle rot in the same places you men do—know what I mean?"

"Jesus," he says, and goes away.

I take a pill and lie down. I dream about a body, a river and a ball of light—the way things would look from the ground looking up, the way someone would describe it if they wanted to be *believed*, and then voices wake me up. It's been thirty or forty minutes, no more. There's a commotion downstairs. I blink, get up and head down.

Everybody's in the dining room around this table, except the two Hawaiian shirts, who are standing around like refs. The windows have been covered with hardstand, perforated steel plate, and little gauzy curtains over that, and there's a big naked bulb hanging from the ceiling. I see Cooper, Bach, the captain and a very stocky guy I don't know who's wearing a wrinkled tan suit with his back turned to me. *He's* the one making the commotion and I can tell by the way he moves there's something wrong with him. There's something wrong with his left side.

He turns to look at me. His left jacket sleeve is folded back, pinned.

A one-armed man . . .

I know him. I know him from the dream.

I stare. I can't look away. He sees me, but hell, I'm a woman in cammies—what's so unusual about that in a fucking war like this?—so he turns back around and starts shouting again.

I look around and find Steve at last.

He's in cammies, too, sitting in the far corner of the room, and when I look at him he looks back. He smiles with all sorts of things in his eyes—those great eyelashes, those great shoulders—and I've never wanted so much to hug someone, take their hand

and go away with them, but I know I can't do that here. The captain's watching us both—he's not even looking at the man in the wrinkled suit, who's still shouting, who's saying that he's not, goddammit, he's not going to sit down, he's *not* going to calm down. I hear a yelp, a scrabbling. The one-armed man has stepped on the dog. The dog's been under the table by Cooper's legs all this time and the one-armed man has stepped on it. All it does— the yelp—is make the one-armed man madder.

There's no chair by Steve, so I take the one by the captain. As soon as I sit down, there's a knock on the front door. One of the Godfrey shirts goes to answer it. I'm looking at Steve and he's looking back. I'm looking at every line of his face, trying to re- member it—to *feel* it. When you dream about someone, you change him in your mind. The eyes get greener. The smile doesn't move the same way on his face, in your memory. When he's there in front of you, you see how he slouches just a little, how he keeps his hands clasped in front of him, doesn't sit up straight with a frozen smile like some department store mannequin waiting for you to walk down that hallway at the 21st toward him—again and again and again—like he does in memory. He's different now, and it takes you a while to get to know him. Every second it takes, you want to cry. It feels so good. He's *here.* Everything's okay now. You're so happy. You're a little girl again and you just want to cry.

I think of the 21st and the 8th, what it would be like to be back *there. This is better.* I tell myself. *This is much better.*

The other Hawaiian shirt is talking to the one-armed guy, saying: "You might as well sit down, Chief. You're not going any- where."

The one-armed guy is shouting: "I don't know *you.* I don't know any of these people. I'm a civilian now."

"You've been recalled, Chief."

"You can't recall some son of a bitch with one arm, you motherfucker. I've got *one fucking arm.* Do you hear me? This room is full of cammo, we're talking black ops, we're talking de- nied areas. You motherfucking sons of bitches lied to me. I can work for a civilian proprietary with one arm, but I sure as hell can't go back into the jungle for you, you motherfucker. I've got a wife and kids and *one fucking arm*. The admiral said *civilian work*—I've got it in writing, asshole. He said *Page Communications*, asshole!"

Harry doesn't blink an eye.

"Plans get changed, Chief," he says.

"I want to talk to Admiral Straub *now*."

"The admiral was told to get you over here however he could, Chief. He did what he needed to do."

"I don't *believe* this. I demand to talk to Admiral Straub *now*."

"Admiral Straub isn't running this, Chief. In fact, he really doesn't know much about it."

"Well, then, someone's going to have to tell him."

"I don't think so."

There's a figure coming down the hallway from the front door, but I haven't turned to look yet. I'm watching Steve and I'm watching the one-armed guy—wondering if he really is the one from the dream. His voice changes suddenly. He's not screaming anymore. He doesn't know what to believe. If it's true, the old admiral can't help him. Even if it isn't true, even if they're lying, what can he do about it? All he can do is say:

"I want to talk to whoever's running this operation, mister. I want to talk to him *now*."

I turn to look down the hallway at last. It's not one of the Hawaiian shirts, it's not another team member in cammo.

It's Bucannon.

Of course.

He's dressed in a nice white tropical suit, clean as a whistle. It's like a dream, a dream I've *wanted* to have, but haven't been able to yet. I've wanted to dream about *him* the way I've dreamed about others, and in that dream try again, and this time really do it. In the dream I'd like to dream—but haven't been able to yet—he's wearing a nice white tropical suit. He's kneeling in his tent for some reason. I'm looking at him, that's all. I'm telling him something, but he isn't dead *yet*. We're talking. He wants me to help him. I'm thinking of what he must have been like as a boy, and then I do it. As I do, his skull comes apart.

The one-armed guy—who's about Christabel's age—turns and sees Bucannon, too.

"Hello, Willie," Bucannon says.

The one-armed guy doesn't get it at first. He says, "Would you please tell these motherfuckers what a fucking mistake this is, Colonel. I haven't had an episode in fourteen months—I haven't seen *anything* glow at all—you know that—and these assholes have me on some mission where I'd need two arms just to hold the motherfucking radio."

"You're underestimating yourself again, Willie," Bucannon says quietly. He says it gently, as he always does: "You've been away for a year and you haven't been using your talent, that's all. It'll come back, but you *do* need to trust it, Willie. You didn't trust it before, and we know what happened, don't we?"

The one-armed man is staring at him, not blinking.

"I've got *one fucking arm*, Colonel," he says.

"And I hear you've gotten pretty good with it, too, Willie. It's been over a year, hasn't it? You've been practicing with it, I'm sure." Bucannon turns to one of the shirts. "It's been a little over a year, am I right?"

Both shirts nod. The one-armed guy is still staring at Bucannon, understanding it at last—whose operation this is, though he can't believe it.

"You're a head case, Colonel!" he shouts. "You don't send a guy with one arm out—I don't care *what* kind of mission it is!"

"You *do*," Bucannon says to him, "if you have confidence in that man's gift, if you know what it can do for him if he'll only trust it, if he'll only let it . . . You send him out, Willie, if it will help him become what he has the potential to become. . . ."

The one-armed guy is looking around, looking at all of us. "He's crazy. Do you hear him?"

No one will look at him. No one will say a thing.

"Why don't you get to know these people, Willie?" Bucannon is saying. "I think you'll find that you have something in common with them, that, in fact, if you're willing to work with them you'll have all the extra arms you need, and, in fact, that you're more important to them than you'd imagine. I think you'll also find that you have the makings here of a good team." He smiles. "You never know, Willie."

"*Goddammit!*" the one-armed guy shouts, taking a step toward the door. "If you think I'm going to stand here and—"

One of the Hawaiian shirts, the funny one who isn't funny, takes him by his arm, takes it again when he yanks it away, and says something quiet to him—something I don't hear.

The one-armed guy stares at him, and then sits down very slowly.

Bucannon's looking around the room. "Hello, Mary," he says. "Steve," he says, nodding. "Corporal Cooper." To the captain he says: "Hello, Robert." He doesn't say a thing to Bach. He isn't really one of us, I know. He's just our dictionary.

I tell myself that Bucannon's going to stay, that *he's* the one who's going to brief us, but that's wrong. He waits a little while to see how the one-armed guy is doing, and then he leaves without another word.

The shirt named Harry is leaning on the table with his arms, leaning over us. When he starts talking, it's not to the captain, or Bach. It's to the rest of us.

"You're going to be here in Vientiane for four days, ladies and gentlemen. You're here for the multiple purpose of, one, getting to know each other; two, practicing the Russian you will need; and three, establishing your cover . . . by presenting yourselves in town in uniforms which we will issue to you tomorrow evening. There are some rules. You will *not* speak Russian outside these walls unless instructed to. You *will* speak Russian within these walls—and as much as possible. Is this clear?"

Someone nods.

"If your guide feels it's safe for you to speak Russian in a bar or taxi or other location, he will signal to you with the phrase *Eto prosto strashny son.* You may respond with *Noo ee strasheely!* or *Podavees tee eteem gorodom!* or *Chortee chto!* or any other expletive on a list you will be given to memorize. After that one exchange, you may use any other expressions you have learned. If, on the other hand, your guide says, '*Nas zdes nee ochen to privechayut,*' that, ladies and gentlemen, is the signal for an *insecure condition.*

The phrase *Eto prosto strashny son* will be used to signal the end of the condition. Is that clear?"

No one nods, but it doesn't matter.

"You will each be given an instruction sheet recapitulating all of this. That sheet, ladies and gentlemen, is *not* to leave this house."

"Tony and I," he adds, nodding to the other Godfrey shirt, "are both Monterey certificates in Russian. The ARVN interpreter on your team, Lieutenant Bach, has also been certified in Russian by a major university in his own country, so we are told. The three of us will be working on your syntax, vocabulary, pronunciation and metalingual and kinesic mannerisms. These last are important as subliminal clues to any individuals you may encounter who have had extensive contact with native Russian speakers—their accents, their idioms, their gestures, their body language—"

The other shirt says: "Now might be a good time, Harry, to tell them how the North Vietnamese see Russians."

Harry stares at him, like they don't always get along but now's certainly not the time to discuss it, and says:

"*Thank you*, Tony. As you begin to think of yourselves as Russians, ladies and gentlemen—and thinking of yourselves this way may mean the difference between life and death for you—you will want to feel, one, not very friendly, that is, not prone to smiling; two, not generous, that is, not free with money; and three, not particularly hygienic. These are the perceptions which the North Vietnamese, given their more extensive contact with Soviet individuals, hold of their allies. In daily behavior this becomes simply: Don't smile, don't tip, don't try to help the natives and don't take baths. If you do this, ladies and gentlemen, you'll be convincing. . . ."

He wants a laugh. He's waiting for one but the other shirt is stepping all over it, saying: "That sums it up nicely."

The funny shirt says something we don't hear, and then to the captain says:

"Anything to add, Captain?"

Kelly shakes his head.

"Ladies and gentlemen," Harry begins again, "you are confined to quarters. Vientiane does *not* have soldiers in camouflage, nurses in camouflage, eighty-five-pound German shepherds running around on its streets. The Pathet Lao have an embassy four blocks away from this house and travel these streets with impunity because they haven't brought the war to the city—*yet*. You may *not* step outside for a smoke. You may *not* walk up and down the block no matter how bad your insomnia is, no matter how empty the street looks. We are, officially speaking, a Christian Science Reading Room—closed now for renovations. You will find newspapers, magazines, books, playing cards in the library at the front of the house. Keep the drapes closed. Keep the hardstand in place. You may play radios. You may use the one television set we have. You may visit each other in your rooms. We want you to be as comfortable as possible during your stay here since you will be living with each other under less than comfortable conditions for the two or three weeks of your mission. Any questions?"

I look at Steve and he looks back. *The two or three weeks of your mission,* we're thinking.

"If not, you're free to go," the funny one says at last and still no one laughs.

It feels like a movie. Like something I've seen before. You know, an adventure story—Tom and Becky, Mickey and Judy, all looking for an adventure. There are going to be laughs, sure, and some good scares, too—because Americans like that—but everything is going to turn out okay. It's an *American* story, an *American* movie. It has an *American* director directing it, I know, so everything's going to turn out okay.

Chapter 20

Steve's room is down the hallway from mine and he's sitting on the bed when I get there. There's a little white vase on the bedstand. There's a ceiling fan turning real slow. There are two little lizards with big heads crawling up the wall by a window. It's a movie. It's one with Bogie in it, I know. Bacall is somewhere, waiting.

I stand in front of him and don't know what he wants. I don't know what *I* want. He stands up with a little smile and gives me a kiss. He puts his arms around me and gives me a kiss, but we don't stay that way long. We're stiff as boards.

"Are you okay?" he asks, and I remember the last time he said that—long ago by a mess tent.

"Yeah," I tell him. "Bucannon's got this little pill."

"It helps?"

"Yes, it does."

He doesn't say any more. We're standing a foot apart, that's all. The hug's over and neither of us knows what to say now. So I say: "I think they're going to stop giving me the pills as soon as the mission starts, Steve. So I saved some."

He nods. His face is familiar again, a face I know.

"Isn't there something we can do?" I say. I want to stand here in this little room, in front of him—no needles, no pills—in this nice French colonial villa with its little library, little deck of playing cards, its ceiling fan turning, and have it no more complicated than that. I want to sit on the bed with him. I want to lie down with him, just touching, but I'm looking at his face now and it's the one I've seen too many times—in the rain, the dark dikes behind him, his body pointing like the hand of a watch, jerking as the rounds go in, in the red red mud.

"The embassy won't help us," I say. "Is that it? Even if we made it there, they wouldn't help, right?"

He nods.

"Can't we get to Thailand and *then* out? Can't we get some clothes somewhere, trade the AKs maybe, and get out through Thailand?"

"Sure," he says. "We could do that." I don't understand the tone.

He sits down on the bed slowly, like he's getting ready for a speech.

"We're going to blow the Red Dikes," he says. "Do you know what that means, Mary?"

"Yes, I know what that means, Steve," I say, getting angry. "It means we're not going to make it. It means we're not coming back."

It's as if he didn't hear me.

"If we can blow the dikes, Mary," he says, "we can *end* this war. I don't like it any more than you do, but if there's a chance—if there's any chance at all of making it, of taking out the Red Dikes and ending it all, it's got to be worth it, Mary. It's what we're *here* for, isn't it? It's what everyone we know who's died here *thought* they were dying for, isn't it? We could be the ones to end it."

It's a voice I've never heard from him. It's the boy who enlisted. The boy who wanted to be one of JFK's Peace Corps warriors, the white Indian who knew God and man's cities and the great forest, too, who would save the savages of the world from those who would make them godless—or at least from themselves. The boy who didn't find these things over here, and now—now wants it to end.

I tell him: "Listen to me, Steve: *We are not going to make it.*"

But he isn't listening. He doesn't *want* to hear it. He's saying: "There's a *chance*, Mary. I know there is. Kelly's crazy, but he's good. He's a telerec, Mary. That's what it's called. He can read minds. The dog scout handler is a telerec, too, but he's bonded to his dog. He sees and hears and smells what the dog does. *I'm* what they call a GESPer, Mary, a good one. I've never gotten a scratch in this war, Mary. The chief, it turns out, is a *waking precog*. He could be *really* good, too, given a chance. Right now the auras he sees on people who are going to die *scare* him. He can't help it. He can't help thinking that God doesn't approve of it—this magic, this talent he has. He's a North Carolina boy who went to Sunday School, Mary—and it's in his bones. If he goes with us, Mary, we'll be able to convince him it's a *gift from God*—nothing evil. I *know* we will. Bucannon does, too. The ARVN interpreter isn't a talent, but he's a northerner by birth, knows Russian, wants us to make it, too, and he'll be an incredible asset. I've thought about it a lot, Mary. There's a chance. We've got to take it."

I can't believe what I'm hearing. *What have they done to you, Steve?* I want to ask him.

"We've got *your* dreams, too, Mary. And you're wrong. Bucannon *wants* this mission to work. Hanoi would go down, the war would be over. How could he not want this? Washington would deny it, but everyone would know that *his* team, *his* experiment, pulled it off. He'd get the credit, but without the blame, Mary. He'd make general, he'd have everyone eating out of his hand—and who wouldn't want that?"

"Listen," I try. "We have my dreams, Steve, and in those dreams—"

But he's still talking. He's saying: "Bucannon will give you the pills if he understands, Mary. I'm sure he will. If we tell him you're not much good to anybody if you're lying on the ground screaming all the time, he'll give you more, I'm sure. *I'll* tell him—and I'll tell him I won't go unless he does it. You're worth more to us as a medic really. Something you dream may keep one of us alive, but you're worth much more as a medic. That's what I'll tell him. The captain agrees. He'll put in a word, too."

He stops talking and I say:

"I've already dreamed the dream, Steve. In it, you die. In it, you're on a riverbank somewhere, by a very big river, and you're dying." I wait a moment and then I say: "I'm there, too."

He still hasn't heard a word. I start to say it again, but he stops me. He says:

"Were you taking the pills when you had those dreams, Mary?"

It sounds like someone else—someone else I know. I know what he's trying to say, what he's trying to do, and I don't know whether to cry or scream. *He's been here ten days—only ten—and he's talking just like them.*

"Listen to me," I say. "The first time I dreamed about you— how you died in the mud by the Red Dikes, NVA uniforms crawling all over them, I didn't even *know* there was a pill. It was the night before I met you, and I didn't even know what the dream meant. I didn't know until I heard about your mission, the single-K, and started dreaming the dream again. I had the dream, and because I did I went and tried to kill Bucannon. Kelly stopped me—he read me like a book—and he stopped me. When Bucannon canceled that mission, I thought I'd won—I thought I'd saved you—and that the dream could stop. But it didn't. I tried to kill Bucannon and because I did the mission changed—but the dreams, Steve, *did not stop.* Do you know what I'm saying?"

He blinks. He doesn't say a thing. I say: "What I'm saying, Steve, is that the dream never *was* about that first mission, Steve. It was about this mission—yours and mine and Bach's and Cooper's and the chief's. I was dreaming about *this* mission all that time."

"I know you tried to kill him," he says.

"What?"

"Bucannon said you tried. The captain and he both told me and they said they understood why and how there really weren't any hard feelings—because they understood the stresses you were under. They *want* this thing to work. I know they do. They want the war to end as much as you or I do. Bucannon's different now, Mary. Believe me. He is. He sees what's at stake and the tapes, his operation, his research—those things just aren't him anymore. He'll walk with generals, Mary—with presidents—if this mission works."

Steve, I want to tell him. *You* can't *believe him. He's never told the truth in his life.*

"I had the dream without any pills, Steve," I say instead, trying one more time, and trying not to hear. "I've had that same dream again and again. If we go on this mission, Steve, it'll come true. If we go on this mission, we will die, and because we do, Hanoi won't drown. If we go on this mission, Steve, the war won't end. . . ."

"The fixity of the future isn't definite," he says quickly, and it's Bucannon. It's Bucannon's voice I hear.

"All we have to do, Steve, is leave. If we leave, *no one's going to die.*"

He looks at me, and his face changes. It loosens, as if giving up, and I feel a chill.

He's been lying, Mary, a voice says, *and* now *he's going to tell the truth.*

"That's all I've ever done," he says to me suddenly, and he sounds so tired. "I leave and others die. The rounds miss me, the mines miss me, so I go home. But the Dogman and Malcolm and Kiowa and all the others have to stay. They *never* get to go home. What is it worth, Mary, if I always leave but the others have to stay?"

"Bucannon will drop the mission," I say quickly, "if we get away, Steve."

"No," he says. "He won't." His voice is flat and dead now, like Christabel's that day. He can't hold it together anymore. All of a sudden, without thinking, I know what he's going to say.

"He'll find *someone else,* Mary. He'll find *five* others if he needs to.

"He'll choose two others from the camp—two other talents— to replace us, and maybe they won't be as good. The mission will go ahead and maybe, just maybe, the people, the two he finds to replace us—*their* talents—won't be as good. And if they aren't, then Cooper and Bach and the chief will have even less of a chance. . . ."

"You can't be sure of that," I tell him.

"Yes," he says. "Yes, I can."

He's right. He *can.* And again, because Bucannon is Bucannon, I know what he's going to say:

That Bucannon or Kelly or both of them *told him.* That they even said it with a smile, compassionately, like: "If anything were to happen to you or Mary, we would have to find replacements for you from the camp. You understand, of course. We're committed

to this mission, Steve. And the replacements we chose might not
be as good as the two of you. And that would hurt the mission's
chances, wouldn't it—that would hurt the team's chances of making it there and back, wouldn't it, Steve?"

When he says it, he says it the way he needs to—with the
words he needs to use. I don't remember them exactly, Major. All
I remember is how it *felt* to hear them—how it *felt* to realize once
again that none of us will ever get away from Bucannon. . . .

They used words like: *In fact, Steve, were someone on the
team, for example, to resist inclusion of another team member, to
take a firm stance on keeping, say, Lieutenant Damico off the
team, because she's a woman, we'd have to replace the team member who was causing trouble, wouldn't we? In fact, we'd have to
replace both Lieutenant Damico and that troublesome team member, and the replacements we found for them might be weaker talents. And the mission's chances—the whole team's chances—would
be hurt as a consequence. You can understand, I'm sure.*

They used words like: *Were someone on the team to take a
resistant stance of any kind, Steve, we would have to keep him—
and anyone who collaborated with him—somewhere safe, incom-
municado, for an extended period of time. Wouldn't you agree,
Captain? Simply for the sake of the mission, I mean. Where and
how long that detention might be we don't know. That's not really
the business we're in. We'd turn the job over to others, I'm sure. It
wouldn't be in the U.S. probably. No, I'm sure it wouldn't. It
might, for example, be in Vietnam, under local jurisdication. Or
perhaps here in Laos, under some subcontractor's care. I don't
know. All I know, Steve, is that it would be for about a year.*

"The fixity of the future isn't definite," Steve is saying again.

I'd rather, he's telling me, *take a chance on your dreams.*

I could have lied, I could have lied in a lot of ways, but I
didn't. I heard Cooper laugh—a memory of it. I saw him kneeling
against his dog. I saw two little white girls, a wife standing behind
them and a one-armed man watching them unwrap things under a
Christmas tree. I saw the ARVN lieutenant with a woman and a
baby, at a park, near a pond, and heard Vietnamese words I
couldn't understand.

Okay, I tell him. *Okay.*

I took off my shirt and Steve took of his and we lay down in the darkness—without a word. We listened to the two little lizards, barking at each other in the darkness, the rush of a car on the wet street below, the ceiling fan turning with a whisper.

I knew Bucannon could see us even now, as he drove through the city. I knew what he was thinking: *She's thinking of me, Captain. She's thinking of me driving through this city, thinking of them. They're lying on his bed now, barely touching, in the wet heat of this night. Because of the corporal, the ARVN lieutenant and the chief, he will stay with this mission. Because he'll stay, she'll stay, too. In a moment, Captain, they will no longer be thinking of me. They will touch each other in the darkness and find other reasons to stay. . . .*

When Steve reached over, I did—I stopped thinking of Bucannon. I'd wanted this for so long, though this wasn't how I'd wanted it to be. We took it slow. We did okay.

Bucannon *knew.*
She'll dream about him now, Captain. She'll try even harder to keep him alive.
She'll dream about them all. She'll try to keep them all alive.

Photostat, Letter, Command Files (Personnel), **Operation Orangutan,** *Tiger Cat, Vietnam*

GENERAL HEADQUARTERS
SOUTHWEST PACIFIC AREA

A.P.O. 500
February 16, 1946

Mrs. Amanda R. Balsam
1145 Narraganset Street
Baltimore, Maryland

Dear Mrs. Balsam:
In the death of your husband, Captain Stephen Robert Balsam, please accept my heartfelt sympathies. Captain

Balsam's service was characterized by his devotion to our beloved country and in his death we have indeed lost a gallant comrade-in-arms.

Very faithfully yours,
Douglas MacArthur

Photostat, Graph, Green Berets and War Resisters, *by David Mark Mantell,* Command Files (Bucannon), **Operation Orangutan,** *Tiger Cat, Vietnam*

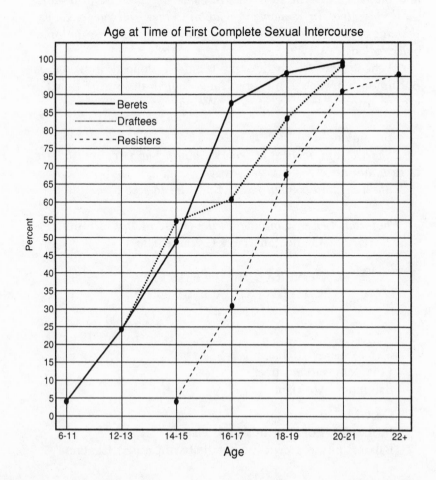

Age at Time of First Complete Sexual Intercourse

Chapter 21

Cooper gives the phrases back. Steve and I give the phrases back. It's early, we're chugging coffee between phrases, and the one-armed guy isn't even there. The Hawaiian shirts—both fresh, no stains yet—don't even look at Bach. *They're* the ones in charge, the ones with certificates from Monterey, and when the lieutenant, sitting straight in his chair, hands neatly in his lap, tries to help by saying, "You should think of it as an Englishman jotting down an *e*—an *ee-jot*—that is what an American captain told me once in Saigon," the shirts look at him like something just died in the room and has already started smelling. At first I don't think he knows, but in a couple of minutes he gets up, says, "Excuse me," leaves with his phrase book, and I know he knows.

"Say it like 'an Englishman jotting down an *e*' if you want," the funny shirt says, "but that's not going to help you much if you're too damned tired to remember the mnemonic, ladies and gentlemen. Just *say* it. *Hear* and *say* it until your mouth has learned it."

We say it with him. *Idyot dozhd! It is raining.* I haven't taken a pill this morning. They gave me one, but I didn't take it. I've got six they don't know about, but I'm wondering whether they do. *Maybe six is what they* want *you to have, Mary. Six on the button.*

I haven't taken a pill and I'm having a hard time concentrating. We're talking Russian. *Is it going to come?* Am I going to see something I don't want to see this morning, just because we're talking Russian, they're making me hear all of this Russian and it's going to be rain and bodies and mud again. Jesus H. Christ. *Take a pill, Mary. Do it for the both of us.*

"Lieutenant Damico," the funny shirt says suddenly, heavy chin out at me. "*Vee zachem prishlee na rekoo?*"

"*Ya preshol po proz' be—*" I say.

"Not good enough, Lieutenant. You should know that phrase by now. Not knowing it could get you and a couple of your friends on this treasure hunt zipped."

I know, Harry. I know.

He spells it out again. "*Vee. Zachem. Prishlee. Na. Rekoo?*"

I know the phrase, but the first time he said it he ran it together, the way *real* Russians do. *What are you doing on this river?*

He tries another one, running it together, too, and I don't understand. I got a C in high school Spanish, I want to tell him. I didn't grow up with the Russian words for *taco* or *olé* or *God-go-with-you* or anything else.

Instead I say: "Are we going to be talking to *Russians*, Harry?"

"That's not the point, Damico," he says, like he's been waiting for this, like he knew some asshole was going to bring it up. "The point is how you sound to the NVA who've heard beaucoup Russian spoken. They're going to know what it *feels* like to hear it, Lieutenant, what it feels like to hear that kind of Russian, to *see* someone speaking it, and if you don't give them the same goddamn set of tickles when *you* speak, you're one dead American. You're not going to be able to move a fucking inch in that region, *any* of you, if your cover's blown, do you understand me?" *Fucking cowboys. Even the woman's a fucking cowboy,* he's thinking.

The serious shirt leans over, says something I don't hear, and Harry says, "Hell, yes."

"Harry here," says the serious shirt, "thinks maybe you didn't take your medication today, Lieutenant, and that maybe that's the problem. *I* happen to think you just don't want to learn this material. Let me stress to you the importance of learning key phrases in such a way that you are able—"

It's beginning. I think I'm imagining it and I tell myself: You're *afraid* it's going to happen, so you're making it up, Mary. You're seeing things because you're *afraid* you will. *Fear* can do that, Mary. Imagination is a terrible thing. There's a river so wide it looks like a lake. There's a heavy gray boat, an old one, with twin Soviet 50s on its prow. We're on board. We've put bags— bags marked *Property of Hanoi* in their language—in the bilge. We've put bags in the little red boats, too—the ones that are roped in a line behind us. There's a smaller gray boat in front of us—a red star on its bow, moving closer, as slow as a dream. No, there are *two*. We're watching them come, and there's nothing we can do.

It's a little movie without sound, and I think: *You're making this up, Mary. There's no sound. There's no death. You're making it up.*

The first gray boat floats closer, machine guns manned, and in the distance I see a bridge, a great dark bridge. I should know it, I tell myself. *Everyone* knows that bridge. We've bombed it and bombed it and it's still there. Behind me the little red sampans slow, as we slow, canvas covering their cargo. All around me on the deck are *Russians*—

No. It's *them*, the others, their faces showing above uniforms with little red stars on them, too. Even the white girl, who's wearing a uniform, too. I'm sitting down somewhere, on duffel bags, because they've told me to, and the angle is strange. The people I know—the faces—are toward the bow of the boat, but I'm sitting here—on duffel bags—

Because I'm not supposed to be seen. Because my skin—

"The medication itself," a voice is saying, "will *not* interfere with her language performance, *Trung Uy*. Isn't that right, Captain?"

The voice says more—in Russian now. I hear Russian all around me. Up at the bow of this old gray patrol boat, far from where I'm sitting on these bags, they're speaking Russian now. Beyond them, the first gray boat and the second have stopped, machine guns ready. There are people streaming from them, little faces, tinier bodies in uniforms the color of sand, but those same red stars. I hear Russian, more of it now, but it's not from them, from the voices I know. It's a voice from the first gray boat, speaking Russian. *"Vee zachem prishlee no rekoo?"* it asks. It's angry.

What are you doing here?

I'm not supposed to get up. I'm supposed to sit here pretending I'm sick, so no one will see this skin. I am not even supposed to look up, because if I do, they'll see it. I understand this. I understand that I shouldn't even be here, and wouldn't be—except that the man who sent us here *always* has reasons. There aren't faces like mine in this country—or in the country whose language they're all speaking—but he has his reasons.

I hear A *nayomniye soldaty pree vas zachem? Zachem vam roozhya?* I can see the faces that are talking, a Vietnamese lieutenant I know, a Vietnamese officer I do not—uniforms the same, but the faces different. I can see them without looking up. The dog is leaning against me, watching them. I can see them because he does.

Something starts—a commotion. Someone's walking back toward me and my heart hammers, my head pounds. I grab my stomach. I groan. I pretend the best I can that I'm sick, very sick. I put my head down between my knees. I close my eyes and *see* them, the way the dog does. The three khaki uniforms coming toward us. Stiff collars, pale red stars, little caps catching the light. The bright hazy sky behind them, making them darker still, small but confident and angry, a little movie in pastel colors. The sounds of their voices are nervous birds. The sounds of the boat, the countless creaks and whistles, the chugging of idling engines, the slap of water on a hull, echoing forever. The smells of *them*—their clothes, the oil of fish-fed skin, the smell of fear, anger. The smells of river—a *thousand* smells. The smells of their boots. The small, clear sounds of their clothes rubbing, coming closer.

"*Vee zachem prishlee na rekoo?*"

"Please repeat that sentence, Lieutenant," a voice is saying.

I try. Nothing comes from my throat. I'm not supposed to talk, to show them my face. I'm supposed to be sick, unable to lift my head. Amoebic dysentery—maybe something worse. I've soiled my pants to prove it—I did that days ago, because someone said to. I don't know the sounds these mouths are making, yet I know the smells of *fear*, just the way the dog does.

Someone's shouting at me. I don't look up. I don't even look around for the white girl. I don't say a thing. I am not on duffel bags anymore—I'm on the deck—and the rounds hit me like fire. I'm scrabbling to get up, my paws are slipping, I'm wetting myself—and I'm trying my best not to make a sound as the rounds hit us, hit again and again. But I can't help it—*I'm sorry*—I make a sound. *I whine.*

I do it again.

I say, "*Vee zachem prishlee na rekoo?*"

I say it as best as I can, the way *he* said it, the face in front of me, suspicious and angry. I hear the khaki uniform, the little face, *say* it, so I say it, too. I say it well. I say it perfectly, an echo.

And then I answer him: "*Mee na spetszadanii. Proklyataya pogoda.*"

It's the right answer, and I say it well, too, but the rounds hit me anyway. They see my face, so the rounds come. The darkness begins not in my eyes, but in *his*, in his bloody matted fur, in his *whining*, which he can't help, and then it bleeds into mine. The rounds hit us both. I give the answer again—and it's right—but it doesn't matter. I feel fingers on my neck, something touches my eyes, my skull. The rounds hit us both again, and I whine. I'm sorry, but I whine.

A man in a flowered shirt is staring at me. He's not making a sound. His eyes are different.

Steve—that's the young man's name—is staring at me, too. The black kid—I know him—is staring, and shaking, like he's felt it, too. The captain is watching.

Did you go with me, Kelly? I ask him. *Did Cooper go, too?*

It's as if I've just screamed, but somehow didn't hear it, though everyone else in the room did. That's what the faces say.

"That was *very* good, Lieutenant," the flowered shirt says. "You've been playing games with us, Damico. You're much better than you've led us to believe."

I'm shaking. I can smell the river, I can smell it all. I can feel the rounds going in and I jerk.

The flowered shirt keeps staring at me. It's bothering him, what I've just done. The accent, the compression. He's not going to move on until he understands. "Did you work with Lieutenant Bach on this, Damico?" he says.

"Yes," I say, trying to hold myself up. If I fall, if I'm on the floor jerking—if they see me jerking—they'll know why. They'll give me another pill. "Yes," I say, too loudly.

The ARVN lieutenant isn't there. He'd wonder why I was lying.

"You have a real ear for languages, Lieutenant. Your vowel reductions are even better than Lieutenant Bach's. That's really what I don't understand. Are any of your relatives Slavic?"

Steve is looking at me with eyes like everyone else's. He doesn't understand either.

"No," I say.

"Go ahead, crew," the flowered shirt says, "give me both question and answer again. That's the question you'll hear once you're past Moc Song." He says it to everyone, but he's looking at me.

Steve and Cooper say it. They say it like high school Spanish, sitting in little rows.

"*Vee zachem prishlee na rekoo?*" I say with them. Then I answer: "*Mee na spetszadanii. Proklyataya pogoda.*"

The others say it again, trying to make it better.

"It was better the first time, Damico," the flowered shirt says, looking away, no longer curious.

I look at the captain, and he looks back. *You went with me, didn't you, Kelly. You're not shaking, but you went with me, didn't you. You were there, too.*

He nods. Or I think he does. I can't be sure, and it doesn't matter.

He doesn't care.

When we quit for lunch, Steve follows me back to my room. I tell him I'm okay. "You're sure?" he asks. I nod. "I just want to lie down for a while," I say. He says: "You sure the medication's okay?"

"Yes, I'm sure."

He waits, like he wants to ask me something, like he couldn't believe the voice that came out of me down there—like a man's an Oriental's, a southerner's, *anything* but mine.

I'm not going to tell him.

I lie down, thinking I should take a pill.

But I don't. I lie there for a while and I go ahead and cry. I cry about the dog, because he's dead now. I'm holding him, his piss and blood on my hands. He isn't moving. I've got round in me, too, I'm not going to make it either, but it's the dog I'm crying about, Steve.

I can't see a thing anymore.

I can't see a thing without him.

Chapter 22

Lt. Comdr. Lawrence Ballet, 290183811, Fighter Squadron 143,
Tape 6 Transcript

They held me at Ap Lao first, and then after a month they moved me to Son Tay. All they gave you was three or four ounces of rice and some fish heads, which were usually starting to go. That wasn't enough protein to survive on. You lost weight and if you got sick, you didn't have a chance. But losing your will to live—that was the worst. We lost Daniels and Simons. They just gave up. You could hear it in their voices. You could see it on their faces. One day they decided they weren't going to live anymore. They couldn't stand it. I wasn't the ranking officer—McLoughlin was—but I was closest to them physically, by physical proximity, so I did what I could. Daniels died in my arms. They let me feed him when he couldn't do it himself and he died in my arms. He was dead even before he started.

I kept a journal on little pieces of butcher paper, on toilet paper, anything. You wouldn't believe how valuable little things like that become. I traded rice for any kind of paper. I wouldn't trade my fish heads though. The guards got a real laugh out of that. Hey, an American who likes fish heads. It wasn't that. I knew I wasn't going to make it if I didn't have protein. They teach you that in training. They teach you to monitor *everything*. I'd write how much urine output I'd had for the day, what medication they gave us, when they gave us any, food and water and how bad the fungus was—how far it had spread on my body. And of course how bad the beriberi was. I was swelled up like a beach ball. My penis was awfully swollen and my testicles looked like two big purple grapefruits. It was awfully hard not to laugh. You couldn't walk but you still had to laugh. We tried to escape twice and we were beaten both times.

When the dysentery got really bad—and also right after the beatings—I got into a very dangerous thing. I didn't have a name for it then, but it was real. It was like breathing or urinating and it didn't matter whether I had a name for it or not really. It was what they call "astral projection," I guess. It was very dangerous. I'd cut my mind away from my body just like that. I'd go any place I wanted to—with physical sensations. I'd be at the top of the cell where they kept me, I'd be looking down, or I'd be floating right behind one of the guards—the one we called Peter Lorre. He'd be on the other side of the cell door but there I'd be standing right behind him, floating right above him without him knowing it. I got information that way. I know that's hard to believe, but it's true. I found out when they were going to move the guys in the Stardust Motel to the Hilton and found out that the guys in the monkey holes were getting medication when we weren't. I didn't find these things out through tap codes. Nobody else knew these things. I'd be floating around and I'd hear the guards talking in Vietnamese and somehow I'd understand it. I didn't know the language but somehow, because I was floating around, I would understand it. When we acted on the information it would turn out to be true. Talk to the others. By traveling I was able to help us. I'm sure that's why it happened. I started doing it when things got really bad—right after we lost Daniels and Simons, when the dysentery was the worst. Something happens to you, to your mind, your *soul*, when you're in a situation like that. You're not the same spit-and-polish guy you were before, the kind who doesn't believe in things like that.

It was dangerous because when I cut away from my body I'd look down and there would be this disgusting body, this terrible mess, and I'd think, "There isn't any way in the world I'm going back into that. I don't have to, do I?" But I knew that if I didn't I wasn't going to live, and I did want to live.

Gunnery Sgt. Scott Sands. 369568032, Sniper Team Two, 26th Marines, Tape 1

I'm on the hospital ship *Repose* with two buddies from Team Two—two WIAs from the same action—and I've coded. They're rolling me into ER on a cart and it feels like somebody's pulling a blanket right up over my feet and my legs and my face. It's not a real blanket—I don't mean that. It's more like a black fog. Suddenly I'm shooting across the room. Not my body, but another part of me. Time isn't moving. I can't feel any pain, even though I can see the doctors working on me across the room. I'm feeling incredible feelings, peaceful feelings and tranquil feelings and I can see this birthmark on the back of one of the doctors' necks. Then I don't see it anymore. I'm standing in a doorway somewhere looking out on this beautiful valley. There are three hills of rich black sand. There's a dark figure, a man, walking across the sand. I don't remember that he said anything to me. He just went over the hills. I don't know what was on the other side of those hills but I know it was something incredible, something incredibly beautiful. When I woke I asked the doctor about his birthmark and he seemed surprised. Ever since, things have been different for me. I believe in Jesus Christ now. I see things and know things I shouldn't. Like, I know when somebody needs help, even though I've never met them before—the kinds of things you've probably heard from Captain Martinez. These things are never for *me*. They're for others and I know this is what He wants, this is why I'm alive. I know that now. I used to be arrogant and egotistical and pretty macho. I'm not anymore. I'm serving *Him* now.

Capt. Oliver Moorehead, 590212756, 5th Special Forces, Tape 3

I was lying there by the bunker, and this tank, this Soviet PT-76, had its gun aimed right at me. It's the only time they've used armor in this war and I'm lying right in front of the bunker, just lying there waiting for this turret gun to blow me away. Nothing happens. *Nothing at all.* There's no sound. Nothing moves. I can't even hear the wind. I look up and there's this figure in white standing about fifteen yards away, almost on top of the bunker. I can't see the face because the sun is behind him, the face is dark— the way it gets when it's lit up from behind. The figure's looking at me and everything's completely still. It's not going to happen, I realize. I'm not going to die. I'm going to lie here until this Russian track with its hundred mike-mike cannon turns around and goes away and I'm not going to die. And I know why. *This is so you'll know,* the figure is telling me, *that I exist, that I am real, that I am here for you forever.* In return, the figure tells me, you will tell others what you have seen today: that I am here for them forever.

The other two experiences I had like this were in Cambodia, when the same figure baptized me in the Song Ma in the middle of a firefight, when I could have drowned but didn't, and then again in Saigon, when I saw Him pointing at a booby-trapped bike and I was able to get myself and four other soldiers away without any harm. I don't always know what He wants from me exactly, but He does want me to live, so I do.

Sgt. Bobby Ray Peters, 570793420, 3d Marines, Tape 2

You don't know what it's like dreaming things like that. I'll be in jail and thinking about what happened last year in the Nam and the dreams will come back like a bad mix. When I was there, man, I'd dream about a face—maybe I knew the asshole, maybe I didn't—and then I'd go out on a patrol with him and he'd get greased. It didn't matter how much bac-bac we saw, how much the guy lay chilly, he'd get greased anyway and I'd have to watch it. Or I'd find him after action somewhere, on a mop-up. I wouldn't remember the dream, his face, until I looked down and saw the asshole. Sometimes I wouldn't recognize the face at first, it'd be so fucked up. I'd get this cold feeling down my back and I'd stare at him and the dream would come back, just like that. Then

I'd walk. I didn't want to look at him anymore. It was like: *Go ahead, look at it until you remember it, but then you better walk.* This went on for five fucking months, man. I didn't know most of these guys, or if I did, I didn't give a flying fuck about them. Maybe in a DX, maybe in a react, any heavy contact, sure—everybody's important to your ass in a firefight, but after that, *shit.* You keep them alive—they keep you alive—but back in the bunkers, it's "Fuck you" and "Fuck you, too." Everybody's an ass-hole in the back.

I got to know this one nigger, though. I don't make a habit of spending time with niggers, but I hung around with this guy okay. His name was Roberts and he was a crazy son of a bitch. He loved ham-and-motherfuckers, so we'd trade ham-and-motherfuckers for peaches. I'd get his goddamn peaches. Can you believe it? We did in-country R&R together. Hell, I don't know *why.* We did it *twice*—can you believe that?—once in Da Nang and once in Saigon. He was all right for a nigger, I guess. I wasn't going to write home to my daddy about him, but he was all right.

This one night I dreamed about his face, this nigger's face, so when I woke up I knew he was going to buy the farm that day or the next day—it didn't matter when, he was going to buy the farm in the Nam. I woke up crazy. I *knew* this guy. I'd just dreamed about him, so I knew he was going to die. I tried—I really tried—to get him not to go out. I grabbed him and I shook him like he was a kid. I was screaming and waving my blooper in his face and he didn't know whether he was supposed to laugh at me or blow me away. *Don't go,* I'm screaming at him. *Don't go, Luther Roberts.* He's laughing so hard tears are coming down his cheeks and he's saying things like "You some fine nigger lover, Peters." He was saying: "Hey, you love me that much maybe we have us a wedding, Peters. Maybe you be my little-brown-fuckin'-machine when we get home?" He didn't know what I was doing. He didn't know why I was acting this way. Maybe I'm jiving him, maybe I'm fucked up on something. Maybe I'm a Section Eight. He says: "I'm goin' out, Peters. We *both* goin' out." I say: "*You are* not *going out, you black son of a bitch!*" So now he gets mad. These soul brothers are standing around, laughing, slapping and dapping, and laughing some more. So he says to me: "This is one splib warrior who is *goin' out*, honky motherfucker!" "No!" I say. "Fuck you!" he says. "No!" I say again, and then I just do it—I shoot him in the foot. I've got this personal weapon, this .45 automatic, and I give him one round in the top of his foot. Now he's lying on the ground screaming and I say: "You got a million-dollar wound now, you ugly nigger. You is goin' *home*." So he doesn't go out on patrol that day. So he doesn't buy the farm that day either. He gets sent home.

Right off they think he's done it to himself, so I've got to go down and tell them who really did it. Next they say he must've *asked* me to, like a favor, so he'd get to go home, and I think to myself: *Fuck it, Peters. Go ahead and tell them.* So I do. I tell them about my dreams and why I shot this ugly nigger in the foot.

They don't believe it, they don't believe it at all, but they see how mad Roberts is, how much he wants to kill me, so now they don't think he asked me to do it. Now they say it must be *racial*. I wanted to shoot me a nigger and the rest is bullshit. They bring down five guys from the platoon and these guys all say, "Yeah, sure, he has dreams. Yeah, he and Roberts are tight." This lifer, this major, stands in front of me the next day and he says, "Listen up, pussy nigger lover. You got your nigger friend on a bird home but *you're* not goin' anywhere. You're not gettin' a Section Eight out of me." [Laughs] He still thinks I did it to go home, so I'd look crazy, so I'd get to go home.

That nigger sure hates my guts, Captain. I've got three letters from him that are just full of piss. He says, "Why you never mention them dreams to me, motherfucker? 'Cuz, you never *had* them, that's why!" He still doesn't believe it. He thinks I'm crazy. He's limping around St. Louie because some crazy son of a bitch shot him in the foot. He's limping around all over St. Louie now because some crazy *white man* shot him in the foot. Hell, I don't know whether he'd have bought the farm or not, if I'd let him go out that day. Maybe he would have, maybe not. I just didn't want that dream *ever* coming true, Captain. And I think he'd have done the same. [Laughs] I haven't dreamed about that nigger once since that day, Captain, but I'll bet you a long one he's been dreaming about *me*.

Sgt. Terrence Mael, 479030278, 3d Marines, Tape 2

In March of last year I was squad leader. We were operating in the Khe Sanh Valley. I carried my squad out one evening to set up a night ambush position. As we were setting up in our position, which was on the side of a hill, we saw this NVA soldier come out of a treeline about four hundred meters from us. He was crossing this rice paddy, heading around another treeline. He was too far off to get a good shot, so I started to take a fire team and go after him, though I didn't want to give our position away. I watched him round the treeline and I saw some smoke coming from the base of the mountain on the other side of the line. I figured there was a village there and that was probably where he was headed. I told my squad that we would check that area out the next morning at daybreak after we broke off our ambush position. While I was asleep that night I had a dream. Everybody stays awake until about eleven o'clock on an ambush and then everyone takes a turn on watch. I go to sleep and I have this dream.

In it I wake up about daybreak and get my squad ready to go out to check the area where the NVA soldier was headed. As we walk around the treeline where we last saw the guy, we find this village in a bunch of trees, right there at the base of the mountain where I thought it would be. It's a really bleak-looking village. There's a fog lying around the trees and the hootches. We've got to walk about two hundred yards across a rice paddy to get to it, though. As we get close I go up front to walk point.

When we get to the treeline at the entrance of the village there's a stream about twenty meters wide with this rope bridge across it. I stop my squad there so we can look around. It's real quiet. We don't see anybody or hear anything. There's this feeling about it that I just can't describe. I tell my men to cover me and I go across first. As I get about halfway, I see a door in one of the hootches right in front of me fly open and there are three NVA soldiers there with one of those machine guns—right in front of me. Then everything goes into slow motion, like a movie. They fire and three bullets hit me in the chest. I see them coming real slow but I can't move. I'm looking down at my chest when the bullets go in and I don't feel a thing. I fall into the stream—I slide into it about halfway. I'm lying there watching the blood pouring out of these holes in me and mixing with the water. I keep thinking that my life is pouring out of me and washing down that stream. I'm not scared. I feel good. It's a feeling like being high. I feel like I'm trying to float away, but something is holding me down and won't let me go. I get real scared because I can't go, I can't float away. I just can't describe it. At that moment I woke up and I was shaking. I was covered with sweat.

At daybreak I get my squad up. I'm still shaking. I want to forget about that NVA soldier and I want to carry my squad back to camp. I keep telling myself that it's only a dream. I'm nervous about it. I've been wounded twice already, so I'm nervous, but we go ahead. I take them toward the mountain. As we round the treeline, I stop. There's this little village just like I saw it in the dream. Right at the base of the mountain, covered with trees and that funny-looking fog over it. I can't describe to you what I felt, sir. I tell my squad that we're going back. We're not going into that village. They want to know why. I won't tell them. They don't understand what's wrong with me. I've got this nickname, "Pilgrim," from that John Wayne movie—I'm always risking my neck on something, volunteering to lead killer teams at night, that kind of thing. They've never seen me acting this way. They can tell I'm shook up from something, but they don't know what.

I start to turn around and then I stop again. I've got to go closer. I don't know why. Something's telling me to go on, that it was just a dream. Something else is telling me that if I do, I'm going to die. I go ahead, I go closer. I've got to see what I'm supposed to see. I take the point across the rice paddy. We get to the treeline at the village. I freeze again. There's the stream, the rope bridge and that quietness, like death, everywhere. I just stand

196 • Bruce McAllister

there. I can't even talk. I'm not scared. I feel like I'm watching a movie, just waiting to see what'll happen next. I don't know what else to do. Something's pulling at me to go across the bridge. Something else keeps saying, *It's your decision—if you go, you'll die.* I've never experienced anything like it in my whole life. I still dream about it. I still see myself in that stream with my blood pouring out of my body and mixing with the water. I'm shaking now—just talking about it. So I turned the squad around and left. I'll always wonder, of course. I'll always wonder what would've happened if I'd gone across that bridge.

Chapter 23

They give us our uniforms and we stand in the dining room helping each other and laughing. "You numbah one tonight, Comrade Joe," Bach's saying to me, pidgin English like a bargirl's, but the shirts don't like it. This is serious business. Who is this dink lieutenant to have a laugh at our expense? "So far I'm only number three, lieutenant—I need help," I say to Bach, but it's Steve who comes over and helps me with the goddamn collar boards.

We're looking pretty strac in these things. Little red stars and shoulder pads, ties and *real* heavy wool. But we don't have all the details right yet.

"Should I do some push-ups to get it sweaty?" I ask one of the shirts. "Or just spill some vodka on it? We have any vodka, Tony? Maybe I can just wet my pants. I hear the Russians wet their pants a lot."

Tony thinks I'm making fun of him, and I am. He wants to say, "Hey, you're a real asshole, too, lady," but he can't. I'm a woman. It doesn't matter to Bucannon—he's sending me North with everyone else—but this guy doesn't want to talk dirty to me in mixed company. It's funnier than hell. "I'm a real asshole, aren't I?" I tell him, and Steve looks from me to the guy and back again, and keeps working on the left board. The damn thing won't stay on. It's hanging like a little store sign off its anchor.

The captain is in the alcove fiddling with his jacket, and the one-armed guy, who's going to be our team sergeant (how can a

chief petty officer, master rank, a Navy SEAL, who's got one arm
and doesn't particularly want to go on this mission, be our *team
sergeant?* Is this for me, too, Colonel—is this someone else you
think I'll like, and dream about . . . . if I haven't already) is still
up in his room. He won't let anyone help him and we can all hear
him shouting, *"Motherfucker! Motherfucking costume!"*

"Go get him," I say to Steve.

Steve looks at me.

"Would you stop worrying about me?" I say. "He's the one
who needs help, Steve."

He leaves and when he comes back he's got our master-chief
team sergeant with him, still swearing, one arm of the jacket inside
out, the star not pinned, the collar boards hanging down like silly
little propellers. Steve's trying not to laugh and I know that if I
look at it too long I'm going to break up right in his face and that'll
be the end of it, he'll go running down the little street outside, into
the bars screaming in English, half dressed, half Russian, and
every embassy in Vientiane will be talking about him. No one,
absolutely no one, will want to claim him as their own.

I go over to him. He's got one of those faces—those open
faces that show every little feeling, and that pink skin Irish people
always seem to have. He's got rosy cheeks, like Santa Claus, this
really thick barrel chest and a good head of wavy hair. You can see
a person's soul through their eyes, they say, and this guy's got blue
eyes like broken glass—like light coming through a pale blue ka-
leidoscope—and he's got crow's-feet around the corners of those
eyes, but they're not a grinning leprechaun's crow's-feet, they're
worry tracks. He looks old, he's got a wife and kids and only one
arm, and he shouldn't be here at all, he knows. He doesn't want to
think about what happened to him that day on the lower Mekong,
right below My Tho—the little balls of light he should have listened to, and didn't, the misery he could have danced past if he
had. He doesn't want to think about it at all, but he's got to.
They've made him a team leader again, like a hundred times before in the Delta, like Bucannon's damn rivers in Cambodia.
They've given him one more fucking team.

It's amazing what you can see in someone's eyes.

"You look like shit, Master Chief," I tell him, taking his right collar board off and grinning at him.

He'd love to get mad, to take it out on *someone*, but I'm not the one. I'm a woman. He reminds me of Christabel, I realize. I don't want him to die either.

I don't want *any* of them to die.

You knew I wouldn't when you chose them, didn't you, Colonel?

A black boy and his dog. A courteous Vietnamese teacher. A one-armed man who's very scared—

Ones I'd be sure to dream about, am I right, Colonel?

"Who in the hell are *you?*" the chief says.

"I'm Miss America, Master Chief." I'm using the address he deserves, even if no else will bother. "I'm with Bob Hope's tour. I'm here to make you happy. You can't touch but you can look all you want."

He tries not to, but he can't. The cracked lips smile.

"Why in the hell is there a *woman* on this team?" he asks, turning, saying it to everyone.

Steve's watching and listening. Cooper is trying to get his own uniform—which is a little too big for him—on, and Bach is helping.

"Because I tried to kill the colonel, Master Chief."

He looks at me for a moment, then says:

"Good for you, Lieutenant. More of us should try it."

"It won't work," I say, nodding toward the alcove. He looks where I'm nodding and sees the captain. I'm trying to get his stump through the sleeve but the steel tip of his prosthesis keeps catching on the lining. It's the color of a pig, one of the three little pigs—this crazy pink prosthesis—and it gets caught on everything. I'm pulling, he's pulling and we're not doing very well at all.

"I'm not surprised," he says.

We get it through at last and I say, "Give me the phrase for *We're agricultural advisers.*"

He tries, but gets the order of the words all fucked up.

"Have you been studying your phrase book, Master Chief?" I say.

"No, he hasn't," the serious shirt says from the doorway.

"Fuck off, Tony," I tell him, and Tony stares, turns and goes away.

"Hell, no, Lieutenant. I just got here yesterday. I can't even get *dressed* by myself. How in the hell am I supposed to learn Russian?"

But he's grinning. I'm grinning, too.

The boards are okay. The sleeves are where they ought to be. The wool's driving him crazy—the jacket's tight across the chest—but he's looking good now. The tip of the prosthesis barely peeks past the sleeve.

"It'll reach the pocket, won't it?" I ask.

He shows me that it does.

I fiddle with his star and shoulder pads and finally do his tie, and he doesn't know what to say. We're alone in a corner now. I feel like his wife.

"I lost it fourteen months eight days ago, Lieutenant," he says to me. "You don't really get used to it for three or four years, they tell me. I can believe it."

I look him in the eye and real quietly I say: "These people are not going to give you three or four years, Master Chief. They're not going to give *any* of us three or four years." I wait a second. Then I say: "If you try to do everything by yourself on this mission, because your goddamn manliness says you've got to, Master Chief Sessions, you are going to screw up the mission and maybe—just maybe—get us all killed. But like the good colonel said, if you'll let us be your arms and hands, we'll do okay."

Anyone else he'd hit or shout at, or at least walk away from, but I'm a woman. I've even helped him get dressed. I've even touched him while we did it, and we know what that means.

He nods. His eyes are getting wet, I can see that, and I know that if I keep touching him I'm not only going to see tears—I'm even going to see how he dies. Just the way Bucannon would want me to.

"Doesn't he look strac, Cooper?" I say loudly, stepping back, looking over at the corporal.

"Boo-coo strac, Lieutenant."

"Numbah one Mastah Chief," Bach says, and it drives the shirts crazy.

"Let's get going," Harry says. "You, Chief, will keep quiet tonight. The rest of you will speak only when your escort gives the signal, and then only those phrases you feel most confident with. Is that clear?"

We nod, grinning.

"You don't say a *goddamn thing*, Chief. Is that clear?" Harry says.

"Chief Sessions understands," I say.

Someone has arrived in the hallway and I think *Bucannon. . . .* I'll have a chance now—I'll have a chance to say, "Where did you get these assholes with the Hawaiian shirts, Colonel? Don't you have enough of them back at camp?" But it isn't Bucannon. This guy—medium height, dark hair—walks in and he's wearing a Russian uniform, too.

When he's twenty feet away and stops to talk to Tony, I see eyes I've never seen before—on *anyone. Jesus,* I tell myself. *They're giving us a pro.*

"This man will be your escort," Tony says, happy that one of the agency's own has arrived to protect him from these camouflaged jerk-offs they've given him to control. He doesn't mention the guy's name, of course, or his real rank, if he has one, or the high school he graduated from, or anything else—and I look at Steve. Steve staring, too. We all are. *Even Green Beanies don't have eyes like those,* I tell myself.

I know the guy standing there looking at us from the hallway is fluent in Russian, that he goes wherever he needs to go and that maybe his face isn't the same every time. It's his voice they use— and so far that hasn't been a problem. Someday maybe, when they've got cheap little machines you can hold in your hand to ID voices with, they'll have to play with his vocal cords, too—change them each time—but for now it's just the face they change. It's a dead, plastic face. The eyes are the things that move.

"Wait for his signals," Harry says. "If you're not completely sure what the status is, don't open your mouths. Don't greet anyone who looks even *remotely* Russian. Don't respond to anyone who *addresses* you in Russian. If addressed in Vietnamese or Lao or English, don't say a thing. Shrug, look to your escort, and let him handle it, please. If the status is clear—if it's *green*—he'll signal you with the designated phrase and you can then use the designated responses in Russian. If you forget and use English even *once*, and someone hears you, you'll have fucked it up royally. You're a group of Russian agricultural advisers, *rice harvest* advisers, and you're about to be sent North to the winter monsoons for the sake of rice and foreign relations—whether *you*, as Russians in a foreign land, happen to like it or not. As it happens, you *don't* like it. Try to be as convincing as you can, ladies and gentlemen. For everyone's sake."

As we follow the face out the door, Steve steps in beside me.

"Good job, Mary," he says. "No one else could have done it."

I don't say a thing.

"If we don't pull together," he says, "we're not going to make it. That's the important thing. You just got a one-armed Navy SEAL to join an Army team, Mary. That's a miracle."

"Right," I say, wishing he were the Steve I knew, and knowing why he isn't.

We're in the same damn Mercedes, all of us except Cooper and his dog, and it feels even more like the Keystone Kops, packed in the back of this old black boat going down dark streets with no one on them, heading toward the bright lights, the whores and hucksters and costumes of an oriental night. We don't go far. We stop on another dark street and pile out the back and bingo, we're climbing into a taxi. "*Mnye eto nravitsa svobody,*" Bach says happily, and the face gives him an icicle look.

"What's Russian for 007?" I ask the captain as we get in, and he gives me the same kind of look.

They're taking the fun out of it, I tell myself, but I stop trying. I'm thinking we should have vodka bottles in our hands, doing those low-kick dances on the street right by our taxis, big furry hats staying on our heads by magic or bobby pins, shouting "Hey!" with each kick and then lying around moaning with terrible charley horses and hangovers the next day. But I remember we're not supposed to smile—we're not supposed to look like we're having fun, or leave big tips, or give candy to kids. *Communism must be a bummer*, I'm thinking.

We drive along silently—not saying a thing—like a bunch of kids in real trouble. The lights get brighter, and finally I can't stand it anymore. I say to Steve, who's beside me, knee touching mine: *"Where the hell are we?"*

"Tu Do Street," he says instantly, and I'm glad to hear a joke. But it doesn't look like Tu Do Street. I see dark alleys the neon lights can't reach, and then, only thirty feet away, like the blazing sun, the nightclubs, the casinos, the whorehouses—Gay Paree. I think of the Mafia, French style, of slant-eyed girls with French accents, of that same Shanghai movie you always watch late at night.

Our escort is in the first taxi with Bach and the shirts, and if our captain is going to play statue right beside me, who's going to be our tour guide? We pass Monica's, the Lido, the Purple Porpoise, the Green Latrine, and no one says a thing.

"Hey, that's the Rendezvous des Amis," the chief says suddenly, pronouncing it with all the *z*'s and *s*'s.

"You've been here before?" I say.

"No."

I wait.

"It's world-famous, Lieutenant," he explains. "It's run by Madame Lulu, an old French mistress with outrageous orange hairdos this high. She's *incredible*. She teaches all her girls herself. The place specializes in blow jobs." He grins. "Sorry, ma'am,"

I'm still waiting.

"You don't believe me? Ask the captain. *He* knows."

The captain doesn't say a thing. He's looking out the window and I wonder what he's thinking. I can feel his leg against mine, too, like Steve's, but it isn't warm—it's thin and baggy and it's not like a boyfriend's would be, in a car, after the prom. It's like nothing at all.

"Hey, Kelly," I say. "Is that place really as famous as the chief says it is?"

After a minute—eyes out the window, staring—he says it. He says, "Yes," and he coughs for the first time tonight.

The chief says: "He ought to know. Ask him, Lieutenant, about the war in '59 and '60. UDTs and SEALs weren't invited. It was a little Green Beanie war and about two hundred thousand Hmong were invited, Vang Pao was the guest of honor. But the Pathet Lao crashed it. *Ask* him."

The captain doesn't answer.

This is something I don't know about, but I don't care. I'm thinking of other things. Riverine aspect, brown-water part of the mission. We needed a SEAL, didn't we, and now we've got one. *I don't suppose you're an RTO, too, Chief, are you?*

"Ask the captain where he got the little tattoo on his neck, too," the chief says.

The captain's head moves around now—like something finally coming to life. An electric shock somewhere, and the head moving. One of his arms starts to move, too, and I stop breathing, watching it. They look at each other—the captain and the chief. They don't say a thing. The car moves on through the lights and night. *No one* says a thing.

"Hey, Master Chief," I say in my best Donut Dolly voice. "Where did you lose your arm—if you don't mind my asking?"

He looks at me like he can't believe I've said it. But it's me asking—I *must* have a reason—so he says: "Near My Tho, down in the Delta, Lieutenant."

"Is that by a river?"

He snorts. "Yes, of course it's by a river. A little thing called the Mekong."

A one-armed man. Angels singing. Halos everywhere.

"Were there *halos* everywhere?" I ask him.

He looks at me strangely, like, *Yes, there were—but how could you possibly know?*

I don't ask him anything else. I turn to the captain and I say, "Captain, if you don't mind my asking, where did you get that little tattoo on your neck?"

He looks at me, too, and he knows what I'm doing—he doesn't even have to *listen* to know. He's got to play. He knows that, too. He knows he's the one who should be doing this, pulling the team together, not me—a woman, a nurse—refereeing like this. And he knows I know. *If you won't, Captain, I will,* I'm telling him, and he knows.

"In Ap Lao."

"It's a prisoner tattoo, right, Captain?" I say—to make it fair.

The chief starts to jump in, but then thinks again. *Don't rock it, Willie.*

Steve looks at the captain and then back to me. *What are you doing, Mary?* He doesn't see it.

I give him a little smile. *Trust me.*

"Yes. It is," the captain says. "It's a prisoner tattoo, Lieutenant."

We all lean back, because it's finished now, and watch the pretty lights go by.

Capt. Robert Kelly, 206794368, 5th Special Forces, Tape 1 Transcript

I didn't know what they were at first. I assumed they were my own thoughts. I assumed they were things I was inventing for myself—in the dark. . . .

Chapter 24

It was called the White Rose and I think it's still there. That kind of place survives every war, doesn't it? There was a big western wagon wheel hanging outside that didn't make any sense, and there were just two kinds of people coming out—drunk and stoned. Americans that just had to be spook pilots—loud shirts, loud jokes, their arms around each other like happy members of a chain gang—were the drunks. Orientals, Europeans and a few American hippies, quiet and mellow, were the stoned. "Grass is legal," the chief was saying. "Opium isn't but there are seventy-seven little dens in this city anyway, I hear. One of them's even called the Detox Center."

It wasn't like Casey's or the Moonlight, I told myself—the places we used to go with the fake IDs Dickie's brother made. It wasn't even like the Long Bar or Jane's in T.J., where I'd go with Jerry and Hank when they let me, before I had boyfriends, and later with Little Bobby Carter, or someone else. It wasn't ten thousand miles that made it different. It wasn't just the slanted eyes and the cyclos and the singsong voices or the old movies you remembered with Bob Hope. It was something else, and I wanted to ask the chief—he'd know, I told myself. But he was gone. I was the last one to get out of the taxi.

We get out as quiet as caretakers and I'm looking up and down the street for Russian uniforms. *This is ridiculous*, I tell myself. We're dressed like Russians, but we don't want to meet any. Who *do* we want to meet, Harry?

I'm watching our escort and I see this little Laotian guy, a pimp, a guy selling whatever pimps sell here, standing near the door. The pimp nods. He doesn't run up to our escort and say, "You want little girls, little boys, my sister, my cousin, my uncle? You want horse, you want dexies? You want nylons?" He just nods and I know it's prearranged. If he nods, the rules say, there aren't any Cossacks inside who can test our Russian. If he doesn't nod, we just keep on trucking.

The bar is amazing. There are little booths and wicker chairs but you can't really see them in the smoke—in the human fog. There are stairs leading up to little cubicles in the darkness. There are doll-like girls everywhere, giggling, taking their clothes off for no good reason at all. They're girls, sure—but they don't look like any you've ever known. They don't look like the ones in your gym class, when you *all* took off your clothes.

But the one girl—a woman, really—that you just can't take your eyes off is right here at the bar, standing on the counter naked and smoking a cigarette with her vagina.

I don't have to tell myself, *Don't speak English, Mary. Don't say "Jesus Christ!"* I squirm a little, as if I'm naked, too, as if people are watching *me*. The guys are looking at me. They're wondering how I'm doing. They're a little worried, which is nice, but it still makes me want to scream, to shout: *Don't look at me! Just don't look at me!*

The Laotians are grinning. They wonder what that Russki woman is thinking. Is she a colonel? Does she like to whip men? Does she like *women?* They know there aren't any women smoking cigarettes with their vaginas in Moscow or Leningrad, so they're thinking this is quite a surprise for her.

I can't grin back. I'm not supposed to. I'm supposed to be shocked. I'm supposed to be serious, severe, basically unhappy. Communism is a bummer, the biggest bring-down you can imagine, *compadres*, I tell them. Vientiane is like being let out of prison. Really. You like it—you like it a lot—but that doesn't mean you're supposed to smile. Russian soldiers *just don't smile*. Russian agricultural advisers are soldiers—*everyone* is—so they don't smile either. Besides, you've got to go home eventually, to some little town on the steppes, and the thought of that helps, too—to keep you from smiling.

How does she do it? Is it a gift like yours, Mary? Is it a skill you can learn—places where you can learn it? Do you discover it one day, lying in bed with him, your pimp—because you're giggling and he's drunk, and he says, "Go ahead and try it—why not?"—and you do, you pull it off. And you discover that people will pay to watch you do it—which is what life is all about, isn't it?

The smoke thins now and then. There's a Thai with heavy eyebrows playing a piano in the corner and a tall blonde woman— a *real* blonde—taking her clothes off beside him. I look around and see a model U.N. I see Laotians, Thais, Vietnamese, Cambodians—maybe even Chinese. I see four Indians from India and two guys who look like ROKs, chunky Koreans in uniform, sitting by themselves. I see uniforms all over the place and women making eyes with every kind of eye. I hear what has to be passes in a hundred languages, *how much* and *ten dollah* and *boom-boom no*. Peter Lorre's out there somewhere, I know, and Bogie's in the shadows copping a look from the woman on the counter with the cigarette in her vagina, which doesn't make Bacall very happy at all.

I know *I* couldn't do it. It makes me dizzy even to wonder.

What is she feeling? Is she feeling like a person? Is she feeling like a toy? Is she feeling the way she's always felt?

The escort looks at us and says: *"Eto prosto strashny son."*

We nod. Some of us say *"Tfoo!"* and *"Bozhe moi!"* Some of us say, *"Tak vsegda byvayet, kogda vryosh detyam."* Some of us just nod and pass on the phrases.

We're at two tables now and our escort is babbling something in French to a woman with the eyes of a cat. The bartender comes over—he's Corsican mafioso, I hear later—says something in French, grins, a cigarette hanging from his lips. The movie keeps rolling.

The bartender grins again and nods. *"Oui, oui, mon colonel,"* he says, and I think of the Yard in the baseball cap. Betel-nut teeth. You learn a language real fast in a war. I'm telling myself his name has *got* to be Jacques or François, but I'm wrong. That's the name of the little Frog in old commando movies, isn't it? Or the name of the Resistance fighter, the one who loves the girl who loves the hero, who is of course American. François will have to die, it seems, because he's French and expendable, and because the hero is indeed American. But that's okay because, as we know, he's dying for a noble cause—his own country—and also so that the hero can marry the French girl, unless he needs to move on. . . .

His name, it turns out, is Emmanuel. Pretty name. A woman's name.

Two women in dresses slit to their rib cages bring our drinks. They're the worst things I've ever tasted in my life. Anyone willing to drink them *must* be unhappy, Colonel. *Communism is a bummer*, I tell myself.

I'm wishing they'd taught us how to drink things like this—without getting sick—when I hear our escort say a word like "agriculture" and another one like "socialist." They're French words, sure, but they sound about the same. He's laying it on heavy, but what's the point if he doesn't? These five Russian agricultural inspectors were in Vientiane last week, didn't you hear? They came—five of the fuckers—through Vientiane, were heading to Yen Bay Province—you know, just north of Dien Bien Phu. They've got some new stiff-stalk high-protein triple-harvest rice for the rain-fed highlands—that fancy 1R16 stuff—to try out. North Vietnam sure gets the attention, doesn't it? Anyway, these four guys and this one woman *never* smile, just never, so you don't know whether they're having fun or not—you don't even know if they're *trying*. I gave them water with buffalo pee in it, and more water and more buffalo pee, and they drank it just like Luong Lan beggars. Communism—it sure must be a bummer.

Suddenly there's a guy in a khaki uniform just like Bach's—little red star and everything—sitting down right next to Steve and the chief. He starts talking.

It's Vietnamese, and hell, I don't know Vietnamese. They don't teach you that at Moscow Polytechnic. Bach is saying something back and the guy's looking at all of us now, every face, smiling, but the kind of smile you could chip off with a chisel.

I'm looking at our escort—trying not to—but maybe I'm *supposed* to. My heart's doing Shirley Temple tap numbers and now the guy in khaki asks me a question. He asks it again. I shrug. I don't say a thing. I try to look severe. I look at our escort and hope to hell he's the ranking officer here or I've just fucked it up.

Bach says something else to the guy and there's this silence.

Then the guy starts laughing. He orders drinks for us all, a second round of buffalo pee, and I think: How long am I going to have to smell these drinks? Is it going to be oozing out of my pores every step I take for the next two weeks? Am I going to be stinking with it in the jungle, for the enemy—for *their* scout dogs—to smell? Is Crusoe going to go crazy walking beside me, having to smell it?

The guy keeps saying things to us in Viet and he knows we won't answer him. They're jokes, after all. They're about us, yes. We're forcing smiles, just like Russians would. We look uncomfortable with his jokes—we look at each other, we look at our escort real puzzled—but no, we don't answer him, we force these smiles. Something—call it a sixth sense—tells us this guy is an asshole.

It's an inside joke of some kind, and a good one this time. Bach and the guy are laughing right in our faces. Bach's laughing right along—two Vietnamese laughing at five Russians—and we're not supposed to know what's going on. Boy, those Russians are dumb, *Thieu Ta*. Even our escort is looking like he doesn't know what's happening . . . though of course he does.

Suddenly our escort says, "*Noo ee doorak.*" It's one of the phrases we learned late, and it wasn't on the list. It means: *What a jerk.* He says it to Steve. Steve looks back, trying not to grin, and says: "*Nyet, ikh dva dooraka.*" *Make that two.* The escort laughs. *I* laugh. We all laugh. Thanks, Harry—thanks, Tony—for making us learn our lines. We're laughing at the two Vietnamese now. It's *our* turn now. Payback. The guy in khaki looks at us, his smile

dying—a real fuck-you-you-hairy-smelly-*moi*-you smile, the kind
that says, *We may do business with you people because occasionally
we prefer you to our great hungry neighbor to the north, but that
doesn't mean we have to* love *you—you hairy, smelly* moi.

We don't need your love, comrade brother, we tell him. We
just need you to believe we're Russian, so we can have a good
laugh about that, too. "*Nas berezhot angel-khraneetel. Takeeye
drooz'ya khoozhe lyubykh vragov,*" Steve says. *Ha, hah, hah, you
little twerps.*

Bach rides in our car this time. "NVA," he says.

"No kidding," Steve says. The chief has gone with the escort
just to get away from Kelly, and I'm wondering whether I should
have taken my pill. I keep telling myself these are just the finer
points of cover, aren't they? This isn't blue-floating-out-of-bodies
and death-flashing and halos-that-kill. *But how can I be sure?* How
can I know when it'll all start up again—when I'll start dreaming,
won't be able to stop and they'll have to carry me out on a
stretcher? Would our talents even save us here? Would they even
work here? Are we scared enough—are our hearts pounding hard
enough—to have them work here? My goodness, ladies and gentlemen, your cover was just blown and those little gifts of yours—
those little curses we've listed in your O&P files as your talents—
didn't save you, did they? You really should have thought a little
more about *death*, about *wounds* and *dying*. Now we're going to
have to try some other scam on these folks.

"I no kid you, Lieutenant," Bach says in pidgin, smiling.
"We have *great* luck."

"You mean *bad*," Steve says.

"No. Great."

I feel something pass over the back of my neck, like always. I
feel it, like always, in my eyes—and I jerk. It's familiar, but it
never feels *good*. I turn. The captain's saying, "We want every
North Viet to know we're here. That's the point."

We wait, but that's all he says. It's a real blue streak. He's
gone again, looking back out at the lights, into the darkness, which
must feel good to him.

"He thought I was Yen Bay boy who hates the Russians, too,"
Bach says. "His province, Phu Tho, is beside mine. He wants our
rice program for 'shallow and intermediate rain-fed regions' to go
to his province next. I tell him I do my very best, but I can make
no promise. Shall we do it, comrade brothers and sisters? Shall we
take our rice program to his province next?"

Steve laughs. I should be laughing, too.

"I tell him, Lieutenant Damico," Bach says, turning to me
with a smile, "that you are the wife of a major, that you are in
disfavor now for certain indiscretions with an officer who is not
your husband, and that you have been 'put out,' so to speak. That
you hate Vietnam, that you even hate rice. Although there are
some *stiff stalks* you like better than others."

I'm smiling now. I can't help it. Bach's on a roll. *Say it,
Bach.* "I'm on a roll." *Say it so we can laugh again.*

We stop at the Purple Porpoise and no one pays any attention
to us there. There's a short oriental girl trying to sing Marianne
Faithfull and the Bee Gees, and I don't drink my drink. I don't
want to have to be carried out of one of these places by *men.*
Russians get fall-down drunk, sure, but they always get up in the
end. Word reaches Moscow that you were shit-faced, conduct un-
becoming a revolutionary sister, and your family ends up in a
place an awful lot like Siberia. Isn't that how it works? You don't
want that to happen, Maria—even if your mother-in-law *is* a
bitch.

We stop at the Green Latrine, turn around and walk away
very fast. No one says a thing, and I get this feeling there are
automatic weapons about to spray us from behind, a squad of
death-dealing commandos about to burst out of the bar at any
moment and nail our wooly asses to these loud stucco walls. We
can't *run*, I know. It would *look* bad, I know.

"Russians," Bach says at last, in English, when no one's
around.

"Good timing," the chief says.

We walk down the street and find another place. I don't even
remember its name. *Last one for the night,* our escort says—in

214 • Bruce McAllister

"It's *okay*, Lieutenant," Cooper says.

"No, *it's not!*" I scream.

Yes, it is, a voice says suddenly, silently, and it isn't mine.

I feel it where I always feel it, and I look up. The captain's looking right at me. The darkness is there in the eyes. There's no light at all.

"There aren't," he says with his throat, *"any Africans in the Russian Army, Lieutenant."*

For a second I don't understand. *Of course there aren't!* I want to shout.

And then I understand.

I wanted to hurt him, I know that now. I wanted to take his team away from him even more than I already had, but I was drunk. I was drunk and I forgot what I already knew.

My face is so hot I'm afraid to touch it.

No one will look at me. Not even Crusoe.

"Well, there *should* be!" I say, and without anyone's help— without Steve's arm—I make it up the stairs to a pill and bed.

Russian, though there's no one to hear it—and we go in. Wh
the hell. I drink my drink. I drink two. These things are bette
They're pink and they don't make your fingers stink.

"Why didn't Cooper get to come?" I say, back at the house
again. Cooper's sitting at the table with his phrase book as we pile
into the room, shit-faced with real honest-to-goodness American
grins on our faces. "Why does Cooper have to stay here with his
phrase book while we get shit-faced drunk?" No one says a thing.
No one wants to deal with a shit-faced nurse.

"Come on, Mary," Steve says. He's squinting in the light,
too. We're all squinting in the goddamn light. We feel like shit.
You don't mix buffalo pee and sugar water, Tony. You drink them
pure and straight. The chief's staring at me, like he's worried—
like the captain's going to do something if the nurse doesn't shut
the fuck up.

"You can't keep Negroes at the back of the bus!" I shout.
"You can't even keep them in their own bathrooms! The Army
was integrated in 1950, Captain Kelly, and you can't do this to
someone like Corporal Wallace Cooper, upon whose skills our
lives may very well soon depend. We're *not* going out again without him, right, men?"

I spin around, looking for the captain, and nearly fall down.

He's walking away from me. Steve's holding my arm.
"Mary . . ."

"We're not going to make it if we're not a team, am I right,
Captain? You know that. We're not going to make it unless we can
all go to a bar where women smoke cigarettes with their vaginas
and drink Tiger Piss beer together and get shit-faced. Am I right,
guys? I don't think our captain is doing his job—"

The captain turns around at last. Cooper's sitting at the table,
holding his phrase book. Steve has my arm and I'm getting madder. Black Americans are dying in the streets at home. They're
setting fire to the cities and none of these assholes give a damn.
"None of you assholes really give a shit about people, do you!
None of you assholes really *care*."

I'm swaying. I'm holding Steve's arm and he's holding mine.

Chapter 25

The assholes wait to brief us until the night before we leave. They do it in the back room of the safe house, where they've got a sand-table mock-up of Dien Bien Phu—that valley where the French lost their war—and another one of a little village called Dong Noi on the Red River, where the Red starts to curve around Hanoi and the Red Dikes are high and thick. It's been determined, they tell us, that 45,000 pounds of TNT or 15,000 pounds of C-2 generation plastic explosive set ten feet under the river at Dong Noi, linked with detonating cord, will release 20 million gallons of water at one-sixteenth the speed of a .45 bullet. They like to think of it this way, they tell us.

The North Vietnamese have lived in fear of something like this happening for a hundred years. The French built the concrete molds and the Vietnamese filled those molds with sand and pebbles, tamping it all down with their little feet. They carried those buckets full of sand and pebbles and filled those holes and tamped it all down and it took them twenty-five years, with the French standing by watching them. The North Vietnamese have *always* been afraid of something happening to their dikes—at Than Loan, Lu Than, Dong Mo, Dong Noi, any of a hundred little fishing villages upriver from Hanoi—and because they have, they've had a million people waiting with buckets, mud forks, little feet, bent backs, for a hundred years, just waiting. Every monsoon season they wait. And now, with the Americans and their technology, they're even more afraid. What will the Americans do? What will the Americans do to their *dikes?*

Twenty million gallons of dirty river water traveling at once-sixteenth the speed of a .45 bullet isn't, Harry says, something you stop with buckets and mud forks. It'll be slow—not some tidal wave like the movie *Krakatoa, East of Java*. It'll take its sweet time and it *won't* stop. The people will go to the hills outside their capital, they'll go there and sit, day after day, just like their nightmares told them they would, and they'll watch their city—their symbol, their heart—drown.

You can't just fly 45,000 pounds of TNT in and drop it on Dong Noi, the shirts say, even if that *is* the best spot on the river. You can't just taxi in at Hanoi Central and say sweetly, "Hey, could you fellows please run this over to Dong Noi for us and while you're at it, maybe detonate it, too? We'd *really* appreciate that." You can't do it with 750-pounders from your B-52s out of Ubon, because if you do, everyone will know and you won't be able to *deny* it, ladies and gentlemen. You won't be able to say, "Gee, what rotten luck, Mr. Secretary-General—how that dike broke last year, in those terrible monsoons, and how Hanoi drowned. When you think about it, climate sure can have an effect on history, can't it? Hey, if there's anything we can do for those poor people, do let us know." *Denial*, ladies and gentlemen, is important. If you can't deny it, you've got problems. You're going to have China and Russia—for some reason these two pop to mind—say, "Hey, Imperialist Friends, because you did that in Vietnam, we get to do it in *Mexico*." You're going to have little countries—like, say, Great Britain, or every little country in Africa—tell you, "Hey, that's dirty pool (and *besides*, Russia and China are going to do the same thing to *us* now!)."

You can't even fly 15,000 pounds of plastique through NVA radar and ack-ack and drop it for your frogmen to play with, because once the drop is made—once *somebody* sees it—you can't *deny* it. The rules, ladies and gentlemen, say you cannot be *seen* doing it. Am I making myself clear? There will, as a consequence, be no air support, no reaction teams, no resupply, no contact after insertion, no diplomats trying to get your living, squirming flesh out of Hanoi prisons *if you're captured*—or your bloated bodies from the Red River if they happen to nail you. *If* you're captured, ladies and gentlemen, you are *not* Americans. You've got sanitized gear. You're not wearing Robert Hall suits and green poodle skirts. We don't know *who* the hell you are, but we know one thing: *You're not Americans.*

Sure, your dental work is North American (Harry adds) but the rules say that doesn't count. According to the rules, we still get to *deny* you if you happen to buy the lower forty with American dental work in your mouths.

I tell him I don't understand.

I make him say it again.

On March 13, 1962 (Harry says), a *métis* from the province of Lai Chau, North Vietnam, contacted an American CAS agent in the North to say there was enough plastique still cached at Dien Bien Phu to blow up the entire valley—if anyone happened to be interested in doing something like that. CAT and Air America records were checked, the last living French generals present at the French defeat were interviewed and the rumor was confirmed.

Somehow, Harry says, there are still 20,000 pounds of old C-2 explosive buried in little bags in Dien Bien Phu Valley.

I tell them I *still* don't understand. They smile. They say, "It's easy."

On April 15, 1954, General Navarre, expecting to be overrun and not wanting to depart this life without taking as many Viet Minh with him as he could, asked the American CAT air force to drop on "Claudine"—the southermost French strongpoint in the valley—20,000 pounds of second-generation plastique. With this material (he announced to all who were willing to listen) he would booby-trap the tunnel systems of strongpoints "Dominique," "Eliane" and "Juno," so that those brave French, Moroccan, Nigerian and Black Tai fighting even now to protect the central command bunkers would not die alone on the final day of battle. "With this," he told the Americans on his little radio, "we will certainly take the *arms*—and maybe even a piece of the *heart*—of Giap's army with us."

The plastique never reached "Claudine." Through a communications error of a kind seen more often than not in the last days of the siege, it fell on the northeast corner of "Isabelle," the isolated strongpoint eight kilometers to the south, the southernmost French presence in the doomed valley, a piece of land only two hours away from being abandoned completely. Only the Nam Youm River—dividing the strongpoint neatly in two with its swamp—had kept the Viet Minh at bay this long. When the sixty-six crates of claylike explosive in their little white parachutes touched down hard on the abandoned airstrip at "Isabelle," the commanding officer—a young colonel by the name of Henri Lanierre—at first considered abandoning them, but did not. Instead, he had the survivors of his four companies of Tai mercenaries carry the crates with them into the foothills just east of the Nam Youm, where the low mountains divided Laos from Vietnam. Here, in the limestone caverns of the foothills, they would, he told his captains, take a stand. Here, when and if the Viet Minh found them, they would use the plastique just as General Navarre would have used it—to bring the caverns and tunnels of the ancient limestone formations down on their enemies as well as themselves.

But (they tell us) it never happened this way.

Lanierre's men placed the thousand bags of C-2 explosive in the largest and closest cave, and waited. Lanierre himself was killed in the final hours of the siege, the bags were never corded and the Black Tai who managed to escape did so across the 4,000-foot mountains into Laos, into the upper Mekong, into the jungles of Cac Tinh, where they waited until—years later—they could return home again. They told a tale—*for Tai ears only*—of the bags of "fire clay" left by the French, gifted by the Americans, hidden in the darkness of the valley's ancient Kha caves—where the Viet Minh would never, as long as the Tai kept their honor, find them. A tale of a long-boned Westerner who had died before he could use what was in the wooden boxes dropped by mistake by the French flying machines near the Nam Youm in those last hours of the battle. And a tale of the flight across the Tua Meo Mountains, and of the hardships in Laos during those years.

The Tai still lived in Dien Bien Phu Valley—as they always

had and always would—whispering these tales at night. In 1961, seven long years after the events themselves, what could be wrong with letting the bastard son of a Legionnaire—his mother a Black Tai from their village, a man who certainly hated the Viet Minh as much as they did—hear the tales, too? Was he not—in his hatred, by his mother's soul—a brother?

You will (Harry tells us), pick up the 20,000 pounds of C-2 in the valley. You will move it by land to the Black River, using roads 41B and 41A on the Soviet maps we have so painstakingly prepared for you. Then you will move it by water to the Red River, and to the spot, fifty kilometers northwest of Hanoi, where the two rivers meet. Then you will move it down the Red River to Dong Noi, where, as expeditiously as possible, you will detonate it under ten feet of water. You will be given a team of mercenary Black or White Tai from one of the highland valleys and these will be your guards, your guides. They will obtain for you the Tai or Mongolian ponies you will need to transport the bags to the Black. Because of the success of Operation Popeye—one of our other projects these days—the monsoons will be especially long and wet this year. The season will run very, very late. Precipitation will be twice normal. This is good news and bad. While land travel will be a royal pain in the ass, my friends, there won't be much traffic on the roads. Road 41A isn't motorable and the natives are staying dry inside. Dien Bien Phu itself, as happens in a heavy monsoon season, is cut off from resupply and communications right now—except, of course, for occasional radio reception.

On the one hand, ladies and gentlemen, the rivers will be swollen and violent. On the other hand, you will have no trouble finding water deep enough for your cargo even as far north as Dao Phu, where the dry-weather mountain road from Route 41 meets the Black, where, in turn, you'll begin your brown-water journey. The swollen rivers will move you quickly.

If stopped by North Vietnamese regulars, Popular Militia or political cadre, you do have a reason for being out in this inclement weather. You're agricultural advisers on loan from Mother Russia. You're specialists, in fact, in "shallow and intermediate rain-fed multiple-harvest" rice crops, that is, in the kind of harvest that may very well make the tribal highlands self-sufficient, even surplus-productive—something Hanoi and the Red River Delta have wet dreams about each night. You may have purchased your 1R16 rice seed from Manila and stolen your rice science from Beijing's Institute of Agricultural Science, but *you're* the ones Hanoi has invited in—given the diplomatic balance Le Duan wants to maintain—and this is not the first time boys and girls from Moscow who know nothing about rice have gone to little revolutionary rice bowls to tell them their business.

You're out in the rain schlepping your goddamn monsoon rice seed from highland province to highland province. You're covered with mud, you're surrounded by little Mongols, the downpour is so heavy you can barely breathe—all of this *not* because you like it, ladies and gentlemen, but because you've been *told* to do it. Because any Marxist-Leninist does what he's asked to do, right? For the sake of the International Revolution . . . if not his own career. If anyone along the way fucks with you, ladies and gentlemen, it's both Mother Moscow *and* Aunt Hanoi they're fucking with. Be sure to let them know.

There's a military academy and a boot camp at Dien Bien Phu. They'll have boots in training but the boots will prefer staying dry, too. Read a little Ho, maybe a little Giap, maybe some Ca Dao poetry. Who knows? They'll be indoors. Their teachers and drill instructors will let them because this is the sticks, ladies and gentlemen. There may be a war going on *somewhere*, but not here. There may be some resupply to the Pathet Lao on Routes 40 and 8, but Dien Bien Phu is too far north for the Ho Chi Minh Trail and B-52s aren't dropping their loads anywhere near this place. There may be American air traffic, but it's electronic surveillance or PJs looking for downed fliers or little recce teams being dropped into Laos. Hanoi has been trying to put ethnic Vietnamese in these northwest valleys since 1962, trying to move them out of the delta, out of a very congested Hanoi, and it's just not working. The Tai *hate* the Vietnamese, the Vietnamese hate the Tai, and there's nothing Marxist-Leninism can do about it. The Tai barely tolerate a Vietnamese political cadre in each village, and they certainly don't like the classes the Vietnamese make them take. They don't like seeing Vietnamese villages being built along the Nam Youm, so you'll find abandoned Vietnamese villages there—as ethnic Vietnamese drift steadily back to their kissing cousins in the Song Hong Ha, back to that swarming beehive of Hanoi. The great Plan of 1962, in other words, hasn't worked, and the Tai are pretty pissed.

The commandant of the academy at Dien Bien Phu proper doesn't, as you might imagine, *like* being in the midst of all this internecine bullshit any more than you or I would, and now, on top of it all, he's up to his little Buddha in monsoon effluvium. If you're lucky, ladies and gentlemen, you'll be the only visitors he's had in eight very wet weeks and he'll be so happy, so grateful, so honored to have five real Russians with him for a night or two that he won't get squinty-eyed and bother to phone Hanoi about you. You'll have your C-2 in ten-kilo bags neatly marked "Very Special Rice Seed—Gift of Your Russian Brothers" for any hick who wants to cop a peek, and you'll *didi mau* your bags and ponies to the Black River as fast as you can. Every day, every hour, every minute you keep your asses in-country, the chance of some nosy slope calling Hanoi out of curiosity if not downright jealousy jumps a notch.

From Dao Phu, you'll take sampans or small barges. You'll have to decide this for yourselves. Either way, the river—given the condition it's in—ought to be *lots* of fun. Where the Black empties out into the Hoa Binh Delta and then, farther north, where it meets the Red, you'll find the broadest-beamed rivers you've ever seen. There won't even be riverbanks, ladies and gentlemen. The water just goes forever. . . .

Keep in mind, my friends, that once you leave the Bam Me Tuong limestone and hit the Hoa Binh Delta, the population triples, then triples again, and finally quadruples near the Red. You're getting awfully close to Hanoi. The Tai and Meo and Kha are long gone. The only tribal minority is Muong and these babies have been living with the Vietnamese so long you can't tell the bastards apart. Once you're in the Black River Delta, the people *are* Vietnamese and the ball game changes. That close to Hanoi, comrades, the citizens get *real* nervous. Anything that glitters in the sky is an American killing machine. Anyone even approaching six feet in height of European stock is a downed American flier— and we know what happens to them—how much every Li'l Abner in those delta villages would love to have a flier of his own to parade around the village, love to bring a killing machine down by his lonesome with his old Home Force carbine, love to be a Hero of the People forever and ever and ever. Who can blame him? There's *rice* and *family* and *Hanoi* and *monsoons*, ladies and gentlemen. That's it. That's all he knows, has ever known, and will ever know.

That close to Hanoi, ladies and gentlemen, there are PBRs— some old, some new—with radar, twin 12.7s and grenade launchers. There are sampans with 75mm recoilless rifles. You name it. The NVA Air Force may be a joke, but its River Navy isn't. As I've said before, Hanoi is Washington, D.C., and Munich and Rome—Vatican, too—all rolled into one. Have you ever stuck an anthill with a stick? It'll be like that. They're mad, they're worried, they're running all over the place, and *you're* going to try to tiptoe in and kill their queen. Pray for rain, comrades. Pray for fog, for rivers that don't have riverbanks, for *lots* of water, and you just might make it.

I don't say a thing. I'm starting at last to understand what he means.

The good news (Harry tells us) is that Corporal Cooper and the olfactory, infrared nose on his dog are going to help you find the C-2. The bad news is that that black face of Cooper's may get you blown up anywhere along the way. There may be Africans studying Marxist-Leninism at Lenin U., but they *aren't* being sent to North Vietnam. They're being returned to their own countries, to lead them, if they've already been "liberated"—or to upset things a little, if they haven't.

"Why aren't we using a single-K device?" Steve asks suddenly. You can hear the anger in his voice. He *wants* to believe we'll make it, but he can't. "Why aren't we using a Greenlight team? Why aren't we getting in and getting out fast?"

Harry looks at him like *You've got to be kidding, Lieutenant. What an incredibly stupid-ass question, Lieutenant.*

He says instead: "It's a little hard to *deny* a nuclear device, isn't it, Lieutenant? Even if the thing's just a cratering device for new canals—the kind you might need, say, in Panama, if someone happened to take your canal away—it's a *nu-clee-uhr* device. You can't *deny* it. Everyone would *know*. Everyone—China and Russia pop to mind again—would say, 'If the Americans can, why can't we. . . ?' They'd really get their feelings hurt, Lieutenant, if we didn't let them try it, too . . . somewhere."

"We wouldn't be using it as a *weapon*," Steve says quickly. "How could the U.N. object? It's a cratering device. We'd be—"

"You don't understand," Harry interrupts, and he means all of us. "You might as well drop a megaton weapon on Hanoi, folks. Read my lips: It's *nu-clee-uhr*. If you use something *nu-clee-uhr*, you've broken the rules. This way—ponies, sampans, old C-2, an act of God—you can *deny* it. You *haven't* broken the rules."

I start to tell him I don't understand—I really don't—but I see Steve's face. He should be standing up, I know. He should be getting up and leaving, furious, but he isn't. He's thinking of the mission, of the team. He's thinking: *If I get up and leave, they'll find someone else.* He's thinking: *The team won't have a chance.*

"Riverine navigation and underwater demolitions," Tony says quickly, "is why you've got a brown-water specialist on this team, Lieutenant. This is SEAL territory we're talking about. Chief, can you tell us what the team can expect on a mission like this?"

The chief's been staring like a dead man, like he can't believe what he's been hearing any more than any of us can. Like: *Even SEALs have never heard anything as insane as this.*

"Chief, would sampans or small barges be the best bet?" Tony is asking.

The chief is getting up. He's wobbly, but he's getting up. He looks around the table, at all of us, and you can see what he's thinking. *How can they sit there like that? How can they even listen to this?* A black kid and his dog. A white nurse, not much older. A Vietnamese interpreter. A POW who isn't *really* cured. It's worse than he ever imagined. It's a bad dream. It's *got* to be.

"Sit down, Chief," Harry says quietly. "We do need your expertise on this. We're really not going to be in any position to get it later."

The chief remains standing.

"*Sit down,*" Harry says.

The chief does not. He turns. He walks out of the room.

I look around. The captain is looking at me, but I knew that. I even know why. I'm thinking what Steve is thinking. I wish I weren't, but I am.

I get up, wobbly too, and I go after him.

Chapter 26

I stand in his bedroom doorway where he can see me. When he looks up, he shakes his head and says, "Has the fearless TL sent Miss America to persuade the reluctant TS?"

I don't answer.

"They're *all* crazy, Lieutenant," he says. "I've never heard of anything this mean, this stupid, this crazy—and I've seen *crazy*, Lieutenant. SEALs are crazy, Lieutenant. SOGers are crazy. I've floated with a fucking breathing tube in my mouth and no floatation device for sixteen hours down a tar-black river. I've stuck leaves in my mouth and stood in mud up to my lips like a goddamn bush for twelve hours. I've covered myself with mud and twigs like some damn fucking log, let someone sit right next to me, eat his lunch and then killed him with my bare hands. I've liberated the souls of five people in less than ten minutes, Lieutenant, under the very nose of an NVA battalion, without a fucking sound, and then made it to a pickup ten klicks away in the jungle that same moonless night. You *do* these things if you're a SEAL, Lieutenant, but *I* wouldn't touch this mission with a twelve-foot poker. I wouldn't send my worst enemies on it. I certainly wouldn't send my *friends*."

I don't say a thing. I go over to his radio and kneel down. I say: "How does this work?"

He's not going to tell me. He doesn't want to, so I start fiddling with the knobs and toggles. I do it for a minute and he finally gets up, comes over and kneels down, too.

"Cut the bullshit, Lieutenant," he says, and looks me in the eye.

I keep playing with the switches and buttons. It's a monster of a radio. How could *anyone*—even with two arms—handle it?

"If we're not supposed to be up there, Chief," I say, "if no one's supposed to know we're up there, why are we taking a radio with us?"

He stares at me. I can feel it. He knows what I'm doing, but he also knows he doesn't have a choice. *You're going to need someone, Willie,* I'm saying.

"Good question, Lieutenant," he says at last. He sighs and makes himself say it. "Bucannon wants us to broadcast throughout the mission. They want to track us. That's what they tell me."

"Can't they pinpoint us that way?"

"You mean Hanoi? Sure." He takes a deep breath, like he's going under water, like he's got to talk whether he wants to or not. He says: "But they assure me that if we keep the repeater—the squelch breaks—to ten-second bursts or less, we'll be safe. They—Hanoi—won't have enough to triangulate with. All I know is what they tell me, Lieutenant. If you think I've ever used a machine like this, you're crazy, too."

"What is it?"

"Hell if I know. It's got Soviet designators. It's probably the equivalent of their PRC-77, but it's got ten or fifteen pounds on the 77."

He's talking, and I let him. And he knows I am.

"I used to be pretty good," he tells me. "I used to be one of the fastest RTOs the SEAL land teams had, Lieutenant. You need a fast hand for that. The old Morse code transmissions, I mean. . . ."

"What gives you the most trouble?" I say real quietly, eyes on the knobs and antennae. It looks like a steel Medusa—you know, that goddess, the one who can turn you to stone.

He's looking at me again. I don't look back.

"The same thing that gives me trouble with *any* goddamn radio, Lieutenant."

I look up at last and it's there in his eyes. He doesn't want it to be, but it is. *Damn right, I'm feeling sorry for myself, Lieutenant. You don't know what it's like.* Nobody *does.*

I say: "Can't you get ahold of these knobs with your pincher there?"

He looks down at his pink prosthesis, the steel gripper tip, and it's as if he's never thought of it that way before—a *pincher.* A crab.

"No," he says, and as he does he forgets what I'm doing. He says: "Not with this one. I ordered two different tips before I left. The VA wouldn't cover them, so Lizzie—that's my wife—was going to surprise me with them on my birthday." There's a grin. "Which happens to be next week."

The grin goes away. He doesn't say anything else. He's remembering what I'm trying to do to him, and who I'm doing it for.

"What happens," I ask quickly, "if you wrap the metal—the part where you'd want to grip it—with adhesive tape, something like that?"

He can't do it. He can't keep the anger going, so he says: "It gets slick. It loses its grip, Lieutenant."

I've got the radio—the motherfucker of a radio—on my lap. I pull it over to me before he can stop me. It digs into my legs, my thighs, but I leave it there, where I can fiddle with the knobs and dials and toggles again. "What's *this*?" I ask, moving the slide bar back and forth.

He's about to say it. He's about to say: *Get your goddamn hands off my radio, Lieutenant!* but he knows what that would mean. If he says that, I'd have won, he knows. *My radio.* I'm holding it for him, yes. I'm trying to understand it, I'm even teasing him just a little—the way a woman would who cared. He wonders if I really do. He'd like me to.

"That's the net selector," he says, pointing with his prosthesis. "And that's for the wattage—the transmission wattage. It's got some goddamn nickel-cadmium battery the size of a meat loaf that'll last a year on full periodic transmission—something like that."

Aware that he's pointing with the prosthesis, he lets it fall.

"And that's the repeater setting." He points with his chin now, the prosthesis in his lap. "We're supposed to keep that on—sending Morse on our own frequency the entire time. Did I already say that?"

I nod, looking down. "Won't Hanoi be able to hear it?"

"Yeah, but they won't know *what* or *where*. The squelch breaks are too short. Or so they say. I'm not sure whether that makes sense or not. It may."

"Is this the transmitter?" I say, flicking the biggest switch I can find. A tiny light—you barely see it—goes on, then off again, and stays off—as if waiting.

"Right," he says. "But not so much amplitude."

"Like this?"

"No." He reaches out—just like I want him to. He does it with his good arm—and I twist away. He *knows* what I'm doing. He knows I'm saying: *You've got to teach me, Willie.*

"Turn it to the left, for Christ's sake!" he shouts, grabbing at it again. I go ahead, I turn the dial to the left. He sits back, a little pale, breathing hard.

"Jesus Christ, Lieutenant. You can't bullhorn like that. Every Pathet Lao with a transistor radio will know we're here."

"Sorry." But I'm grinning.

After a second he says, "Okay."

"*Now* what?" I say. "After I set it like that, then what?"

He doesn't answer. He's looking at me, and I know he's thinking: *Do I really want this? Is this what I really want?*

"Slide the bar, Lieutenant," he says. "Yes, *that* one—to the left about halfway—and flip those two toggles at the same time. *No, not like that!*"

He can't stand it anymore. He reaches for his radio and this time he doesn't care whether he grabs it with his good arm or his bad. *Anything*—anything at all to get it away from this crazy nurse.

I don't let him touch it. I slip it over on the floor right beside me, on the other side, where he can't get it. Then I say slowly: "Tell me what I'm supposed to do, Willie. It'll take a while, but if you stick it out, I will, too, and in the end I'll learn it. I'm a nurse—I can learn these things. I'll certainly learn enough to help you with it. There'll be two of us who can work with it, Willie."

He's looking at me again. He's thinking: *Is this Miss America, or is this a woman who cares?*

"Want me to get some adhesive tape?" I say. "We could try some harness padding with adhesive tape to hold the sides down—if you think it might work."

He doesn't say a thing for a moment. Then he says:

"Hell. Why not."

You're no different from Steve, a voice keeps saying. *What you're doing isn't any different.*

We go ahead and fix the Soviet Prick-77, so that both of us can use it. We teach each other a number of things.

Chapter 27

"Sampans from Dao Phu," Willie says at the table, everyone watching him, "and then patrol boats, any make, any model—if we can put our hands on them. The closer we get to the target, the more we'll need to have the C-2 in one place, moving as fast as we can move it. With the rains this bad, the Song Hong Ha tributaries—including the Black—will be what we call 'rollers,' but by overloading no more than thirty percent we should be able to stabilize the sampans. We need Vinh Choi sampans. They're broad-beamed and have a decent keel and they shouldn't be that hard to find in Tai river country. We won't be able to handle the cargo ourselves. We're talking 20,000 pounds. Yes, I know, we've got Tai coolies to do it, but isn't the plan to ditch them before the Hoa Binh Delta? Right. It's not going to work. It's too early."

The shirts wait. He's giving them what they want, even if they don't like what they're hearing.

"Is there any chance, Captain," he says, "that we can get Nungs? We want mercs who can make the entire trip with us. We can't take the Tai into Muong country. You don't take your Appalachian cousins to New York. Nungs we can take all the way to Dong Noi and no one's going to look twice. The provinces north of Hanoi are full of Nung—merc Nung, rice-farmer Nung, any kind of Nung you'd like. If you can put your hands on a dozen Nungs with northern accents—steal them from the American Embassy in Saigon even—that's what we need."

The shirts are looking at the captain and the captain's nodding. *Yes. He's right.* But he isn't looking at the shirts as he nods. He's looking at *me.* I look away. I don't want to see his mouth mouthing something else, something like: *Thank you, Lieutenant.* I don't want to see those eyes and *hear* him thinking: *Thanks for bringing him back into the fold.*

I didn't do it for you, I tell him.

"All right," Harry says. "I suppose we can do that. Half of the Nungs in the South have northern accents. *If* you both think it's necessary. . . ."

"We do," the chief says.

The captain doesn't say a thing, but Harry nods anyway. We'll get our Nungs—those remarkable hereditary mercenaries who came south from China a thousand years ago, keep coming even now, who were so good the Trung Sisters—the one in Hanoi, the one in Hue—kept them as their personal bodyguards; who live in the foothills and valleys between Hanoi and the Chinese border in the North; who sneak out of the North every day to come South, where American Special Forces fall in love with them—because they're disciplined, loyal, feisty. We'll have Nungs to travel with us all the way, to move the bags to the PBRs, to set the cords, to float down the rivers with us—or head into the mountains if we fail—or die with us if *we* die, making yet another legend of courage and loyalty for their own people, for whom, the chief says, manhood and duty mean very different things.

We'll have them because the chief wants them—because he'll *walk* if we don't get them. He's made that clear in his own way.

We might as well have a third moon for the insertion, Harry tells us—for whatever light the cloud cover will allow. I get the feeling that Steve, the captain and the chief already know this. It's what you *always* do, but Harry is a Remington Raider, so he's telling the Green Beanies and a SEAL what they already know. After that (Harry adds) you'll want the worst possible weather you can get.

We know.

"We'll push the insertion back six days," Harry says, "for your Nungs and for your third moon."

"What'll we do with six dead days?" someone asks.

"More study of essential Russian phrases," Bach says. "Accents still number ten, comrade brothers."

"Kiss my ass," the chief says. Bach smiles.

"Hey, Bach, teach us some Nung," Steve says. "I've got a list of four-letter words in Rhade and three or four animist prayers in Jarai, but no Chinese. It may come in handy."

Bach shakes his head. "Not necessary," he says. "Nungs not talk. Nungs eat, shit and shoot." He says it with his best b-girl voice again and we laugh. It isn't really funny, but who does it hurt to laugh?

Someone's leaning against my leg, and I look. It's the chief, head down, elbows on his knees, thinking. I pull away. I don't *want* to touch him. I don't want to touch any of them. I don't want to dream his death. I don't want to see halos again. Even if I can hear angels singing, even if it feels *good* to die, to float so high like that, to see the whole world for once, to hear all that singing—I don't want to dream his death.

I pull away slowly and he doesn't even look up.

Cooper is petting Crusoe, like always. Steve leans over to me and says, "I've got a few details to work out with the captain, Mary." I look at him. I know what he wants. He wants permission, even forgiveness—*something*. He wants me to understand why he's doing it. "I'm ATL, Mary. I've *got* to," he says.

"I understand," I tell him.

I do. I really do.

I'm almost asleep when he finally comes to my room.

"Bucannon won't do it," he says after a while.

I make a sound and try to sit up.

"He won't give us the pills."

I lie back down. I close my eyes. I want to be cruel. I want to say: *Did you really think he would, Steve?* I want to be even crueler than that. I want to say: *Was it more comfortable that way? Did you tell yourself he* would *just so you could get this far, so you could work with them this long without* feeling *it—so you'd be able to say, "Gee, I'm sorry, Mary. He won't give us any. But it's too late to turn back now, isn't it?"*

I don't say it. He looks like Christabel and it's not his body, or his eyes. It's the look on his face—the hurt—and it's only going to get harder for him. *It's not his fault, Mary,* I tell myself. *We've all been lying to ourselves.*

"I've still got five of them left," I tell him.

He doesn't seem to hear me. It's not just the pills.

I trusted him, he's thinking to himself, *so I could avoid feeling it. . . .*

I shut my eyes and keep them shut. "All we've got is our talents, Steve," I tell him, and breathing isn't easy. I go ahead. I take deep breaths between the words, the thoughts. "Bucannon isn't going to help us. All he wants is to see how long we can last up there, to see whether we have inside us the talent to *do it*—to stay alive, to keep each other alive—to see whether what we have inside us can be used in this or any other war, whether it's worth the trouble of trying it. It's a test, Steve, and whether we live or die he'll have learned something. Either way, he wins. Men like him always win, Steve. *You* know that." I take another breath. "This isn't *really* a mission, Steve—the kind where it really matters whether you succeed or fail. This isn't *really* war, Steve. This is a kind of science, where things are wonderful, because there's always something to learn. . . ."

I don't ask him again. I don't have to breath to do it. I don't say: *Can't we get out through Thailand? Aren't there expatriated hippies there who could help us, because we're fleeing the war? Even some French who wouldn't mind helping us? Even some candy-assed gringo tourists who probably don't even know there's a war, would be horrified to find out, so of course they'd help?*

"We'll stay alive as long as we can," he says. Or I'm the one who says it. Or it's what we're both thinking, though no one says it. "That's really all we can do."

We sit there on the bed, not saying a thing. I'm looking at his face, the way his shoulders roll, as he sits there. I say: "We may not have another chance, Steve."

He shakes his head. He starts to say no. He's coiled tight as a spring. He's exhausted. It's the last thing he'd have thought to do now, and it's sad. We're kids, so it's sad. *We're kids but we're old. We don't even want to make out in the back seat of a car.* . . .

Maybe he *is* tired—maybe he *is* worried about whether he can even do it, but I don't care. I look at him. I make him look back. I hold those eyes of his, those great eyelashes, and I don't let go. *We're just kids, Steve. It may be the last chance we have.*

He gives me this little smile and I give him one back. I punch him in the arm, and he laughs—the way he's laughed before. I pull the blanket over my head and the light goes out. I listen to him getting undressed and for a moment, the briefest moment, I see Bucannon undressing instead. But I make it go away. I change the body, I make it younger, I make that picture go away.

He's warm. He's hot as a fever and we giggle. He's better at it this time—better at all the things he's supposed to do—and I go ahead, I tell him that. He's had women before. Of course he has. He's had bar-girls and high school girls—you can't be a Green Beanie and not have, but boy, were you bad that first time. I go ahead and tell him. *We're both a lot better,* he says. *Thanks,* I say. *Thanks a lot.* Every time his breath, his body, starts to leave me— every time he starts thinking of the details he's got to work out with the captain and the shirts if we're going to have any chance at all of staying alive—I pull him back to me. I know we don't have a chance and I pull those eyes, those shoulders, that little boy back to me. I say, "Hey, lover," and he comes back.

We get there together. I say "Oh, God!"—just like women do in those books. We laugh and moan. We make all the sounds boys and girls make when they're doing it—"first base," then "all the way"—and we try not to laugh. We really do. We don't want him to say, "Oh, shit, Mary, I'm laughing too hard." We don't want *me* saying, "You know, honey, it isn't very romantic, laughing like this." So we finally settle down. We get serious, just like lovers. Hot and sticky, legs around his hips, holding tight, we get there— we get there together—and then fall apart like the halves of a clam. We lie there on damp sheets and catch our breaths, waiting until we can do it again.

When it happens, I think I'm dreaming the way everyone dreams. A *nightmare*, nothing more.

He's on top of me. We're doing it a little differently. He's arching his back, the way men do, and I'm thinking: *How would you know what men do? How many men have you done it with, Mary?*

The jerking starts. For a second I don't think a thing about it—it's just his way, I tell myself, jerking like this. Boys feel it differently than women. I think: *They're little spasms, that's all.*

But they aren't, and when I realize what they really are, I want to scream, and can't.

He's jerking. He's jerking from the rounds. I *try*, but I can't get up. I can't get him off. I can't scream because his forehead, his hair, his skin are in my face, my eyes, my mouth, his arms are around my head, the dead, dead weight of it—I can't even turn my head, spit the hair from my mouth, and scream.

The mud is like a cold wet bed that won't let go. The smell of silt, muddy water, a river so wide you can't see it end—washing the paddies clean, carrying the fish away, boiling like a storm only yards from our legs—where we lie, in mud, on a slope, the uniforms above us silhouetted against a gray, rainy sky. I try—I really do—I try to pull my arms free, but the mud holds me. There's a sucking sound. But the mud holds me tight. I try to lift one leg, sliding it up under me, so I can raise the body that weighs me down. But the leg slips and I sink back into mud again. I don't want to—I don't—but I keep thinking: *If he's on top of you, Mary, the rounds will hit him first.* I don't want to, but I'm thinking: *He's dead, Mary, so it doesn't really matter . . . whether the rounds hit him first.*

The river is rising. The rain falls in sheets. The water, slowed by marsh grass, eddies nearer and nearer to our boots. The uniforms stream over the brow of the dike like a river, little red stars on their caps just like points of blood, their bodies like a wave about to break.

He's inside you, Mary, a voice says. *Why do you want him to go away.*

He's dead!

I try again, and my leg slips again. He's jerking. He isn't alive, but he's jerking—from the rounds going in. I try both legs, and they both slip now. I lift my chest, and his body—at last—slides a little, slides down between my legs. I rise up on elbows and his body slides a little more—and then the mud, the eddying river by our boots, the red river, all begin to pull. *No!* I grab at his hair and hold on. The sliding stops. The waters lap, pulling at his legs, but the sliding stops.

The hair slips in my fingers—an inch—then another. The fingers are cold, the knuckles white. The hair slips again, and again. His body jerks, jerks again.

Please, God. No.

The hair slips free at last, through fingers that barely feel it. The body disappears. Its arms move almost as if it were swimming. The river takes it away.

The weight on my chest is gone, as he rolls away. He lies beside me, shaking. "Jesus," he says.

"You felt it?" I ask—in someone else's voice—trying to breathe.

"Yes," he says. "Jesus, yes."

He knows what it's like now, and it's made him feel afraid.

It takes him a while to get dressed, and as he does, he doesn't speak. I close my eyes, but see mud again, the coldness, something pulling. I open them quickly to the darkness, to the rustle of his clothes.

When he finally leaves, I keep my eyes open. I *know* what it means.

We're all going to make it happen, Colonel. We're going to make it happen in very small ways.

Subject: If someone wasn't going to die, Major, I didn't dream about their wounds. I didn't need to. I know that sounds unfeeling—but it's the truth. I thought about it a lot. I even talked with Bucannon and I remember we agreed: *You won't dream about someone, Mary—no matter how badly hurt he is—unless he's going to die.*

If I had dreamed about Willie, it would have been something like this:

The bone sticks out of the flesh. It looks like a shattered tusk, Lizzie—pink and gray and a lot larger than the gorgeous scrimshaw my daddy gave me—when he came home that year. I'm seated cross-legged in the mud, Lizzie, like an Indian, trying not to fall over. There isn't much pain, I guess. The dirt and the leaves have stopped raining down. There's even sunlight in the rain. Shock is a very wonderful thing, Lizzie. I can see my arm over there in the dirty leaves, by the canal where it should've been easy, where there shouldn't have been any mortars at all, or I—I should have paid attention to the way my arms glowed, the way my whole damn body glowed. Have I told you about that, Lizzie? Have I told you how they glowed?

The question I have, Lizzie, is simple: Would God really want me to believe in things like that—in things that glowed like that? Wouldn't it be magic, a sin, not a miracle at all? Wouldn't it be a gift of the Great Liar—not the Lord God? What would Reverend Acres say, Lizzie—on a sunny morning in that white room under those windows when I was young? Wouldn't he say: "Don't listen to it, Willie. Listening is the first step toward the fire?" Wouldn't he say: "It's not His blessing. It's not His grace. It's the Prince of Liars asking you to believe in his world, in Darkness. The Lord God of all wants you to believe in Light. There is, yes, a power we can't see in the world, Willie, but it's God's—and it's not for men like you and me. Those who hunger for it, Willie—those who are willing to accept its curse in trade—only sell themselves to the Liar, to live lives of eternal Hell." He would say: "It's better to lose your arm, Willie—it's even better to let your best friend die—than to lose your soul in that way, Willie."

I'm a man. I know that, Lizzie. I'm not a kid in Clayton anymore. But the questions stay the same—they just don't go away. The reverend, the room, those windows—they just don't go away.

If they move, if the fingers lying there in the dirt start to move,

I know I'll scream. Anyone would, Lizzie. It isn't the pain (did I say that?). It's the fear—of dying, of leaving this world, and wondering whether I've lived it right. You can't take an arm off like that, have it lying on the ground like that—the stump of it pumping all your blood away—without dying, can you, Lizzie? You can't look like that and not die.

I should take my boots off. I know that. I should use my socks as a tourniquet maybe. But I don't wear any. SEALs just don't wear socks. We don't wear socks on a mission. They gather up on you. They give you that other kind of blister. Only cherries wear socks. No SEAL ever wore socks—or underwear—not even underwear. I can't take off my pants and use my underwear for a tourniquet, because I'm not wearing any. SEALs love the air. They love running naked through the rain. They love the water, too. Even if you drown them, they love it. Right, Cutter?

Someone's handing it to me. I'm not sure what it is at first. It doesn't make any sense. But then I see that someone has picked my arm up from the mud, someone has picked it up—like something I might have lost—and he's giving it back to me. "Thank you," I tell him. He's putting it in my lap. It's got to be Honcho. It's got to be. He's tying the tubing around the stump where the bone grinds when I move it, and the tubing—this IV tubing—is a helluva lot better, believe me, than any sock or underwear you could use. I say: "Shouldn't we be trying to get it back on me?" He doesn't answer. I really don't know why. So I try him again: "Aren't you supposed to put it back on when it comes off? We did that, I know, with Sally's finger—that's my cousin—and it stayed on fine, Honcho." It's Honcho all right there, but he isn't talking. He's giving me an ampule—right in the thigh—but he isn't talking. There are little holes in my thigh. Jesus, Lizzie. There are little holes all over me, I realize, and I hear someone say: "Aw, shit." It's me. I'm the one saying it. There are little black things all over my chest and I brush at them. They're holes maybe. No, they're something else. I feel like I'm going to fall over. I'm a lot heavier on one side, Lizzie, when I try to brush the things away. "Stop it," someone says. It's Honcho all right. I can get the little pieces off me if I brush them away.

"Stop it," he says. "I want to get the shrapnel off me," I tell him. That's why I'm brushing like this, even if it's only with one hand.

I tell him, "If you hold the hand, Honcho, I'll take the stump end and we'll get it back on, I know we will. It'll take both of us, but we can do it. I know we can." But Honcho won't. He doesn't take ahold of the hand. It's hard, Lizzie, to believe your friends can change like that, but they can. He's there right beside me, watching the tubing, and telling me to "Stop it." When I say, "I know it'll work," he nods, but he doesn't do a thing. He doesn't take the hand.

People are like that, Lizzie. They lose their compassion, their feelings for you, in a situation like this . . . in a darkness that grabs you like this. . . .

Subject: That's wrong. That's what the *captain* heard, what *he* saw and heard when he looked at Willie that day—when he touched Willie with his eyes and heard him. Or at least that's what the captain told me. That's what he told me in the dream—the one I dreamed in Vientiane that night.

It was changing, Major.

It was changing in so many little ways.

Photostat, Telegram, Command Files (Personnel), Operation Orangutan, *Tiger Cat*, Vietnam

350P CDT JUNE 10 69 NSA24
NS A1A204 (NS WA002) XV GOVERNMENT PO
WASHINGTON DC10 1124P, EDT
MRS ELIZABETH SESSIONS
323 OAK AVENUE
RICHMOND VIRGINIA
THIS IS TO CONFIRM THAT YOUR HUSBAND
MASTER CHIEF PETTY OFFICER WILLIAM
DEAN SESSIONS USN WAS INJURED 2 JUNE 1969
IN THE VICINITY OF MY THO REPUBLIC OF
VIETNAM. HE SUSTAINED TRAUMATIC AM-

PUTATION OF AN ARM AND FRAGMENTATION
WOUNDS TO HIS CHEST FROM HOSTILE MOR-
TAR ROUNDS WHILE ON AN OPERATION. HE IS
RECEIVING TREATMENT AT THE FIRST MEDI-
CAL BATTALION. HIS CONDITION AND PROG-
NOSIS ARE GOOD. WE SHARE YOUR CONCERN
AND CAN ASSURE YOU HE IS RECEIVING THE
BEST OF CARE. HIS MAILING ADDRESS RE-
MAINS THE SAME.

HENRY M GREENE JR ADMIRAL USN COM-
MANDANT OF THE NAVY (47).(to be mailed)

Chapter 28

Subject: There's something I forget to say. I think it's important. Can I go back?
Interviewer: Of course, Lieutenant.
Subject: I mean, being able to talk about events even out of order is important, isn't it? We lose things—important things—if we can't go back. Don't you think?
Interviewer: Yes, I do.
Subject: Once we lose them, they're gone forever.
Interviewer: Yes. Go ahead.
Subject: It was our fifth day in Vientiane, I remember. They brought this doctor to the safe house—a regular doctor. Bucannon wasn't there when he arrived, but that's not what I want to say. He was a regular doctor. A civilian, the kind you'd go to if you had cramps or the flu—the kind the whole family would go to. He wasn't a shrink. He wasn't a combat surgeon. You wanted to trust him. That's what I'm saying.

He's wearing corduroy slacks and a button-down Oxford shirt. It's a real shock. He *looks* like a civilian. He *moves* like a civilian. They've got the kitchen cleaned up for him with a little cot and a few basic outpatient instruments laid out on a white cloth there on the table. It's as if he's going to take warts off our thumbs, maybe a precarcinoma from our foreheads, that's all.

"Can I help?" I say, and Tony gives me his what-an-asshole

look, which he's trying to perfect. "I mean it," I say. "I'm a *nurse*, Tony. Ask Bucannon."

The doctor won't even look at me.

I'm wondering who's going to tell us what's going on. No one's jumping up to do it.

"Penicillin shots?" I say, looking at Tony, at the doctor, anyone. "Warts?" We're all there watching the kitchen get washed, the surgical steel get laid out, the doctor get scrubbed in the little kitchen sink. "We don't want to spread VD up North, right? We don't want to spread any viruses that might cause warts, right?" I'm feeling pretty good. It's Vientiane, after all. We're still having fun.

"Actually," the doctor says all of a sudden, matter-of-factly, like it really is worth considering, "that wouldn't be a bad idea. We could vaccinate you all and give you something to spread around up there. Hollow out a molar or two, put some hybrid *Pasteurella* in one and a bacteriophagic wash in the other. When the time was right you'd crack the tooth and cause some trouble. Rural to urban vectors. *Very* natural-appearing."

I wait for the smile—for the joke. Everyone waits. It doesn't come. He's a family doctor, like ours, isn't he, Mom? It's a deadpan joke—that's it. It's sarcastically serious. He's married, has a wife and kids, is working for USAID, and remember how in med school he was such a deadpan cutup? They used to say, "Hey, you ought to be a stand-up comic, Jules." Maybe it runs in his family. Maybe *no one* in his family smiles when they're trying to be funny. His father doesn't, his older brother doesn't, so Jules doesn't either. But family doctors shouldn't sound like guys from the Atlanta Centers for Disease Control, should they, Mom?

Harry, the funny one, snorts. No one else makes a sound.

I look at Steve. He's waiting. Even the shirts are waiting, like even they aren't sure what our doctor is going to do.

Who is he, Harry? Who've you brought to the house now?

The doctor rearranges the five steel basics—the outpatient cut-and-stitch kind—and suddenly Tony is clearing his throat. Ah. I understand. It's *Tony's* turn to lecture:

"You're not," Tony says, "going to have access to pharmacies up there, and the wet season *is* the infection season."

"We know that, Tony," Steve says, and Tony pretends he doesn't hear.

"You're also not going to be very happy if you have to worry about losing your transponders. So we've got a little surprise for each of you." He's looking at us the way a real Professor Tony would, the way they teach you to look in public-speaking classes: *How to Hold Their Attention. How to Look Sincere.*

"Morphine you'll have in the standard ampules," Tony proceeds, "and of course you'll use that when and where you need to. In a firefight—which is the last thing you should be praying for, of course—morphine may not be what you want to use—"

"We *know*, Tony," Willie says.

"*Some* of you may not, Chief."

"Right, Tony," Willie says.

"What we're going to do," Tony says, "is ask you to join a little experiment—one that may very well save your lives." There's a pause and no one says a thing. Steve and the chief look at each other like *Can you believe this?* Real fast Tony says: "We'd like each of you to carry an antibiotic drip in you throughout the mission, but *only* if you agree it's worth it. A little cut can turn into a flaming pseudomona out there and you don't want to have to pop pills for it, right?"

"Right, Tony," I say.

"You want us," the chief says suddenly, "to have a thousand miles of IV tubing running from our asses back to this house, Tony?"

"Wouldn't that much tubing," Steve says quickly, "get caught on trees and bushes, Tony? Wouldn't the NVA just follow it through the jungle and eventually find us?"

Tony should be getting mad, but for some reason he isn't. He's smiling and I don't like the feeling. It means we've *helped* him—we've somehow helped him. *The fun's over, boys,* it means. "We won't have to do that, ladies and gentlemen," he says, sounding just like Harry now. "First, you'll have a little transistorized release ampule under the skin of your weaker arm. Second, the drip will be self-regulating for up to two weeks. Third, to kill two birds with one stone, the transistor will also power a low-frequency pulse. In other words, ladies and gentlemen, the device will also be your transponder."

"I've never heard of anything like that," I say, meaning the drips. *Transponders?* I've never even *heard* the word.

"No, you wouldn't have, Lieutenant," Tony says pleasantly. The smile stays. He's got a script, that's clear. And it hasn't failed him yet. "They're from Bell Labs—the autodrips. They're brand-new. All the transponder is, Lieutenant, is a miniaturized version of what SEALs already use anytime they're picked up by a sub on Yankee Station. Right, Chief?"

The chief doesn't nod. The doctor doesn't nod. He's prepping and arranging, getting ready to do his work.

"It's a Bell Lab prototype, the autodrip," Tony says once more, liking us where he has us. "No risk to the carrier and a solid ninety-six percent effective rate. You'll see them used with diabetics in a couple of years, with cardiac cases, too. Right, Doctor?"

The doctor looks up from his tray but doesn't say a thing.

"You're familiar with these things, Doctor?" I say. "They're in the literature?"

"Yes," he says at last. And then he says: "I don't know what the fuss is all about, Lieutenant."

"Who's the *we*?" Steve says to Tony.

"What?"

"Who's the *we* who would like us to carry these things in our arms?"

"*Everyone*, Lieutenant," Tony says. "The consensus is, if they're going to make the trip, why not have them try it out? It's not going to blow up on you, I promise. It's not going to poison you. It's not going to take control of your mind in some strange way. You'll be helping science and medicine and your respective branches of the military. You'll be helping any long-range teams that follow you in this and any other war that requires unconventional warfare. You may very well be helping yourselves as well. Ask SOG about the infection rates on longer LURPs. Ask the Navy what happens when you lose your transponder in the Gulf of Tonkin. Let me repeat, ladies and gentlemen: This is *not* the kind of device that carries a risk factor. The broad-spectrum antibiotics it will introduce in your system are the ones you'd be taking orally or intramuscularly anyway, here *or* back home."

No one says a thing. And then I say:

"We're heading into an infection zone, Doctor. Why should we want fresh stitches on our arm?"

Tony doesn't miss a beat. He's *ready*. Everything we say helps him along. "I'm glad you asked that, Lieutenant," he says. "The stitches *won't* be fresh. It'll be an outpatient operation. Dr. Langer will use the finest monofilament money can buy and the stitches will be pullable in forty-eight hours. The holes will plug in another twenty-four, and if there's going to be a rejection, it'll be within seventy-two hours—*before* you leave—or at around three months . . . after you're back. We're not expecting either. The plastics the guys at Bell Labs use have a 96 percent acceptance rate. And the rejection, were one to occur, would be a simple inflammation the autodrip itself would keep under control."

"Right," the doctor says, and it sounds ridiculous. *He* should be the one telling us these things, but he isn't. *Maybe they don't trust him, Mary. Maybe they think he'll tell us the wrong things.*

Or maybe he just doesn't want to be bothered.

I'm looking around. I see Steve staring at Tony, then at the doctor. I see everyone staring, everyone trying to understand, and I start to say: "Why aren't you putting it on our abdomens, Tony—for better absorption? Why isn't it a lot bigger—say, the size of a tuna fish can—if it's going to have to drip that long?" But I stop. The chief is sitting up. There's a look on his face and I'm thinking: *Shit. He's about to leave again.* Tony sees it, too, gives the doctor a glance, says quickly: "A question, Chief?"

"No," the chief says quietly. "No question. I just have no intention of doing it, that's all."

Tony looks at the chief for a moment, *thinks* he understands, and says: "I think we have a little misunderstanding here, Chief. We're not going to slap one of these things in your *good* arm. We'll put it anywhere you want us to—any low-contact surface you're able to reach with your good arm so that you can press the device in the correct manner and activate the transponder when you need to. Upper arm on your good side, lower back, thigh near the groin—there are any number of places. You choose the place, Chief."

The doctor looks around the room again and continues to wait.

The chief gets up suddenly and heads for the door. He'll do it more than once before we leave Vientiane, but we don't know that yet.

Harry takes off after him and catches him in the dining room. We can't see them, but we can hear them.

"You're going to terminate us," the chief shouts. "You're going to have these things in us so you can terminate us when you goddamn well please. Maybe it's time-set. Maybe you've got a Buffalo Hunter to trigger it from 20,000 feet—I don't care—one way or another you're going to do it and I know it and you know it."

"*That*," Harry says, voice calm, "is the *stupidest* thing I've ever heard."

"It isn't!" Willie shouts. "You fuckers terminated the Doom Cats in '62. You terminated 77s in '66, and don't give me any of that bullshit about fucking inclement weather. You left them out in the cold because *you didn't want them back*. Everyone knows it. Now you want to put something inside *us* so you can abort the mission whenever you damn well please, you fucking son of a bitch."

"Why," Harry says, still calm, "would we want to terminate *this* team, Chief? This isn't some SOG recon. This isn't some over-the-fence combat tracker job. This mission *matters*, Chief. It matters to an awful lot of people. You should know that by now. We wouldn't have taken it this far—involving this many resources—if it didn't. I'm talking Casa Blanca. I'm talking JCS. Why in God's name would we start you people out on something like this and not want you to *finish it*? We don't want bodies up there with American technology in their arms, Willie. We don't want to start a mission like this—and then stop it for no reason. . . ."

It feels like an hour before the chief answers him. Willie's voice is low and soft, but it's the kind of voice you wouldn't want to hear at night, in the dark, lying in your bed. The voice says:

"You are out of your league, Harry. You're talking to a Navy SEAL who's lost more friends than you'll ever *have* to mission aborts issued by your motherfucking controls. There are a thousand different reasons for terminating—you may know a few of these, but I've been *down there* and I know a hell of a lot more, Harry. You may tell that son of a bitch Bucannon that I have *absolutely no intention* of submitting to this surgery. That I'd sooner cut off my other arm."

I don't hear footsteps, so I know Willie hasn't left. They're still standing in the dining room, neither moving, neither saying a thing now. The chief is staring at Harry. Harry is staring back, thinking to himself: *If I have to get Bucannon over here to fix this, I've fucked up.*

"Captain Kelly," Harry says at last. "Will you please come in here?"

The captain gets up from his chair and walks through the doorway. Harry's voice says:

"You're going to let us put one of these things in *your* arm, aren't you, Captain?

"Yes," the captain's voice says, "I am."

"If *he's* willing to do it, Willie," Harry is saying now, "if a man in his position—a member of your own team, a man who's been in on this project from the very start, who's been briefed all along, who certainly isn't blind—is willing to have this done, why aren't you, Willie?"

The chief doesn't answer.

"I *swear* to you, Willie," Harry says, "that the device we want to place under your skin for this mission does *not* contain bacteria or toxin—*any* substance that could possibly hurt you. It is *not* a device for termination, Willie. I swear to you."

No one says a thing in either room now. The doctor just stands there in front us, waiting.

There's a sigh from the dining room and Willie says, "Is the device what he claims it to be, Captain?"

"Yes," the captain says, but I can't tell what he's feeling.

"Will they be putting in your arm the exact same device they're putting in mine, Captain?"

"Yes, they will."

"Can we shuffle the devices, Harry?" Willie asks. "Can we each choose the device that's going to be put in us?"

"Of course," Harry says.

"All right," Willie says. "All right."

The doctor gives a topical block, four pricks, makes the incision neatly and slips the little thing—like the smallest pen you've ever seen—under the skin. Then he puts the flap back, stitches it as if he did this kind of thing all the time, and gives us something with codeine for when it starts to hurt—which he says it will. That's all he says. He looks bored, but maybe that's a family trait, too. Maybe he's really *very* excited, upset, worried about his job, about whether we're going to make it up there and back and end this war. You can never tell with some people.

I'm the last. Steve, Bach and Cooper stand around, worried about me. The chief looks away. No sweat, I say. I'm used to little blades, I say. I'm a nurse, guys.

When he's finished, I get up. I get a cup of coffee and sit with the others. I'm not worried at all.

Chapter 29

Subject: I remember taking one of the pills. I just don't remember when.
Interviewer: [unintelligible]

There were four choppers that took us out of Wattay, Major. We did it right beside a Lasky Skymover with Russian pilots in civvies and a Chinese C-130 imitation that probably had a Pathet Lao crew. We did it within sight of three civilian airlines and we did it wearing our very best pressed cammies. That wasn't etiquette in Vientiane. Even if you were chunky Chinese agents heading for the upper Mekong or an American Special Forces team planning to put a thousand pissed-off Meo mercs on the Ho Chi Minh Trail near the Plateau des Bolovens, you *still* didn't wear cammies in Vientiane. You wore short-sleeved shirts like Harry's, or nice pressed slacks like the good doctor's. If you were running a war, it was supposed to be a *secret* one.

You certainly didn't want to advertise it.

We had our weapons and other gear in a big team locker, like a Green Beanie A-team would—and our Russki uniforms in personal duffel bags—and even with all of this we barely filled one Hornet. The other three choppers stayed empty, and I was the one who said it: "Why all the extra room, guys?" No one answered. I was just supposed to know. "Hey," I said. "I'm a nurse. I don't know these things." The Russian pilots were walking by us to their big gray whale with the big red stars on its jaw, and the traffic, in general, was picking up. Big day at Wattay. Laotian sunshine. Not much rain. Time to *di di.*

I was the only one saying a thing.

"Decoys?" I said. "Is *that* it? What if they shoot all *four* of them down?"

"I'm a woman," I told them. "I have a strange device in my arm, I smell like a gym, but I'm still a woman. Give me a break, guys."

"Yeah," the chief said. "Decoys. And I do know what you mean."

With all the air traffic we stayed the night, taking off at first light. We moved up the Mekong valley, flying low enough to be under the radar, but not so low some AK could bring us down. The empty birds flew fore and aft and when we took fire, they'd do one of their little runs, swinging their M-60s. I wondered whether we were going to go all the way to Dien Bien Phu dancing like that.

I'd never seen anything like it. I could remember going to see *South Pacific* with my first real boyfriend, Craig Norbert, who wore a crew cut with butch wax, and how my mother chaperoned us. I could remember that big crazy woman in the movie who loved life (and the sailors, too), who sang about a beautiful place called Bali Hai. Those scenes with the fake palm trees and the clear blue water on some back lot were just wonderful. The endless green below us was how I'd always imagined it—Bali Hai. Pineapples and palm trees and rivers like silver snakes going forever. A place you could get lost in and never mind, a whole bunch of people singing in the background, and laughing—having a great time. Nothing could be dying down there in all that greenery. How could it? It was green and growing, just like Jack's beans. It was a Walt Disney movie—you know, *The Living Jungle*, where snakes try to get the birds and the furry little mammals, the ones we like best, but always blow it. After all, we don't want those furry little mammals to die, do we? Monica the Monkey gets away, so does Stevie the Squirrel, and the snake, who isn't like us at

all—and who'll starve to death someday because he isn't—keeps
on trying, because Mother Nature wants him to. But we know
whose side Mother Nature is really on.

If there are people living in the jungle, they always respect the
animals, of course. They know what Mother Nature wants, too. In
fact, the Living Jungle is a lot like Paradise. No one wears clothes.
No one really sins. Only the hunters and the jewel thieves and
builders—who are out to destroy the land—ever wear clothes, or
sin.

The people who live there eat fruits and nuts. You never see
them kill a thing. The furry animals get away, and if the snake
does starve to death in the shadow of some big green leafy tree, we
really don't have to watch it. It's not exactly something we want to
watch.

The chief sees me staring out the door, hands in my lap, and
slides over beside me. These choppers aren't as loud as the Hueys,
I tell myself. The turbine whine is higher and the doors keep the
howling wind out. The chief doesn't have to shout.

"Sure is beautiful, isn't it?" the chief says.

I nod. I smile.

He doesn't say anything for a while, just sits there beside me
on the metal bench. I wait. I keep waiting for him to smile, too.

He doesn't. I wonder why. And then, all of a sudden, I know.
Please don't ruin it, Willie.
We're going to be there soon enough. Don't ruin it yet.

"There's this little snake down there, Lieutenant," he says
suddenly. "It's about this long." He makes a line along his prosthesis with the fingers of his good hand. "If it bites you, you die
two steps later, Lieutenant. That's how they measure it. That's
how it gets its name." He waits. There's more coming, I know.
Don't do it, Willie. Please. "There's another snake, too, Lieutenant—about the length of your arm—the most beautiful green
thing you've ever seen. It'll kill you, they say, in just one step.
Everyone jokes about it, of course. What else can they do, Lieutenant? It's real. It's down there, Lieutenant, and it's been there for
a long, long time."

Please, Willie.

"Some even say there's a quarter-step snake. Your leg is up in the air. It doesn't even have a chance to come down once. I believe it, Lieutenant. Do you want to know why? Because any place that can kill you in as many ways as this one can, could have a snake like that, Lieutenant. Any place as beautiful as this one with so many, many ways to kill you, could easily have a snake like that."

Charlie Two-Step . . . the Two-Hop Chuck . . . I've heard of these things, but I always thought it was a joke—the kind people make when we're afraid. *Why are you doing this?* I want to say.

"The Viet Cong, Lieutenant, use the littlest one as a booby trap in the tunnels around Cu Chi, Hung Than Tich and Long An. They tie a string around its neck and slip the creature into a fresh section of bamboo. When your shoulder hits the bamboo in the dark, the snake drops out on its little string and it bites you. It *always* bites you. They know this, the VC. They've lived with this little snake for thousands of years. They *know.* I've seen three tunnel rats—these three little Americans—laid out on a sheet of plastic, Lieutenant, all three of them the same day—black and bloated from the venom, the tiniest teeth marks you've ever seen." He clears his throat. He takes a breath. "There are pictures of snakes like those in *National Geographic.* Maybe you've seen them. They really are a beautiful snake, Lieutenant."

I don't move. I don't say a thing.

"There's a booby trap, Lieutenant," he says. "It's made of mud and about four dozen bamboo points. When you touch the trip wire, it swings in low and catches you in the groin. The VC *know* a wounded man will keep one or two others busy. They know how afraid any man is of being hurt in that place. There's also a booby trap that's made with a C-ration can, a grenade and some string. That's all it takes. The C-rat can and the grenade are ours. Sometimes the string is, too. When you set it off, Lieutenant, the little string pulls free and you lose a leg or two, maybe a little more. Maybe you've seen the results. There are over twelve hundred different booby traps, many of them made from the junk *we* leave behind, the metal we've dropped on their villages, even our own dud rounds. What these people don't use to feed their families with, Lieutenant—to keep their families fed and dry with—they use to kill us with. Twelve hundred different devices, all of them designed just for that. They've been down there—these people—for a long, long time, Lieutenant. And they're going to be down there for a long, long time to come."

I nod. I know what he's saying.

"It's the most beautiful place in the world, Lieutenant," he says quietly, "and it wants to see you die."

We haven't taken fire since Nua Than Chu. The engines roar with a rhythm. Our bodies are numb from the vibrating steel. Some of us are almost asleep. The chief is still beside me, silent.

"Like that," he says.

At first I think he means the jungle, that he's going to say it one more time, just in case I haven't understood it. But then I see them—the little things rising from the jungle like pale green birds, the littlest birds you've ever seen—flying up from the trees by the river.

They're flying right at us. They're flying right at us, yes, but now they're veering away. They look—I want to tell him this—like little green hummingbirds, like little green sparrows, bigger and bigger, closer now, then veering away.

"Have you ever seen anything as green as that, Lieutenant?" he asks me.

The Emerald City of Oz, I think. *"The Girl with the Green Eyes"—that wonderful movie. Robin Hood's merry men? Baby booties when you can't get them in pink or blue.*

I nod. They're beautiful, but what are they?

"There's nothing prettier at night than those things, Lieutenant," he's saying. "You've never seen a Spooky, I'll bet. You've never seen the red rain of its gattling guns streaming down on the jungle, the weird light from its flares, the green vines of light that reach back up to it from the jungle, trying their best to pull it down. . . ."

When the rounds—the *tracers*, he calls them—start hitting us, they're *plinks* and *thuds*. I start shivering and can't stop. The men arrange their flak jackets under them like little old ladies, then help me arrange mine. The chopper banks and before long I can't see them anymore.

He's beside me again, his prosthesis hard against my leg. I want to say: *Do you see something, Willie? Do you see a light, like a halo, like napalm, starting up my arms, inch by inch, the minutes ticking by? Am I covered with it now, Willie? Is this why you want me to know about beautiful things that kill? Is my halo still to come—though you're sure, you're absolutely sure, it will? Is it beautiful, Willie? Is it terrible, but beautiful, to behold—like the face, the radiance, of God? Is it a lie prepared by the Liar, or is it a blessing from our Lord?*

Is violence ever sacred, Willie? Do the holy ever kill?

I don't say it. He doesn't want me to die, that's all. He doesn't want me to die any more than I want him to. He's seen me glow—I know he has. I've dreamed his death. He knows that, too. Slowly but surely, Colonel, we're becoming what you've always wanted us to become.

I was scared, but didn't want to think it.

In six hours it would be night. We would be there. The choppers would drop out of the darkness, we'd jump out with our trunks, the choppers would leave. We'd *be* there. We'd take a step. We'd start walking through the night and never stop.

Did the jungles of North Vietnam look the same as these? I wondered. Did the rivers? Did the night?

Any place in the universe is different when you're afraid, Mary.

I know.

We'd have our third moon, but it wouldn't give us much light. Clouds were gathering to the north. Rain, hard rain, was beginning to fall—

Like cold rice. . . .

How had Willie put it?

Like cold rice on your father's grave.

That's the oldest curse they have, Mary.

We refueled at a little camp sixty klicks north of Luang Prabang, the ancient royal capital where the Mekong makes its crazy loop and the narrow Nam Eu joins it. I saw why we needed more choppers. Ten of the fastest Orientals I'd ever seen came trotting out of a corrugated shed at dusk—team locker and duffel bags in their hands—and piled into one King Bee, while we threw ourselves into another. Steve went with them and I didn't know what I felt. *Let's go. Let's stay. Let's get it over with, or never do it at all.*

Chopper pilots weren't supposed to fly in weather like that, I knew, but ours were the two best storm jockeys—the two best night fliers—SOG had, someone said. What did that mean? Did it mean that bad weather really *is* all right to fly in, if you're good enough, if you don't get blown from the sky? Did it mean that some pilots were talents—whether they knew it or not—and it somehow kept them alive?

Or did it mean we might not even make it to Dien Bien Phu?

One of the Nungs has to speak English, I'm telling myself. *That's why Steve went with them, right?* Steve doesn't speak Chinese, so one of them *has* to speak English, right?

Let's go. . . .

Let's not.

We make it. A couple of shots from AKs in the jungle, in the fading light—just to let us know they're there, they're going to be there for a long, long time—and the choppers are up and the little camp spins away.

"What do they dream of?" I ask Lieutenant Bach.

"In the North, Lieutenant?" he says.

"Yes," I say.

"*Many*, many things, Lieutenant," he says. "But most often, perhaps, of those who have mistreated them."

Chapter 30

We hit the western side of the mountain range—just below radar from Lai Chau and Son La—at nightfall. The two empty ships head north to make noise—engine trouble, botched insertion, what you will—and we drop like boulders to the mountainside, to the coal-black darkness. To the south, I know, is Road 41-A, down from Dien Bien Phu, across the Laotian border toward the upper Mekong. At our backs, northeastern Laos—its share of the Golden Triangle. To the north, a little piece of North Vietnam, and as the mountains rise to ten thousand feet, China, the Himalayas, headwaters of the Mekong—three thousand miles from where the great river enters the sea. You can see all of this in the *darkness*.

To the east, I know—on the other side of this little mountain range—is *our* valley, waiting for us in the night. High in that range—looking down on Dien Bien Phu, the forty or fifty villages there, the ten thousand people who inhabit them and have done so for three thousand years—are the last Meo tribes, the ones who know opium, how to grow it, who to sell it to, to keep their villages alive. On the valley floor, by the Nam Youm River, by the Pavie Track built by the French, by Road 41-A, are the Black Tai—children of the Lai Chau Federation—who buy the Meo opium and know, in turn, where to sell what they cannot use. These are the ones, dressed in black—not white or red like their cousins to the east and north—who helped a French officer hide those bags of "fire clay" in the limestone caves of the foothills, at the end of that long siege, on a dreary May 7, 1954, as the northern monsoons began again. These are the Tai whose prostitutes, trapped in the bunkers with the French, joined the "Angel of Dien Bien Phu"—the lone French nurse—to keep the wounded alive as long as they could. *These Tai are still there,* Harry told us, *distrustful, fighting the arms of Hanoi, loving the lowland Vietnamese no more than they ever have—and the Vietnamese, in return, knowing no better what to do with them than they ever have. Except to pretend that there are no real differences between them, to make them obey, and occasionally—when a general, a colonel, a political commissar can arrange it—to take some of their opium away.*

Just past the valley of Dien Bien Phu, I know, is Road 41-B, the one Ho and Giap used to bring ten thousand Viet Minh to the valley, arranging them with their genius on the surrounding hills, like a great dark necklace, the artillery pieces so well hidden the French Air Force *never* found them, the barrels aimed *down,* into the valley, so that nothing could get in or out; the road over which Giap brought his "army of ants," which no one, he told a French general once, would ever be able to defeat.

If you take 41-B northwest, ladies and gentlemen, you'll reach 41-A in a day—and just beyond that, the winding dry-weather road through the Tinh Ma Mountains, to the River Noire. If you take the Black south by southeast, you will, in two days, leave the ragged karst mountains behind. You will enter the Hoa Binh Delta and the paddies that never seem to end. And then, if you head north from that famous Bridge of Peace, you will reach the River Rouge, and thirty-five kilometers down it, toward the sea, a little innocuous village called Dong Noi—

And the dike that has been there for a hundred years.

We drop, we rise again in the darkness, clouds boiling above us, rain tearing, wind howling. We don't *have* an LZ where someone's been kind enough to pop purple smoke, a flare, flash a mirror, show us cards. Our LZ is wherever the pilots, with their infrared and starlight scopes and talent—if they have it—decide it will be. "The blades won't clear," someone shouts in the cockpit.

"Yes, they will," someone says right beside me, standing up in the dark. *How would* he *know? He's a SEAL.* Does he know? Is he wearing goggles, too? Do his halos work this way? Or has he been inserted so damn often like this that he just *knows*?

The pilot thinks so. We plummet and this time we don't stop. Somewhere Steve, our ATL, wears starlight goggles, too. It isn't a dream. He's in the chopper with the Nungs, because the captain is in ours—wearing goggles of his own.

It's as dark as any darkness I've ever seen, Mom, and I'm thinking: *There's no moon—they lied—they even lied about the moon.* But no. It's there—the moon is there. It's behind the boiling clouds.

I'm thinking a scream or a moan or a shout would help—*anything* to break the nerves that are making it harder and harder for me to breathe. But you can't scream here. *Someone might hear, Mary.*

There are little lights at the front—red and green and white, a tiny Christmas tree, and for a second I think it's the valley—or fire on a mountain peak, or a factory that isn't on our maps, but of course it's not. It's the cockpit. It's the lights the pilots see. *They're the only lights in the world, Mary.*

We're going to jump—I know that. "When your feet hit the ground, Mary, *bend*," Steve said. I can hear him saying it. He *ought* to know. He's got his wings. I'd be a fool not to listen, but. . . . "The instant you hit, let your body keep going and you'll be okay. It'll be ten feet at the most—soft ground, mud and leaves, I promise. You may hit a log or a branch, but don't fight it—just let go and roll."

"You'll be sore," the chief said. "You'll twist an ankle, you'll scrape a fucking shin, but you won't break a bone."

How can it be only ten feet to the ground when it's so dark, Mom—when you can't see a thing?

"It might be a good idea," Steve said, "if you took a pill, Mary."

We're dropping, nose up, tail down, rocking side to side like a great metal cradle. "Go!" someone shouts over the rain and wind.

Someone's gone. The darkness beside me is empty. "Go!" the voice shouts again.

"No," I say.

A hand takes me by the arm and the voice it belongs to shouts: "I'm going to wait for you to jump, Lieutenant. I'm going to be jumping behind you. I'm going to *help* you do this." When I don't move an inch, the voice shouts more: "The choppers can't stay here, Lieutenant."

I still don't move. I don't say a thing.

"Bach and Cooper are already down," it's saying. It's the chief—I know that. I can even see his face. I can see it in sunlight, crow's-feet, the Irish eyes, free of the darkness where people die. "Steve's down there, Lieutenant. The dog's jumped, too. Let's go."

I nod. He *feels* me nod. His hand squeezes once more, moves me toward the door. The wind howls—inches from my face. The rain moves every which way but down. The whole world bucks and swings like a hammock in a hurricane. Something hard touches me.

His pincher, I tell myself. *That's all it is.*

He squeezes my hand again with his and I go ahead. I do it. I jump.

I'm wishing I hadn't taken a pill, but now I'm glad I did. *Am I going to land on someone? Am I going to land on the damn dog? Am I going to turn my ankle, my knee, and they'll have to carry me, body without a body bag, for two whole weeks?*

If Bucannon were here, I'd push him out, I know. I'd tell him we were three thousand feet up and I'd listen to his heart stop—then push him out. Or I'd wait until we were heading home at last, and I'd do it then—above the jungle—when it wouldn't be a lie at all.

My left leg hits, sinks into something cold and wet. My right leg hits something slicker, twists, and I go ahead—I fall, letting myself do it, the pack too heavy, all of it moving so quickly I don't have time to shout. I lose something—the AK—grab for it in the mud and leaves, which I *know* are there, because I'm in them—I don't need to *see* them to know I'm *in* them, grabbing for the AK.

Two bodies hit beside me—a grunt, the other only a hitting sound. Boots suck through mud near my face, my hand, scrambling, and I find the goddamn AK at last. It's cold—like metal, like wind. It's as cold as the mud and rain where we're going. *It's the North, Lieutenant*, Bach told me. *A place makes you the thing you are. It is cold in the North, Lieutenant. There isn't much food. The rice bowls there are smaller, Lieutenant. In the eyes of southerners, northerners are cold. They never tell a joke. In the eyes of the northerners, southerners are lazy and slow—no longer "Vietnamese" at all.* . . .

My boots suck mud. The rotorwash lifts rain and leaves, everything whirls, and the choppers, suddenly, are gone. The silence is rain, only that. The choppers—with all their noise—are finally gone.

A hand slaps my back, my front—the signal—the direction we're going to take. I take a step, but my knees don't work. The patellae, the cartilage—did I hurt them after all?

I take a step, fall, knees sinking into mud, shins slipping with sharp little pains down *something*—something hard that hurts. I get up, legs shaking. *Adrenaline, Mary. That's why you're shaking.*

"Get up, Lieutenant," a voice whispers. Was it spoken at all? My neck tingles. Something brushes my eyes—inside my skull— and I know who it is, who's there. A thin hand—bony and cold— grabs mine. *He's wearing goggles, Mary. He can see you. He can see everyone here.*

Even without them, Mary, he'd know.

Will I dream his death? Will I see his death, too, Steve, because he's touching me now?

You took a pill. Remember?

Will I dream it anyway, Steve?

Another hand—bigger now—grabs my other arm. The thinner hand lets go.

Did he see Willie grab me? Did he see it with his goggles—or did he hear someone thinking: "I'm taking Mary's hand now. I'm worried about her." Did he hear a woman thinking, "It's Willie. That's his hand now"?

"Move it uphill—five minutes," the voice with the goggles

says, the words nearly lost in the wind and rain now. Boots suck and slip, rain slaps the tops of the lockers which arms and shoulders are lifting, and we move—we move. It's leaves now, not mud. I can feel them under my boots. They're wet and slippery, but at least they're not red red mud. We'll be away from the landing zone soon. We'll be safe from that.

We stop. I hear clasps and hinges swing free, items pulled from the lockers in the hissing rain. A uniform is pushed in my face. *He can see you, Mary. With the goggles—he can see you and he's handing you your clothes.*

We're going to become Russians now.

Will he watch me? I wonder. *Will he watch me undress in the dark?*

I'm trying to remember and can't: Steve? The captain? The chief? How many of them have goggles?

Should I ask them *all* to turn away? Should I say, "Steve, *you* can look. You've seen this body before. But you, Captain—you can't. You can't either, Willie, if you don't mind."

Which is worse? I ask myself. *Naked in the green ambient light of those goggles—the eyes ten feet away? Or a man who can hear your thoughts, Mary?*

I can't help it. I see a picture—of myself, naked in a mirror in the dorm at St. Mary's, worrying that my hips are too wide, my breasts too small. As I do, I know what I've done.

If you *see it, Mary* he *sees it, too.*

I go ahead. I undress in the rain.

We move again. I'm going to do it by sounds, just sounds, I tell myself. I'm at least going to *try*. I take a step. I hear rain on leaves. I don't hear the trees—I can't hear logs and limbs. I take another step, slip and try not to fall. I cock my head like a dog—that should help, I think—slip again, getting up as quickly as I can. Why can't I *do* it, Steve? My knees are holding. Am I walking with my weight too far back? Is it the *leaves*—would anyone slip on leaves like these even if they could see them?

I don't know—and now it doesn't matter. Someone's taken me by the hand—and I know that hand. It's wet, it's cold—like everyone's tonight. It's the *fingers* I know. They know me well, too. They touched that body in the mirror . . . because I wanted them to.

I squeeze the hand back and neither of us says a thing. The hand pulls. I follow. I don't fall.

Are Cooper and his dog at point, or is the captain the one now? A scout dog with a nose and a good set of ears and eyes much better than ours in the dark? Or a man—our team leader— with goggles, who can hear others think in the dark? *Who's up there tonight, Mary?*

I hear bodies behind us and I know it's Nungs. *They're carrying our things, Mary. Guys like them have always carried our things.*

I want to stop him. I want to say: *In a darkness like this, Steve, it's easy to see too much.*

I see a hundred different teams like ours, inserting on a thousand different nights. I see every *movie* I've ever seen. I see Bwana, his porters, his girlfriend in khaki shorts, who twists her ankle and has to be carried. I'm the girlfriend—and then I'm not. I see Kirk Douglas blow up a dam, blow it up again and again and again— and I'm with him, helping him. And then I'm not. I'm waiting for Kirk Douglas and a man who looks a little like Steve to come back, but they never do. I see John Wayne trying to save a Vietnamese village—running back and forth across the screen. He keeps trying. But he dies in the red red mud right beside us. He keeps dying, again and again, so it must have meaning. He keeps dying so the audience will know it does.

Keep holding my hand, Steve, I want to say, *and don't die on me, please.*

Everything grabs you in the darkness. Everything's wet and slick and it grabs your feet, your arms, your neck. Little limbs that dig against your face, then snap away—they grab you. They grab you again and again. Broken branches that snag you, holding on too long—they do it, too. And the vines—the ones they call *wait-a-minutes,* because that's what you say when you stop, try to undo them and *can't*—they grab you and they never let go. They're *alive,* you tell yourself—they've got to be, you think—Sleepy Hollow, dripping trees, a grinning head tucked under a horseman's arm, a horse rearing, a terrible voice in the rain. These are woods the Prince must travel through to find her—to kiss her again and again, like a dam blowing up in another world—so that she can wake at last after the long, terrible sleep.

I fall. I don't *want* to, but I do, Mom. If I can stay on my feet at the 21st, if I can stand there for seventy-two hours straight, why can't I stand up here? Why do I need these men to hold me up?

Steve takes me by the arm and I push the hand away. I get up myself, I take a step, I keep on walking. When I fall again, I let him. I can't slow the others down. So I let him.

Near us another body falls. It scrambles. It gets up. I shouldn't, but I do: I grin. I'm thinking: *See, Mom!* A man *is falling, too.* I imagine a hand pulling that body up—making it feel weak, making it feel like wide hips and little breasts. But that's not true. *He's a man, Mary. He'll get up by himself. And even if he doesn't, he won't feel the feelings you do.*

Beside me, Steve stumbles, grabs my shoulder and almost falls.

It isn't men *and* women, *Mary. It's darkness. It's mud and rain, that's all.*

The jungle in the highlands is thicker, I remember hearing. It isn't as tall, but it's thicker. We're moving slowly and finally we stop.

A body passes near us in the darkness, and a moment later a machete starts hacking toward the front. *No one will hear it,* I tell myself, wanting to believe. *The sounds will be lost in the rain. No one will hear it.*

The rain is quieter now. I hear bootsteps on twigs, stones and leaves. I hear giant drops, too, gathered on leaves as big as platters, dripping down to other leaves. It's loud, I tell myself—it's louder than boots could ever be, right? I cock my head. A nurse's dreams are worthless here. But we've got a captain *listening.*

We move faster, then slower, then faster again. The jungle *always* grabs. We stop again. We start up again. An animal crashes through the trees beside us. A bird cries—a harsh sound—without an echo, swallowed by the rain. Our boots slosh, wet sticks crack in the darkness. The rain falls even harder, drowning every sound out. I shiver. I'm wet. I don't like this one bit, but the fear—the fear of other things—says: *You don't know what a* really *bad night is.*

His hand is in mine. He's waiting, I know, for this darkness to turn some wonderful shade of blue.

I don't know what I want, Mom. Do I want—walking here in this darkness, *toward* an enemy instead of *away* from him, remembering dreams that no one else has ever had—to know what will happen, because we're walking *toward* it, and not *away*? Or do I, Mom, want to be safe from knowing? What did *you* want, Mom? What did you want when you were a girl, and then later a woman? There was a war. You told me. There was a Depression, which was hard. You told me that, too. Did you want to know what was coming—when the war would end? When *he* would be coming home? The answer to a question like *Will the world ever be simple again?* Which presidents would die—and *when* and *where* and *why*? How long you would live in Long Beach—when you would move there—and why. How much money he would make—and what that would mean. Did you want to know, so long before it happened, what your husband would be like at forty-five—what kind of man, what kind of human being—angry and unhappy, though he'd never think of leaving? If you'd known these things, Mom, would you have gone ahead and done them anyway—married him with all that anger, had children with him, a football player and a nurse, lived in a house you never liked because that's what *living* means?

All *I* want, Mom, I think, is to have his hand in mine tonight, to walk through the Pike and pretend I'm scared, because boys always want it that way. I want—I think, Mom—to have his hand in mine, to laugh and say, "Gee, it's dark. Think any junkies will roll us? Think any tattooed bikers will kidnap us? Think our parents will be willing to *pay*?"

I want him to be a boy *forever*, so I can be a *girl*. I want to go home once more, not knowing I've even left it, and feel sure that a country with red red rivers couldn't possibly exist—or if it did, that people like us couldn't possibly live there.

I want to see all three of you in the car, Mom, on Pacific Avenue, the sun coming out of the rain, the three of you waving—coming toward me to hug me and say: *"You've made it, Mary! You've come home!"* I want to hear that—or feel the other feeling: *that I never even went away.*

That's what I *think* I want, though I'm never sure.

The machete barks like a dog, stops barking, barks again, clears a way through the darkness to a ravine (you can tell by the sounds, Mom) where runoff rises to our knees. The darkness *is* water. It would be scarier, I know, if we could actually *see*. Perfect ambush sight, AKs and carbines sighting on our necks. *Some things are worse than darkness, Mary. One of them is* light.

We climb through another stream, slipping on streambanks we never see. The Nungs don't make a sound. They're there but you wouldn't know it—if you didn't already know. They'd like to take off, I'm thinking, to leave this craziness behind as much as I would, but a thousand years of hereditary pride, bone-deep loyalty, their fathers' dreams, keeps them walking alongside us in the dark. *Manhood and duty*, I'm thinking, *mean many different things.*

We start up the other side of the ravine (you can feel the slope in your feet, in the muscles of your shins, Mom) and I'm thinking: *Is this the last—is this the last ridge we'll need to climb?* Our valley, with its ginger fog of winter, with its swollen, bankless Nam Youm, its people staying as dry as they can inside, is just on the other side. It's waiting on the other side.

Dien is what they call it now, I remember.

The place where so many have died.

When we reach what *feels* like the top of the ridge, it *is*, thank God, the top. Your muscles know it. Your ears hear the absences, seeing better than eyes. There aren't any lights—no skylines, no airfields—to say, "This is it. The valley's down *there*." But the sounds you're making in the wind and rain bounce off nothing—no trees, no rocks, only air—and you *hear* it. You can *hear* them disappear.

We're covered with mud. We're wearing uniforms that aren't ours. How can we really think they'll believe us?

I squeeze Steve's hand. He squeezes back. *It's just like a date, Mom,* I want to say.

Walkin' . . . with my angel.

Letter 9/18/71, 1st Lt. Stephen Balsam to Katherine Narbush, Command Files (Personnel), Operation Orangutan, *Tiger Cat, Vietnam*

Dear Kath,

Sorry I've been such a bad letter writer. I won't give you any excuses like being out on missions. That may be true, but it's no excuse.

I guess you're right—that we ought to be seeing other people. I don't want you to have to be the Nun of Atwater, and there are American women here at the bases that I'd at least like to be able to talk to without feeling too guilty.

What we have is pretty special, Kath. I just hope we can be honest with each other.

Love,
Steve

Chapter 31

It's hard to describe, Major. It was sounds and things touching you in the darkness, just like a field trip, a camp-out, but one that makes you *afraid*. Things that wouldn't normally mean anything—the leaves, the branches, the rain—make you *afraid*. The darkness only makes it worse. Do you remember lying in bed as a kid, afraid to put your hands over the sides into the darkness, because you *knew* something was there? How much *darker* it was under the bed—how much *darker* it was in the closet—and how *something* was there?

I'm sure you felt these things, Major.

It didn't help that we were heading toward *caves*, of course. Toward the biggest, darkest closets in the world.

We went down the side of a 4,000-foot mountain, sliding at least half of the way. We went down slick slopes that didn't have a thing growing on them. Ravines that had too much. The valley was there but we couldn't see it in the dark. Clouds covered the moon. Fog covered the valley. The world ended a yard or two from our boots.

I kept thinking of those sand-table mock-ups they'd made for us in Vientiane. I kept filling the darkness—my head—with things like that, to make it a little better. We were moving, I told myself, down the eastern face of the Sop Nohm Range, north of Road 41-A as it left the valley, heading south. We were just east of Strongpoint Isabelle. The caves were just west of that. We were, I told

myself, moving down foothills to the limestone caves where people
had been hiding things—weapons, gold, poppies, even themselves—from Chinese warlords, Kuomintang bandits, roving Tai
and the lost tribes before them for ten thousand years. To the caves
carved by water washing through karst substrates, carving it for fifty
million years—until some of them were big enough now to hold
an army or a thousand bags of clay.

I kept thinking of Tom Sawyer and Becky, filling the darkness
with them, too. Was it going to be like that? Were we going to find
a *dead man*, a treasure, all sorts of scary things we could laugh at
later—a story to tell our friends, our families years from now,
when we were grown-up and had kids of our own and could look
back with a smile?

Or would my dreams come true?

Would we die? Not here, no, but on a riverbank somewhere.

In the red red mud.

We group in the darkness at a stand of young trees. That's
what it *feels* like. Slick bark, trunks like posts dripping rain around
us. We crouch. We wait. The wind is gentler here, near the valley
floor. The rain has stopped. If anyone is following us, we'll hear
them. The dog will—the captain will—even if the rest of us don't.

A hand slaps my back, I jump, I hear muffled slaps around
me, and we pull in tight. If we're going to talk things over, it'll be
here, yes—near the valley floor, heel of the foothills, far from the
villages where *ears* might hear.

I close my eyes again. *How long will the pill last? How long
will it be until I dream again?*

"Plan change," the chief whispers. "Cooper, Kelly, Balsam
inside. Bach, Damico, the Nungs *outside*."

There's a cave? I want to say. *We're near a cave?*

"No," I say, thinking of all those movies where the men try
their best to leave the one woman behind—but she won't have it.
She's spunky, yes. She's as good as they are. She doesn't, goddammit, *want* to be safe.

"No," I say.

"It's not your call, Lieutenant," the chief says. They're not going to let me go. Even Steve will say, *You'll be safer outside, Mary.*

"No," I say.

The chief sighs. He says: "Captain?"

I can feel the captain *listening*, but I don't care. *He's seen you in a mirror, Mary. He's seen you undress in the night.* I don't say: *Get out of my skull, fucker.* I don't say: *I hope they kill you last.* I'm thinking to myself: He'll hear the enemy coming, Mary. He'll hear what they're thinking when they come. He'll be the one who keeps us alive here . . . so that the dream of a riverbank can come true.

He hears it all. He *knows*. I go ahead and let him.

"Okay," he says at last, and it means: *Let's see what you can do for us, Lieutenant.* It means: *I know why you want to go.*

I want to be with Steve. I want to be with them all a little longer before they die.

I know, he says. *I know.*

The chief sighs again. "All right. Let's move."

Someone takes my arm, my hand.

"Steve?" I say.

"Yes," he says.

"We're going to be okay here, I think."

"Glad to hear it," he says.

The rain starts up again, hard—

Like cold rice on a father's grave.

It takes us another two hours to reach it. It wasn't near us at all. No one says a thing the whole way. When I see the light at last, I think it's *moving*. I think it's someone holding a light and moving with us through the trees. The bootsteps behind me stop. I stop. So does the light. *It isn't moving. It never was.*

A hand in front of me finds my shoulder, squeezes twice, and I do the same to the body behind me, the way we were told.

We move quietly, no rain to cover our sounds, and when we stop once more, it's inside the treeline—where we can crouch, where we can watch this light.

It's a fire. It's a fire inside a cave. The cave is so huge the fire lights only a corner of the mouth. I stare. We're like animals, crouched, staring at the light.

Three young men in NVA uniforms are arranged around the fire, and we're closer than I thought. The fire is small. The three young men wish it were larger, of course. One stands in front—between us and the flames—arms raised, uniform backlit like some dark angel. One squats to his right, resting on his heels, the way these people do. The third stands by the lip of the mouth, almost in the rain. They're inside, keeping dry, that's all. *Are they really that stupid?* A fire too small to keep them warm, a cave too large for the heat, the young men themselves too close to the opening to stay warm. *Why don't they move back, Mary?*

We stay crouched. We wait.

Quiet pats move down the line—*Wait*, they say—and we do. I lean forward, craning for a better look, and an arm stops me: *Don't. Don't even move.*

The young men have AKs. They have what looks like an LMG, too, tipped against the wall of the cave. *What does it mean, Steve?* I want to ask him. *Why are they* here? *Does anybody understand?*

They don't have rucksacks. They remain near the mouth of the cave. One paces, one kneels, one doesn't move at all. But they're nervous. They glance again and again back into the cave. They could be warmer back there, but there's something that's making them nervous.

I get out my little envelope. I open it with barely the whisper of a sound. I take another pill. *This is enough*, I'm telling myself. *I don't want any more than this inside my head.*

A wind brings a smell. Something dead.

There's something dead, a voice says suddenly, *in that cave.*

The rain is too quiet. One of the three soldiers gets up and turns, as if hearing us, says something to the one silhouetted by the fire, and that one nods, saying something back. A no? A yes? An *Are you kidding?*

They're waiting for something. You can see it in their bodies, the way they move.

The rain stops again. The silence is the kind you hear your

own heart in, roaring, and one of the three speaks again. The one squatting makes a sharp sound back—if it were us, it would be swearing—and the other shrugs, maybe agreeing. The trees drip. White ginger fog rolls past the mouth of the cave. Without knowing it, they've moved even closer to the overhang, dripping with rain, too. The fire is behind all of them now.

They're not waiting for someone, I realize. They're waiting to *leave.* Something's making them nervous. They're about as close to leaving as three bodies could be, without actually stepping from the cave. *Someone's given them their station. They've been here a while. They want to go now. They want to return to those dry barracks at Dien. They're nervous. They just want to go, Mary.*

The one who likes to talk checks his watch, says something. One of the others grunts back.

They're a patrol, Mary, that's all. They have their valley rounds and schedules—caves, road, Nam Youm, five or six villages—whatever the CO at the garrison wants them to do. He's not really worried about area security, but this is what he wants them to do. They're cadets at the academy—it's nothing more than a kind of KP. Or maybe it is. Maybe there *is* a threat to the valley's peace and quiet—from disgruntled Tai, angry at all the transplanted Viets, at the Viet villages that were built, half of them abandoned but half of them hanging on with surly looks. From *moi* who live in the mountains. Perhaps the CO even daydreams of American commandos choosing *his* valley—passing through it on their way to some action in Hanoi. He's bored. He dreams of excitement, and his cadets have got to help. Perhaps he's a stickler for military discipline—something you need out in the boonies, right, Colonel Ninh?

They check watches again and again, and finally, laughing, pick up their AKs and walk from the cave. We watch them. They take the path—the only one we can see—toward the valley floor, which is there in the darkness, in the rain and fog, even if *we* can't see it. We don't get up yet. We wait.

I check my watch, too—the Soviet Krostu luminous face they've given each of us. It's thirty minutes before we finally get up. Legs straighten, nerves tingle, blood starts to move, we sway, moving paralyzed legs. *We're going in at last.*

We do it at a running crouch, so the fire won't catch us in its light, turning us to dark angels, too. We do it low and we do it running.

When we reach the mouth, there's that smell again—filling everything now.

There's something inside, the voice says again. *That's why they wanted to leave.*

"Jesus!" someone whispers. It's an incredible smell. Burnt hair, draining wounds, open bellies, old blood—all of it filling the air. The kind of smell you never think is possible until you work on a ward, in Graves Register, or visit an open mass grave.

You *can't* be sick, Mary. You *can't* bend over and make that silly noise and do it here. You're a nurse, Mary.

So I don't. The dog whines once, like he's going to die, his nose on fire, acid in it, and I feel better. Even this dog—who never makes a sound—is whining.

Someone swallows loud enough to hear. Someone else coughs, and these things help, too. *It's affecting them, Mary. It's affecting them, too.*

Even commandos throw up on occasion, Mary.

Our eyes adjust, but our noses don't. I see other hands, faint in the firelight, covering their noses, touching their throats, trying to keep the coughing from ever starting—because once it does, it'll only get worse.

This is the biggest, closest cave to Strongpoint Isabelle, someone says.

It's the one Lanierre would have used.

Chapter 32

We slip behind the fire, keeping to the shadows. Even thirty feet inside, the smell is a lot worse. We stop. We listen. There isn't any wind, any rain, any light. The silence—the silence and the dark—makes it worse. You can't *think*. It's that strong. You can't *see* and you can't *think*.

"What *is* it?" someone whispers.

No one answers. I'm trying to breathe through my sleeve—through anything at all that'll keep the smell away. The sleeve is wet and muddy. It won't let me breathe.

"Yes," a voice says suddenly. There wasn't a question, but the voice says, "Yes," and coughs. It's not the smell that makes it cough—it's the voice that always coughs. *How can you stand it here, Captain?*

"They're here," the voice says, and for the first time I hear the fear.

They're dead, the voice says—someone says it, or I think it—*but they're still here. They're still here.*

I'm listening, too—for sounds outside the cave's opening and sounds farther into the darkness. I'm thinking of that tunnel rat from Long An, lying on the gurney at the 21st, wondering how he stood it—nine months in those tunnels until the day he took the bayonet in his gut and two small-caliber rounds in his pelvis as he dropped down through the hidey-hole, where they were waiting—so patiently—for him. I'm thinking of his friend—his face clear enough in the dream—the peace sign on his jacket, his initials, hiding their love this way. What was the earth like down there, Billy? What was it like not to *see*, but to *smell* and *hear* a world— the dark damp one to which all rotting things, enemies and lovers both, must go?

"Yeah, right," the chief whispers. "There's something dead here, but we've all had our shots, so let's go."

"Chief?" Cooper says suddenly, his voice tight—like he can't breathe either. "The dog can't work in this, sir," he says, and he means: *We* can't work here. He means: *I smell it the way he does, sir. I'm sorry, but I do.* He stops. We wait, listening. When he's through getting sick, we keep waiting, wondering who's heard it— if they're going to come.

"Fuck it," the chief says—and he means the dog. We're all getting sick and now—*Fuck it*—the dog's nose won't even work.

"You all right, Corporal?" Steve asks.

"Yes," Cooper answers, then starts to lose it again.

If the smell makes *us* sick, what must it be like for the dog, Mary? Flowers don't mean a thing to his nose. Metal doesn't either, and neither does stone. These are things that have never mattered to his kind. But *bodies? Flesh? Blood?* The *rot* of flesh, buried and dug up, this has mattered for a million years. What must it be like to smell air like *this*? Air that makes you crazy?

What must it be like for his handler, who smells it, too—

Because that's how it works, sir.

When the dying fire is behind us, all of its light lost to the dark, we stop again. We listen. We listen in every way we can. Someone starts to say something, doesn't, and flashlights appear at last—blinding us—because someone has decided it's okay. Our eyes adjust. The beams of light rise slowly and we see the faces we are. Someone has decided it's okay. Even if it isn't, we still need them to *see*. In darkness like this, starlight goggles are worthless. There *is* no ambient light, Mary.

The flashlights are like the ones at the movie theaters—little cylinders on the ends of them to guide the light, to keep it out of others' eyes. We move. The lights are bright moths, flittering ahead of our boots, on the cavern floor, along the walls—where the trip wires, pressure pins, booby traps, would be.

The air change—a current—a little draft. You notice these things, Major, when there's so little to see—your nose in your sleeve, the flashlight beams jerking across the cool, damp floor. You don't understand it. You're moving deeper into the mountain. *How can there be a draft?* Is there a room? Are you coming to it? Is there a fault, letting air in, a sinkhole, carved by the same waters that carved everything else?

Does the draft lead to the dead man's treasure, Tom?

Something flies over, beating raggedly. A bat. Another. Like those little strings hanging in the darkness at Disneyland—on Toady's ride. The breeze from its wings—to make you scream.

I can't see the flashlights. I'm at the end of the line. Someone reaches back, touches my front—the right-turn signal—and I follow it. I follow the wall as it curves to the right. The air changes. You can feel the tunnel open up, the smell hitting you harder as you step into a darkness that's got to be *big*—a *chamber*, another *cavern*, the reason for the draft? The wall—the slick stone—is *cool. Everything* smells here. Even your fingers. Even the stone. The smells of a jungle are far away, and these—the smells here— will be on your skin forever. Where are the stalactites, Steve—the stalactites that have been dripping here for a million years, the ones they love to make with cement and yellow paint on the Matterhorn, another Magic Kingdom ride with a thirty-minute wait? The tunnels of Cu Chi and Long An are different, I know. They're not *karst*. They're black earth, red clay, airless, pressing against your chest and neck until you want to scream. This is spacious—like an ocean, waiting, at night. *Try to enjoy it*, I tell myself, *even if it does smell*. Telugo would have loved it, would have taken his friend—the one with the peace symbol—here and said things to him that he could never have said outside.

I don't see a thing. I don't even try. I walk faster and the flashlights, curving along the chamber's wall now, come back into view. A flash of limestone—a stalactite at last. Smooth rock, a molten puddle, no longer dust. The flashlights move to the left, getting smaller, and I feel the *fear*. I walk faster to catch up. *The wall is curving, that's all*, I tell myself quickly. *The flashlights are following the wall.*

"Steve?" I say.

No one answers. I walk faster, trying to hear a breathing that isn't my own. *"Steve?"*

He answers with a *Shhhh*, like Tom would. His bootsteps stop, his hand takes my shoulder, then my arm, pulling me on. I breathe again—and wish I hadn't.

The smell is even *worse*. How can that be? *Handkerchiefs. Why didn't we bring handkerchiefs, Captain?*

There's something in this room—you should have foreseen it, Captain. You're team leader.

I want five sixteen-layer gauze masks to increase team effectiveness. I want them through S&R immediately. Throw in a muzzle while you're at it, so we'll have something to hold on to the dog's face with.

The gagging stops. It's mine. There's a whine at last, a cough, the one he always makes, and something touches my neck. We move again because we can't stop. The cavern is *immense*—you can feel it in the air.

There's something here, Mary.

I know.

It's there—in the center of this great room.

I know. . . .

Everyone feels it now. Everyone stops, bunching up in the darkness. The flashlights quiver, taking a moment before doing what they know they've got to do. We don't *need* to see it. We know it's there. We can *smell* it, crawling in our eyes and throats.

The smell of pseudomonas, gangrene, clotted blood. I know that smell—but from another place, from the hallways, ER and post-op rooms. How can a smell like that be *here*? How can it be *ten times worse*?

It's right next to you. In the center of the room, Mary.

I know.

I want to leave. I want to get away, stop fighting the smell and finally breathe. One of the flashlights moves, does what needs to be done, and when its thin beam of light touches the center of the great chamber, I go ahead—I do it—I get sick again. What else is there to do?

The flashlight passes over it again and it's different now. I *want* to see it, as the beam passes again. I think of Auschwitz or Dachau, those old black-and-white pictures in *Life* magazine. Those black-and-white movies some American soldiers took— when Americans opened the gates of places like those for the very first time. No. It's different.

It's in *color* here. There's a color for every smell you smell.

They're like strange dolls, sleeping like that together. An arm pulled from its shoulder, hanging by a slick white thread. A leg twisted back, like it never really had bones. The faces flattened into themselves, sinking the way the faces of the dead always do, as if they had never had skulls. The chests are thick with gas, bellies bloated, the women's legs spread apart, hands to their genitals, as if afraid something might touch them there. In the flashlight beams the penises are shriveled, as if cold. The hair is like wigs— matted—drifting free of the skulls. The bodies have settled into one another like brothers and sisters, sleeping.

The eyes are either closed and sleepy or open and dull—like sanded glass, like windows in the fog. The black paint is blood. The things that move like rice and corn under the skin of those bodies are exactly that: *things that move.* I can't help it. I get sick again.

Someone else does it, too, and I think: *It's all right. It's all right to get sick.*

The beams of light don't stay long in a single place, but that isn't a help. That doesn't make it any better.

No one makes a sound. If there's a buzzing, it's on the bodies—or in our own blood, moving behind our eyes, across our necks, as one of us *listens* and the rest of us watch.

The bodies on top have more color. As they should. They're thinner but more solid than the ones below. The earth hasn't taken them yet.

I'm not telling it the right way, Major. Those weren't bodies.

You tried—you wanted to see them that way, but they *weren't*. They were a single draining thing, changing in the dark, trying its best to become something else. The air, the earth. . . .

"Captain?" the chief whispers.

The captain doesn't answer.

"Captain?" the chief says again.

A flashlight moves from one muddy pair of boots to the next, looking for the pair it wants. It doesn't touch faces. They would look like the others, I know.

Fifteen or twenty feet past me, the flashlight finds the boots it wants. The light goes up the legs—to make sure—and then down again. The body that holds the flashlight follows the beam, brushing by me, heading toward the boots, and when it reaches them at last, says:

"Captain, are you all right?"

"Yes," a voice says. *No, it says.*

What are you hearing, Captain? I want to ask him. Is this what it was like—in the dark, hearing what the others in their cells couldn't—listening, even though there was no sound? Is this what it was like—the smell of flesh turning to fluid, eyes as blind as ours, while you learned to listen, when the others could not?

What are you hearing now, Captain?

"I'm sorry," the voice says suddenly, and it isn't speaking to us. "I didn't know. I'm sorry."

"What, sir?" the chief says.

The voice doesn't answer.

And then suddenly—to *all* of us—the voice says:

"Please. Please get me out of here."

Photostat, Journal Article, Command Files (File: Kelly, Robert E.), Operation Orangutan, Tiger Cat, Vietnam
Vietnam Era
The Prisoner of War: Precaptivity
Personality and the Development of Psychiatric Illness
by Robert J. Ursano

In contrast to the apathy syndrome identified in

Korean War POWs, the subjects in the present study showed a marked movement toward character rigidity, a decreased interpersonal relatedness, and a heightened drive to master and achieve, accompanied by the experience of time pressure. Such alterations are neither pathological nor beneficial in and of themselves, but depend on the starting point of the personality structure. What may produce an obsessive-compulsive style in normal subjects may lead a basically dependent individual with little self-motivation to a more productive personality style (subject 4).

Personality changes reflect both adaptational and intrapsychic shifts. Character rigidity (manifested in isolation of effect and a stubborn, unifocal determination) and a decrease in interpersonal relatedness clearly served an adaptive function in the captivity environment. . . .

Chapter 33

"Balsam," the chief whispers. "Get over here."

Steve's hand lets go of mine and his body moves away. The flashlights are off. There isn't any light now.

When his bootsteps stop, the chief's voice says: "Do you understand what's happening here?"

A flashlight clicks on, flashes on a face—the sunken eyes open and staring—and then clicks off again.

"No," a voice says loudly, but it isn't Steve's. It's the captain again, answering a question we haven't heard.

Then the same voice says: "*I can't.*"

"What the hell is he talking about?" the chief says. "Do you know?"

"I'm sorry," the voice is saying, almost crying.

Someone is going to hear us, I want to shout. *We're being too loud*.

"It's the room maybe," Steve's voice says at last. "Maybe he's picking up something from the room. . . ."

Of course he's picking up something, I want to scream. *He can hear them.*

"There's no one here," the chief is saying.

We're all talking louder, as if nothing could harm us in a room like this.

"We don't *know* that," Steve says.

No one says a thing and then the chief says: "Let's get him out of here. He wants out, let's get him out."

It starts again. I can feel it in the sockets of my eyes, as always, moving on like a beam of light I just can't see. The chief is saying, "Jesus. What was that?"

Don't you know, Willie?

"That's what it feels like," Steve says, "when he's *listening*. Haven't you ever. . . ?"

Don't you know, Willie? Don't you know why Bucannon chose him?

The feeling comes again, touching us all, tingling, moving faster and faster around the little circle we've made. The chief's voice makes an *Uh!* like a stomach punched. The dog whimpers. The black kid whimpers. It passes through us, frantic, as if trying to hear, trying to understand something, unable to, and then the captain's voice, nearly crying, says:

"They're dead, but they're here. They're still here."

Back in the tunnel the smell comes with us, but the voice is calmer. The chamber—with all its bodies—is a hundred meters behind us. It isn't talking to him, it isn't breathing in our faces anymore. The voice says nothing. The body it belongs to is finally able to walk on its own.

The wall turns and we stop. Slaps move down the line and we backtrack to the "Y" where the branch began. Another slap—*let's talk*—and we bunch toward the flashlight that's on.

The light counts our boots and paws.

"How's he doing?" Steve whispers. The flashlight stays low, and I don't know which *he* he means.

"Better," the chief answers. And then: "How's the dog, Corporal?"

Cooper has a hard time starting, but he manages to say: "It's driving him crazy, sir."

"If it weren't," the chief says, "you'd be able to work in the dark, right, Corporal?"

"Yes, sir," Cooper says. "There's a touch code, sir."

"Captain?" Steve says suddenly.

The flashlight moves to the captain's boots and waits. The captain doesn't answer.

"We need to talk about that room," the chief says, loud again, and I want to scream.

"Isn't someone going to hear us," I say, "if we keep talking like this?"

"Lieutenant," the chief says—and you hear him take a breath, like *Be patient with her. How's she supposed to know?* "There's no way in the world anyone's going to be in these caves. To the people of this valley there's nothing in this place worth breathing this stink for, and if there were, the garrison down the road would have removed—or burned—these bodies a long time ago and posted guard forever. Again, Lieutenant, don't we need to talk about that room?"

"Yes," Steve says.

"I saw bracelets," the chief says. "The bodies are tribal."

"Yes," Steve says.

"They can't be Meo. We're too low."

"Yes."

"Besides, Meo don't treat their dead like that."

"No, they don't."

"The Meo are civilized."

"Yes."

Why aren't you asking the captain? I want to shout. *Why aren't you asking the man who can* hear *them?*

Because they don't want to believe it, Mary. They don't want to believe he can hear *things in that room. No one wants to believe that, Mary.*

"You're the Yard expert," the chief is saying. "Have you ever heard of a burial like that?"

"No," Steve says.

"A reprisal?"

"Don't think so. Viets wouldn't have left the silver on them. And there aren't many battle wounds."

"No, there aren't, are there?"

"They died of natural causes and someone put them there and no one is planning to take them out."

"Because they're *afraid*," the chief says.

"Yes. That's the *point*, isn't it?" Steve pauses. "It's got to be."

We stay crouched in the darkness anyway, waiting—not completely sure—and finally Steve says: "They don't look *Tai*. They don't look Tai at all."

"Meo, then."

"Not at this elevation."

"No, I mean, what if *someone else* brought the bodies down from three thousand feet? Someone who didn't care about Meo superstitions? The bodies could be Meo, couldn't they?"

"The dress is wrong," Steve says. "The *faces* are wrong."

"Maybe the dead don't get dressed up," the chief says.

"They do if they're Meo."

"Okay. Okay. Then who are these guys?"

"Maybe they're Kha."

"What?"

"There's no one left."

I found his boots, his legs, not far from mine, and I whispered to him: "Captain, tell me who they are. Tell me why they're here . . ."

I whispered it again. He didn't answer.

"It's the smell," Steve was saying. "It's got to have something to do with the smell."

What we were looking for, I kept telling myself, was impossible to find. A hiding place that could've fooled the Vietnamese for fifteen years—billeted soldiers, transplanted Delta farmers, anyone else of the Vietnamese persuasion. A hiding place that could've fooled the Tai all those years. The only ones it wouldn't have had to fool, I knew, were the Meo, who believed that if one of their kind ever stepped below three thousand feet, into the land of the valley dwellers, he'd up and die.

Look for changes in the wall texture of the tunnels, the shirts had told us. Use your fingers or a light. Look for pits covered with wood, or tin, and a layer of dirt. Hit the floor with your boots, and listen for a difference. Look for ledges eight to ten feet up. Feel along the wall, feel for a lip of any kind (there won't be *ladder rungs* in the limestone, friends). Think like a Frenchman. Think like a platoon of fleeing Tai. Where would *you* hide it—and *how*—if you wanted to keep people just like yourselves from finding it for fifteen years?

Given ten or twelve hours to do it in—no more, ladies and gentlemen—where would *you* have stashed those goddamn bags of clay?

The smell would keep people out, I'm telling myself. Whether they were afraid of their ancestors' ghosts, of *phi*, of one god's anger or another's, the *smell alone* would keep them out.

They're trying to keep everyone away, a voice says suddenly.

"They're trying to keep everyone away," I say.

"Right," the chief says. "That's obvious. But why?"

Because something's there, the voice says.

I say: "Because there's something there, Chief."

"Okay. But what?"

What? I ask.

Something, the voice says, *we're not supposed to find*.

"Something," I tell them, "that we're not supposed to find."

Even in the dark I can feel the chief staring at me like I'm crazy.

"Of course, Lieutenant."

I know whose voice it is, so I go ahead—I tell them:

"The captain says there's something there."

The chief hasn't heard the captain say a word, so he snorts. Steve says:

"If she says it, she means it, Chief."

They're hiding something, the voice says.

"They're hiding something, he says."

"Who?" the chief says.

Who? I ask.

The voice won't say.

"It doesn't matter," I say.

"It fucking well *does* matter!"

"Shut up and listen," Steve says.

They're afraid someone will take it.

"They're afraid," I tell them, "that someone will take it."

"Take *what*?" the chief says.

I listen. I don't hear a thing.

"I don't know," I say.

"This is *bullshit*," the chief says. "You want me to believe he's getting a reading off that room. Okay, so he's getting a reading. But it can't be the fucking bags. That was fifteen years ago. *Those* bodies died *yesterday*."

I am—

"He is," I say.

—talking about the same room.

"He's talking about the same room," I say.

"We don't understand, Mary," Steve says quietly.

They don't know it . . . but they've got them in the same room.

I'm shaking like a leaf. I don't like hearing things this way, I don't like what it feels like to *hear* them, but I keep thinking: *He's chosen you for a reason.*

"They don't know it," I finally say, "but they've got them in the same room."

"Now how in the hell," the chief says slowly, "am I supposed to understand *that*? I'm sorry, Lieutenant, but I just don't believe you—I don't believe any of this shit."

You don't want to, I want to tell him. *It scares you and you don't want to . . .*

"I don't," Steve says, "want to pull rank on you, Chief, but we've got a problem. The captain is a *telerec*. Whether you accept it or not, he is. He *reads* people, and that's why he's with us. In fact, that's why he's TL. If you find this difficult to accept, I'm going to remind you that you had a hard time accepting someone else's talent a little over a year ago, too, and you know what happened. We *cannot* afford, Chief, to have your problem become *our* problem. I think you know what I'm saying."

The chief won't answer.

"Who's he reading?" Steve says to me.

"The bodies, I guess," I tell him. "I mean, whatever's there because the bodies are . . ."

"Nothing older than that?" Steve asks.

I listen. I don't hear a thing. I say:

"I don't know. I really don't."

"Why is it happening to him *here*, Mary?"

Because it's Dien Bien Phu, I want to say. *The Valley of the Shadow of Death. The French died here. The Viet Minh died here. Laotians, Nigerians, Moroccans, and Tai—all of them. There are more ghosts here, Steve, than you'll ever dream of knowing. . . .*

But I don't say it. I'm *listening*.

Yes, the voice says suddenly, *older than that, Lieutenant.*

"Yes, older than that."

"Thank him for us," Steve says suddenly, and to the chief—who's still angry—he says: "Let's take a look, Chief."

We try to take the captain with us, but he stumbles, keeps stumbling, and it just isn't going to work. We stop.

"You three go on," the chief says. "The captain and I'll stay here."

They're trying to keep everyone away, the voice says.

I know, I tell him.

The dead want us to be with them, but the living want to keep us away.

I know, Captain. I know.

We begin at the great chamber, holding our noses however we can. "Is it under the bodies, Captain—this thing that is hidden?"

Steve is the one who asks it.

I listen. I hear something. I say:

"I don't think so."

We try each tunnel that spokes out from the chamber. The first ends in a small room. The second deadends in nothing. The third has old shovels—wooden handles cracked, the metal rusting—and four piles of powdered limestone. *What are these things for?* I ask him.

He doesn't answer.

"Coal," Steve says suddenly. "Someone mined coal in these caves."

The air is cleaner here and we want the dog to try again. "Is the dog's nose working?" Steve says.

"No, sir," Cooper says.

"How do you know, Corporal?"

Cooper doesn't answer.

Believe him, Steve, I start to say.

I do, Mary. I do.

"All right," Steve says at last. "But let's give him a try anyway, Corporal, if you don't mind. Over by those shovels, say."

With the smell, we don't get hungry. We get thirsty, though, and we drink from our canteens. Our legs get tired. We stop where the tunnels end, where the smell somehow isn't as bad, where we can rest while the dog tries to sniff it out, keeps trying, doesn't turn up a thing.

I keep thinking we ought to go back, find the chief and the captain. I want to say: *I can't hear him this far away. I want to go back, Steve.*

We don't go back. We keep looking.

It takes us four fucking hours, Major, to find that little ledge.

Steve's flashlight is following the wall where it joins the ceiling, just like Harry told us to. There's a wall and a ceiling and then suddenly no wall at all.

It's here, the voice says—distant, but there.

"It's here," I say. Everyone stops.

There's a wall beside us. The flashlight shows it again: Three feet from the ceiling the wall disappears.

Hey, there's a *ledge*—a ledge eight feet up, three feet from the ceiling—just like you thought there'd be, Harry. A ledge no one was *ever* supposed to see. *Everready batteries, ladies and gentlemen. The miracle of American know-how.*

The flashlight follows the ledge. The ledge travels for ten feet, and stops.

An ambush ledge, like you said, Harry. *The caves should be full of them. The Tai have used them for a thousand years. When you use something that long, ladies and gentlemen, you often use it again.*

The flashlight crawls along the wall once more, trying to understand what it's found.

"I don't think it *is* an ambush ledge," Steve says.

"What?"

It's here, the voice is saying. *It's always been here*. . . .

A knife appears from the darkness, falls inside the beam of light, and begins to scratch at the limestone.

"Someone *made* this wall," Steve says.

The flashlight turns off and for a moment no one says a thing.

"The captain said, 'It's here'?" Steve asks.

"Yes," I tell him.

"Is your animal getting anything, Corporal?" he asks.

"No, sir. No, he isn't."

We make a ladder with our hands, Cooper and me, and we hoist Steve up. He plays the flashlight into the darkness on the other side of the wall and says: "There's a room. Can you get the dog up here?"

Hands still linked in mine, Cooper steadies his legs. The dog stirs in the darkness beside us. "Not like this, sir," Cooper says.

"What, Corporal?" The flashlight casts eerie shadows on the ceiling above us, then disappears again into the darkness beyond the wall.

"We need to trade places, sir," Cooper says.

"Right."

Steve gets down and we hoist Cooper up. The flashlight shines in our eyes for a moment, then on the ceiling, then on Cooper's face, too, out of control. It steadies. "Are we supposed to *lift* the dog up to you, Corporal?" Steve says.

"Yes," Cooper says, "you'll need to do that."

"He won't object?"

"No, sir. He may *wonder* a little, but he won't object."

"Give me a little light, please," Steve says. Cooper does.

Steve leans down and says something to the dog—the way you would if you were just a little worried—and turns his face, just in case. When he puts his arms around the dog's middle, the dog gets nervous. Cooper says "Easy," Steve grunts, and the dog is rising in the air. He's too heavy—he's starting to tip, to slip ass first into Steve's face—so I step over to help and pushing and pulling we get the dog up where Cooper can grab and pull and get the dog all the way to the ledge.

Something falls into the darkness on the other side, lands lightly, makes the patter of paws in dirt. Cooper reaches down to me, Steve grabs me around the legs, and up I go too. The wall's thick. It's enough of a ledge, thank God, that we don't all pitch over it together. Steve scrambles up with our four arms pulling him, and then, one by one, we help each other down the other side into the darkness.

The flashlight steadies on the floor. The dog shakes once, dust flies—motes in the flashlight's beam—and then the flashlight begins to crawl around the room.

It's not another great chamber for the dead. It's twenty feet across, that's all. But it is a *room*. It has the feeling of a *room*.

The flashlight moves. Dust. The curves and bumps of lime-stone walls. "It's a crude cement," Steve's saying. "Limestone's perfect for it. Powdered rock and a little water. You don't need shoring."

No one's been here in a long time, I tell myself. Dust from the tunnel—dust carried, ever so slowly, up and over that man-made wall—covers the floor like the surface of the moon. There are footprints, but they're old. They're covered too.

"No one's been here in a long time," Steve says.

I know, I want to tell him.

The flashlight moves on, checking the floor, the ceiling, the walls, and when it stops, it's on the farthest wall. It stops the same way it stopped before.

Steve walks over. We follow. The light touches the wall like braille.

"This is manmade too," he says.

You store opium in these caves. You store whatever you don't want other people to find. You put your son, your brother, your cousin on a ledge up high like that, around a corner, and give him a big field of fire. You shoot anyone who comes by. You throw their body on the pile. The smell of it will keep people away. You take any room you like. Or you make your own room. Limestone's soft. You build a phony wall—one you can climb back over. You make it look like an ambush ledge, because then, if people see it, they won't even give it a second look.

Is that it? Is that what we've found?

"Could you please bring the dog over here?" Steve says, flashlight still touching the wall.

Boots and paws move toward him.

"Is it any better for him here?" Steve asks.

The smell isn't as bad—but there's still a lot of it.

"I don't know. He's acting funny, sir?"

"In what way, Corporal?"

"He thinks he hears people."

"Does he? Does he hear people?"

"I'm not sure, sir. Yes. Yes, he does."

Yes, the voice says suddenly. It's as if the body it belonged to were standing beside me.

What? I say.

There are people, the voice says, *on the other side of that wall, Mary, and the animal hears them.*

"Is the captain talking again?" Steve asks.

"Yes," I say. "Yes, he is. 'There are people,' he says."

"Where?"

"On the other side of that wall."

"Your dog's right, Corporal."

"He can *hear* them, Corporal?" Steve asks.

"Yes, sir. He can't smell them through a wall like this, but he sure can hear them."

"What exactly does he hear, Corporal?"

"Excuse me, sir?"

"Voices, footsteps or what?"

"Metal, sir. He hears metal."

"I don't understand."

"He's hearing metal hitting against metal, Sir."

"There's a signal for that—some signal from him to you that means metal, Corporal?"

"No, sir, there isn't."

"Then how do you know?"

Cooper doesn't answer. I say: "He doesn't need a signal."

"I see," Steve says.

Believe him.

"I believe you, Corporal. I do. . . ."

Cooper and I sit in the darkness with Crusoe, waiting for Steve to bring the chief and captain back. We have a flashlight, sure, but we don't turn it on. We talk as loudly as we would back home. I say: "They can't hear us, Corporal?"

"Not unless," he says, "they have a dog like ours."

Or a captain, I want to say.

When they arrive, we help them over the wall, too. We stand in the darkness, the six of us, and play the flashlights around. We stare at the farthest wall, cock our heads, and hear nothing. We make the dog sniff the floor, even if his nose isn't working. We wait for the captain to say something.

Who are they? I keep asking. *Who are the people on the other side of the wall?*

He doesn't say a thing.

When we're tired of standing there, we climb back over. We check the closest tunnels.

We find two shafts leading to a vein of coal—low-grade—abandoned by the French long ago. More shovels, more little piles of limestone powder to make the shoring walls. We have the dog sniff them too. We have him sniff *everything* just in case. We have the captain stand like a doll beside us, too, even if he's not saying a thing. We do this until Steve and the chief have had more time to think.

"The entrance to it," the chief says finally, "has got to be outside."

He's talking again. He isn't angry anymore. He's had time to *think*.

"Right," Steve says.

Yes, the voice says, the body right beside me. *But they're in the same place.*

292 • Bruce McAllister

I say: "The captain has just said: 'Yes, but they're in the same place.'"

"All right. All right," the chief mutters. "I believe you. I do. But what does it mean?"

That's all the captain will say.

"Did you check the floor by the inside wall?" the chief asks as we head back through the darkness toward the entrance, toward the rain, toward a valley cloaked in fog.

"Yeah, the dog gave it a sniff," Steve answers.

"I thought his nose wasn't working."

"It isn't."

"Great."

The captain is walking beside me. I can feel the crawling on my neck—on the skin of my neck.

There are people on the other side of that wall, he tells me suddenly.

Yes, Captain.

I—I just wanted you to know. . . .

Letter 8/11/71, Command Files (Personnel), Operation Orangutan, *Tiger Cat,* Vietnam

Dear Aunt G and Uncle Joe,

I'm a lousy letter writer, and I'm sorry. I think about you both every day and wish I had the discipline to put those feelings down on paper right when they come. You know what I'm saying.

Please keep clipping those articles. The last one was very good. The writer didn't have all of his facts straight about Thieu, but he made some *very* good points.

We've got a long-range mission coming up, which means that none of us on the team are going to have much of a chance to write for quite a while. Even if it's a little longer between my letters, please don't worry.

Give each other a big hug for me. I love you both

very much and want you to know how much I appreciate everything you've done for me.

Love,
Steve

P.S. Do you remember if my father ever talked about having premonitions or anything like that? Do you remember if my *mother* ever talked about him having them? I'd like to hear when you have a chance.

Chapter 34

I don't know how we found our way back to the mouth, but that's what Green Beanies and SEALs are for—like cats and bats and owls. At the "Icebox" at Fort Bragg, Steve told me once, they're put in drums of water. The tops are welded on. If they've got the same fears you and I do, they start screaming, they have to be let out, and they don't get to be Green Beanies. *Better to find out here than over there*, someone tells them. At Coronado they're dropped into a swimming pool at night, hands tied, buddies fouling their air lines, their masks, to see if they'll go crazy—the way you and I would. At Ft. Bragg they're tortured, too, *just a little*— kept awake, slapped and grilled until they're crying—so they'll know what it's like to have *friends* do it, and it won't be so bad when the enemy does it too. At some point they even start to like it, Steve said. The *darkness*. The *water*. The *jungle*. The *night*. They eat snakes and keep eating them and after a while it isn't strange anymore. They learn how to build walls with limestone and a little water, bridges with chicken wire and rocks, schoolhouses with anything you can think of. Then they learn how to blow the bridges and schoolhouses up, using piss and fertilizer and thinking to themselves: *I've been able to do this since I can remember. I was born to do these things, wasn't I.*

Soon they can slip out of a canal, out of the familiar stale-milk stink of it, and make their way down a tar-black path—one they've been down so many times before—dressed in black pajamas just like the natives—down to a village like all the other villages they've stolen into, ever since they can remember. They can enter a hut, just like every other hut, and know where the province official and his family are sleeping, where they've always slept—even what it feels like to lie on those mats, the way the province official and his family are doing. They can hear the province official's family breathing. It sounds to them like their *own* family—back home—breathing in *their* rooms at night. They can pinch the nose of the man they've come for—gently, as they would a child's—and know even without seeing it that the mouth is opening slowly in the darkness, needing air, not waking. They can stuff the rag into the mouth, bind the little body quickly, lift it as if it were laundry—their hearts calm, not missing a beat, because everything is so familiar—and steal away without anyone ever waking. Just like they could back home—just like they can remember doing as kids, ever since they can remember. As they return up the tar-black path smelling all those familiar smells, they know it's over, that they'll be drinking beer with other SEALs on a familiar barge in an hour, maybe two, that they'll climb out of that same canal—or one just like it—tomorrow night too, and the next, and each time they do, it'll feel familiar. Like coming home again.

Anything can be familiar if you live with it long enough, Mary, Steve told me. *Even war. Even death.*

Even death can feel like going home again, Mary.

Getting back to the mouth of the cave was easy, Major.

Bach and the Nungs were right where we'd left them. We stood for a while with them, right inside the treeline, gulping air. It was dark still. First light was beginning *somewhere*, but not here. The clouds wouldn't let it start here.

The Nungs take perimeter guard, and their leader, this stocky guy who speaks Vietnamese, joins us in a blind huddle.

"How long is it going to take Crusoe's nose to clear, Corporal?" Steve says. This isn't a cave anymore. We're whispering and the drizzle is barely enough to cover it.

"I don't know, sir. An hour. A little more."

"They teach you things like this at Benning?" the chief asks.

Cooper waits and then says:

"Some things they teach you. Some you learn."

The chief starts to laugh, but doesn't.

"We can't wait," Steve says, and turning to me, he says: "Do you think he's going to tell us where it is, Mary?"

Are you? I ask him, the body somewhere in the dark.

He doesn't answer me.

"No," I say.

"Then we'll have to find it ourselves."

"Please tell Son Chem," Steve says to Bach, "that as soon as we have light, we're going to look for an entrance. Tell him spider holes, air vents, the usual. Ask him if he has any suggestions."

Bach's voice whispers a stream of Chinese and another voice whispers something back. "Yes," Bach says. "He understand. 'Standard tunnel system design,' he say."

The chief laughs, can't stop himself, and we all say *Shhhh.*

"He's probably dug one himself," the chief whispers.

"You correct," Bach says, the b-girl again. "He say he has, Mastah Chief."

"We *don't*," Steve says quickly, "want people walking around on this slope like some damn Easter Egg hunt."

"No," Bach says, "we sure don't."

"Let's try a grid and make assignments, then. And tell them what they already know, Lieutenant—that there's no sense bothering with any open spaces."

Bach sings a little lilting song in Chinese and the other voice sings something back. "He say best bet is *co muc* bushes," Bach says. "Everybody use those, he say. For pee, boom-boom, everything."

"Jesus H. Christ," the chief whispers, and you can hear the smile on his face. "That guy ought to write a book."

By the time it's light enough to see, Crusoe's nose has cleared and he's the one who finds it. It's under a *co muc* bush, yes—thank you very much—and the bush is by a small rock slide. After all, *Tiensao*, who would *ever* look there?

"*Air vent*," someone says. "Eight inches across. Standard design."

"Nothing's new under the sun, is it," someone else says.

Crusoe is pulling at his leash, nose in the vent, drinking air as if it were rabbit blood. Cooper's got his eyes closed. He's breathing hard to me. I'm beside him. I can hear how heavy his breathing is.

"Did you know, Lieutenant," Cooper says to me quietly, "that a dog *sees* what it smells?"

He says it to me, just me. It's the first time he's ever said anything like it. But the chief is right behind us, hears it too, and says: "So what do the Yards down there look like, Corporal?"

Cooper's voice changes a little. "I'm not sure, sir."

The chief goes away. Breathing hard, without looking at me, Cooper says: "There isn't much color, Lieutenant. The colors are real pale. There are *two men*. The smells tell him this, so this is what he *sees*. They're the same kind—they're *men*—but they're different too. They don't *smell* the same—to him. They aren't *our kind*, and that's the biggest difference to him. The dog *smells* the difference, so he *sees* it too. They've been eating. They've been cooking with smoke. They go to the bathroom right there in the room, and he smells that, Ma'am, so he *sees* it too. They've been there for a *long time*. It's their *place*, he knows. He *sees* these things, Ma'am, so he *smells* them too."

I wait. I think there's something else he wants to say, but it doesn't come. It's the most he's ever said to me, I realize.

"It isn't something you can really draw a picture of though, Lieutenant," he says.

The Nungs break into groups of three. We do the same. We start to look for the entrance hole. "We find downhill," Bach whispers. "Entrance always downhill, he say."

"Chapter Five," the chief whispers, grinning, "of his goddamn book."

It's daylight and we're lucky. Sixteen people and a dog parading around a hillside—like they've lost their wallets. But the ginger fog is everywhere, glaring bright as snow. Visibility is fifty feet at the very most—enough to see, but not enough to be seen. *Someone's watching out for us, Captain,* I tell him. *Someone must like Russians. And ginger fog too.*

It's a Nung who finds the entrance under another *co muc* bush, this time by a hardwood tree. The tree's roots are cut away. The bush can be entered without breaking a twig: But the hole, I tell myself, is way too small. It can't possibly be for a *human being*.

There *couldn't* be all those things you hear about where the little tunnel ends: kitchens, cots, weapons caches, flood guards, boobytraps, and surgery rooms. Air vents hidden like bird's nests. Smoke chimneys hidden the same way. A little city underground, the kind the Chinese and the French and all the others who wanted to rule them had encouraged them to make. *They can't rule us if they can't find us, can they, Tiensao.*

That, Harry told us our last night in the house, *is the kind of thing that will defeat us all. We have bombed the shit out of the Trail, ladies and gentlemen. We have bombed the panhandle, Hanoi, and Haiphong. It doesn't seem to matter. In the nightmares we're having these days, we see tunnels in the South, tunnels that never end. We see underground cities and the endless supplies stored there. We see that it doesn't matter how much we bomb above ground. It doesn't matter where. Because all those supplies, all those tunnels, all those underground cities are sitting there, and we're never able to touch them.*

Resupply is the secret, ladies and gentlemen. It always has been. You won't read about it in the papers, no. You won't hear about it from Tricky Dick's lips. The truth, after all, is too terrible to talk about. Our nightmares, like yours, Lieutenant Damico, seem to be coming true.

That's why we want to see Hanoi drown.

And even then, Harry added, *who knows?*

It's about the size of a badger hole—something your dog might wiggle into, whining and digging like crazy after the animal that lives in the darkness down there. It certainly isn't something a *human being* would use. It isn't something an *American* would ever dream of using.

But somewhere, down below, there are people making noises, aren't there, Crusoe? You can hear them, I know. Your handler can, too. Is it metal on metal this time? Is it things cooking? Is it *voices* now?

"Yes," Cooper whispers. "He hears voices now."

"Can they hear us?" someone asks.

"Not if we're very, very quiet," someone else says.

Steve is smaller than the captain and the chief. The chief's got one arm. Bach, the smallest, isn't really the tunnel-rat type. And no one's going to send a black kid down. I keep thinking of bayonets, of little sections of bamboo with snakes tied of them. I keep thinking: *Please, God. Don't let Steve be the one.*

Why are we doing this? I want to shout. *Why are we risking* anyone *this way?*

But I do know why.

Because what we want, Colonel—what we've come all this way for—is in there, isn't it? We know that now.

The chief is looking at Bach, squinting in the glare of the fog. He juts his chin toward the smallest Nung in the group. The Nung stares back, then looks at his leader. He *can't* say no. He *can't* say, "Shove it up your lily-white ass, honky." After all, he's a Nung. He's been in tunnels like these before. He knows better than we do what's there to greet him. And as Buddha in his exquisite wisdom knows, a Nung is worth at least three Americans in a fight—and certainly six Vietnamese.

"Nungs will do *anything*," the chief says, grinning. I wish he weren't.

The little Nung nods at last. He has a family, witnesses, and his own pride, after all.

I'm looking at the chief and I'm thinking: *You're an asshole, Willie.* But I'm wrong. The chief has done things like this. SEALs and Green Beanies always do. He's had people point their chins at him, and he's nodded, too. He has a family, witnesses, and his pride.

"Please tell him" the chief says to Bach, "that we've heard a lot about Nung courage. Tell him it is certainly true."

The instant the little Nung lies down at the hole and starts to pull himself in, the captain steps over, grabs him by the legs and drags him back out. Taking the flashlight from him, he puts it in his own armpit, holds his Makarov in his other hand and gets down on the ground.

We're looking at each other. We're looking at the Nungs. They're looking at us, too, thinking: *Americans are sure* dinky-dau. *It's their giant—their tall captain—who wants to go.*

I'm thinking it, too, but I'm wrong again.

I *know* why he's doing it. I do. And he knows I know.

He'll hear their thoughts, Mary.

Yes. . . .

He'll kill them before they kill him.

Yes. . . . Yes, he will.

We wait by the hole, squatting like mamasans and papasans or Cherokee Indians at least. The Nungs don't move. They're so still you think they've gotten up and walked off into the fog.

Steve looks at the chief. The chief looks back. No one is going to say a thing.

When it happens, I jump. The sound is faint but you know what it is. You wouldn't even hear it if you were ten feet away, but you hear it *here.*

We look at each other and the sound comes again—another round muffled by the earth. Handgun? Something larger? You can't tell. Two shots. That's all you know.

We wait another twenty minutes and I listen, trying to *hear* him. When I can't, I think: *He's dead, Mary. They've killed him down there.*

And then a head comes up. Covered with red and yellow earth, it comes right out, wiggles like a baby being born. A torso follows it, and in a minute—no more—the whole long body with its dirty Russian uniform is free. Everyone's grinning. Nungs and the Russians both.

Standing up, the captain knocks the dirt from his uniform, doesn't even look at us, doesn't say a thing. I *listen.* I don't hear a thing. The captain steps to a rock, sits down and begins to take his Makarov apart. He does it in his lap.

It's dirty, of course, so he's taking it apart.

"How many?" the chief asks him, and then waits.

His fingers keep working on the gun. His throat doesn't move—it doesn't make a sound.

Two, the voice says to me.

"Two," I tell them.

"Two," the chief echoes. "Okay. Okay."

We move back to the treeline. We take the captain and the pieces of his stripped handgun and we wait inside the treeline for another hour. When no one comes—when the fog doesn't change, when the sky lightens only a little—we go ahead, we leave the captain with the pieces of his weapon lying in his lap, seated in shadows inside the treeline, and we go back to the hole.

"What's the plan, Balsam?" the chief says.

"What do you think it ought to be?"

The chief knows what Steve is doing, but it's okay. He's the team sergeant, so it's okay.

"You and the corporal and the dog," the chief says, "go down and check it out. You take a couple of Nungs with you—just for the sake of face. One-armed guys have a tendency to get stuck in holes like that, so I stay here with the captain, to make sure he gets his little weapon back together. Damico here—I don't know what she ought to do."

Steve nods and says, "Did you take a pill, Mary?"

"Yes."

"Then there's no reason for you to go down there, is there?"

Steve, Steve, I want to say. *I've been hearing the captain all this time. It's happening even with a pill. . . .*

When the last of them wiggles down through, I sit and stare at the hole. I get up, take the flashlight from the chief and go over to stand by it.

"How far down is the room, Chief?" I ask.

"Ten meters, maybe fifteen. The captain didn't exactly tell us, did he, Lieutenant?"

"Does it get any bigger?"

"*Of course* it gets bigger. There's a whole room down there, Lieutenant."

"I know."

I get down. I put my legs into the hole. I can feel a shiver go through my hips.

"You can't do it that way, Lieutenant," the chief says quickly, getting up. "You can't crawl *backward*. But you don't really want to go down there anyway, do you?"

He takes a step. I take a deep breath. I turn around. I stick my head into the hole, start to wiggle and pull myself in.

When I say, "Fuck you," he lets go of my boot.

It isn't the smell of rotting bodies, Major. It's other things—metallic, damp, bitter. Something wiggles with me, just under my hand—something that belongs here a lot more than I do. I jerk, thinking: *You are not going to scream.* My elbows hit earth. Earth falls on me. I can feel it on my shoulders, in my hair. The thing they've put in my arm *hurts now.* It really hurts, rubbing along the ground. I aim the flashlight. I aim it again. The earth falls into darkness ten feet ahead. The tunnel falls away. *This is where things crawl, Mary. This is where things hide so we can't find them.*

I'm breathing too fast. I'll hyperventilate. *I'll breathe in the earth. I'll get bronchiectasis. I'll suffocate with clods in my lungs. I'll die here and they won't be able to get my body out.*

The tunnel keeps sloping and I turn the flashlight off. It isn't worth the fumbling. I don't *need* to see. *There's a spacious room,* I tell myself, *only thirty feet away.*

If a little snake doesn't get me first . . . if a little piece of bamboo doesn't fall on me . . . if an Arc Light doesn't bring it all down.

When I see the light, it's awfully faint. I think: *They'll shoot you, Mary. They'll shoot you if you don't tell them who you are.* It doesn't make sense but that's what I'm thinking.

So I say: "This is Lieutenant Damico. Don't shoot, please!"

When I finally stand up—in a room at last, shaking the dirt free of me just like a dog would—I see their faces, and it's strange. They should be laughing. They're not. Their faces are saying:

Uh-oh. There's a woman here.

Chapter 35

I don't know what I thought I'd see in the room, but what I saw wasn't it. The room was no bigger than my parents' living room in Long Beach. It was lit by four wicker lamps that were hung by little smoke ducts carved in the low ceiling. Three of the walls were limestone. The fourth—the one I'd just come through—was dirt. The entire room was full of bales of something wrapped in big dry leaves.

The wall on the right had the white smears of handgun rounds. *Limestone does that*, I remembered someone saying. On the floor lay two moon-faced Montagnards in loincloths, black blouses and silver bracelets. Neither was moving. Even the blood in their wounds wasn't moving anymore. Ten or fifteen rusting shovels—the same kind we'd found in the tunnels—were tipped against the walls. Two woven mats, like cots without legs, lay near the nearest body. A third mat had what looked like food wrapped in smaller leaves, a lidded basket and a cast-iron pot half full of rice. The fire under the pot glowed. The rice wasn't even burned yet.

One of the bodies had knocked some bales down as it fell. The other lay spread-eagled in the middle of the room, like some crazy snow angel. Standing by the far wall—the one someone had made from powdered limestone—stood three Orientals in NVA uniforms, a young Russian with a flashlight and a young African in a Russian uniform, too. A dark, wolflike dog rooted and pawed behind the bales, its tail barely showing.

That's how it looked, the figures flickering in the lamplight, the faces turned toward me, saying: *Why is there a woman here?*

I knew these people, but I also didn't.

For a long time no one moved.

I *knew* what the bales were. The Meo raised their poppies like clockwork. In December, the juice began to run. There were Meo to bleed it, Meo to dry it, Meo to sell it—so the village of the Hmong, those "Free People," could make it through another year.

"Don't smell it, Dorothy," the Tin Woodman said. "If you do, Dorothy, you'll sleep forever."

They would need a place, dry and safe and near the valley, to store it. They'd hide the entrance near a hardwood tree, in a *co muc* bush. They'd—

No, that's wrong. The Meo don't—

"They're Kha, Mary," Steve says, looking at me as he says it—as if the others already know.

"Yes," the captain says suddenly, using his throat, his voice, which is hoarse, as always. "Yes, they're Kha, Mary," he says.

"He's *talking* now?" I say.

"A little," Steve says. "He does seem to understand what all of this is about."

Of course he does, I want to tell him. *Of course he does.*

Instead I say, "What's a Kha?"

"They've got the stuff, but they didn't grow it, Mary," Steve tells me. "They may have built this wall, but they didn't build the one inside—the first one we found. These shovels lying in the tunnels are *French*, Mary. There's a *fabrique* on every one of them."

"He told you all this?" I ask.

"He told us they were Kha."

And we figured out the rest, Mary, Steve is saying.

That's what Green Beanies are for, he's saying.

There are twenty-three major tribal groups in the North, I remember Steve saying once, when we first reached Vientiane. *It took us two weeks to learn them, Mary.*

That's what Green Beanies are for.

When he finishes, I *know* what it was like for them. The Kha are *shit*. They've always been *shit*. They were shit before the French arrived—and the French only made it worse. The Meo, a proud people, have always owned the peaks. The Tai, proud too, have always owned the valleys, the river farmlands. Even the French looked down from heaven and judged this right. The Kha went the only way they could—to the scrub jungles of the foothills—hating everybody and loved by none. They were shit when they first fled from Burma two hundred years ago and they're shit—the *moi* of *moi*—now.

Wouldn't you—if you were Kha, Mary—steal the poppy from the Meo, hide it below three thousand feet so they'd *never* come looking, hide it in caves where the NVA had rules against Tai—or anyone for that matter—gathering in unlawful assembly? Wouldn't *you*, if you happened to find it, prefer a room that already had a phony wall? Wouldn't *you* build another just inside that, to be safe, to make your room accessible only from *outside*? Wouldn't *you* leave your dead in the great chamber, rotting, keeping everyone away—smelling the smell, finding the bodies, looking in the great chamber if they looked anywhere at all, and even if they found your wall, even if they found your room, finding only the empty half of it?

Wouldn't *you* leave your dead to remind them of what they had done to you?

Wouldn't you?

"Who built the first wall?" I ask.

"Who do you think?" Steve says, picking up a shovel.

There are ghosts that old in this place? I ask the voice.

Yes, it says.

There are ghosts that old in this place, and you found them, Captain?

Yes.

"The Frenchman and his Tai," I say quickly. "*They* built it."

Yes, the voice is saying.

"Yes," Steve says, too.

The young African and his dog—Russian uniform and coal-black fur—are back behind the bales of dried-out sap wrapped in big dry jungle leaves. I can smell it. I can smell it like the dog can—not death, but dreams dreamed in a burning bush. I can see their dreams. A cash crop better than rice could ever be. *Can you blame them? What else will there ever be?*

I don't like what I'm thinking, but I think it anyway.

You didn't dreams their deaths. You were thirty feet away, that's all—and you didn't even dream their deaths.

I couldn't, I argue. *I took a pill—*

That doesn't matter. You know it doesn't. They're shit, Mary. That's why. That's why you didn't dream about them.

Yes. . . .

"How's the dog?" Steve asks, and Cooper says: "Fine, sir. His nose is working better here."

The air is clear. Fresh blood, not old. Bodies that haven't started to rot. Opium, yes, but that's okay. His nose can still work here.

No one's looking at the bodies.

"That's what I thought, Corporal," Steve says. "He's having fun digging, isn't he?"

"Yes, he is, sir."

"Does he know what he's digging for, Corporal?" Steve is grinning. Cooper is grinning back. They're having a good time.

"He sure does."

"He knows it won't blow up on him, Corporal?"

"That's right. He knows it's not that kind."

"You notice how much lower the ceiling is in here, Corporal?"

"Yes, I do, sir."

"Can you think of any reason why that might be?"

"Yes, I think I can."

"How about the ceiling on the other side of that wall? Is it as low?"

"Yes, sir, it is."

"Is the ceiling in the tunnel that low?"

"No, sir, it isn't. It's a good two or three feet higher."

"You're pretty good at this, Corporal—and I don't think it's your dog."

"Thank you, sir."

They're smiling at each other like idiots, like kids. They're not looking at the bodies, and neither am I.

"What is it like, Cooper," Steve asks suddenly, "to smell it the way he does—to find the things we've come all of this way for and *smell* it the way he does?"

"It's a little difficult to describe, sir."

"I'm sure it is. You want to do the digging, Cooper, or you want me to? Or do we just let the poor dog scratch his paws raw?"

Did you know it might work out this way, Colonel? I want to ask him. *The right talents traveling together, a dog, a cave, a room, a wall—a little luck?*

Or is this, Colonel, more than you ever dreamed?

Lanierre found a room deep in the tunnels, put the thousand bags on the floor and corded it. When he realized it was too far from where it would do the Viet Minh any harm—when he admitted to himself that he didn't really *want* his Tai to die that way—he had them cover the bags with earth, using shovels from the old coal shafts. He had them wall the little room up with the powdered limestone mix the coal diggers once used. He had them stop it at eight feet, so it would look like an ambush ledge, so he could feel certain no Viet Minh would ever find it . . . even if Black Tai from his valley just might, someday.

Which, of course, would be okay.

That's the story the captain told me, so it was the one I told everyone else.

The Kha found the room, seeing only a hiding place they might use, built a second wall for sound, and then outside, a tunnel to their stash. It was ingenious—and why not? It was how they'd *always* lived, scuttling like rats, stealing from others, while their world went on dying.

All of these people believe in ghosts, Steve tells me. *All* of them. The garrison soldiers stay away from the cemetery where the French and the Viet Minh martyrs lie. The Tai stay away—from anything reeking of death. No one in this valley—on these peaks, in these foothills—is going to come near that chamber, except the Kha relatives who bring their dead. The Kha are *real* smart, Mary.

Their own gods might be dead, but they know that other people's aren't.

What is it like, Captain? I ask him. *Are the ghosts of those dead Kha unhappy? Do they mingle with the French, with Giap's martyrs, with everyone else in this valley who's ever died—and call this valley their little heaven? Are they happy at last?*

Or are they waiting—*wanting so much to leave?*

Do they want you to help them get free, Captain? Do they say: Come join us. You're really one of us, Dai uy. *You're already dead,* Dai uy.

Do they scream at you in that great room when you can't help them?

Is it a little quieter here?

I dig with them. We all do. The dog steps back from the hole he's made, cocks his head, paws the air once with his right front leg and lets us do the digging.

I *know* it isn't nitroglycerine—a little glass vial you tiptoe around with in some old movie, afraid of blowing everything up—but I start shaking anyway when my shovel hits it. The shovel cuts through earth, takes earth out, cuts through more and then finally touches something different. It catches on canvas. The old canvas tears. It catches again—on something that *isn't* canvas—something that isn't earth—and I step back, shaking hard.

"It won't bite you," Steve says.

"Glad to hear it," I tell him. "But why don't you do the honors?" He looks at me. I look at him. He takes my hand. It's cute, it's sweet—and it does stop the shaking. "Thanks," I say. "No big thing," he says, and we hold hands just a little longer. No one sees it. The bales are in the way.

And then we lean over and do it together.

We pull the first bag out—rotting canvas and faded French letters, smell of earth, the pale "clay" barely cracked. We pull out another bag, then another, wiping the earth from both. The canvas on the second isn't even torn. *We're digging backward,* I think, *in time. We'll hear their voices, Steve—speaking French, then Tai? We'll hear* their *shovels digging, digging—the way the captain does.*

I look up. Steve's watching me.

"You're doing fine," he says.

"You bet I am."

When we've dug up every inch of the floor and every bag under it—moving the bales back and forth across the room like little bodies—we stop and count them.

We count them again.

"*Shit*," Steve says, looking at the phony wall. "Shit."

"You mean," the chief says, up in the daylight, where we've all gathered, "that some of those *fucking* bags are on the other side of that *fucking* wall?"

"Right," Steve says. "The floor goes right under it. They built the wall on top of it."

"*Shit*," the chief says, too.

It takes us all day and all night. Bag by bag through the little badger hole, while the chief and his Nungs go back through the cave's entrance, gathering shovels in the tunnels as they go. Inside, they work like crazy, digging up the floor on their side of the wall, pitching the bags up and over the phony ledge, carrying them through the darkness, through the smell, all the way back to the cave's mouth.

The patrol is punctual, of course.

They're the same young men, or maybe they're different—it doesn't matter. They build their fire. They stay two hours. They leave—glad to get away from the smell of ghosts and things. The chief and the Nungs don't make a sound. None of us do. *You'd be proud of us, Colonel. We're getting good.*

When we're finished digging up the room, we don't bother to take the bales.

We don't even bury the two Kha we've killed.

That's not what Green Beanies are for, Mary.

When we had our thousand bags—half a freight car, as the chief put it—and an extra fifty-three just to be safe, we moved everything half a klick into the treeline, bag by bag, and barely made it before the next patrol arrived. We kept quiet, and when they left ate our Russian rations. We hung ponchos from the trees.

We slept in darkness. "Jesus," the chief kept saying. "If they'd dug their little fire pit just a *little* deeper, Lieutenant . . ." It didn't take talent to know what that meant. "It doesn't really *explode*, Mary," he went on, "but my, does it burn fast."

Just before first light, the captain got out his NVN scrip, gave it to Son Chem, and Son Chem took six other Nungs away—to buy us ponies in Muong Tip, twenty klicks to the south. CAS agents out of Laos (run by you know who) said Muong Tip was the best bet, because: (1) There were ponies there—the tall Tai kind. (2) The White Tai who lived there were isolates—they wouldn't be chatting with anyone soon. And (3) even if they chatted, Muong Tip was southwest—the direction our ag team was supposed to be coming from.

"Do you want to take the poppy?" Steve asked Son Chem.

Bach translated. The head Nung said something, shook his head.

"It's *Kha* poppy, he say," Bach said. "Very bad ghosts, he say."

The Nungs who stayed behind started cleaning the bags with little brushes from the big lockers we'd brought. If one was torn, they sewed it. If it couldn't be sewn, they tore it off and put a new one on it—from the lockers, too. When the bags were ready, they stamped them with the words for "Special Rice—Property of Hanoi," or whatever *Nong Nhiep Lua Tan Nhong* means. They did it with little kits someone in Vientiane had concocted for us, and they did it in the dark, hitting each bag a couple of times. They didn't really care how it looked.

I offered to help them, but they stared, said nothing and I went away.

I lay on my poncho, in the leaves, under the rain, and thought:

Are you worried about us, Colonel?

Are you wondering how we are?

Wish you were, I told him. Just like a postcard. *Really wish you were here.*

Chapter 36

PH2 Leroy Culver, 224632690, U.S.S. Forrestal, *Yankee Station,*
Tape 1 Transcript

You're going to laugh, but it's the truth. I was on the *America*
in July of last year. I was performing camera maintenance on a
recon bird—an OV10 with a spotter dome. A bunch of red
shirts—those are the ordnance guys—come running by all of a
sudden. They're looking back over their shoulders and people are
shouting, "Clear the deck! Get out! Get out!" I look over and
there's this one red shirt, a kid—no rating stripes—sitting with a
500-pound bomb across his lap. How he got that way I have no
idea. Nobody does. He's reaching for the fuse but can't seem to get
ahold of it. I check the distance from me to the nearest catwalk
and I know that if the bomb goes off, I'm definitely going with it.
I'm not moving—I'm looking at the kid and I'm not moving.

Then this light, this pale white light, comes over the whole
picture. Just like *The Ten Commandments*. This beautiful light
falling all over Charlton Heston because he's so holy—that kind of
thing. Suddenly I'm not in control anymore. I know it sounds
funny. Something grabs me in this gorgeous light and I see myself—a hundred of me—stretched out in a neat row leading from
where I'm standing to this kid who's got this 500-pound bomb.
Time's completely stopped. Whatever's got ahold of me pushes me
forward and I flip through all these bodies—I mean, I move from
where I am to where the kid is through all these bodies. I'm think-

ing: "What the hell *is* this?" I'm thinking: "What *are* you up to, Leroy?"

You forget what it was *really* like—you always do with something like this—but I can remember thinking to myself: "This is what it must look like to God. This is what every second of the time we live in must look like to *Him*." I wasn't a churchgoer. I'm not now. I didn't get religion that day or anything—I'm not saying that. I'm just saying that for a second I felt something amazing and that as far as the people who were standing there were concerned I did something I really shouldn't have been able to do. I got to the kid and took the fuse. I did it awfully fast. People came up to me afterward and said, "How'd you get your ass over there so fast, Culver? We could *hear* it start to go." Some people didn't want to be near me. They wouldn't even talk to me—it made them feel that strange.

I dream about it sometimes, Major. Every once in a while I can remember what the light was really like, and I wish I could see it again, and know I never will.

Maj. Robert Consejo, 729574898, 35th Tactical Fighter Squadron, Tape 3 Transcript

They'd take your mosquito netting and say they had to wash it. That was the kind of torture they were into. They wouldn't beat you. Your natural painkillers would start to work if they did, and they knew it. After a couple of blows you'd just feel the pressure, that's all, so they had to find other ways. Without the netting, you couldn't sleep. It was a nightmare. You'd wake up and wonder what this black thing was lying by your face. It was your hand. It'd be crawling with them. Your face would be so swollen for a while that you wouldn't be able to eat unless someone helped you. You wouldn't be able to see, I mean. They'd take your mosquito netting and they'd tell you they were doing it for "humanitarian" reasons—"a dirty mosquito net carries diseases," that kind of thing— and they'd get more out of you this way than they ever could with a beating.

I don't think I signed anything I shouldn't have. You tried to make them work hard for it in any case. Just when they thought you were going to sign, you'd say, "No, the words aren't quite right. I'll sign—don't worry about that—but I want to make sure the words are *exactly* right." They'd go away and change the words and come back again. So you kept this up as long as you could. If they caught on to what you were doing—if you did it too many times, or if you asked for the wrong changes—they'd get mad and put you in the hole or let the guards beat you—or take your netting away. You had to be careful. If you could sign something— help them in some small way—without getting the other prisoners or your country into any trouble, you went ahead and did it, because then they'd think you were sincere. You'd have more influence with them that way. If you could get the words so garbled they didn't make sense, you'd feel all right signing it, too. If you could give them information that was out of date or so general it wouldn't help them, you could sign it. You gave them things that didn't matter so they'd leave you alone—so you wouldn't accidentally give them something important under duress.

If they weren't angry with you, they'd say, "If you show us that you know your errors, if you show us you understand what you have done wrong, we will let you go home." If they *were* angry, they'd say, "We can keep you here forever, Captain. We have French officers here—did you know that, Captain?" That was the last thing you needed to hear. It was the most frightening thing of all—that there might be prisoners who'd actually been here that long. And you knew that if they could scare you, you might give them something important under duress.

I remember more than once being so sick, so delirious, that I'd have signed anything if there hadn't been someone to keep me from doing it. Every time I was in that condition, there was this guy who would keep me from doing it. That's what I want to tell you about.

I'd be ready to sign whatever they had in front of me—I'd be telling myself, "Go ahead, Robert, sign it. Then they'll leave you alone"—and I'd see this guy in the corner of the room. He was an American. He'd be standing there just looking at me from the corner of the room. So I wouldn't sign. Having him there kept me from signing.

I didn't know who it was at first. Every time I'd get sick they'd take me into that room and I'd see him standing there in the corner. He was wearing the same prison clothes we were all wearing and I couldn't figure out why he was there—why they'd let an American stand in the corner like that when it was obvious what effect he was having.

It happened three or four times, I remember. Whenever I was sick. Once I went ahead and picked up the pen—I was going to sign it anyway, even with him there—and when I looked over at him he was actually shaking his head. They were *letting* him shake his head at me. I didn't do it after all. I didn't do it for one simple reason: he was shaking his head.

I didn't find out who he was until I was released. His name was William Schorr. He'd been captured in '64, one of the first PWs, I guess. He was a marine—an intelligence guy—an adviser. He knew French and German and Vietnamese and Russian—a lot of languages. He was a real intellectual. An Annapolis graduate from a good family. That kind of thing. He was very good with the Vietnamese, too, and with the Yards—the kind of guy you just knew was winning the war in his own AO. When the VC finally caught him, they caught him with two other advisers in the highlands. The VC executed the guy with him who was wounded, but they let Schorr and this other guy live. He did a number on them for two whole years. He was so smart he had the NVA writing coded messages for him to sign—messages to his family, to his commanding officer—and then he'd sign them and they'd send them out thinking they'd gotten some propaganda from him. They didn't know he knew all those languages—that he was sending prearranged codes that way—and when they found out, of course, they killed him. Just like that. They killed him in '66.

That's what I was told anyway. When I described the guy in the room to the people who were debriefing me they got up and left. The next morning they bring in this other guy who's just been released. It was the guy who'd been captured with Schorr. I described the tattoo on the guy's lower arm, this scar under the eye and a missing tooth, and maybe a couple of other things, and the guy sitting in front of me says, "Yeah, that's Bill all right."

He used to hassle them in that same room, the guy said. Schorr was part German—his father was German—and a week before they killed him they made him sign a letter to the President of the United States confessing his crimes against the North Vietnamese people. He told them sure, why not, but the letter had to be in German, he said, because his father was German—that it was a matter of German pride. This was something the NVA could understand. They knew about "face." They knew about pride and he *knew* they knew. He told them how he wanted the letter to read and the first thing they did was get some professor from the University of Hanoi to translate all that German for them. They didn't want another trick, but they did want that letter out of him before they killed him. The letter looked okay, so they went ahead and sent it.

It turned out there was a lot of slang in it—the kind kids from Munich use—double-meaning words, that kind of thing—and the whole letter really said the same thing. "Fuck 'em," it said. It said it in a dozen different ways. It looked pretty much like a confession when you read it one way, but in Munich slang it kept saying: "Fuck 'em." The press had fun with that. The NVA didn't get any propaganda use out of it at all, of course.

He died in '66, they tell me.

I was there from January of '69 to May of '71, Major, and he was in that room with me three or four times. I swear it.

I don't know if anyone else saw him, no.

Chapter 37

They found fifteen ponies in the first village, twenty-two in the second and twenty-three in the third, and nearly didn't have enough scrip to cover them. The White Tai knew suckers when they saw them and the Nungs had to trade Makarovs and an SKS carbine—all of the weapons Soviet, thank God—to get the very last eight. They should, someone remarked, have taken the poppy.

Getting the ponies to the caves from Road 41-B—which split at the southern end of Dien valley and which the Nungs would have to cross from White Tai territory to the southeast—was a bummer. There wasn't much cover, most of it was in daylight, and they had to divide the ponies into little groups, hustling them across the road like chickens. A *couple* of long-necked ponies you can hide—if they're not in heat—but a herd of sixty animals is straining Buddha's blessings. It took them until nightfall, Bach said, just to move them across the road.

On the third and fourth trips across, they had visitors—two Black Tai families about an hour apart. But the ponies looked local, the Nungs had AKs—comrade lowlander steel—and the crossing looked natural enough. The father in the first *pantai* wanted to buy four of the ponies. A brother in the second family wanted a rifle. Son Chem told him in Viet: "No way. Property of Hanoi, comrade brother."

Both families were traveling west, into Laos—which was lucky, too. The last thing we needed was a family heading north, up the valley, where they'd talk to their Black Tai cousins, or, worse, to a chatty patrol from the garrison, whose commandant might, just might, decide—weather allowing—to call Hanoi to check it out. A cover story's fine, guys, but not if it falls apart before you even get there.

When the first group of ponies reached us, the two Nungs who were doing the herding looked just like Don Quixote and Sancho Panza silhouetted on little swayback horses—AKs instead of lances. You tried to imagine Genghis Khan on animals like that—he rode them, they say—and it was hard not to laugh.

It was raining when we started to load them. It was going to take all night.

The eyelets on the bags were wonderful. The hemp rope the Nungs had purchased was wonderful. It was the ponies that gave us problems, whinnying and stomping and making it clear that they didn't like being felt up like this in the dark.

Waiting inside the treeline with sixty midget horses, all of them just aching to let out a squeal, was crazy, I kept thinking. *What if someone finds us in the trees before daybreak, Chief? Why can't we just hit the road right now and get it over with?*

"Think *Russian*, Lieutenant," he whispered. "You wouldn't mess with these roads at night if you were *Russian*, would you?"

"Only American commandos full of piss and vinegar would, right?" I said.

When first light comes, it's an incredible scene. Muddy uniforms, everyone drenched and shivering. Sixty ponies, heads down, covered with bags that are dripping, too. "Look sick," the chief tells Cooper, and bingo, Cooper does a great job. He slumps over on his pony—the only one of us who gets to ride—and yes, he does, he looks like a very wet, very ill Russian. Maybe it was the water, *Trung Uy*? Maybe it's something worse? You certainly don't want to walk up and look in his face, *Trung Uy*, because you just might catch it. *See*, he's getting even sicker now. He's leaning even farther forward on his horse.

And that Soviet woman—the one holding that leash, *Trung Uy*—she's got her killer dog with her just in case any of your locals think to pinch some Soviet ass. All of them—the Russians, their

Nung guards and porters, their NVA interpreter, too—aren't a group you want to mess with at all. They're wet, they're cold, they're miserable, and you have absolutely *no idea* what they might do. Moscow and Hanoi are bedfellows these days, *Trung Uy*, and you really shouldn't jiggle the bed.

If we were lucky, that's how we looked.

We got to the road without making contact, took a deep breath and stood there for a moment. We were at last what we were supposed to be: Russian rice experts traveling the dry-weather roads of the Northwest in *very* wet weather, because the seed we had demanded it. We could be *seen* now. We *wanted* to be seen. It would be easier this way. On the road, wet and convincing. Not having to sneak around in the darkness anymore.

It really *was* like a high school play, Major.

I remember how we kept to the high ground as we entered the valley. The valley entrance was *always* swampy, but the silver-nitrate monsoons our friends in Vientiane had arranged for the North this year had flooded it completely. It took twice as long as it should have just to enter it. The bridges across the Nam Youm were flooded, too, and it took us two hours to find one we could cross.

There were good things about it, though. The river was so high we could travel by the treeline without looking suspicious. We could travel right by the treeline and never be in the main line of sight of the valley. We could travel almost all the way to the garrison that way.

That was one of the good things. There were other good things, too. . . .

We didn't see anyone for a long, long time. The villages looked abandoned, the water lapping at their stilts. I remember thinking how slow and patient our ponies were, moving through that mud, that water, over one flooded bridge after another, in the incredible flood.

I remember Willie walking beside the pony that carried his radio, swearing in whatever language he'd decided to use.

I remember Bach. I remember walking and talking with him in the rain, feeling safe.

I remember Bach saying, "Do you know, Lieutenant, what we Vietnamese mean when we use the word 'sincere'?"

I said no, I didn't.

"We call a man 'sincere,' Lieutenant, when he dedicates his life to what he believes in, when each action he takes follows his beliefs—whether he kills or shows mercy, whether he takes up arms or lays those arms down. To the Vietnamese, Lieutenant—even to the ones he killed—Ho Chi Minh was the 'sincerest' of men. Do you understand what that means?"

I nodded. But I didn't.

"Do you know, Lieutenant, what you Europeans have done to us? Your French taught us to desire freedom. Our best and brightest young people wanted to be educated, like the French. They went to Paris and London and many other places. There, they discovered your political philosophers. Then they returned to their own country, which the French still ruled. They could not stand it. One of these was Ho Chi Minh. You could have had him in your pocket, as you would say, in 1945, for a few weapons and your public blessing of the idea of a free Vietnam. After all, you nursed him back to life from malaria in the Tonkin jungles, did you not? Did he not help you against the Japanese when you asked him to? But the French were Europeans, too—like you. They were colonialists. Of this you did not approve, but in the end this sin was less important than the shape of their eyes, or ours. Who knows, Lieutenant, what might have happened if you had helped Ho early on, if you had kept him, as you might say, away from Moscow back then? If you had helped him to be just a little more Vietnamese, a little less 'communist.' Or before that—if you'd helped his country gain its freedom before he was even born. . . .

"What is saddest to me, Lieutenant Damico, is that even now you are fighting the very people you could, in another universe, have loved. I do not mean the Viet Cong at their cruelest, their most insane. I mean the real heart and soul of the South—the best of the NLF, the bravest of the 'third force' nationalists, who are the real patriots of a free Vietnam . . . though you will not see this. You will not see that you are fighting your own finest legends, Lieutenant. *Woodsmen* with their flintlocks and the terrible *Redcoats* who won't set them free. You are the Redcoats now, Lieutenant, and that is why you will never win.

"There have always been 'third force' patriots in my country, Lieutenant—in the North and in the South. When Ho Chi Minh began, there were thirty-seven groups—that many of them. They were wonderful people. They were kind, romantic, nationalistic and, as such people always are, naive. The French killed them. Ho Chi Minh killed them. Diem killed them, too. They are not the kind of people who survive these things, Lieutenant. They could not imagine why a man like Ho, a *nationalist* even if he was a communist, would want to kill *them*. They were 'communists,' too, were they not? They wished agricultural reform. They wished a free Vietnam for the Vietnamese, as Ho did. Why would he want to kill them? They never understood, Lieutenant, that a 'communism' which places the homeland second can never be truly Vietnamese. Or that an idea—no matter how beautiful it may sound—must always take the shape of the heart of the men who follow it. . . .

"Our own tragedy, Lieutenant, is twofold. America will not win because, by its very ideals, it is fighting itself. But neither will the heart and soul of the South—which will defeat you—win. They will defeat America for the North, and the North, despite its promises—*because we are indeed two peoples*—will never let the South have what it has won. The South will not have a position in the new order. The North will administer the South as the mandarins once administered Tonkin, Cochin China and Annam.

"In a universe somewhere, Lieutenant, I believe, you are fighting beside the sanest, the most loving of the Mat Tran Den Toc Giai Phong Mien Nam. You are fighting beside the bravest of the 'third force' nationalists. You are fighting with us against every foreigner who has ever tried to enter our land. In that universe, Lieutenant, you are winning, because in that world your dream is the same as ours."

I remember not answering. I remember waiting and hearing him say:

"Have you ever seen Ho Chi Minh's Declaration of Independence, Lieutenant? It begins: 'All men are created equal. They are endowed by their creator with certain inalienable rights. . . .' Strange, is it not? You know now why I have joined you, I think. You know now why this mission may be *sincere*, even if we die trying."

I ask it. I ask the question I've been wanting to ask.

"Do you have a wife and child, Lieutenant?"

"Yes."

"Does your child have your wife's eyes?"

"Yes, she does, Lieutenant. Why do you ask?"

He isn't stupid. We walk for a while in silence and then he says:

"You have had a dream about me?"

"Yes, I have. . . ."

She lies with him on the banks of the river. On the grass they eat a lunch of pho and rice. He loves her for her beauty, for things no photograph can ever show. The child rolls over on the blanket and squeals. She has her mother's eyes. When the little girl is older, will he tell her the story of Kim Van Kieu, the wonderful verses in rhyme—of the young woman who does her duty and because she does she will have completed her obligations on earth? Will he tell her about the American girl—on a road, in the rain? How she dreamed the deaths of others, but was sometimes wrong?

Will he even be there at all to tell her such things?

"Do I die in this dream?" he asks me.

"No," I say. "It's a wonderful dream, really. There's a park, a river and a pond, Lieutenant. The three of you are having a picnic on the grass. You are laughing, Lieutenant, and your child rolls over and looks up at you. No one is dying. No one is dying in the dream."

"I see," he says.

Why did she dream it then? he's thinking. Why did she dream at all, if it doesn't mean death?

Maybe I was tired, I want to say. Maybe I was tired of death, and wanted to dream a beautiful thing.

I remember a village that was an island, Major, staring back at us from the flood and rain. I remember a Black Tai family—not at all like the Siamese in *The King and I*. They wore heavy black blouses and pants, hollow silver collars, and conical hats. Their heavy eyebrows were the first things you noticed on their faces. Their bodies were hunched in the rain. They didn't want to buy anything. They just wanted to keep moving, moving in the rain. *They've been moving for a long, long time, Mary*, I remember thinking.

Will he die, Mary? Will he die because *you had that dream?*

I remember a patrol, how it stopped us a little ways past Drop Zone Etienne—the place where, if the chief knew his history, the Legionnaires had run screaming like banshees at the Viet Minh, who outnumbered them ten to one.

Will he die with us ? *Will he die on that riverbank with us?*

I remember not being worried then. The captain was up front. He was *listening*. He would *know*. Steve was up there, too. *They'll know what the soldiers are thinking, Mary*, I remember thinking. *They'll kill them before they can kill us.*

I remember the patrol, how easy it was to fool them. Three young men—the Russian we spoke, our sour looks—Bach doing all the talking. It was just like a high school play.

They stayed with us all the way, happy to be escorting their Russian guests to their garrison the few kilometers to the north.

They grinned. They were feeling proud.

They're kids, I remember thinking.

Just like us, a voice said.

Chapter 38

It's dusk when we reach the Bailey Bridge—the Nac Tau Bridge, the "Bridge of the Victory of 1954"—and their commandant, a colonel, comes out with his entourage to meet us. They're shadows in the rain, under the dark clouds. They're barely *real*.

He's concerned, of course, this little man. He doesn't understand what has happened. The leader of the patrol tries to tell him, happy for the chance, and the commandant nods. But he's thinking: *Why wasn't I told? Why didn't the Ministry of Agriculture tell me?*

They'll want to remain the night with us—maybe several nights, he tells himself. *They're covered with mud, these people. They're miserable. They're Russians and they do not understand this land.*

We nod but do not smile. We stare. We let Bach do the talking.

You're right, Colonel. We're wet, we're miserable and we're going to stay the night with you. We've got sixty ponies, a thousand bags of rice and two goddamn weeks to finish this job in. Forty-one B to the Black, and the Black all the way to Hoa Binh. All those highland valleys with their ethnic minorities and their "shallow to intermediate rain-fed rice." We'll even leave you a bag or two of *real* rice—which we were smart enough to carry in our lockers from Vientiane. We just can't stay around to plant it for you. Your valley, Colonel, is just too flooded for us to work in, if you must know. If Hanoi has failed to warn you that we were coming, that is Hanoi's fault—and we *know* you won't complain. You'll do what our interpreter suggests: You'll let us, us wet and muddy Russians, do the complaining when we get back. If you handle it right, we won't complain about *you*. You'll apologize to us for Hanoi's failure, of course, citing inclement weather. You'll tell us you're sure that Hanoi did its very best, that Hanoi really *tried*. You'll be the very best host you can be, so that when we complain to Hanoi, we won't complain about you.

The woman is a captain (Bach tells you). She is the wife of an officer with the Commissary of Agriculture, and she is being punished, by this assignment, for romantic indiscretions of a very ordinary kind. While her husband is angry, he also must not lose more face. So he has provided her with a dog for her "protection"—for the pretense that she needs protection in a "backward" country like ours. In a country like ours, Colonel, where dogs are *eaten*— where people themselves do not have enough to eat, so dogs cannot be coddled like children. Colonel, there may or may not be an insult in this—of the Moscow kind. I really cannot say. Yet the fact remains: The dog weighs forty-five kilos and can tear a man's throat out with its jaws.

In other words, Colonel, like so many other Russians you have met, these people do not really trust us. The woman's husband won't even trust us with his unfaithful wife.

We should treat them, Colonel, with that in mind.

The Russians have asked me to request trucks from you, Colonel, and I have told them that is impossible. The garrison would certainly oblige, I've told them, but trucks would be worthless in this mud. I did not tell them that most probably there are no trucks to spare.

They have reprimanded *me*, Colonel, for the failure of Hanoi. Which is not surprising. They should not be out in weather like this, they keep telling me. I have done my best. I have told them that the Democratic Republic could not have predicted such a season—the worst monsoons in twenty-seven years—and that, of course, had Hanoi indeed been able to predict it, it would certainly have advised against this trip. I have pointed out gently that I am suffering these travails with them and that perhaps they should view this as evidence of Hanoi's good faith.

I have also reminded them of the importance of the rice they are carrying—of the instructions they must give to our rural minorities and transplanted fellow Vietnamese in the planting, tending and harvesting of this special wet-weather rice—of the profound importance of such an experiment to a young revolutionary nation like our own.

I have told them, as well, how willing you will be as commandant of this garrison to make it up to them in any way you can. By giving them dry barracks for the night, by providing what medicine you have on hand for the member of their team who is ill. By whatever you are able, as their host, to do for them tonight—with the exception of trucks, which I keep telling them would be useless in weather like this.

I have told them, too, that only a man profoundly committed to our great international socialist future would be willing to face conditions like these in a distant valley, year after year, as joyously as you obviously do, Colonel. And, of course, that having such a man as their host even for a night should help them view their journey—even Hanoi herself—in a more favorable light. . . .

Do you suggest, Major Bach, that I send a patrol by foot to Son La—to make sure that Son La knows they are coming? I could call, of course, but the land lines are not working and radio reception is unreliable at best.

No, Colonel Tranh. I will inform our Russian guests that you have offered this but that I have turned your offer down, because Son La *already* knows. They were contacted just before we left, Colonel. I was there to witness it. I am sorry that you were not contacted as well. I feel certain Hanoi has *tried*. Is there any chance that one of your radio operators, perhaps new or young and inexperienced—

No. That isn't possible, Major.

Of course, Colonel. I was merely wondering. In any event, Son La does know.

I understand. I will at least, Major, send an escort with our Russian guests when they depart tomorrow morning.

I will convey that offer as well, Colonel, but that is not necessary. My impression, in fact, is that they prefer—

I am perhaps in a better position than you, Major, to determine what is "necessary" and not. I am their host, after all. I do not wish that they—or others who might hear of their sojourn in this valley—feel that we have abandoned them to the rain. . . .

I understand, Colonel. I am sure they will, too.

I remember thinking about Bucannon. I remember thinking how much he would have wanted to record it all—whisper by whisper, lie after lie, bootstep after bootstep in the rain and mud. How sad he would be that he couldn't. How, in his sadness, he would be thinking: *There are lessons to be learned from every breath they take, every hammering of their hearts.* He would be thinking this, I knew.

Wish you were here, I said to him again.

Wish you were here to feel it all.

I remember thinking—maybe even dreaming—that this was how it seemed to them:

We gave the Russians their own barracks and the Nungs their own barracks, too. We gave them five metal sheds for their ponies, which they guarded like opium through the night.

We gave the Russian woman her own divider, too—good black cloth hung on a wooden frame—and on the other side of that put a clean metal cot.

Their interpreter, because he was one of us, and a major, we invited to our barracks. He accepted with grace. The Russians, he told us, would of course want to be alone—to curse our weather, to curse our land, if nothing else.

To the young Russian who was so ill we gave a divider, too, and a sulfa drug, passing it along to him through the major. What he had was contagious, the major said, and no one ever saw his face.

The heavyset Russian with a bad arm carried his large radio into the barracks and did not seem at all happy. The Russian woman helped him. That's all we know.

If they were trying to raise Hanoi or any other station that night, we never heard. We monitored them briefly on our own equipment, and then gave up.

Their Nung escorts guarded the bags as if the rice seed were priceless.

Which of course it was.

We cover the windows, just like Russians obsessed with privacy would. We turn out all but one of the three overhead bulbs. We even say good night to each other in our best Russian.

I touch the thing they've put in my arm. The stitching is purple. It *hurts* when I touch it the wrong way. The scar will turn pink, then white, I tell myself. When they take it out, will it hurt?

I don't understand why you did it, Colonel. Why you let us set out on this journey without any way for you and yours to know, day by day, how it goes. A pen, a pad, a tape recorder, a camera—those instruments of learning which you love—any of them would make your deafness, your blindness, more tolerable, would they not? Any of them would let you say, sitting there in Vientiane: *I'm going to learn from this. I'm going to learn what can be learned.*

I know you awfully well, Colonel. I know what you need most and how you suffer for the things you love.

The chief holds the radio between his legs. He curses quietly, using the only Russian curses he knows, trying to get the radio to sit up straight. It tilts again, he curses again, and I get up off the cot at last.

I kneel down beside him. I start to speak. But I don't have the Russian I need.

We're broadcasting, I know. The little lights are on. We're telling Vientiane we're *here*, that we've made it.

That shouldn't be enough, Colonel. That shouldn't be enough by itself.

I think of plastic and circuitry and the vibrations that move through our bodies as we speak. I think of relays, augmenters, all those things the chief described. I think of a radio as large as this one, of skin healing over little transistors, of the little lights that always stay on.

I think of what Bucannon needs.

I'm not supposed to talk English, but I do. I whisper:

"Is there any chance that this"—I touch the little bulge in the skin of my arm—"is a mike, Willie? Is there any chance that we're transmitting—through this radio—what those little mikes hear?"

Willie stares at me. I can see the radio behind his eyes, each little piece of it as he starts to take it apart, and then puts it together again. I can see the physics of a *transponder*, the way an audio relay works, what it would take to make a transceiver that small. I watch him build it, give it juice and then—piece by piece—take the thing apart again.

His mouth opens. It isn't Russian he's going to use.

"Yes," he says. "Yes, it is."

Neither of us says a thing.

I look at my arm in the dark, trying too think of all the things it has heard by now. On the floor, cross-legged, Willie is twisting around, trying to reach his back—where his own mike is—and with his one good arm.

He's here! I want to shout at every one of them, jerking them from their cots. *He's been here all along.*

I don't.

Instead, I tell him things. I whisper them—in English—into my sleeve. "You son of a bitch," I say. "You fucking son of a bitch," I say.

I don't remember who took guard duty that night, Major, or how much I really slept. All I remember is lying on that cot, holding the AK to me and whispering things into my sleeve.

U.S. Army FM 31-21, "Guerrilla Warfare and Special Forces Operations"

1.2. *Definition*

Unconventional warfare includes the fields of guerrilla warfare, evasion and escape, and subversion against hostile states (resistance). Unconventional warfare operations are conducted in enemy or enemy-controlled territory by predominantly indigenous personnel usually supported and directed to varying degrees by an external source.

1.3. *Delineation of Responsibilities*

1.3.1. The responsibility for certain of these activities has been delegated to the service having primary concern. Guerrilla warfare is the responsibility of the United States Army.

1.3.2. Within certain designated geographic areas—called *guerrilla warfare operational areas*—the United States Army is responsible for the conduct of all three interrelated fields of activity as they affect guerrilla warfare operations.

1.3.3. The United States Army shall work closely with appropriate intelligence agencies when necessary. . . .

Photostat, Transcript, EGLO Transmission 11/3/71. ELINT gathered for Codeword Little Boy Blue, Command Files (ARK Mission) Operation Orangutan, *Tiger Cat*, Vietnam

Page 1102, 11/3/71 1258:53

Sound (overlapping): *Automatic weapon fire.*
Sound (overlapping): *Body falling(?).*
Voice #1: "Do it if you can, Mary."
Voice #2 (overlapping): "Yes, do it if you can."
Sound (overlapping): *Automatic weapon fire continuing.*
Sound (overlapping): *Explosion (air?).*
Sound: *Explosion (water?).*
Voice #3: "He loves us, doesn't he?"
Voice #1: "Of course he does."
Voice #2: (laughing) "'This I know. . . .'"

Sound (overlapping): *Automatic weapon fire ceases.*
Sound: *Body falling (?) a moan (Voice #4?).*
Sound: *Breathing (Voice #3?).*
Voice #4: "It's beautiful, isn't it, Willie?"
Voice #3: "Yes, but what is it?"
Sound: *Automatic weapon fire resumes.*
Voice #3: "Right. It doesn't matter. There's something we need to do."
Voice #1 (overlapping): "There's something we need to do."
Voice #2 (overlapping): "There's something we need to do."
Sound: *Engines (PBR?), water.*
Sound (overlapping): *Automatic weapon fire fades.*
NB: *Voices lost 11/3/71 1301:56 to 11/5/71 0533:62.*

Chapter 39

I remember dreaming. I hadn't taken a pill, so I dreamed. I dreamed of the river—the one we were heading to—and of the bodies lying there in the mud. I dreamed about Bucannon, too, kneeling in a tent in his nice white suit. I was going to help him. It didn't make any sense.

I dreamed a dream I'd never dreamed before—of a man in a wheelchair I'd never met, but somehow knew. Everyone knew him. He died in my dream, but it wasn't a violent death. He died, that's all. He was sick, his body weak. They heard him on the radio—they knew him that way—and then one day he died. I did all I could for him. I tried to fix the muscles, the sheaths, the nerves. I held him. I told him about his cousin, and what she thought of him now. I tried to keep him alive, because I knew what that might mean.

But he died. He went ahead and died, like the others.

When I woke up, I thought I'd screamed.

But no one was looking at me. No one was saying a thing.

Bach tries to argue. The commandant insists: The Russians *will* have an escort. It is the least he can do. *Remember this,* he's telling us, *when you are sitting high and dry in Hanoi.*

When we're five hours from the garrison—five hours of mud and rain—one of our three young escorts begins walking toward Cooper, and I know—I just *know*—how it's going to end.

* * *

We spent two whole weeks on Vietnam in Mr. Laidlaw's' class. I remember because that was homeroom, and you never forget homeroom. He was more interested in the war than most of the teachers were. "And what of history?" he would ask us. We never understood what he was talking about, but he was good-looking and had a great voice, so at least the girls listened. "Is there nothing in their past," he would say, voice so dramatic, "nothing at all to make this—this thing we call 'communism'—attractive to them? Is there no Confucian marriage of church and government in their past . . . so much like the Marxist-Leninist State? Is there no long tradition of *duty*? Is there no Buddhist acceptance of personal fate in the larger scheme of things? Is there nothing in their past that should make them feel that the *end*, after so much patience, might indeed justify *any* means—even one as hideous as those Viet Cong atrocities, with children, in the night? Is it possible, Miss Damico, that when you sow a field with dragon's teeth you always reap what you have sown?

"Can you, Miss Damico," he would say to me, "think of anything the French might have done in Indochina during their hundred-year reign that might illustrate this?"

I couldn't, of course. No one could. He was a "communist," we heard later. I didn't know what that meant. *They don't believe in God* was all my father said. He didn't come back to teach the next year, which was okay. He wasn't a very good teacher. But I do remember thinking: *Communism sure has a great voice.*

I'll never be able to justify what the VC did, Major. I'll never understand the life a hard-core cadre leads—prisoner to an idea, doing anything, anything at all, in its name. But sometimes, Major—sometimes, at night, in my room here, I start to see it the way he must have seen it. I see a man in a field. Someone—either that man or a man before him—has planted these dragon's teeth in the ground, and he—the man in the field—has got to dance with the skeletons now, the ones that have sprouted from those teeth. It's like the *Seventh Voyage of Sinbad*, but it's worse—because he can't stop dancing. He's got to dance forever. He should have known that before he started, and he didn't. He really didn't.

Bach was saying the same thing, I know that now.

Which is something I don't understand, Major.

Bach wasn't a *communist*. He couldn't have been.

They'd never have sent him with us if he was, would they?

The road is mud. The rock and gravel have been washed away and the logs of the "corduroy," if there ever was one here, have washed away, too. But the ponies are happy. They'd rather walk on mud than logs like those.

Along the roadside are the little piles of rock and gravel for repairing the road, but there's no one to do the job.

Even with an incline like the one we're on, the runoff reaches to our ankles. The ponies are *slow*. The dog isn't even straining at its leash. The young escort—a soldier, a kid—takes his time moving past me, moving toward Cooper—I understand that now—moving toward the sick Russian on the pony.

Why?

He's curious, Mary. He just wants to see the sick Russian's face.

I see a picture—I dream a quick little dream:

That boy—that Vietnamese soldier—lying in blood. Lying on this very road, in blood.

I haven't taken a pill, so I *know*.

It'll happen. . . .

The body mutilated, face slashed like zebra stripes. The arms across the chest, stiff like a straitjacket. The fingers snipped off at the middle joints. The front of the jacket laid open, belly laid open, the bowels arranged like letters in the mud.

It'll happen, but it won't be us, I tell myself. *It can't be us. It'll happen after he leaves us—when we're not around. Things like this happen all the time up here, Mary.*

The captain drops back from the lead, catches Steve's eye. Steve nods and falls back.

Bach looks around with a jerk—as if someone's called him—and starts talking to the other two escorts, who are beside him now, and who never turn around.

The boy is almost to Cooper when I hear the voice from the caves say:

He thinks—he thinks the skin of the sick Russian is awfully dark. He's curious. He wants to see it better.

I know, I tell him.

The captain is ten feet from him now. The boy doesn't even notice. His two friends haven't turned. Cooper leans as far forward as he can without falling off the pony, and Steve, up ahead, jerks, too—as if someone has called him. He begins toward the two escorts who are talking with Bach, and who still haven't turned around.

The chief understands and moves with him.

The Nungs just look on, pretending they don't see a thing.

He's thinking of a black GI he saw once on a street in Hanoi, paraded for the people there, the voice is saying—to all of us now.

The instant the captain reaches the boy, Steve and the chief reach the other two. The Nungs just look on.

The captain says something in Russian. The boy turns his head, puzzled. The captain smiles and says it again—using gestures to make it clear: *Won't you come over to the interpreter with me, comrade? I have a question I would very much like to ask you—about your life, your garrison, your career.*

The boy is annoyed. He doesn't like having a Russian this close.

He won't do it, the voice says. *He won't go with me. He thinks it's strange, in fact, that I'm here—*

The boy has turned back around, is talking to Cooper now, trying to get him to turn. Cooper's poncho runs with rain. Cooper keeps pretending he doesn't hear.

The dog strains suddenly at the leash in my hand.

He's telling himself, the voice tells us, *that there's something wrong—that we're acting strange—that there's something about the sick Russian that doesn't make sense—*

We don't have to kill him, do we? I ask, but the captain has already moved. There isn't even a snap—the kind you hear in movies. There isn't any sound at all in the rain. He hugs him— that's what it looks like—and the boy falls to the ground.

Up the road Steve and the chief are doing it, too. Neither uses a weapon. Steve touches his boy's throat. The chief hits the other boy on the side of the head, where the jaw meets the skull. The Nungs just look on. Cooper looks on, his face upturned at last. The dog whines. The ponies keep moving through the rain.

"Jesus," the chief says, checking the steel tip of his arm.

You're right, Mary, the voice says. *The dream is right. That is how their bodies will look, here in the mud.*

Two of the bodies are still jerking. Even wet, their pants legs make loud, rubbing noises. The body by Steve makes a sound with its throat, and then stops moving altogether.

Steve and the chief check their uniforms for blood.

The captain turns to Bach: "Tell the Nungs we need some mutilations done, Lieutenant. Ask them if they know any *vung ti.* Meo or Tai will do."

Bach and Son Chem talk quietly. Then Son Chem turns and talks to his own.

"They know Red Tai execution style," Bach says, "and they know ceremonial Lao. They can mix, they say."

"Fine. Have them do it."

Four of the Nungs are given knives. They step over to the bodies. One boy still jerks a little in the mud.

I don't have to look, I tell myself. I close my eyes.

But I see it anyway. I see the dream. I see them part the jackets, pull the shirttails out and expose the brown stomachs to the rain. I see the knives slip in, the hands grab the bowels and pull. I see the knives move toward faces.

I hear a sound and turn. It's the chief. He's staring at the bodies. "Oh, God," he says.

I know what that means.

He can still see it, Mary. He can see the fires burning on their arms and legs.

He knew they were going to die, too, Mary.

He just didn't want to *believe.*

The captain didn't have to *listen* to the boy's thoughts. I know that now. He didn't need to. He could listen to me. He could see my daydream, and know what would happen that way.

He could listen to the chief, see the fires the chief saw and know it that way, too.

Either way, Major, he knew they were going to die.

"Will it work?" someone asks.

"Sure," the chief says. "Bodies like this appear every month. The ethnic indigs get pissed at the soldiers or each other and there's always someone who ends up paying. Deals are cut every night, my friends. They won't know exactly *why* these three died, but they'll *believe* it. Of course they will."

"They were heading back," the captain says calmly, staring into the rain. "They left us at Muong Reo and were heading back early. We told them to. Other than that, we don't know a damn thing."

"Right."

We move the ponies as fast as they'll move, to put distance between us and them.

I go ahead and say it. I put my mouth near my arm. I tell Bucannon what we're becoming, whether we want to become or not. I tell him about the strange dreams people have, about children who kill, who giggle and laugh as they do it. I tell him about the monsters people have always sent into the world out of fear.

Yes, he says. *Yes,* he says, and it sounds just like the hissing rain.

Chapter 40

Even with the rain, the children come from Tai villages to travel with us as long as they are able. The women wear white, if they're White Tai, and black, if they're Black. Either way they're the most beautiful women I've ever seen, and I think: *How can they be—in this mud and rain? How can they be so* beautiful *here?*

Yul Brynner, with all his Mongolian blood, would want to marry them. Hollywood would want to hire them. Soldiers would want to write them letters every day, and when the war was over, bring them home.

For a moment I think I'm getting my period—that all this stress, this fatigue, has thrown it off, that's what's happening. Or that it's cancer, that I'm going to die, that *that's* what's thrown it off.

But it's a stomachache, that's all. A little queasiness from the Russian LURP rations we were given perhaps. A little nervousness, which would certainly make sense here.

What do they do out here, I'm wondering, *when they start to bleed—in those white clothes—when it happens every month?*

A village called Ben Jai sends a greeting party. Six men with silver armbands, black pants, black shirts all walk alongside us in the rain, wanting us to stop. They ignore the Nungs as if they were ghosts. They watch the dog carefully, and stare at me as if I were odder still. But they do talk to Bach. They trust him. He knows their language, after all. He answers them as the NVA have never done. Even the way he carries his body tells them he is different—

he is different from the NVA they know. They want us to spend the night with them, they tell him. They have questions for us—like: *Are the Americans so different from the French?* Like *Who will win this war, Major?* Like *What will happen at the end of eternity?*

We don't answer them. We speak Russian among ourselves. We don't smile. We don't want to be rude, but after all, we're Russians. It's a bad habit.

We let Bach make it up to them with his graciousness. A North Vietnamese soldier who treats them this well may become a legend, we know.

We travel as far as we can that day. We don't stop for a rest. We keep moving and when we can't move another step, we find a stand of dripping trees in the darkness and try to sleep, shivering in the rain.

We reach Khe Vo by the next nightfall. They give us a longhouse and big bowls of sticky rice. Word of our presence has preceded us, and we've had greeting parties all day. At each village the children seem bolder.

There is a fruit that smells god-awful, but tastes sweet, and we eat it with the glutinous rice. We eat a fruit with knobs on it, too, and a soup made of buffalo meat. We use as little *nuoc mam* as we can—not wanting to smell like it when we sleep—and do our best, our very best, not to smile at these people.

The Nungs guard the ponies, sleeping under their ponchos in the rain.

When we're on the woven mats in the longhouse they've given us—when we're ready to fall sleep at last, warm and drying—the children come to us. Little brown bodies with big eyes and sensuous lips climb the longhouse posts, climb the woven walls like skinny brown geckos, peek in at us. The headman comes by, shoos them away, says, "You need food? You need mats? Please, tell us what you need." When he's gone, the eyes come back again, peeking through the holes in the walls and giggling, whispering things to each other. *With those eyes in it,* I tell myself sleepily, *the wall looks an awful lot like a peacock's tail.* I blink. I lie back. They giggle again. I tell myself I'd rather have them *here*—giggling, bothering us—than down with the Nungs, where there might be trouble.

I'm sleepy. I can barely keep my eyelids up.

There's one hole bigger than the others and in it a brown face that will not leave. The nose—broad, like a koala bear's. The Siamese eyes. It's a girl and she giggles.

Finally a mother comes by and the eyes disappear for good.

In the morning, they're back. We speak Russian to each other—and even to them. We go ahead and do it. We let ourselves smile. The little girl with the koala-bear nose is back at the biggest hole. Her eyes slide up and away. Her mouth takes their place. She smiles at us. She keeps smiling. That's what she's been wanting to do all along.

The eyes at the holes changed. Little shrieks followed little shrieks—brothers, sisters and cousins fighting—and new eyes take their place.

The chief waves his prosthesis, and the eyes, terrified, disappear. The giggling stops. He waves it again and says: *"Touket lut."* Is it Bangkok Thai? Something else? The eyes reappear slowly. The chief picks up a piece of the smelly fruit with his pincher—slowly, showing off—and puts it in his mouth. He's done this before, I realize. *He's done it with children back home.*

He chews slowly, makes a face, and the eyes giggle. He picks up another piece with his steel tip.

"*Vostna met,*" Cooper's voice says, from under the blanket. It's Russian. It means: *Stop farting around, Chief. I'm tired of lying here with a goddamn blanket over my face.*

Down with the ponies, back in the rain, we get nervous again. And it shows. We're checking the straps on the bags and keeping one eye on the children. The Nungs are better at it—*bogeymen*, their parents have told them, *so you'd better keep away!* We shouldn't have smiled, I know. Now they trust us.

All it would take, I tell myself, is one kid grabbing one rotten bag, giggling as he does it—smiling right at you—for it all to end. For the voice—the one from the caves—to say:

We've got to kill everyone in this village, Mary.

Two little brothers giggle. They want to touch my pony. They dance away when I say *"Nyet!"* They keep on giggling. They keep trying to sneak a touch. All I can do is stand between the bags and their little arms and go crazy hoping it just won't happen.

I turn. The captain has crouched down. I stretch a little, trying to get a better look.

When I do, I freeze.

He's crouched down with a little girl.

Dear God . . .

He's talking to her. He's talking Russian, and though she doesn't have a single clue, she's listening. She's smiling, listening to him talk.

Why?

I take a step, trying for a better look at the little girl. He's stopped now. He isn't talking to her at all. He's just looking at her, and she's got an itch. She's scratching it. She's scratching the back of her neck.

All of a sudden I understand.

Why? Why is he reading her?

I don't like what I'm thinking. I don't like it at all.

There are men like that, Mary.

I know.

Even with the itch—even with what he's making her feel—she doesn't stop smiling. She's scratching an itch. That's all she knows.

What are you seeing, you bastard? What are you looking for in a little girl's skull?

If I take another step, the two brothers will sneak in. So I stand on tiptoe. I stretch a little more.

Do you see a woman undressing—and dressing—in the dark?

There's something about the little girl. The shape of her head? Her jaw? Her hands?

I see what it is at last.

She isn't Tai. *She is—but she isn't.*

The epicanthic folds of those lighter eyes. The thinner lips. The brass-colored hair . . .

She's Eurasian, Mary.

But why?

Why is he talking to *her*?

There are patches on her cheekbones that look like freckles—
the kind mulattoes sometimes have.

Who is she, Mary?

She's too young to be the daughter of a Legionnaire. She'd be
grown by now if she were. Is she the *granddaughter* of one—
quarter French—daughter of a *métis*?

She's lucky to have a village, I know. *Some Tai wouldn't be so
kind.*

They've been squatting for a long, long time. They've been
squatting as if nothing in the world mattered—his years at Ap Lao,
in the darkness, her years of being different from the others here—

Why her, *Mary?*

When I see it at last, I wonder why it took so long.

*Is it a boy or girl, Captain? Does it matter? Was it Da Nang
or Nha Trang or Saigon? Do you send the mother money? Is she
living, and wishes she weren't? Does her family speak to her? Do
her friends? Does she have any? Does she live on the street with
others like her? Was she a whore who did her best, but blew it? Was
she a b-girl, dreaming of what an American's child might mean?
Did she fall in love with you? Was it a mistake? Did you love her
for a week—or was it longer? Do you love her still? Do you miss the
child, Captain—though you've never seen it, or you have, but only
once? Do you wish it—*

When he turns around, it's like a rifle shot. I stop breathing.

He's heard you, Mary.

I know.

The eyes are dark.

The voice says;

Goddamn you, Lieutenant. You can't possibly understand.

No one comes from Dien Bien Phu or Son La to question us.
The bodies—the mutilations—are convincing. If there are questions in any official minds, they are familiar questions, having
nothing to do with us. They are certainly not accusations.

We are free to keep moving through the rain.

A rain we are somehow making.

There are more and more villages as we near the Black, more and more greeting parties to be rude to.

At the little village of Bao Uyen, we stop. We don't have a choice. A group of women have appeared, pleading and pulling at our sleeves. We let them, this time. We let them lead us to a house on stilts.

There is rudeness, Bach would tell us, *and there is cruelty. Even Russians know the difference.*

On a woven mat a thin, yellow man is dying. I *know* him. Of course I do. I've seen him in a dream, the kind you forget until it comes true.

His name is Khon Sak. His wife is named Lom Phae. I know, even without thinking it, what his brother in Som Long two valleys away thinks of him—the respect he feels, though he has never said it to his brother's face. I know also what Khon Sak feels about the child—the one they lost, years ago, the year so many babies died. I know how long—the weeks, the very number—his wife, who is pulling at my sleeve, will mourn for him.

I take a step, trying to remember what we have in our packs.

You can't, the voice says suddenly. I jerk but I don't turn around.

You're not a nurse here, the voice says. *You're something else, Lieutenant.*

I take another step. *I'm a woman, I'm a nurse,* I tell him. *I'll always be.*

I'll tell him things, Captain. That's all, I say. *I'll tell him what his brother feels, though he's never told him face-to-face. I'll tell him that for every child who dies ten more are born each morning. I'll tell him—word by word—what his wife will say, so many good things, when he is gone.*

You don't know the Russian, Lieutenant, the voice says.

I don't need Russian, I tell him. *I can hear the words. The Tai words his own brother would use, has used in his own mind—and the Tai words his wife will use, to praise him, after he is gone. I will use these words, Captain, not Russian.*

No, he says, *you won't.*

It would be a miracle, Lieutenant, he tells me. *Word of the Woman Who Knows would spread like holy fire. Son La and Dien would hear of it. They would wonder, too. They would send patrols. Within days we wouldn't be able to travel these roads at all. I'm sorry, but you can't, Lieutenant.*

I stand with these people. I watch the man on the mat, the woman who is kneeling beside him, the faces who are watching *us.* In the worst Russian I know I say, "Please, Lieutenant Bach, tell them how *sorry* we are. Tell them how if one of us were a doctor, even a nurse—instead of the agricultural officers we are— we would *of course* help them. But we aren't. . . ."

I turn. I look at the captain.

You could do it, Kelly, I tell him. *You could let him hear what his brother thinks of him, what his wife will say when he is gone. . . . You could take what I know and give it to him, Kelly.*

The voice doesn't say a thing.

Goddamn you, I tell him.

You can't possibly *understand,* I say.

The children do not come to the holes in the longhouse walls in Lang Bieu. The jungle—its black face, its black body so near us—looks in through the holes instead.

We could have given them a miracle, and we didn't, Captain.

The world is different now.

They didn't tell me at first and I'm not sure why. A man—an older man from the village—slipped through the guards, cut two bags from a pony, and fled with them on the smaller road to Nha Nam. He knew what "special rice" would be worth to *someone*— to farmers in a highland valley, to Son La, even to Hanoi itself. He had stolen things before from the soldiers who traveled these roads. Official anger didn't frighten him.

The Nungs caught him five kilometers away, killed him and buried him where no one would find the body.

The captain had known the man would steal them, of course. He'd *heard* the man considering it over his bowl of glutinous rice.

He'd even *heard* the man as he did it, in the night. But he'd waited until the man was far from the village—

He didn't want to kill him *here*, he said.

What are we becoming, Colonel? I ask him on the road the next day, without raising my arm.

What are your five children becoming?

Chapter 41

PFC Gregory Williams, 908924827, 4th Infantry Division,
Tape 3 Transcript

Subject: I was given a prisoner to guard in a ville once. I'd never been that close to a live VC before. I was shaking like a leaf. I'm twenty years old and this guy was probably fifty. You really can't tell with these people. They're out there in the jungles or working their asses off in the paddies and they start looking old real fast.

Anyway, I was given this prisoner to guard until the S-2 and his ARVN counterpart could get there. There wasn't anyone else around. I was standing up. He was sitting cross-legged on the ground with his hands tied. I don't know an American who could've stared that guy down. He never stopped looking at me— this hatred in his eyes—and the way he watched me made me think he knew what I was thinking. You get feelings like that over here, Captain. Why else would he be looking at you like that if he wasn't *listening* to what you were thinking? That's what you start telling yourself after a couple of weeks of it, Captain.

He was looking at my uniform, my boots, my M-14, my hair, my eyes—*everything.* He was looking right through me with this look of hatred and I was doing my best to stare him down, too, but I couldn't. Something was making me nervous, so I got up and walked around a little, and the feeling just got worse. Every time I'd look at him he'd be staring at me. It was driving me crazy. I finally couldn't stand it and I walked over to him and hit him with the butt of my M-14. I hit him in the temple. I'm not proud of that, but at the time I did feel better.

He fell over and just laid there blinking. He was alive and all of a sudden that weird feeling started up again. I start to hit him with the rifle again but I could see the sergeant coming, so I stopped.

Sergeant said: "Apparently, Private, we do not have a live prisoner."

I just looked at him like an idiot. I was cherry. I didn't know what he was saying.

I said: "Sergeant, sir, I'm not really clear on this. What are you telling me, sir?"

And he said: "Jesus, Williams. Read my lips: *We do not have a live prisoner.*"

He waited and finally I nodded that I understood. He said, "I'll be back in ten minutes, Private. If you need someone to help you with the load, get someone. Just don't fuck up." He left. I just stood there, wondering whether or not I could do it. It was an order, right? Even if he put it that way, it was an order and I could be court-martialed if I didn't do it.

The prisoner was shaking now. It was the strangest thing I'd ever seen. I was shaking and he was shaking—like he *knew*. I thought, "He speaks English. He's got to." But I knew that wouldn't have been enough. The sergeant didn't say, *"Kill him."* He said it in a way a Vietnamese wouldn't understand. Maybe it was just the way I was acting. I wasn't exactly acting like I was about to go on R&R.

I was shaking. He was shaking and I kept having this crazy thought that he *knew*—that this prisoner knew what I was thinking and feeling. I kept having these crazy thoughts, like suppose this guy knew he'd be caught in the tunnel. Suppose he did it *on purpose*—let us catch him—so he could sit with one of us, like he was sitting with me now, and hear the guy's thoughts, get important information from him and then escape. Like: Suppose there was a VC who could listen to your thoughts. Isn't that exactly what he would do? He'd know what we were thinking, so he could easily get away.

Like I said, you start thinking crazy thoughts.

I stayed as far away from the guy as I could. I just stood there looking at him, trying to get up enough nerve to do it. I kept saying to myself: Gregory James, you were raised in a good Christian family, with the Bible, with the Ten Commandments. How can you possibly *do* this? I kept thinking: John Wayne was no saint, but he certainly wouldn't just off a guy like this.

I argued with myself. I said: He's a baby killer, Gregory James. He's killed people in a lot of villes. He's probably cut their heads off and strung them up by their feet. He's pulled their guts out while they were still alive and had the village pigs eat them while their wives and children watched. He's probably done *terrible* things like this, Gregory James. You *know* he has. You're not going to get any closer to evil than this man and you know it.

Maybe that was true, but I still didn't want to do it. I didn't want to kill someone like that. It wouldn't be *war*. It would be something else.

I knew people would say: By not killing him, Gregory James, you'll be killing the next Americans *he* kills. You'll be raping the next little girl *he* rapes. You'll be making the next family watch someone they love being eaten by pigs.

Maybe that was true, too, but I didn't think God would see it that way.

I stepped over to the guy and took my M-14 and shot him in the shoulder—in the meat, away from the bone, I mean. Then I also shot him in the thigh, away from where I figured the artery was. All this time I was saying to myself: The sergeant is out there listening, Gregory James. You've fired two shots. That's all you need.

The guy was screaming, of course. What else can you do when some guy shoots you in the shoulder and the leg. But I knew that if he kept it up the sergeant would come back, and find out, and say: "I told you not to fuck up, Williams, and you've fucked up. We have a *live* prisoner now, Williams. We have a prisoner that *you have mutilated.*"

I put the barrel on the guy's forehead. I stared at him as hard as I could. I shook my head real slow, so he'd understand, and he did—he finally stopped.

Then I got him up on my shoulders. He wasn't that heavy. None of these people are. He was shaking, making this sucking sound with his mouth, but that was all. He wasn't going to scream anymore. He knew what I was doing. He'd *heard* what I'd wanted him to hear in my head, I guess.

He was bleeding all over me and I knew what I'd have to say. I'd have to tell the sergeant what a dumb fuck I was, how I thought I was supposed to carry the body away by myself. The sergeant would piss and moan, but that's all.

The guards at the gate nodded at me, like it had been prearranged—like they knew what the hell I was doing, if I didn't—and I took him outside. It took us ten fucking minutes to get outside the gate to a spot where no one could see us. All that time I kept thinking, "What if you get shot out here, Gregory James? What if you get yourself killed over this gook, you dumb fuck? What if he starts fucking with you, flailing and screaming just to be a son of a bitch? What's going to happen then?

I laid him down by a tree and diddy-bopped back as fast as I could. They picked up their dead and wounded *real* fast, I knew. They never left you a body to mutilate, I knew. Just blood trails. They'd find him fast and he *wouldn't* bleed to death, right? They had ways we didn't know about for communicating, right? In fact, they were probably watching me right now and they weren't going to shoot because they didn't want to shoot him by accident, or they kind of guessed what I was doing and were thankful. Right?

It was crazy, sir, I know. If I'm going to get court-martialed for it, that's fine. But I do believe that God gave me the right to do it, that He gave me the *duty* to do it, so I'm very willing to take whatever punishment the United States Army decides I deserve. *Interviewer:* That's a little outside our jurisdiction, Private. If *you* want to tell your commanding officer, fine. What happened next? *Subject:* [Pause] I got a confirmation three days later, sir. I mean, I found out that the feeling I'd had that day—about the guy—was right on. God gave me the proof, I guess. [Pause] One of the cooks—this guy from My Tho—came to see me in my bunker. I wasn't thinking about what I'd done. The cook looked at me like he'd seen a ghost. He said to me, "This for you, Williams-san." Then gave me a little book all wrapped in butcher paper. I said, "Who's this from, Doan?" And he said: "Not know, sir." He knew. He was just scared. He was shaking like a leaf, so I knew he knew. All the Viets know who's VC and who isn't at a camp like that.

Like I said, it was butcher paper. The wrapping was folded the way you'd fold one of those paper animals, those Chinese things, so it stayed tight even without any tape. I wouldn't let the cook leave. I made him stay while I opened it.

It was a book. A beautiful little book. The paper wasn't high quality—you know how the paper is here—but the cover was this drawing of a Chinese girl, really beautiful. I found out later the guy who wrote it was considered to be their best writer. It was called *Kim Van Kieu* and it's about this girl named Kieu who does her duty, because that's the most important thing in life. There's this guy she wants to marry, but she's got to leave him in order to support her father. So she does. To support her father she's got to agree to become someone else's mistress. She does that, too. It gets even more depressing after that. I didn't read it—how could I read it? But a guy in S-2 told me about it later.

Inside the book was this little piece of paper with Vietnamese writing on it. I still hadn't let the cook go, so I made him tell me what it said. I made him read it to me. He read: "I hope that the gifts you have purchased for your parents and sisters please them, Private Williams, and that you are able to give them the finest gift of all this Tet: their son and brother returning home to them on his own two legs. I hope as well that your fiancée Sheila has recovered from her illness and that your life with her in Louisiana is a happy one."

I didn't understand who it was from. I thought it was a joke—something one of the other grunts would do. It was signed "Nguyen Dai Ta." When I asked the cook what "Dai Ta" meant, he wouldn't tell me. I told him I'd get him fired if he didn't, but he still wouldn't. He was really shaking like a leaf.

When I asked the S-2, he said, "It's a Viet Cong rank. Same as colonel."

I knew right away, with this chill down my back, who the book was from. I didn't want to know, but I did. I could remember clearly what I was thinking the day I shot him. *Presents.* I'd needed to buy presents. And I'd been worried about Sheila, because of her letter.

He was alive. He'd made it. He really *was* able to do the things I'd imagined he could do. And it scared the living shit out of me. I knew exactly what he meant about returning home—having two legs to walk on. That scared me, too. I remember thinking to myself: *A VC colonel is going to shoot you in the legs, Gregory James. A VC colonel is going to get even with you, you dumb fuck.* I remember thinking: *Why can't we just send books and messages to each other, God? Why do we have to shoot each other in the legs?*

I wasn't sorry about what I'd done. I just was scared.

I found out later how good he was, and how much information he'd gotten from my head that day—what he'd been able to do with it. Not just things about Sheila and the presents, but about the camp, the patrols, the bunker layout. Four days after I got the book, we were hit bad. Maybe it was just what some VC cook had learned about us—that's what people said—but I don't think so. The sergeant was killed in his bunker. He was shot in the forehead before he could even get out of the bunker. He was lying on the medevac with me, so I saw him.

I was shot in both of my legs when I ran from my own bunker. He was a damn good shot. He knew exactly where they wouldn't do much damage. He knew it a lot better than I did.

I was able to walk, like he said. My parents came out to meet me at the New Orleans Airport when I went home and I was able to walk out to them on the tarmac myself, just like he said he hoped I would.

Chapter 42

War isn't what you think it is, Major. You wait and you wait, and when the firefight finally starts, it's over before you know it. Then you start waiting again. You're tired. You're tired of *waiting*. You're tired of the fear, so you figure out how to stop feeling it. You save it—you save that feeling—for when it *really* matters.

Nothing happened for two days. I guess that's what I'm saying. I didn't have any more pills to take, so I dreamed—but the dreams were old. The bodies by a river, mud. A long, dark dike— or wall. A man in a white suit, kneeling. Three bodies mutilated on a road.

Nothing happened for two days.

A patrol from Dien Bien Phu caught up with us on the third day as we started up the road to Loc Nghia, and just beyond, the Black. The patrol had eight young men in plastic ponchos just like ours—just like the ones everyone used, even American soldiers in the South. They had questions: *When did the escorts leave you, Major Bach? Why did they not accompany you the entire way? Why did you bypass Son La? Did you observe any groups of Tai on the road before or after the escorts left you?*

Even these weren't accusations. They had to ask them, that was all.

We gave them answers. They left. No patrol would be coming from Son La, they told us. Son La hadn't even been notified, they said. We knew what that meant.

Dien Bien Phu would wash its dirty laundry by itself.

We were tired. Two hours into the foothills of the low mountains that stood between us and the Black River Valley, we stopped at a stream so swollen we weren't sure we could cross it. Like the chief had said. We'll be a thousand feet from the peaks, he'd said. The runoff there will be outrageous. The streambeds, the gullies, the earth itself, just can't handle that much water. "We may drown up there," he'd said, and we were sure it was a joke.

Even back from the streambed twenty or thirty yards, even up where the road crested, the ponies were wading in water up to their hocks. "They're going to go under, I tell you," the chief said. "We're going to lose five or six ponies right here, goddammit, and we're not going to have enough plastique when we arrive. You *never* lose one animal in a mess like this, Captain."

We roped everything—and everyone—together. When the ponies stumbled, the Nungs could hold them up.

I helped, too. I couldn't hold a pony up, but I could hold a German shepherd's leash. I held it as tightly as I could as we stepped into the stream, as he began to paddle the way all dogs paddle, and I stumbled and fell.

I was screaming as the water swept him away. I was thinking terrible things—things I never ever thought I'd think.

I was thinking:

Please, God, let him die here. Let the dog die here.

If he does—

—one of the dreams will be wrong—

—and if one is wrong—

—others can be.

We ran along the stream for what seemed like blocks, the humus sucking at our boots, bringing us to our knees again and again, trying to see his body in the torrent rushing through the trees.

When we found him, it was in an eddy, the leash caught on a branch. He was swimming like all dogs swim, his head up, his legs paddling in a circle as if nothing really were wrong.

We pulled him out. He shook, he shook again, and when he was through shaking, he stood there.

He didn't die. No one did, Major. Even the ponies—every last pony—made it across.

Is it luck, Colonel? I remember asking. *Or is this the dream you're dreaming?*

I don't remember what happened next.

I don't remember the people at Nghan Son Lap that well. I don't remember their dogs or their children. I remember that Willie wanted to give me something, because I was shaking and couldn't stop. Steve said no, I remember. He said: "No, Willie. Don't give her anything else."

I remember that they put me in a longhouse. One where I could listen to the voices by the fire pit, voices I don't really remember. I was lying on another mat, Major, another woven mat in another longhouse—or I think I was. It may have been another village earlier, another longhouse, another mat. I don't know.

I was remembering the little gray boats as I lay there, I think, though I can't be sure, Major.

I was thinking to myself: *That's* where the dog will die, Mary. On one of those little gray boats. . . .

I remember waking up once in the night, sitting up, waiting for my eyes to adjust to the darkness. I remember crawling over to the chief, bumping into Cooper as I did, and whispering words in English to him:

"One of the Nungs is going to die in a village, somewhere. There isn't any river in the dream, so it's going to be soon, I think."

Do they care? I remembering wondering. *Do they* really *care if a Nung is going to die?*

They must have, Major.

They tried to stop it.

The captain asks me and I tell him what I've dreamed—the man's face, lying in mud by the dark posts of a longhouse, somewhere. There isn't a river, so it's going to be soon, I say. His throat is gone. I don't know how. That's all I see, Captain.

He asks me with words and I answer him without them: *That's all I see, Captain.*

They make me walk down the line of ponies until I find the face. When I find it, I give a little nod to the captain. They move the little man up the line with us, but tell him nothing. He's grinning. He likes all of this attention. He's got a scar on his chin, but it's a friendly face. He's small and wiry—real Nung.

The chief says, "She's right, Captain. He is *burning.*"

Or the captain says it for Willie—Willie never has to say a thing. I don't remember which it was, Major.

At the village where we stay that night they put him in the longhouse with me. They put the dog in with us, too—so the dreamer and a dog will be there with him, so the dream won't come true.

Cooper stays at the foot of the longhouse ladder, guarding, hiding his face while he does it. The others leave to sup with the headman and his family, as they should. *I'll be listening*, the captain tells me.

I don't remember everything, Major. I remember sitting in the longhouse with the Nung, and not wanting him to die. I remember trying to talk to him, using little hand gestures in the very bad light, laughing when the gestures didn't work, when nothing either of us did worked at all. I remember both of us laughing, Major. I remember the young man grinning and I remember thinking: *This is what kids do, isn't it?*

I remember him taking me by the arm and not letting go. I remember that he *didn't* hit me. I remember he grabbed my arm and pulled me down to the floor and I didn't know whether to laugh or scream. I remember thinking to myself: *What does this mean to him? What does this really mean?*

I don't know if the other Nungs would have done it, Major. I don't know what women are to them, what *duty* and *manhood* mean. I don't know what any of these things mean to anyone anymore, Major.

I remember—I remember wanting to scream, and not being able to, and then screaming, and wishing I hadn't. I hit him twice—I hurt him, I know. He would've stopped, I'm sure, Major. *All he wants,* I remember thinking, *is to be able to say he touched her—he touched the Americans' woman. That's all he wants.*

The dog was there in the darkness. When I screamed, it got up. I do remember that, Major. I remember hearing its claws on the wood floor, hearing them speed up, and then suddenly nothing—no snarl, no growl, no paws. And the hand that was holding my arm let go.

I tried but couldn't get the dog to stop. I said everything I could think of. I pulled at its harness, at its fur. I tried to *hurt* it so it would turn on me, and let the man go. I kept thinking he should be screaming—*why wasn't he screaming?*—his arms and legs were pounding on the floor, but he wasn't screaming. I didn't know he couldn't.

I kept wondering, too, why the dog wouldn't stop—why Cooper, standing there at the bottom of the ladder, hearing it all, hadn't come up to stop it.

He didn't want the dog to stop.

I understand that now.

I remember how the Nung stumbled to the doorway. I remember how he fell. I remember climbing down the ladder by myself and finding it—the body—by the longhouse posts. The light was bad, but I could see what had been done to his throat.

I really don't remember anything else, Major.

I remember crying into my arm, into the circuitry. I remember saying: *You knew, Colonel. You knew we'd try to save* someone, somewhere, *and by trying, help it come true. . . .*

I thought of Christabel the next morning. I remember that, too.

I wondered how he was doing. No, I don't know why.

Photostat, Telegram, Command Files (Personnel), **Operation Orangutan,** *Tiger Cat,* **Vietnam**

1106P CDT NOVEMBER 21 71 NSA309
NS TIA937 (NS BE005) XVI GOVERNMENT PO
WASHINGTON DC 10 654P EDT

MRS DOROTHY W CHRISTABEL
323 MAPLE STREET
LAFAYETTE NORTH CAROLINA
THIS IS TO CONFIRM THAT YOUR HUSBAND
MASTER SERGEANT GEORGE CHRISTABEL
USAR WAS INJURED 15 NOVEMBER IN THE
VICINITY OF PLEIKU REPUBLIC OF VIETNAM.
HE SUSTAINED PENETRATING WOUNDS FROM
HOSTILE SMALL ARMS FIRE WHILE ON AN OP-
ERATION. HE IS RECEIVING TREATMENT AT
THE EIGHTH SURGICAL HOSPITAL. HIS CONDI-
TION AND PROGNOSIS ARE GOOD. WE SHARE
YOUR CONCERN AND CAN ASSURE YOU HE IS
RECEIVING THE BEST OF CARE. HIS MAILING
ADDRESS REMAINS THE SAME.
WILLIAM R. NOBLE GENERAL CHIEF OF STAFF
US ARMY
(176). (CALLED IN 11/22)

Chapter 43

It stretches below us west to east and bigger than any river I've ever seen. I'm standing in the doorway of a longhouse. I'm looking out at the river valley and rubbing sleep from my eyes. It's Loc Mao, first village on the Black—and the others are down buying sampans by the headman's hut.

I remember this, Major. I do.

They have been down in the village center all morning, dickering, just as men should. Any less would be an insult to the headman, one he would never forget.

It is the most beautiful valley I have ever seen, even with the river flooding its banks. I want to stay here. I want to stay with these beautiful brown people, their black blouses, their silver jewelry, their dogs yapping in the morning fog, sampans moving swiftly down the river, children stretching in a moment's patch of sun—just as *I* am, in the doorway of this longhouse.

I want to stay in Bali Hai.

This is the river, a voice says suddenly, and it's only my own, *where the black kid and the dog will die, Mary.*

I know. . . .

It took all the ponies we had. It took three of our last four bags of *real* rice seed from the big lockers we'd left back in the trees at Dien. And it took our last hundred dollars of kip. In return, we received ten sampans, the kind with three-foot keels.

I don't know what I expected. A fire on stilts—like Apaches.

The body wrapped in white cloth sent downriver in a little boat. Crosses. Little Buddhas. *Someone* to pray to—or *for*. But the Nungs buried their comrade in the earth of a hill not far from the river, standing over him for a long time. The Tai and the Russians stayed away.

The Nungs know how to work a sampan, and the chief, who's ridden in one only twice, whispers: "It's a goddamn boat, isn't it? I know *boats*." The villagers want to help us—they want to move the bags from the ponies to the boats—but Bach says quickly: *We need to check them first*. He says: *It is amazing how much precious seed can be lost through even the tiniest of holes*.

The Nungs, unhappy, check the bags, patch the ones that need patching with their little kits, and then hand the bags reluctantly, one by one, to the arms of happy Tai—who deposit them, just as gently, in the sampans, which are painted red and blue.

The rice is special, they're telling themselves. *If the bags happen to be heavy, is that so very strange? Is that so very strange for* special *rice*?

What is precious, they know, *is often heavy*.

I wade out into the eddying water, where the sampans float. Arms reach down to pull me up and over and when I'm seated on the plank—far from White Tai ears—the captain leans over to me and in English says:

"We're very close. I need to see your dreams."

"So we can *help* them come true, Captain?" I say.

"No."

Why should I believe you? I ask him.

It doesn't matter what you believe, he says.

He's right, of course, and I go ahead.

I tell him how the kid and the dog will die.

I need more than that, Lieutenant, he says.

Get it yourself, I tell him.

It's not the same that way. It's better if you help.

All right, I say. *All right*.

So I give him more.

I give him every drop of blood in every dream.

The river is a boiling brown body. I'm holding the gunwales and sitting as low as I can. My knuckles are white. They *hurt* if I try to let go.

The sampans somehow stay upright.

The current is fast—faster than anyone thought it would be. "It won't," the chief says, grinning, "take us any three days."

We hit whitewater more than once. I remember that, Major. I don't remember the names, the places, though. We hit whitewater and the sampans have a hard time of it, but I'm not scared. We're not going to die here, I know. *We're going to die later.*

I knew what was coming, Major. All I could do was wait.

The chief had our tiller. He was keeping us from *pearling* on every swell. Everyone else was hunkered down by the wet bags of clay. The sampans rolled, righted themselves, rolled again, moving like eels downstream. The villages on their flooded banks went by like telephone poles, like trees on a highway in a country far away.

There weren't any patrol boats this far up the Black. There weren't any aircraft either—in the rain. The clouds were like a dark gray dome so low you could touch it. The rain stung. The river boiled like a school of bonita off the Coronado Islands, where I'd fished with Jerry once.

All we could do was wait.

We pass the Mountain of Light, near Bay Ca, and the cave villages of Me Xuyen. They're like photographs, misty—now there, now gone.

We eat with one hand and hold the rail with the other, and sleep squatting down low. The rain stops. It starts again. The river widens and the boil of it slows. Someone takes out a pack of cards and grins. I think of Christabel at camp.

"Hit me," someone says in English, and we play until the rain comes down hard and washes the cards away.

"Do Buddhists," I asked Bach, "ever return to earth as Catholics?"

He smiled, the rain dripping from his chin.

"Only," he said, "only if they are *very*, very bad."

I dreamed another dream that day, Major. Something long and black shining in the sun. I wasn't asleep when I dreamed it—I was kneeling in the sampan, in the rain, in the sudden light. I was holding the side of the boat, my knees in dirty water.

It wasn't a dike, Major. I thought it was, but it wasn't.

It was just a long black wall.

I remember exactly how they died, Major. I really do.

That is something you never forget.

We made it past Hong Gai and the garrison on the cliffs.

We made it past Hai Duong and the flooded wire bridge to Xuan Mai Province.

We made it through the rapids of the Van Yen Gorge and lost no one, lost nothing at all.

When we reached the fishing village of Uong Bi, it was dusk. We had one bag of "special rice" left, a few bars of soap that would be meaningless to the people here and two tins of Soviet C-rations. They took the rice and the rations—a gracious gesture only—and made us welcome, too. We checked the sampans and bags with our flashlights. We posted our guards. We ate with the headman's family, as always, and did our best to sleep.

There wouldn't be another village after this, we knew.

The Tai of Uong Bi wore red, not black or white. They fished in red blouses. They farmed their rice in red hats. Their favorite fish was the little bright red *chopolet*. I wanted to ask them what red meant to them, what it really meant, but I never had the chance.

The next morning, we're the only sampans in the fog. For hours we see no one else. The Black has begun to flatten, to broaden here. We're near the last limestone ridges of the Bac Can Cordillera, the great Hoa Binh Delta lying just beyond. We won't know it when we reach it in all this fog.

The fog lightens. We see a river that goes forever in every direction—the way Harry said it would—and then the fog closes in again.

The river has no banks. The water reaches into the green

hills, into paddy canals, like long fingers of mist, all of it lapping at limestone cliffs carved by water before any human beings were ever here. Were it not for the current, I keep telling myself, we'd be lost. We'd be lost forever. . . .

The river isn't boiling. I start to ask the chief where the schools of bonita are, what has happened to them, but then stop. *This isn't California, Mary. They aren't fish. They're "rollers," like Willie said. They're "waves that roll."*

I shake my head, trying to clear it.

No one is talking. No one is saying a thing.

We're being carried by the current forever and ever, that's all.

All of a sudden Steve is staring and I turn and look.

A few klicks downstream you can see it—a boat heading up the opposite shore, skimming the water like a big gray hand. A *big gray boat, Mary.*

We're not on it, I tell myself. *No one can die yet.*

No one is shouting. No one is grabbing weapons as if the world were about to come apart. The river is wide. The boat doesn't see us. We're ten little sampans, that's all. It's a gray day. The clouds are low. It'll start raining again any second. Why should they even see us? Why should they even care?

Then Steve says:

"It's *blue.*"

"What?" I say.

He glances back at the captain, who's kneeling with Cooper in the sampan just behind. The captain raises his chin: *What's wrong?* Steve stares at him, as if answering, and then turning to the chief says it again: "Willie, it's *blue.*"

The chief sighs and moves the tiller. The sampan begins to slow. The sampans behind us slow, too. The current rushes past. Our stern rises and falls, rises again, falls. The sampans behind us drift closer.

"It's *blue,*" Steve says again, and all the chief can do is nod. The captain, a few yards behind us, *knows.* The dog, lying on the bags beside me, squirms, as if knowing, too.

The corporal and the dog don't die in sampans, I tell the captain, but he already knows. He remembers the dream I gave him. *They die on the deck of a big gray boat.*

Yes, he says, *they do.*

"Every last bit of it," Steve keeps saying, "is *blue.*"

When we killed our escorts, Steve, I want to ask him, *was everything blue then, too?*

The patrol boat slows, holds for a moment, begins to grow. *It's turning.*

I know.

We reach for our AKs very slowly. We rest their stocks on the sampan's rails.

"Shit," the chief says. No one laughs. What he means is: *We're not close enough to Dong Noi.*

I look at Steve. He knows I'm looking but he doesn't turn around.

"It's still blue."

I know, I tell him.

"Goddamn son of a bitch," the chief says, the patrol boat bigger now, higher and wider as its engines carry it toward us.

Is there anything—anything at all you can do to help, Mary?

I close my eyes.

I see a long black wall.

The patrol boat cuts its engines and drifts, letting the river carry it to us. At the last minute it turns, swinging its hull against ours, the current holding us together like good friends, very close.

Three AKs on its foredeck stay aimed at us. The twin 12.7s on its prow—manned by men in khaki—stay aimed at us as well. We don't move an inch. We act like we don't know we're even holding weapons. *We're Russians, after all,* Dai uy. *We're not exactly the enemy, you know.*

Bach shouts something to the coxswain at the wheel.

The officer shouts something back and walks to the patrol boat's wire. A voice—which isn't mine—says:

We've got to get on that boat.

No, I say. *If we do, Cooper will die.*

Bach steadies himself in the sampan with one hand, reaches up to the patrol boat's deck with the other and hands the officer our wrinkled papers. The officer steadies himself—uniform dark with rain—and studies them carefully, just as he should.

We've got to get aboard, the voice keeps saying.

No! I shout.

Bach turns, glances at the captain and turns back again. *Yes,* the voice says suddenly. *Yes, Bach, that's fine.*

Bach speaks to the officer and the officer looks annoyed. Bach repeats it—something about needing to use their radio because *ours* is broken. The officer finally nods, gestures, shouts something a little louder in the wind: *If they must, Major, but have them do it quickly, please.*

Bach and the captain climb aboard—helped to its deck by cautious but respectful hands—and are led to the coxswain's den, where the wheel, the radar screen and the radio sit. I glance at Steve. He's standing in the bow of our sampan. He's ready. *How blue is it, Steve?*

The chief's hand is barely on the tiller, much closer to the AK in his lap. *How many of them are burning now, Willie?*

The dog is sitting beside me again. Cooper is sitting hunched in the sampan behind, face hidden as always.

No, I say. *No.*

Can you smell it? I want to ask.

Can you smell it coming?

We took the boat away from them, Major. It wasn't very hard to do. I can tell you exactly how, if you'd like.

When it was over, Major, I was thinking:

They'll never stop us now. They'll never stop a team like ours.

We were all thinking it—

Because the captain was.

I understand that now.

We let the Nungs load as many bags into the patrol boat as they could. We let them puncture the lungs and bellies of the crew, so their bodies would sink. We let them push them overboard.

We set all but three of the sampans free, and put the remaining bags in those. We arranged those bags neatly along the patrol boat's gunwales and also down in the bilge. We covered the three sampans with canvas and roped them to us in a line. We didn't let the Nungs do it *all*.

The patrol boat rode low and slow. The sampans rolled like cradles, the way we'd known they would.

I saw the chief with a knife in his good hand. He was standing alone on the foredeck, just staring at the Nungs.

I went and stood beside him, and didn't say a thing. I *knew* it, too.

"They're burning," he said. "Every last one of them is burning, Mary."

"I know," I tell him. "I know."

Subject: I haven't told you the truth, Major. I've tried to. I really have. I've tried to tell you what we went through, but to do that, Major—to do that sometimes I've lied. Am I making any sense?
Interviewer: Can you give me an example?
Subject: Yes, I can. [Pause] Those details about the first patrol boat—how we took it, I mean.
Interviewer: Yes. What about them?
Subject: I don't know if those details are true. I don't remember really. All I know is what it *felt* like to do it . . . and what it *felt* like when we were through. . . .

Photostat, Journal Article, Central Files (Narda), Operation Orangutan EVAL
The Testimony of Political Repression as a Therapeutic Instrument
by Ana Julia Cienfuegos and Cristina Monelli
Method and Procedure

In our treatment of these patients, the initial contact, consisting of one or two interviews with a therapist, is devoted to eliciting basic data on patients' life history and political repression, and to establishing a therapeutic relationship. Patients are encouraged to tape-record a detailed description of the events leading to their present state of suffering. The therapist explains that although recalling the details of such experiences may be very painful, the procedure will allow the patients to understand more fully the emotions associated with their trauma and will allow them at the same time to denounce, through a written essay, the violence and injustice to which they have been subjected. A series of three to six sessions is held in which all details of the detention, torture (physical and psychological), and other political suffering are recorded. The patients' obvious history is included in the testimony so that the traumatic experience may be integrated and understood in the context of each individual's life.

Patients are urged to tell their stories in their own words and their own way. The therapist may ask questions to clarify or elicit more detail with respect to particularly significant events. When the testimony is transcribed into written form, the text is revised by the patient in conjunction with the therapist. The final version is a document that has been revised and edited jointly by patient and therapist. Written testimonies have ranged from 15 to 120 typed pages.

Discussion

The use of testimony has been found to have significant therapeutic value for victims of torture and political repression. Patients reexperience their suffering in their own words and their particular tone of voice, through tape-recording which allows the therapist to understand the special meaning attributed by the patients to their traumatic experience. Afterward, when the tape is put into writing, the testimony acts as a "memory" that can be shared, reviewed, rewritten and analyzed at any time by therapist and patient. It has the ability to preserve the past exactly as remembered and experienced. It constitutes an important step toward the elaboration of past experiences for the patients themselves, and creates a document of historical value for future generations. . . .

Chapter 44

We left the Black River Valley at Quy Boum—last of the great limestone ridges, "gateway to the farmlands of the merry Muong," as Harry liked to put it. We were slow, sampans in tow, our own gunwales nearly to the water. We entered the Hoa Binh Delta at dusk and at nightfall, chose a flooded canal where the chief could be sure of clearance. We anchored a klick up it—by a windbreak of river trees. "You just don't risk night running on a river that doesn't have *riverbanks*, Lieutenant," Willie said.

We didn't answer the boat's radio, which kept calling all night.

We didn't talk much either, even though there wasn't anyone to hear us.

A voice somewhere kept saying:

Another ten hours, that's all . . . if the little gray boats let us.

The three PBRs of the Soviet PC class, lighter and faster than our own, met us at dawn just south of the Hoa Binh Bridge.

They knew what they were looking for.

We knew they knew.

They'd gotten the word by now and it went something like this:

Dien Bien Phu garrison and Tai province reporters report team of Soviet agricultural advisers on rice seeding mission to extreme northwest. Relevant ministries unable to confirm. Group size and cargo volume inconsistent with enemy infiltration teams, but caution should be exercised. Four Russian males, one Russian female, one DRV officer and nine tribal escorts with cargo last reported at Van Ban on the Song Da traveling south by motorless vessels. Locate and detain. North and east of Hoa Binh consider threat to the Republic. Addendum: Central radio contact with PBR PA class River Police Unit 76 lost at 0245 hours on 11/2. . . .

They came at us out of the fog and we let them, their quad 12.7s aimed down our throats.

We *let* it happen.

We let Bach wave. We let them board the sampans, lift the canvas, read the lettering and move on—as we'd known they would.

We let them board *our* boat.

We let them look *everywhere*—in the coxswain's den, in the twin fifty buckets, every nook and cranny, starting at the bow and moving to the stern, where Cooper sat. We let Bach walk with the ranking officer of the two boats, right by his side, on our deck, giving him our history.

The bags from the deck were in the bilge, where we'd hidden them quickly, thinking it made sense. The little section of deck that raised up to reveal the bilge was a yard from the officer's boots now.

They're going to open one of the bags, the voice said suddenly. *They're going to climb down in the bilge, wonder why we're letting our rice seed get wet, and open a bag. The lettering won't be enough.*

I looked back. Cooper was sitting on the duffel bags, keeping his head down, the way he was supposed to.

It's the dream, Mary.

I know.

Please, I said. *Please. . . .*

They were confused and angry—that was obvious. They were embarrassed, too, but weren't sure why. They felt tricked, but didn't know whether they had been, whether Hanoi had been, whether anyone had been tricked or not. They wanted us to understand, of course—without having to say it—that this was *serious.* That Hanoi said it was. That the relevant ministries *couldn't* confirm, so that as far as they, the patrol boat officers, were concerned, we *couldn't* be what we said we were. Whether they wanted to or not, please understand, they had to treat us as a *risk*, because the relevant ministries *couldn't* confirm. As soldiers—as comrades in the fight—would we respect them if they didn't? There would be apologies later, of course—oral and written—when matters were resolved, but for now, they were obligated to treat us as a *threat to the State.* Hanoi said so. We could understand their position, could we not? We would do the same in their places, would we not?

They didn't want to be the little men who caused a diplomatic commotion—who made it necessary for Hanoi to dance with Moscow in ways it didn't want to—but they didn't want to be the ones who let *enemies of the Republic* through either. We could understand that, certainly. And now that the ranking officer thought about it, there *were* things that looked odd—

What are you doing with this boat? he asked Bach.

We spent the night in That Khe, Commander, Bach answered. *We found this vessel drifting in a canal. We saw no one in the vicinity to report it to. Observe the holes made by bullets. These made us wonder, too. They made us think that the River Police Unit at Hoa Binh would want to know about it. We tried to call them, of course, but the radio was not functioning. Our project in the Northwest is finished and we are returning to Hanoi. As you can see, Commander, our Russian guests are wet and tired. This has not been pleasant for them. They wish to go home now.*

The ranking officer was listening but he didn't stop walking. There were *odd* things here. He gestured with his hand. He gestured again. His crew kept their weapons trained while walking and gestured toward the stern of our boat, toward Cooper.

We let him. We let him walk toward the stern.

We didn't try to stop him.

Why, Captain? I was shouting. *Why are you letting him walk toward Cooper?*

I step up to the two of them. Though it will look odd to the commander, I'm sure, I start walking with them. I look at Bach. I'm going to say something in the best Russian I know—say *anything*—anything that might make a difference, that might keep him from walking to the stern.

Something touches my neck. I look around.

The captain is by the gunwale. No one is paying him any attention. He's looking at me. He's shaking his head a little. No, he's doing it without moving his head at all. *No, Mary*, he's saying. *No*. The AK in his hands is moving ever so slowly up. . . .

I'm aiming it, he says. *I'm aiming it at the commander's heart*.

I understand now. He was going to do it all along. He was planning to stop it this way all along. I just didn't know.

I step back—I step out of his way.

The boat lurches a little. It's something we could have foreseen.

It lurches at the very moment the captain fires. It lurches, the barrel tilts, the bullet that leaves it goes somewhere else, hitting Bach, hitting him the only place it can.

The dream starts now.

The commander doesn't know where that bullet came from. He heard it, but isn't sure where it went. He thinks for a second that one of his own men fired, looks around him, looks around again. When he turns back, he sees Cooper—who's looking up because of the sound. He sees *very dark skin*. It's wrong, he knows this, and he steps toward it, the face, sees *dark skin again*. He thinks of American GIs who have skin like that and all of a sudden he understands.

Somewhere sailors dressed in khaki are firing now. They've noticed the captain with his AK raised. They know who fired the shot. They don't like seeing an AK aimed at their commander.

I've stepped away. I've stepped back so far I'm standing in front of the captain, so I step aside. Bach is down on the deck, twisting. The captain fires again, but it's late. The commander has his Tokarev out because of the *dark skin*, because of the *dog*—which is leaping now. The dog is leaping because Cooper is afraid. Cooper is afraid because he has no weapon in his hand—because a sick man wouldn't—because a man in an NVA uniform looms before him, like a dream, shouting, "*Vee zachem prishlee na re-*

koo?" and Cooper is trying his best to answer, *"Ya zdes po deloo."* But it doesn't matter. It doesn't matter because the dog is leaping, and the commander is firing, and the dog, hit, is rolling away. Cooper stands up. The commander turns toward him the instant the captain fires, and fires himself. He fires because a black man he's *sure* is an American is standing up and it scares him. It scares him because he's *sure* the black man has a weapon—why wouldn't he? He fires, *hoping* he is right. The bullet from the captain's AK enters the commander's head and the captain ducks, seeing himself in the eyes of sailors aiming their own, and, ducking, kneeling, shooting, the captain hits them at last.

I look at Cooper lying on the deck. I look at Crusoe, his back leg kicking. I look at Bach and I can't stop screaming.

I didn't dream about you! I tell him. *I didn't dream that you were dying!*

Yes, you did, a voice whispers. *Yes, you did.*

I've got an AK. It's my own. The sailors don't fire at me until I have it—and I remind myself what Christabel said, what I learned in that village with all the bodies and the clothes. I go ahead. I *hug* them. I steady my legs, I put my foot back, I watch the left arc (it's a killer, Sergeant) and I *hug* every one I can.

The chief is firing. Steve is firing. The captain is up again, firing.

It's very hard, Major, to really know which of us did the killing.

The chief takes a round in his bad shoulder. Blood blooms in heavy wool. The captain takes a sliver of the deck in his thigh, cries out and pulls it loose. A little cut over Steve's right eye blinds him with the blood. Bach and Cooper, five of the Nungs—and the dog—are lying on the deck. They're dying.

You just didn't know that's what it was, Mary, the voice is whispering.

I remember screaming even after the firing had stopped. I remember screaming for quite a while. I remember Steve, the way he danced—like a snake, a cat—how time slowed for him and how he was able to float, to *see* what he needed to see to keep the bullets away.

I remember this, because the captain showed me. He showed me what it was like.

I remember the captain, skinny, moving, too—seeing his own face in a sailor's mind and knowing when the man would pull the trigger, turning and rolling and shooting until his face wasn't there anymore, until there wasn't a mind there anymore.

I remember the chief, too—his good arm holding his AK, the silver tip of his prosthesis holding it, too—shooting until all the *burning* sailors, just like Buddhist monks, weren't shooting at him anymore.

I remember Cooper. I remember feeling what it was like when the bullets hit them *both*, when they both felt it, because that's how their talent worked.

I remember seeing a river, a park and a blanket. I remember walking toward Bach.

All of these things are all true.

I remember kneeling beside Bach and thinking: *I didn't know.* I said this to him. The captain *helped*. I wouldn't lie, Major.

I remember holding his hand, the way I'd done with so many others. How he looked at his own stomach, confused, as if thinking: *What is that hole doing there, Father?* As if saying to me, confused: *Will you please help me push it back in, Lieutenant?*

I remember how he used words, too. How he said: "It's all right."

I remember him saying: "We are given as many chances as we need in eternity, Lieutenant. I only wish—"

I remember seeing the last things he saw:

A park, a baby and a blanket.

That's what they were, Mary, the voice whispered. *The very last things he saw. . . .*

I remember kneeling by Cooper and taking his hand, too, and pretending I knew so many, many things about him. That I knew his mother and his father, but had somehow forgotten this. That I knew what they *felt*, what they'd always wanted for him, what they'd do for him when he came home on his own two feet. That I knew the streets where he'd lived, the friends he'd had, that dog—the one he'd owned at fourteen—how it had died, and what that

"Was it blue, Steve?" I ask, the wind tearing through our hair, engines screaming their limit. "Was the world all nice and blue for you?"

I want to hurt him. I want to hurt *someone*.

"Was it blue, Steve?"

"Yes. . . ."

"Why didn't you at least *try*?"

He doesn't answer, but he doesn't have to.

It doesn't work that way. I wish it did, Mary. But it doesn't. I can save myself, but I can't always save others. . . .

I say:

"Didn't you see them *burning*, Willie? Didn't you see the fire starting on their arms?"

He doesn't answer me with words.

I didn't know what the fire meant, Mary. I didn't know one of us would do it.

And neither did you, Mary, the voice says.

We take the bennies the captain offers. We've got to stay awake for the next five hours, I know. There isn't any reason to argue. There isn't any reason to take a chance.

The chief takes the wheel in our boat. One of the Nungs takes the wheel of the other.

I turn once. I see the captain steering, the chief kneeling and beginning to cord the bags. *How is he doing that?* I wonder. *How is the captain navigating these currents?*

But I know.

The way he's done everything, Mary. By listening. *By learning what all of us know.*

The chief looks around at me—because the captain, without words, has told him to. *She wants to know how we're doing this, Chief.*

"I'm teaching him," the chief says, grinning. "He's quick, but he ought to be, don't you think?"

We're a team, I remember thinking. *Even with two pieces gone, we're a team, Colonel. Isn't that what you wanted?*

Wish you were here, I told him. *Really wish you were here.*

death would always mean to him. That his father was a min
his uncle a sergeant major—the most decorated Negro in W
War II, the one who'd told him once, "Try the Army, Wal
Ridley. Try it with dogs if you prefer it, but try it." That I e
knew what it meant to be black, to forget it once in a while and
laugh at a white girl's jokes.

I didn't *know* these things. So I had to pretend I did, Majo

You could've asked him, Mary. You could have asked him ⠶
camp or in Vientiane—in the jungle, in the cave, in the boats—a⠶
those days. But you didn't. You just made him laugh.

It was safer that way, wasn't it, Mary?

If he was going to die, it was a lot safer that way.

I remember kneeling by him—by the dog, which was still
breathing. I remember listening to the breathing until it stopped.

I tried to pack the wounds. I tried to help the Nungs, but
Steve kept stopping me. I hit him—I thought he was my father—
but he kept saying: "They're dead, Mary. You can't help them."

Five of the Nungs were wounded. One would die within the
hour. Two would die before we reached Dong Noi. I *knew* that. I
knew all of it even without thinking.

The chief's wound was a fleshy one, a small chip from the
bone. He didn't want morphine, no. Steve's cut clotted soon,
didn't need a bandage. The captain's puncture wound wouldn't
bleed, but he wasn't worried. He said: "I'm on autodrip, Lieutenant. I'm being taken care of just fine."

We've got to go, the chief says, starting the engines with a
little help from the captain. We're on one of those little boats now,
and I'm not sure how we got here. I'm not sure what we're doing.
"I don't think I can do this any longer," I tell them, but no one
hears. I start to turn, but then don't. Somewhere there are bodies
being pushed into the river. Somewhere the last living Nungs are
moving our bags into two lighter, faster boats. *Which do you want
to do to help, Mary?*

I take a bag. I move it.

I take another.

Steve and the captain took the 12.7s. The chief took the wheel again. The wounded Nungs sat against the gunwales on the deck. The others manned the boat behind us. I stood by the coxswain's window and held an AK that wasn't mine.

I remember other things, Major, but they're just not as important as these.

Is it life or is it death that shows us best what it means to be living, Lieutenant? Bach would have asked me then. *Is it the dream of a park, or is it the bullets that take that dream away?*

From USARV USPW/CI Detainee Files and MIA Board Proceedings of the 5th Special Forces Group and MAC-SOG

MAC-SOG MIA to Date

Shaffer, William, 209085676, PFC, Americal Division, TDY Command and Control North, MAC-SOG. Born 12 July 1950 in Concho, West Virginia. Entered service on 16 May 1969 at Colcord, West Virginia.

Missing in action since 30 November 1970, 10 miles inside Laos east of Tchepone returning from patrol aboard Vietnamese H-34 helicopter. Aircraft was struck by 37mm antiaircraft fire, lost control at 3,000 feet and according to witnesses exploded upon impact. Ground search in denied area not initiated.

Trevino, Anthony, 786539045, SGT, 173d Airborne Brigade, TDY Command and Control North, MAC-SOG. Born 23 March 1941 in Atlantic City, New Jersey. Entered service on 31 May 1965 at Atlantic City, New Jersey.

Missing in action since 16 January 1971, when reconnaissance patrol inserted 10 miles inside Laos west of Muong Tip engaged enemy at landing zone; CIDG and LLDB survivors reported his capture and summary execution but confirmation of death has not been recorded.

Klein, Daniel, 497234094, PO3, SEAL Team One, TDY Command and Control North, MAC-SOG. Born 14 December 1939 in San Diego, California. Entered service on 17 June 1959 at San Diego, California.

Missing in action since 10 May 1971 when long-range reconnaissance team entered western Quang Nam Province by ground two miles east of Cambodia on May 3; past initial radio contact, no further contact was made. Ground and air search conducted.

Takakuni, Peter, 576892007, PFC, 2d Air Cavalry, TDY Command and Control North, MAC-SOG. Born 24 July 1946 in Northampton, Massachusetts. Entered service on 22 June 1964 at Springfield, Massachusetts.

Missing in action since 24 March 1970, when UH-1H helicopter carrying his patrol attempted departure from landing zone in the tri-border area 14 miles inside Cambodia, aircraft experienced multiple explosions during ascent, continued forward for 200 yards and according to witnesses crashed in the jungle. No ground search initiated in denied area.

Christabel, George, 980774852, SSGT, 5th Special Forces Group, Command and Control North, MAC-SOG. Born 5 September 1930 in Charlotte, North Carolina. Entered service 22 March 1954 at Charlotte, North Carolina.

Missing in action since 16 October 1971, 1½ miles inside Laos west of the DMZ with a reconnaissance patrol which engaged the enemy twice on 29 November; last seen by Vietnamese patrol survivors attending to the team's wounded officer.

Chapter 45

We make it past the Hoa Binh Bridge, the one that America has never—in all its years of bombing—been able to bring down. It was there in the fog all along. It was there—only a few klicks away—when Bach and Cooper were dying. *The dreams are never wrong, Mary.*

We make it to where the Black is broadest, right before it reaches the Red. Here the river is split by long flooded islands, sea monsters just below the surface, and you've got to know what you're doing, which of course Willie does. We make it past the flooded paddies of Xuan Mai, past the flotillas of sampans ferrying stranded farmers and their families to wherever they need to go. We make it past these things because of Willie.

The sun comes out. It burns through the fog. Willie swears. No, the captain swears for him. And then, like an answer to a prayer, the fog comes rushing back again.

We may make it, someone says. It doesn't matter who. We all say it. *If the fog holds. . . .*

No one says: *We'll have time to set it.* No one says: *We'll have time to stay there and watch it blow.*

Only: *We may make it to Dong Noi . . . if the fog holds.*

We won't have a chance to set it. PBRs and spotter planes and the few choppers the North has are looking for us now—they've *got* to be—waiting, just like us, for the fog to clear. They'll be looking even harder at the little villages north of Hanoi. The dikes all the way from Hanoi to Son Tay are crawling with soldiers.

They've got to be. Peering through the mist, tracking the river with their weapons now. They don't know where we'll land, but by now they certainly know *why. Four patrol boats are missing*, Trung Uy. *And a cargo that size* . . . They don't know *where*, but they know *why.*

We don't have an interpreter anymore, no, but it doesn't matter, does it, Colonel? We won't be *talking* anymore. We don't have a dog or a dog handler, and that doesn't matter either. What we needed them for was finished in another valley, long ago.

What we really need, Colonel, is *air support.* What the grunts always pray for. *We need Sabers and Intruders and Broncos—anything that flies, Colonel.*

What do we sound *like, Colonel?* I want to ask him, but I don't want to raise my sleeve. *Are our voices muffled? Is the blood in our veins a little too loud? What has it been like, listening day after day? Do you have machines to record it and other machines to write it down? Can they separate our voices, so that we aren't one single voice—so that we aren't a single scream?*

Do you sit night after night in a shack, listening, trying to figure it all out. Trying to see what it all means, Colonel?

Is it maybe a little harder work than you imagined it would be?

What did you hear when Bach died, Colonel? When he lay there and said, "It's all right. It's all right"?

What did you hear when Cooper and his dog died, neither making a sound? Did you want them to? Were you hoping they would make a sound?

In a universe somewhere, Colonel, we do make it out of this alive. In fact, we come back to you, Colonel. We find you. We help you see and hear and smell it the way it was. . . .

There's got to be a fail-safe, someone says, *in case we got this far. Some way for him to stop us, or he'd never have let us start.*

I'm standing next to Willie. He's leaning against me, hurting.

He's the one who asked it.

I'm not so sure, someone else says. *He may not have thought . . . He may never have thought we'd get this far.*

It's Steve. We all nod. We don't say a word. We just nod.

The wind, the waves on the hull, are loud enough. We'd never hear each other with words, so we don't use them.

We get past Xuan Tet and Na Bao. In a fog like this all they can use is boats, we know. We tell each other. We agree. *We're lucky*, someone says. It doesn't matter who.

We're the luckiest team in the whole wide world, someone else says.

Will it last?

You know better than we do, Mary.

So I say to God:

When we finally stop, when we finally get out and hold our breaths and sink into the river, feeling for the dike with our feet, planting those charges ten feet down, will you let us change *it, God? Will you let us change the world you have made?*

Will you let our luck *go on like this?*

Two hours into the bennies I fall down. I see the bodies on the riverbank just as if I were lying beside them. I see a little red flag waving in the village three hundred meters upstream. The bodies—the ones I'm lying beside—are jerking, jerking the way they always have and always will. In the mud. In the red red mud.

No, I say, and I'm not the only one saying it. The others say it, too, though it doesn't do any good. We're moving through the fog. We're moving *toward* the dream. We're not even there, Major, but we're already lying in the mud.

Someone with a hard pink arm helps me up. I don't understand. I say: *Who's steering this ship, Willie?* He says: *Robert is, Mary. He tells me what's happening out there and I tell him what to do. I go where I want to on the boat and I feel fine, because I know the rest of you are here. I'm here picking you up, Mary, but I'm also telling Robert how to run the ship. Everything is fine.*

I fall down again ten klicks from the Red, where the Black sheds its tears into its sister, who, according to legends, turns them red out of love. Willie is at the wheel. The captain is in one of the buckets, staring ahead, telling us about himself. I can hear him using words, giving them to the wind.

Steve is the one who picks me up. I'm jerking on the deck—

the rounds are making me jerk—and he holds me while I do it, while I tell him *with words* what he already knows without them.

The important things about the captain's life.

I start screaming as we make the big turn into the Red, where all the islands are under red red water. I see Willie getting hit, the round opening the side where his good arm is, spinning him around until he's there with us in the mud—jerking in the mud.

Willie sees it and his heart stops—I feel it stop—and then starts again.

Jesus, he says. *Jesus, Mary.*

Turn around, I tell him, *and it won't happen. It won't happen if you turn the boat around, Willie.*

None of it will come true, I'm telling them, *if we turn around right now.*

But I'm wrong.

If we turn around, Mary, it'll be another riverbank—somewhere. It won't be Dong Noi, but it'll be a riverbank on this river—somewhere. By turning we'll make it happen—somewhere else—if not in this world, then in another . . .

Steve sits on the deck. He holds me as if I were sick. He's wishing the captain hadn't given me bennies. He's saying:

It's too late, Mary. The captain hears them. He hears them looking for us only two or three kilometers back. He hears them thinking about us, Mary. They can see us on their radar, though they aren't quite sure. They want to find us so badly, and they're faster, faster than we are, so they will. They're just not carrying the load we're carrying, Mary.

At the wheel, in the fog, Willie is saying: *PC class. RPGs. And probably the only two minicannons the North has. You're right, Robert. They know we're here.* He says it staring at the radar screen, at the fog, without blinking.

There isn't a sound anywhere, except the engines, the water and the wind.

I remember how the fog held. I remember how one of us—it doesn't matter who—said: *There are three boats now. We look just like them, so they're not sure—they're not completely sure who we are.*

Is it luck? I remember asking a young man sitting beside me. *Or is it something we are making?*

Is this what you wanted? I remember asking a colonel somewhere, who was listening. *Is this exactly what you wanted us to become?*

When we were ten klicks from the village we wanted, we pulled to the north shore. *Ten klicks*, someone was saying, and the wheel turned. Everyone helped it. Whose hands they were didn't matter.

The fog was lifting at last.

We could see the fishing villages—one by one—the little red flags, and then, as the dike began to curve, the one that had to be Dong Noi. The villages east and west of it *crawled* with soldiers, but this one—its dike—crawled even more.

Yes, Mary, Robert was saying. *You can even hear them thinking it: Are they coming here? they're wondering. Are the American commandos coming here, to our little Dong Noi, where the Great Dike begins to bend?*

The boat turned. Willie's hands and the captain's were on the wheel, but we all turned it together.

The patrol boats are behind us. We can hear the officers thinking. The captain can, so we all can. There's no difference now. We can see what *they* see in the clearing fog. There are patrol boats downstream, too, where the fog is clearing. When the fog is gone, all of it, they'll see us—they'll have to—like a shaft of light from the sun, like sunlight on an enormous black wall. *We'll* see *them seeing us, Mary.*

Of course we will.

The shore rushes toward us, waves slamming the hull, the fuel more than enough to get us there. *Is it luck, Colonel?*

Or is it something else?

On the great dark gravelly dike rushing toward us—swollen river lapping higher than it has lapped in years—khaki-colored figures move like insects, like short sand-colored grass moving in the wind. Wisps of fog drift between us and the shore. The figures disappear, the wisps move on, the figures return—larger, closer now.

We've got to scuttle the boats, someone shouts, and he's a SEAL, so he ought to know. *It's the only way*, he shouts, and two Green Beanies agree. *It's the only way*, they're shouting, *to get the bags where they need to be.*

Willie raises his arm, waves it at the coxswain's den on the boat behind us, and the Nung who has the wheel waves back. Willie gives our boat full throttle. The Nung does the same.

The shore rushes toward us like a dream.

They know we're here, someone says, a joke, the echo of a joke. *It's a battalion*, someone else is saying. *A fucking battalion. . . .*

I'm in the coxswain's den. I'm the one steering it, giving it full throttle. Somehow I know how.

I look down.

The radio—where Willie put it—is blinking. Its lights have never stopped.

If a liar lies, I'm thinking, *can he ever stop? Can a liar ever stop lying, Mom?*

If Bucannon lied to us, I say to Willie—just to him. *If the transmission was constant or more frequent than he said it would be, could the NVA have tracked us? Could they have been following us for a long, long time? Could this be the fail-safe, Willie?*

I don't know if he answered. It doesn't matter. In a universe somewhere he did.

Sure, Mary, he said. *Sure it could.*

When the boat turns at the very last moment—under my hands or Willie's or the captain's or Steve's—when we turn from the riverbank where the automatic rifle fire is starting up at last, where the figures on the shore are *people* now, not ants, and the air is full of popping sounds—I fall against the gunwale. I just can't help it.

I get up, holding the gunwale. I look again at the shore.

We're flying past a marsh now, an eddy, another marsh, another eddy, looking, I know, for a place where the figures aren't as thick. A third marsh, a fourth—and the dike at our starboard is a long dark wall.

I look at the deck. The chief is on the floor of the coxswain's den, slapping at himself and crying. He's trying to hit it—the thing they put under his skin. He wants to get at it. He wants to crush it, to see if it will bleed.

I look at my own arm—the good one. I touch the little bulge under the dirty wool and I say: *I see you kneeling on the ground. I see you there in your nice white suit, kneeling on the ground. In a universe somewhere, John Bucannon, we've come home to you.*

The captain fires into the deck with his AK, then runs back to the stern. He waves at the Nungs, telling them to do it, too—to shoot at their deck, scuttle their boat the same way we're scuttling ours, because it's the only way to get those bags where they need to be. The deck splinters. Theirs splinters, too. Pieces from both decks rise, sailing into the wind. Engines scream, turning. We've chosen a marsh at, I realize, an eddy—at last.

The captain jumps into the bilge, firing at the hull. I can't see him but I hear him: *Don't worry, Mary. Bullets won't make it blow.*

We're sliding into the eddy, sinking lower and lower, water filling the bilge, engines straining to move us forward at all. We've got a minute, maybe two, to get those bags ten feet down, up against the dike, where they'll make a difference—if they can make a difference at all. I'm firing with him. I'm firing at the deck, at the hull down in the bilge, while the figures shift again and again on the shore. We're all firing, we're all steering, we're all checking the det cord which the captain's *body* is setting below.

It's a beautiful day. It really is. The fog is completely gone.

When we hear the rotors at last—two sets of them—there's a steady buzz with them, too, a saw, a zipper that won't stop—and the deck rises in bigger pieces now. But none of us are hit. The captain *knows*. He can hear the doorgunners aiming a hundred meters up. He tells us where to step, and we do it, and none of us are hit.

What a help, someone says, and it isn't a joke. Anything that helps us *sink* is a help. Our own boat turns, starts to lose control under all the hammering, under the buzz saw of the rounds raining down. We're almost there—to the marshy shore. I'm laughing. Someone else is, too. We're laughing because it *is* a joke.

They can't grenade us. They can't rocket us, mortar us—because they aren't sure we won't blow them up, too.

We hit the dike. We hit it where the waves are lapping hungry and high. I fall down. We all do. The bow sails up into gravel and mud and a voice, my own, says: *This is where it happens.*

I know, I tell it. *I know.*

The stern is sinking. The whole boat is. The Nungs have hit the dike beside us and are firing, firing into their deck. Both boats are sinking now.

I get up. I get up again and again. A Nung who hasn't fallen is laying cord on their deck—twenty feet away over water. The chopper above us is hitting *both* boats, plastic and wood rising into the air. A Nung screams. The figures move toward us in a wave, firing. The gunwales come apart, rising into the air.

Steve is in their field of fire. None of us move. He's finishing the det cord, jerking so the bullets he sees in his blue blue world will miss him. I see the bullets. We all do—because he does—and we tell him when to jerk, where to move.

The body that belongs to the captain is in the coxswain's den helping Willie to his feet. He's listening. We're all listening. We're telling each other *everything.*

I can hear them, Robert is saying. *I can hear them more clearly than anything I've heard before. I can hear them aiming—I can hear them thinking before they aim—*

And he can. He tells me where to move and I do. He tells me again. I do. He tells me—he tells Willie, too—so we both move now. He's moving with us, because he's got to, too.

The uniforms are almost to us. Their fire shreds the canopy and the radar, eating away at the hull.

Get off the boat! Robert screams. He screams at me and I step to the gunwale and slip. The deck is 45 degrees, as we sink in ten feet of water, which is where the bags of *special rice* need to be. We need to get away, he's telling us. We need to get away.

No! I tell him.

Steve is down in the bilge with the rising water, with our bags of special rice, which he's linking with the detonation cord. *No*, I say.

He's coming, Mary, Robert says. *Don't worry. He's coming.*

I *see* what Steve sees, a blue, blue world—I *feel* what he feels, hands cold and cramping in the water, holding the cord. I *feel* what he feels as he pulls himself—muscles screaming—up through the hole.

He's beside me. We can go.

I *feel* the captain's hands, warmer, under Willie's arms, helping him up. I *hear* what the captain hears. I hear what the door-gunner, high above us, is thinking: *I am taking aim.*

Steve is standing in bilge water to his chest. He raises himself on screaming muscles up through the hole in the deck. *I do it with him.*

He raises himself up through the hole to the deck. He does it again and again. I do it with him. I watch him do it and I do it, too. The dream keeps going.

Jump, Mary! he shouts at last, standing beside me.

I do it. We do it together. We jump together into the marshy water, we flail, we make it through the splash of automatic rifle fire, to the shore. We stand up now. Steve pulls my arm, keeps pulling.

We stand up again on the shore. We keep standing. I don't move. He keeps pulling.

It's going to happen, Steve. Mud and gravel tamped by a million feet. The mud is red. The river is red. The uniforms are sometimes khaki-colored and sometimes blue. You know what that means, Steve.

I tell him again, but he keeps pulling.

You know what that means, Steve.

He yanks my arm. I fall forward. I get up.

He yanks me hard again, and the dream begins.

We're running, Steve. We're running in the red red mud.

We've got our AKs at least. We're pulling Willie with us and he's making a terrible sound. He's trying to gouge out what they put in his back. He's trying to reach around, he's trying to do it with his barrel. *We don't have a chance, do we?* I say.

It's blue, Steve is saying.

I can hear them, Robert is saying.

They're burning, Willie is saying.

I see it—how the burning starts in their eyes, takes their bodies, becomes the halos Willie's always seen and always will. Willie sees it first, so the captain sees it, so we all do—starting, as always, on their arms and in their eyes.

It doesn't matter. It doesn't matter, Mary.

They want us alive, Robert is saying. *To embarrass our country. To parade us down a street in Hanoi—like that black GI. They'd like to take us alive if possible.*

We help them the best we can. Steve jerks and the little blue bullets miss him. Willie show us the *fires* he sees. Robert helps him. I show us—Robert helping—every little second of the dream. Robert finds our faces in a hundred pairs of eyes, shows them to us—so we know once more *where* to move and *when*, so the little blue bullets will miss us all, so we'll know where to send *our* bullets, so those bodies will start burning and Willie will *see* them burn, and we'll make it happen, and our faces will fade from those eyes.

We drop, we step, we spin. We see what we've already seen and will always see. We keep moving away from the boats, from the river, the marsh grass, toward the uniforms—sometimes khaki, sometimes blue—and we do what we need to do to keep our own bodies from burning, even if we're making the dream come true.

I didn't know how weak a body could be. I never really thought about it. We could *see* what we needed to do—we could *hear* them aiming, so many, and we *knew* what we needed to do, how we needed to move—to keep moving—so that those bullets would keep missing us. But our bodies couldn't move like that, couldn't duck and jerk and jerk again—*forever*. Our muscles were starting to cramp. Our boots were slipping even now in the mud. We couldn't turn as quickly as we had. The bullets were missing us, yes, but they were getting closer and we knew that in a moment or two we'd be lying there, Major, jerking and jerking in the mud, until the bullets weren't missing us anymore.

I kept thinking of the Nungs, Major. I kept thinking we ought to be doing something for them. I didn't know they were dead.

I'm on my knees crying. Willie—who's been hit again—is

crying with me. Robert is staring at the uniforms moving toward us in a wave. Steve is getting up and taking a step. He jerks, jerks again, and falls. The three minutes of the fuse we've set have passed. The fuse—

Now, a voice says suddenly. *Now*—

And the world—the entire world—rises up in light and gravel and mist. The river rises like a fountain. The ground rolls under us like a rug being pulled, and a shock wave—brown mist now— hits and lifts us away.

The uniforms around us stop firing. A river of rain begins to fall. The four of us are curled together just like kids, trying to get our breath, jerking even though there isn't any reason to be jerking now. We can't hear a thing. We can't breathe, but we keep waiting for the second sound.

We were curled up in the mud just like kids, Major.

The sound doesn't come.

The roar of the dike collapsing doesn't come.

It never will, we know.

Willie is crying—I'm crying—Steve is up on one knee, eyes closed, but staring. Robert is, too. We're *all* staring—at the dike. Our eyes, full of mud and water, are closed, but we're staring. We're seeing what Robert sees, because the uniforms see it:

The dike, holding. The C-2 not enough. *Buddha be blessed*, one of the uniforms is thinking. *Buddha be blessed.*

Motherfucker! Willie screams.

What figures did you use, Willie?

The ones they gave him, Steve answers.

Oh, Jesus, a one-armed man is saying.

He had *two* fail-safes, I remember thinking to myself then. He'd had *two* fail-safes all along, Mary.

In a universe somewhere, Colonel, we are coming home.

We can go ahead, I remember thinking. *We can go ahead and lie here as they start shooting again. We can lie here jerking, dodging them the way Steve does, the way Robert has told us to—until our bodies tire and can't do it anymore. We can go ahead and do it that way . . . and make sure the dream comes true.*

We can go ahead and lie here like kids, arms and legs akimbo, shivering like a very disappointing camp-out in the rain. We can lie here waiting for the lactic acid to gather in our muscles, the synapses to tire, and the bullets to hit us at last—so that we're jerking and jerking in the mud the way I thought we would be.

And make sure the dream comes true that way.

Or, I said to the others, *we can get up and move.*

I was wrong. I know that now. I thought—in the dream I thought—we were lying there because we *had* to. I thought we were jerking because the bullets were hitting us, because the bullets were hitting our bodies and making us jerk, jerk in the mud. I didn't know we were jerking so they'd miss us.

We got up.

We got up out of the mud.

You thought we were dying in your dream, didn't you, Mary?

Yes, I did.

You didn't know the bullets never touched us, that we got up before they could, that we got up—we got up out of the mud.

No. I didn't.

Shouldn't we help the real dream—the one you never really understood, Mary—come true?

Yes.

Shouldn't we get up now and move?

Yes, we should.

In a universe somewhere, Major, we got up. We were *already* getting up and moving, had always gotten up, always would be getting up—but now we were doing it in my dream, getting up and making the dream come true.

There's something we need to do, a voice was saying. We were *all* saying it. We couldn't say a thing without everyone saying it now.

There's something we need to do, we said.

You don't lie there in the mud and let bullets hit you, Major, when there's something you need to do.

Chapter 46

Do you still want to die? I remember asking the captain. I remember asking just *him. You did once, Robert. Do you still want to now?*

No, I remember him saying. *No, I don't.*

I really don't know how to describe it. There isn't any way. I've tried to—for myself, I mean—and I've never found a way. Cooper would understand it. *Some things aren't meant for words,* he would say. *Sometimes words just get in the way.*

We're so bright, the chief says, and that's when it happens. We *move.* We're just not there anymore. I really don't know how to say it. We're lying in the mud one moment, not wanting to die, and then this voice says, *Motherfuckers!* This other voice says, *You can do it, Mary.* A third voice says, *There's something we need to do*—we all say it—and suddenly we're floating high, looking down at everything, just the way Steve would. Looking down at our bodies, still breathing, curled in the mud. At the uniforms moving toward us, barrels aimed like the beaks of birds—like needles—like anything you can think of that isn't very nice.

We're so bright, the chief says—and we agree. We see ourselves as *they* see us. We're looking up at the sky, seeing ourselves as the uniforms see us:

The sky's on fire. The air's on fire. That's what it looks like. The uniforms stop moving. They stare up at us. The popping of automatic weapons fades. Their faces keep looking up at us and we keep looking back down. We're the fire, Major, looking down. We don't have faces. We don't have bodies. We're the air, the sky, and we're burning.

There are four bodies lying there in the mud. We can see them. We *know* whose bodies they are. We tell them to stand up, to get up out of that goddamn mud. *It's embarrassing*, we say, *seeing you four like that.* We tell them to hold Willie's body up, because he's the one with the really bad wounds. They do it, of course. They know whose *bodies* they are.

We look down at the uniforms, at the faces of the uniforms looking up. Out of all those faces, only ten or twenty go ahead and fire—at the sky, where we're burning. But we don't say to those four bodies: *Well, shit, if they're going to shoot, we're going to shoot back.* We don't tell those bodies to pick up their rifles and fire back. We're not really the sky. We can't really be hurt up here.

Only the four bodies can be hurt.

The rotors above us are *inside* us, like slow heartbeats. The gunships see the fire, the burning air, and they bank away. *Why are you out here today?* we want to ask them. One of the gunners fires at the ground, at the mud, at the four bodies there. He shouldn't do it. We tell the body that belongs to Steve—or maybe the one that belongs to Robert—what to do. We tell it to pick up the AK, where to aim it, where the bullet will mean something. It's funny, we think. One of those four mud-covered bodies is going to bring that gunship down—with just a rifle, like any real Hero of the People should.

We watch Steve's body—or Robert's—bring the gunship down.

We watch him aim again and bring the gunship down.

I remember it all from the dream.

We know where the bullet should go and we help Steve—we help him aim. *You can do it*, we tell him. The bullet leaves the muzzle, floats pretty through the air, strikes the fuel tank where the pilot has told us it should be. The spark it makes is *blue*. The pretty flower the spark makes is *blue*. The bodies inside it turn *blue*. The machine falls into a river that is just as *blue*.

In the river there are three boats—all of them blue, too. They're not firing at the fiery sky, but they *are* firing at the four

muddy bodies on the shore—since one of those four poor bodies
has just brought a gunship down.

Someone sighs. *They're* always *shooting at the bodies, Robert.*
Yes, and they always will.

The four bodies start to dance. They jerk. They know how.
They jerk in the sun, dodging, and the rounds from all those muz-
zles go whistling by.

The captain goes ahead. We *all* go ahead and do it. There's
no argument really. There's no one to argue *with*. We tell the
sailors in the first boat a little lie. We show them some things that
just aren't true—a submerged island that isn't there, five
motorized sampans that really aren't either—and the first boat hits
the second and the third boat turns to hit the shore.

Motherfuckers! Willie says, but he doesn't mean the sailors or
the uniforms. Or the dike. Or the two bullets in his body that hurt
like hell.

There's something we need to do, we're saying.

We saw the future, Major.

We saw the little lies we would make for all the uniforms
there, and what those lies would do. We saw the first boat turn
into the second even before it happened. We saw the third boat
swerve to hit the shore. And *then* we saw it really happen.

When we did, everything opened up—like a window, Major.
We saw the places where some things had started and the places
where they would end. We saw it like a window, all of it opening
at once.

And then, after we'd looked, the window disappeared, because we didn't need it anymore.

I remember floating. It wasn't *me*. It was *us*, of course.

I remember looking down at our bodies—having looked at
them so many times before—and feeling: *there's something we*
need to do.

There were still too many uniforms near those four bodies, so
we helped the uniforms see *other* things. Other uniforms were
coming down a road in trucks—with some weapons that might be
a problem, but that was okay, too. We could stay there on the

riverbank and help the uniforms that were coming on a road see other things, handling it that way.

Or we could simply get up and leave.

In the blue blue river we found a patrol boat—you know what color it was—and made sure this one wasn't at all damaged. We helped its captain and its sailors see a fire, one that certainly could—in another universe at least—have been burning on their boat. They knew as soon as they saw it what they needed to do. They got off. They started swimming and made it to the shore okay.

We kept the coxswain because we needed him. We didn't show him the fire. We didn't show him his friends swimming to shore, their eyes as wide as quarters. We just showed him how the fog was clearing and we told him some jokes—ones he'd already heard, but had somehow (because we helped him) forgotten. He brought the boat to us, nosing it onto the shore. Then we let him go.

We let him see the four muddy bodies he had helped get into the boat, and then we let him go.

We told the four bodies to board the boat. We told one of them—Willie's, Robert's, it didn't matter now—to take the wheel, just the way we had before. All the bodies knew how. We could see it—we had already seen it—how one of the bodies would take the wheel and steer the boat away.

All the way down the river we *helped* the uniforms. We helped the uniforms on the dike and in the sky and in those boats see *other things*. It wouldn't be as easy in Haiphong, we knew, but we'd do okay there, too. We'd seen it in the dream. We'd seen it when the window opened.

In the dream we saw everything had gone okay.

We knew how it would end as long as we didn't stop, as long as we went on helping it—helping the dream—come true.

Do these transponders work? someone asked.

Does it matter? someone answered. *They'll hear us coming one way or another, Willie.*

We could have found trucks in Hanoi and led them to us, full of ordnance of all kinds. We could have reached up with a little picture or two and brought one of our own B-52s with its payload down—four or five or six MIGs, their payloads, too. We could have *tried* it—to see if it would have worked. We could have added to the stress and pressure on the dike and seen if it would have worked.

We could have added to the pressure until it cracked, until the river pushed hard enough and it cracked, and the dike let go.

Somewhere—in a universe somewhere, Major—we did it.

The supplies were there, just like a man in the Hawaiian shirt had said. Like a treasure buried in caves. Like a cancer you can't scrape out. Buried on every kilometer of the Trail. In a thousand tunnel systems carved with patience in the South. Crated on the docks of Sihanoukville and Kompong Chnang, then taken and buried everywhere else.

Even when we did it, Major—even when the dike let go, when the city called Hanoi drowned, the supplies were buried everywhere and the war didn't stop.

Fifty thousand people in that city died—then or later, from one thing or another—but the war didn't stop.

We could have blown the dike that day, Major—that's what I'm saying. We could have done it. It wouldn't have been hard.

But we knew what would happen—we'd seen it—so we didn't bother.

There was something else we needed to do.

We saw many things that day, Major.

I was crying on a boat when we did. I was heading out to sea. I was muddy and tired and hurt and I was crying about what we'd already seen, were seeing, and would always see. I wasn't the only one crying. We were a team, Major. It wasn't just *me*.

We would reach the harbor. Or we already had, and always would. We would make it out into the gulf because of what we would do to the sailors and soldiers and gunship pilots along the way. Later, someone in a room on a carrier—using spoken words—words in English—would say: *I know. They don't have working transponders, but that's what it sounded like, sir.*

I was kneeling on the deck as we saw the things we saw. Steve's body knelt beside mine. He held me. I was crying. He was watching everything I saw.

I saw the same man in a wheelchair talking in a room that had a beautiful wooden desk. He could sit behind it. He just couldn't stand up. I could hear his voice—the New York accent, upper crust. It was a voice a whole nation knew. I heard him say: "The French are fools, Cordell. Colonialism is dead, as it ought to be." The dream changed. There was darkness everywhere. A voice said suddenly, "He's down at Warm Springs, ma'am." The dream changed again. The man in the wheelchair was dying now. I didn't like him, not really—I didn't like the way he treated women—but I didn't want him to die. He was arrogant, but he was smart, and his legs, his weakness, made him *try*. I didn't want him to die either.

He was in bed. I could see that now. His cousin wasn't with him. He didn't want her to be. Another woman was. He wasn't speaking to her, because he couldn't. His mouth wouldn't move. I tried to tell her—*for him*—but I couldn't speak either.

He died. Like all the others.

He's the one, a voice says—four voices, or one. *If he'd lived—*

We watched it happen in another world. The man in the wheelchair lived. We heard him say: "We are no longer able to support your position in Cochin China, Tonkin or Annam, General. We are, in fact, General, unable to support the Gallic position *anywhere* in Indochina, I am sorry to say. You can appreciate our position." As he said it, the universe changed.

The general and his people did not stay in Tonkin or Annam or Cochin China—because the man in the wheelchair would not support them, because he believed colonialism was dying, as it ought to be. Because the general and his people did not stay, a man named Nguyen That Thanh became president of his country earlier. Because he did—because he did it earlier and because his country was a nation at last—he did what he had always planned to do. He asked for the help of a North American nation. Because he did, and because the French no longer ruled his country, and because that North American nation no longer supported colonialism, and because that North American nation did not want that man, whose name was Ho, to ask another nation for help—that North American nation said yes. Because it said yes, that man's country did not ask another nation for what it needed and wanted. It did not ask Russia. It did not ask China. Why should it? Why should it ask Eastern Europeans with all of their border fears and imperialism? Why should it ask the Chinese it hated—the giant that had always stood over them? Why should it ask anyone else when that North American nation, founded on a document so much like its own, was willing to give it?

In that universe, Major, that North American nation did not fight two wars. It did not fight in a country called Korea—because the nation of the man called Ho did it instead, at that North American nation's urging. It did not fight a war in the country that belonged to Ho—because that war never happened.

Even though the North of his country and the South of his country had *always* feuded, in *this* universe that war never happened.

Because a man named Ho was different.

Because a man in a wheelchair lived.

We saw other worlds, Major. We saw worlds where the man named Ho died early in his life, killed by the French in the Triangle near Yen Bay, killed by malaria that summer, where the "third force" nationalists made a coalition, where the coalition never *felt* like "communism" to that North American nation, and so it helped them—just the way it helped a man named Ho in another universe. Because it helped these "third force" nationalists, a teacher named Van Bach was never born. Because he was never born, he couldn't die on a boat. Because he couldn't die, a kid named Cooper couldn't die with him.

I saw—*we saw*—many things, Major. We saw the deaths, one by one, of the people who had died, were dying or would die in the war we were fighting. We saw their faces, one by one—like blossoms floating on a long black pond—and we changed it. The man in the wheelchair lived. The general and his people went away. The blossoms never fell to the dark water.

We saw their *names*, Major. We *felt* what it was like—one by one—to have those names ourselves, and to put them—one by one—on a long black wall.

I saw, Major, how all four of us would die—in *this* universe and in so many others. Most often it wasn't here—in the North, on this river—but sometimes it was. I'd known that. I'd known that all along.

You forgot, Mary. That's all.

Yes.

In *our* universe, Major, it wouldn't be here—in this gulf—on this open sea. It wouldn't be in this little country. It wouldn't even be in this war. It wouldn't, for most of us, be for a long, long time, though somewhere, Major—at this very moment—we were, of course, dying. We were already dead. I could see it. We all could, Major.

You just forgot, Mary. You forgot you knew.

Yes. Yes, I did.

I didn't try to save us, Major. There wasn't any reason to.

I showed the others. I was the one who saw it, so I was the one who showed them. I showed them what it would be like for each one of us—who would be there by their beds, if it happened on beds, who would be there on the street, if they fell, or a car, if that's how it happened. How many of their friends were still alive then, what their children—if they had any—would be like, and what they would *say*—if anything—*or* feel *or* think in those last moments.

They *let* me show them, and then, Major, they made sure they forgot.

I saw Cooper's life, his mother, his father—a minister—his uncle, a sergeant major, the most decorated Negro in the U.S. Army, the man who'd told Cooper to "give the Army a try." That dog—the first one—and how it had died, though somewhere, right now, Major, it was still breathing. Those books—*Robinson Crusoe, Beautiful Joe, Big Red*—the ones he read, though he never found a black kid in them. I got to know Cooper at last, Major. I got to know him the way I always had, and he said, *It's about time, ma'am*, and laughed.

I saw the captain's son. In Vung Tau, selling junk on the

beach, fingers as long as his fathers, chin identical. He was getting
older. He knew a hundred words in English and his mother, yes,
was still alive. She took him to see his grandparents, who weren't
cruel, who did their best to pretend they understood. Ten years
later she would die of cancer, I knew. I saw this. I showed the
others. We watched her dying. *You never get it all out, do you?*
someone said. We watched the boy at twelve losing his eyesight.
He needed surgery. *Who would pay?* someone asked.

What do you want to do about it? I asked Robert.

I want to find him, Mary, he said. *I want to find them both.*

She won't go with you, I say.

I know. . . . And he did. He knew it as well as I did.

You can find them, Robert, I tell him, *when we've done what
we need to do.*

I saw the woman and the child from the blanket. I saw the
park and the pond and the river and the sky, heard laughter so
familiar I thought it was mine.

What, Robert asked me, because someone needed to, *do you
want to do about it, Mary?*

I want to find them. I want to tell her the truth.

You can find them, Mary, he said, *as soon as we've done what
we need to do.*

I saw where they lived by the Saigon River. I saw her open
the door to me. I saw myself, standing in the doorway. I heard
myself say it—in the Vietnamese he would have used. I saw her
hands move to her mouth, the child inside on a mat, the blanket
different. When she cried, I stayed with her. I didn't leave.

I saw Christabel lying at the 87th Surgical Hospital getting
sewn up, doing fine—getting sewn up again and again, and doing
fine. I saw the report in Bucannon's files. I saw Bucannon write it
himself, knowing it was a lie. I saw him put it there, put it there
again and again, in case it was ever needed. I saw him write it, file
it and write it again. I saw the telegram to Dorothy lying on her
dresser in the dark. I saw their daughter, Kristy, asleep in the next
room.

I saw myself telling a major everything I knew. I saw him

listening, trying his best to understand. I saw him put it in a report, because he believed it mattered.

I saw him in a room with another major, and a colonel, later on, trying to decide. And then, at last, deciding. I saw what that decision would mean.

I saw a woman in the tunnels whose name was Mai Van Vo. I saw her die of her wounds on the fifteenth of May. I saw her spend seven years trying to keep others from dying. I saw another woman, another time—finding her made me dizzy—in a harbor, steel ships sinking, the water itself on fire, a beautiful city called Pearl. She was a nurse, too. I saw a girl in the very same war who wasn't, but who could have been—writing letters to a hundred men to keep them all from despairing. And I saw the Angel at last. I even heard her name, *Galard-Terraube*. I saw her face. Moonlike. The childlike softness even after the march. I saw the Tai prostitutes who worked beside her until they, too, were marched away. I saw the Angel of Dien Bien Phu.

I saw a boy named John and the way he lived. The things he would forget from childhood. The people who would forgive him. He couldn't, but *I* could—I could see the houses where he would live when he was grown. I could see the friends he would have—another colonel, a college professor, a congressman and a scientist with a nice sailboat. I could see the women who would want him, lover, father to their child. I could *feel* what they were feeling. I could see the two women he would marry—the one who would give him a son.

I could see him in a jungle talking to a white girl too young to be a nurse. He wanted to understand. I could see the needle raised in her hand and what did, and didn't, happen later.

I saw how *they* saw it, Major—as they stood there on the dike not far from our four bodies, sky afire, a miracle they just weren't supposed to believe. I saw how *he* wrote it—word for word—so I wrote it down, too. I translated it for you, thinking that might help.

You'll want it for your report, Major.

I know you will.

Photostat, After-Action Report, Colonel Truong Doan Nhu to
General Nguyen Dinh Hoa, 135th Regiment, Army of the
Democratic Republic of Vietnam. Reported and translated from
the Vietnamese by 1st Lt. Mary Damico, Operation Orangutan
EVAL

To: General Nguyen Dinh Hoa, 135th Regimental
Headquarters
From: Colonel Truong Doan Nhu, 2d Battalion
Subject: Enemy Commando Assault at the Village of
Dong Noi

At General Toi Lan Bay's suggestion I am herewith submitting to Regimental Headquarters a detailed after-
action report with supportive documents on the recent
enemy aggression at Dong Noi, including enemy commando infiltration through That Khe and Thuan Chau
provinces and tactical use of the Song Da and various
riverine craft. I must ask headquarters' patience with the
tardiness of this report and its patience as well as with
certain unorthodox features of it.

(Material deleted.)

From the ground this phenomenon—or "apparition"—
resembled, in the words of many witnesses, a "ball of
pale fire." Size and distance were difficult to establish,
but the phenomenon appeared to be hovering at thirty
meters, with a diameter of twenty. One's first impression
was that the object must be related to the detonation itself. The atmosphere appeared to burn and the overall
effect was of a foggy lunar night. It produced no sound to
the extent that witnesses are able to report; and because it
was moving, many of those present thought it to be life-
threatening. Command disagreement over the nature of
the phenomenon (chemical or physical by-product of the
detonation, chemical weaponry, chemical illusion or

commonplace diversion) did, I am afraid, interfere with timely action.

The seventy-five to one hundred officers and enlisted men standing nearest the bodies of the four commandos on the dike bank report a later phenomenon as well. As they observed the bodies of the four commandos—who were no longer moving—all four "disappeared." One would be tempted to explain this phenomenon in a conventional manner, e.g., the ease with which trained commandos might slip away during a distraction of such magnitude; but witnesses have testified that at least three of the four commandos were wounded, that they were twenty meters from the river and in open terrain, that they were not camouflaged but were instead wearing uniforms of the Soviet Socialist Republic Army (or facsimiles) and that they were being watched by at least half a dozen witnesses at all times.

(Material deleted.)

These distractions, it should be mentioned, include not only the "fireball" but also the explosion of one SV Hova helicopter and the collision of three PC-class river patrol boats, which arrived momentarily.

(Material deleted.)

For a list of the officers and enlisted men able to corroborate the claims and interpretations submitted in this report, please see Attachment 1. For a description of the cases of hysteric response to these events, please see Attachment 2. (These cases, please note, total no more than 11%.)

If other information would prove helpful to your investigations, please do not hesitate to request it.

Attachment 2. "Van Menh Trong Tay Ta."

So luong linh mac chung ixteri ca trong va sa cuoc thi dan Khong Khi nao vuot qua 11%. Hanh vi cua nhung nguoi mac chung ixteri duoc Ke Tu Luc Khoc van ban sung. Danh Sach nhung nguoi da bi loai Khoi. . . .

Chapter 47

I don't know how we got on the carrier, Major. I remember kneeling on the deck of the little boat—I remember that the captain and the chief were steering it—and it was Haiphong Harbor. No one was shooting at us. No one was coming alongside us with a bullhorn, telling us to stop and lay down our arms. *They can't see us,* I remember thinking, *because of what we're doing.*

We made it out of the harbor and then something happened to the boat. I don't know what. All I remember is Steve standing on the deck with the twin 12.7s, aiming them at a MIG and laughing. After that, the little boat wasn't there anymore and I was hanging on to the chief to keep his head from going under. The water was pretty cold. I remember thinking: *Is Willie's wound going to attract sharks? Do we* all *have wounds?*

It was me—but it wasn't me—thinking these things. It was *all* of us, floating somewhere above the waves, watching. That's the way it felt, anyway. Ask the others.

We were looking down at the waves. The patrol boat was gone. There were just these four bodies, rising and falling in the swells, in the Gulf of Tonkin, in water that was awfully cold.

How we got onto the carrier, I don't know, Major. We were on the deck and two corpsmen had the chief laid out on a stretcher and were taking him below. I had a wound on my foot and I was telling everybody to get away, just get away, that the chief and the captain needed it more than I did. But I did it by shouting—which didn't convince them at all. They gave me a needle. I remember that. *That's reasonable*, I remember thinking.

I also remember thinking: *Isn't there something we need to do?* We all said it. We used our mouths, and we said it. We said: "We're going home, ladies and gentlemen. But first there's something we need to do."

The corpsmen, the nurses, the doctors nodded like we were crazy and went back to their work.

Steve had a lacerated forearm. The chief had two penetrating wounds in his shoulder. But the place where he'd gouged out the thing on his back—using the barrel—was the worst. The captain had a broken tibia and I had a shattered ankle. The doctors and corpsmen were good. They were pretty nice, too. They were the kind of people you need in a war.

But they did a stupid thing. They tried to break us up.

They wanted me in another ward just because I was a woman, and that didn't make sense to us at all.

I don't know exactly *what* we did. I don't know whether we made the air in the room actually burn or whether we just helped the people there think it was burning. Whatever we did, the doctors and the corpsmen stepped back, stared at the ceiling and then called someone to put a fire out. We started laughing. It was pretty funny. Someone came and tried to put it out, and when they couldn't do it, everyone started screaming.

And then everyone went away.

We talked during the night even though they'd medicated us pretty heavily. For some reason it didn't seem to affect us. We weren't floating out over the carrier's deck, no—or over the waves of the gulf—nothing fancy like that—but we were able to do other things we probably shouldn't have been able to do. Like talking in the night with all that medication in us, or doing it without words.

We were still the thing we'd become at the dikes, I guess. We just weren't thinking about it.

We could have told Bucannon we were coming. We could have told him right then, and he'd certainly have heard us:

We're coming, Father. We're coming home to you.

But we didn't.

Three days later they moved us to the hospital ship *Repose*. We asked them to. We said, "That's really where we'd like to be, Commander," and they put us on the *Repose*. They didn't want to do it, but we convinced them to. We did a few things, I guess. The point was, we didn't want to be shipped to Okie or Japan. We wanted to be as close to a certain camp as we could be. We wanted to surprise him.

I remember the doctor who didn't want to do it. He said he'd gotten word from MACV that we were "sensitive"—he liked using that word—and so he'd cut papers for us to Japan.

We were still so doped up that we started laughing again. Four bodies in a little row. All of them laughing. Willie said: "Hey, Commander, your ass is starting to *glow*." Steve said: "What he means, sir, is that someone is going to shoot you in the *butt*." It wasn't *that* funny but we sure thought it was. We kept on laughing. The doctor was getting mad. He knew a case of insubordination when he saw one, so he started talking about tranquilizers and MPs and hey, even *physical restraint*.

We stopped laughing. Robert looked at him and in the calmest voice you've ever heard said: "Listen, Commander Echison. You've been screwing that Air Force flight attendant for months. You've got a wife and kids and you've still been screwing that woman blind. You've been laying out money on her that you'd *never* ever lay out on your wife. Your wife, Commander, nearly died of a tubal pregnancy last year, but did you know that? Of course you didn't. You were too busy screwing the Air Force, and your wife didn't want you to worry. You should be *ashamed* of yourself, Commander. Ashamed."

The doctor had backed away. He wasn't even blinking now.

"You did *that*?" I said to him, and threw my pillow at him and called him all the names I could think of—the ones his Air Force girlfriend called him when she was *really* mad.

"Where's my AK?" Willie said. "I want to be the one who shoots this guy in the *butt*."

We never did have to go to Japan.

In comes this guy from Vientiane. We're doing something right below the ceiling, a little floating, a little slipping and sliding, so we see his chopper land on the deck. We know this guy, even if we've never met him. His name is Pete. That's all. Pete. He walks into our ward and as soon as he opens his mouth to say something, we use our very best voice to say: "You touch us, Pete—you let any of your people touch us—and we'll follow you around like puppies. We'll find your family and we'll kill them, Pete. After all the money you've spent on Debbie's and Carl's teeth, that would be a real waste."

We say it together in a voice from this horror movie Pete has seen—one about men who want obedient robots for wives.

This time they leave us alone for a whole week.

When it's time to leave—when our wounds have healed and we're really ready to go—another guy in civvies comes from Vientiane and even brings some marines with him. Can you believe it? The marines are carrying M-14s and they're very strac—like those guys who protect the embassies. Real honor guard types. The man in civvies has heard about us and he ain't taking chances. He signals with his hand. The marines lock and load. They do it together like the June Taylor dancers. Then they point their guns.

Jesus Christ, Willie is saying.

We're dressed. We're all ready to go, so what's this all about?

"Let's go," the guy in civvies says, "and let's not have any trouble." He sounds like Harry, but he dresses better.

We go ahead and let them take us to their chopper, because a chopper is what we need.

I remember standing in the treeline and looking at the camp and wondering how many fucking-new-guys there were and whether Christabel was back yet. I kept trying, but I couldn't remember *everything* we'd seen as we floated over the dikes—the worlds, the truths and lies. I closed my eyes, but I just couldn't do it. We were losing it—we were changing, I guess. I didn't know it then.

I remember taking a step and starting to walk. I remember the

406 • Bruce McAllister

chopper was behind us in the jungle somewhere. I remember, too, wondering if the guy in civvies and his strac marines were still standing there in the leaves trying to understand what had happened, why they'd landed, whether they should stay right where they were—which is what we'd suggested.

We were wearing civvies. I don't know where we got them, but that's what we were wearing. It was more comfortable that way.

They've got a new mess tent, someone said—or all of us said it. *Very strac,* someone else said.

Hey, Bucannon's got a new tent, too.

We keep walking.

We're a hundred yards from the perimeter wire when this guy at an M-60 emplacement starts shouting at us. He's new. He's pretty cherry. He shouts those things you'd shout in a movie, like "Halt! Who goes there? What's the password? Who's pitching for the Yankees this year?"—those things you shout so you can tell who's an American and who isn't. He can't *believe* what he's seeing, and he doesn't know what else to do. This isn't a situation that comes up very often.

Three men and a woman dressed in civvies, who look very American, are walking toward his wire. *What if they don't know the name of the pitcher?* he's wondering. *What if they're Americans but they still don't happen to know?*

Robert closes his eyes and *listens. He isn't a talent, no,* he says.

We shout "Sandy Koufax!" and "Marilyn Monroe" and "Ipana Toothpaste" and all sorts of things to let him know how American we are. He isn't a talent, so he won't know it otherwise.

We help him *see* it, too—just to be safe. Steve remembers what the uniforms look like, I remember what Gidget wore, so we go ahead and slip them on. The guy sees three men in Yankee uniforms suddenly. He sees a woman dressed like Gidget in *Gidget Goes to Rome.* It's suspicious as hell, he knows. He *wants* to fire— he wants to start rockin' 'n' rollin' so badly it hurts—but he also doesn't want his ass in a sling.

"Stop or I'll shoot!" he shouts. He's figured out how to handle it. If the four people in front of him *don't* stop—if he's warned them and they don't stop—it won't be *his* fault.

He's seeing the Green Bay Packers now—Jerry's favorites— and it's a miracle, a real miracle, because one of them is a woman—a woman with shoulder pads on.

"*Are you guys American?*" he's screaming. We're walking *real* slow now. Guys are running toward him. ROKs and Yards and round-eyed fucking-new-guys all running, wondering what the fuss is about. No bullets yet—no grenades, no claymores, just some- one shouting lines from some old movie. His radio is crackling at last—he's getting someone at the CP. *What's the password, Ma- jor?* he's screaming.

For Christ's sake, Corporal, this isn't Double-U Double-U Two. If they look *like Americans, if they're wearing civilian clothes like Americans, if they have bodies like Americans, Corporal, then that's what they are!*

But to be safe, we do it. We leave.

We disappear again.

Chapter 48

We were just inside the gate when we let them see us again.

Don't start to glow, Willie, one of us said. *They'll think it's some dink hocus-pocus, and innocent bystanders will get shot. You know that. So don't.*

All we need to do is walk and smile, Willie. Big, pale Chinese with eye-jobs wouldn't be doing *that*.

Two of the perimeter guards turn and see us first. They can't do much except stare. *Jesus, Carmine, they don't look like dinks.* We're inside the gate. We're walking. We're smiling. We're wearing awful PX clothes. We must be on R&R, right? We must've landed in the wrong place, that's all. We're laughing and dapping and saying *really* funny things, like, "Bob Dylan's earlier lyrics owe a profound debt to the more political resonances of traditional Celtic ballads, don't you think?" Or "Did you hear—Jackie O and Timothy Leary are living together but they are, yes, planning on getting married."

If we were supposed *to shoot at them,* the perimeter guards are telling themselves, *someone would already be shooting, right?*

Larry—the guy at the M-60 emplacement—is one of the last to turn around. I go ahead. I wave. His mouth is open like a hole. We keep on truckin'. We're CBS. We're Cronkite. We're taking our tour of the base for the six o'clock news. Lines of guys form on either side of us like some wedding reception. We know some of them. It's *our* camp, after all. We're coming home.

Everyone wants to know what's going down. We can *hear* them wondering. They're excited.

There's this little guy I've never really seen before with red hair and ears that stick out like handles, whose mother tells him *when* mortars and rockets are going to hit and *where*, and who's a little stoned right now on Mary Jane. He's thinking: *These guys really look great in baseball suits.*

I smile just like Gidget at him. I do a little Gidget step. I use words and I say: "You're going to get that GTO with wire wheels, Paul. You're going to survive this world of hurt, but most important of all, you're going to get that bitchin' car."

He looks at me like I'm a madonna. And then he grins.

No one tries to stop us.

Not even a black lieutenant by the name of Bush, who's got a gift just like the captain's but isn't nearly as good yet. He stands there wondering if he really ought to do something as we walk by.

He *knows* what we're planning to do.

Don't, Carl, we tell him. *Be happy. Be alive.*

There are guards at the flaps, but what's new? *We've done this before,* one of us says. *We'll do it again. World without end, amen.* The guards have Swedish Ks, those little submachine guns Bucannon likes so much. They're cooperative, too. We show them a couple of things. One faints and the other two step aside.

Bucannon hears the commotion. He knows what it means. He knows we're here and he must know why. We step through the flaps and he's getting up from the table now, a Browning automatic in his hand. An MD type stands up with him. The guy they've been taping—this staff sergeant from New Jersey named Rose, who wishes he hadn't told them about the menorah—doesn't stand up. Bucannon's wearing his ice-cream suit.

"What," the MD type says, "do you people think you are doing?"

He's a stupid man. He doesn't understand. Bucannon does. He understands so *many* things. He isn't afraid really—he's just surprised. Like *I really didn't expect to see you here. . . .*

"Sorry we didn't call first, Colonel," Willie tells him, using words.

You knew we were out there on the ship, Colonel, I tell him, too. *You knew everything that was happening, didn't you?*

You just didn't think we'd drop by, did you?

"Get Christabel and Pagano, please," Bucannon says quietly to the MD type.

He thinks they'll be able to talk us out of it, doesn't he? Robert says.

Yes, I answer, *and in a universe somewhere they're trying. And in a universe somewhere we go away. . . .*

Does he think we wouldn't hurt them?

He thinks we'd hurt his favorite XO.

Yes. And he's right.

"No, sir," the MD type says. "I'm not leaving, sir."

We look at the MD type—Bucannon's favorite boy. His name is Andrew. He is thirty-five. He thinks he is being good. We open our mouths at once and the voice we use is his father's, telling him not to play with himself in the closet like that or his mother will find out. That if he keeps doing it, terrible blisters will grow on his hands.

We show him his mother and father in their bedroom—the way he saw it once, but this time we change it. In this little movie his father beats her, and *that* is why she moans. He beats her until he's satisfied, and when he's finished—when she's lying on the bed beside him, barely able to make a sound—he does it himself. He plays with himself. The child standing in the doorway, watching. The blisters growing on his father's hands.

The XO named Andrew is on the dirt floor of the tent now, hands over his ears, white smock getting dusty, eyes closed. We go ahead—we tell him with his mother's voice what it was like that night—a man so hard inside her, beating her face until she couldn't see him anymore, knowing in her heart that that was what he'd always wanted.

"*Leave him alone,*" Bucannon says. He knows what we're doing. He isn't stupid.

We look at *him.*

We say: "Would you do it again, John?" We say it together—
a single voice—because that's what we are, what he's always
wanted us to be.

Yes, he says.

It isn't what he wants to say. He wants to tell us how *good* we
are—this miracle we've become, this team that nothing can stop.
He wants to say: *I didn't really think you'd make it. Travel that far,
find the C-2, navigate the Black and Red, make it all the way—
lose only two team members and, of course, the Nungs.*

He wants to say how *proud* of us he is, how he hadn't really
expected to feel something like that—something a *father* might
feel—but he feels it, he does. *It's wonderful,* he wants to tell us.
*You've changed how war—certain kinds of war—will be fought,
you four. You've changed the future itself, by showing us all what
can be done.*

If I'd only known how painful it would be, he wants to say, *I'd
have found an easier way for you. . . .*

But he can't.

He can't lie to us.

He can't lie with words.

Yes, he thinks to himself. *I would.*

We go ahead. We show him what he needs to see.

In a tent somewhere a man is screaming, in the dirt. His
mouth is filling with dust as he rolls, like a dog, like a man on fire,
like a black boy rubbing his own skin away.

We show him what he needs to know. We show him
everything.

We show him how Cooper and Crusoe died, how it *felt*—to
both of them—to die. We show him what Cooper's mother will
feel when she hears it. We make him *feel* it, for as long as she will.

We don't let that feeling stop.

We show him how Bach died and the similarities—so interesting, we think—between what the young Vietnamese woman in
the park by the pond will *feel* when she hears, and what Cooper's
mother will *feel*. *It's interesting, Colonel, don't you think?*

There are so many things to be learned, aren't there? we say.

We show him a long black wall that will not be built for

years. We set him down by it, in the shining sun. We let him read
the *names* on it. We make him memorize them—so he'll remember them forever, whether he wants to or not.

When he's learned the names—and it takes him a long, long
time—we let him *feel* what each name felt like to the man—or
woman—who had it.

And then we take the names away.

We make him *feel* it.

We make him feel it forever.

We show him how his son, Patrick, will die in Willamette,
Oregon, when he's twenty-five. How he, the father, won't be there
to see it and what his wife will think. We let him see it the way
we've seen it—again and again. We let him *feel* what's it like, how
long it lasts, the pain—for a young man dying. And then we let
him be a father again, one whose son has been taken away.

We show him the decision that two majors and a colonel
listening to a woman who was once a nurse will reach. And what
that decision will mean.

When we finally let him go, someone in the doorway—by
the flap—sends for a medic, an O2 tank, a needle full of something to start a heartbeat with.

He does all right. He doesn't fly to Saigon. He just sits in his
tent—in his nice white suit, a little dirty now—and looks as if he's
thinking.

I was the one who went back to his tent that night, Major. I
went back to make *sure*.

Because of what we'd seen.

Chapter 49

What we saw as we floated above Dong Noi was a little movie, I guess. I don't know how else to describe it. After everything else we'd seen, what mattered most was this little movie—something you'd see on TV at night, watching it with friends. We didn't know what it meant at first, but that doesn't mean we stopped watching. We watched it until we understood what it meant.

We saw a square—the kind of square you see in Europe or South America—the one I'd dreamed about with blue jeeps and blue trees and blue weapons that fired pure blue light.

We saw a man. We saw him standing in a hotel room overlooking that square. It wasn't Vietnam. It wasn't Southeast Asia at all. The man was looking at a light on the ceiling. That's all. He was stocky, like Jerry, and he had muscles like a weight lifter—like Jerry when he used to work out. He had blue eyes like Steve's, but darker hair, and neat little scars on one cheek—the kind you see on African natives. We could see an earring—a stud, I mean—in his right ear, the way sailors from some countries wear them. The room was shaking and we didn't know why. It wasn't Southeast Asia. We didn't even think of war.

He was standing in the middle of an old hotel room and his head was cocked like a dog's, listening for something—that's what it looked like—while the room just kept shaking. It was rockets and mortars, but we didn't know it yet.

He had two arms, but one of them was making a sound, like

a purring, like a cat. We didn't understand that either and then all of a sudden Willie said: *It's a prosthesis. It's the kind they'll someday have.*

It was old and scratched, but not like anything we'd ever seen. Like a rusty spaceship—*old*, but not old to *us*. It purred and moved and the man used it as if he didn't want to use his good hand for what he was doing now. He grabbed the ceiling light with the purring arm and started to pull the light apart. His head stayed cocked, *listening*, as he pulled the light apart.

I know what he's doing, Mary. Steve said. *He's waiting for the world to turn blue—for everything to turn blue.*

You know who he is, Mary, Robert whispered, and I said: *Yes. Yes, I do.*

There was something happening outside the building, but we really didn't understand what it was. Here was a man we would someday know in a hotel room pulling a lamp apart and waiting for the room—or the lamp—to turn blue. We didn't know why. We didn't even know *where*—or *when*. We watched it anyway, because we had to.

The stocky man found a key inside the lamp. We could see it in the chalky white fingers of his artificial hand, and then it was gone again as he dropped it into a little bottle he was holding with his good hand. The good hand, we noticed, never touched that key. The building was shaking again. *It's mortars or rockets, isn't it?* Willie said, and we knew that was true.

The man turned to the window. We saw what he saw. We looked out with him—at the plaza, at the little square I'd already dreamed of, at the side of an old brick building that was somehow really a screen, like a great TV set. He stared. We stared, too—at the face that had been there, on that screen, all along. The face moved. It opened and closed its mouth. We couldn't *hear* it in all those rockets and that automatic weapon fire in the square, but we certainly could see it—the head tipped back, the words taking so long a time to come out. It was a song. We just couldn't hear it.

The face was Asian, and it wasn't. We knew that face, too. We'd seen it as we floated over a river so many years ago, when it belonged to a child then. It was a man's face now. The long hair the color of brass, the eyes that amber so many Amerasian kids have. The epicanthic folds of the eyes made it Asian. But he had his father's chin, his father's fingers.

The face was full of feeling. The eyes were upturned in what had to be compassion. It believed, it really believed, what it was singing. It had sung the song before, we knew.

I know that face, Robert was whispering.

Yes, I said. *You do.*

It was South America, yes. We knew that now. We understood other things, too. The *campesinos* and the students in the square—who'd come to listen to that face, to that singing and to what that singing made them feel—weren't really listening now, because they couldn't. The students were throwing pipe bombs. They were *firing homemade pneumatic dart guns with sodium cyanide*. They were shooting *the few FN FALS they had*. Someone was thinking these things, so we thought them, too.

The soldiers in the jeeps with weapons that fired pure light were firing back now. The students and the *campesinos*—who'd come to hear the *singer*, to hear him sing his songs—were dying now.

The stocky man watched this without feeling, so we watched it, too.

We see what the stocky man sees: a dream, a memory. In this dream or memory we see a boy and an older man, a man old enough to be his father or grandfather, though he isn't. The man wears civilian clothes, though he doesn't always. We know his face, too—the crow's-feet at the eyes, which never ever change, the broken capillaries of the cheeks, the full head of hair even now. The boy, already stocky, is ten or eleven. The man has his hand on his shoulder and is telling him something, like he always does. "I know it's painful," he's saying, "but it's better than not knowing, am I right?" The boy nods. He nods again. He wants to be back in the compound with the other children. He won't see his father for a month or two, and that's fine. He's not happy in his father's house anymore. His father's a coward. He knows this. The older man—a general now—has helped him to understand. What a coward his father has been.

The dream, or memory, fades. There is no feeling.

The man, arm purring, walks down the fire escape and into an alley. Nothing has turned blue. He is calm. *He isn't worried*, Steve says, *unless the world turns blue*.

He trots to the corner and when he rounds it, there it is again—their little war, what he calls their *carnaval*. That's the way he thinks of it: their little wars, their little *carnavales*.

He's remembering the *carnaval*—another kind—in a town called Ixtla. He's thinking of the woman who stayed with him while he waited for confirmation to come. He thinks of these things as he runs, feeling nothing. We feel nothing, too.

She had the eyes of a *meta* user, he remembers. She saw the scars on his face, the stud in his ear, and believed he could give her what she needed. He was a *traficante*, was he not? He had that look.

When he left her, she was writhing on the floor in what the people in this land call "mother's hunger." For three days she'd been inexhaustible, doing whatever he wanted.

We remember these things with him.

We try to understand and can't.

The confirmation came (he remembers, so we remember it). They wanted the *singer*—the slant-eyed man who could move 200,000 bodies at a concert, who could make them *feel* what he wanted them to feel—eliminated. Before he could do any more damage, before he could encourage the *campesinos*, the unionists, the students even more than he had—before the problems got entirely out of control. The singer was meddling. It wasn't his country. He was meddling as so many of your people do, they'd said.

The job was his if he wanted it, they said. He was one of the three best in this hemisphere in his line of work—trained by the general who was also doctor, trained by the years with the other children who also had his gifts. The men in the city of cherry blossoms, of clean white monuments to the north, had said so— how very good he was—and they would know. They had used him themselves, had they not—just as they had used the *singer*, before he went feral, before he became a problem for little coun-

tries like this, where he meddled—where he was an embarrass-
ment to his own country, too.

The money would let him retire for five years, get a place in
Kalki, a woman if he wanted one and a new arm if he wished to
spend the money that way.

It was a contract, nothing more.

He was thinking these things as he ran, Major, so we thought
them with him.

He knew the face on the screen. He knew it from a long time
ago. He knew it the way you or I, Major, would know our
brother's or sister's face, if we felt nothing for them.

It was a contract, nothing more.

The *singer* is in an adobe house in the hills near San Andres,
he knows. There will be a concert tomorrow evening in the stadium, and this is the event he must stop. If the *singer* appears, if
he does to the 300,000 people here what he has done to crowds in
Uruguay and Peru, the National Guard and the police will not be
able to stop it. It will mean the end of many things, *Labrador.*
These are the terms, if you wish to work.

How well guarded the *singer* will be, he has no idea—but it
doesn't matter. The world turns blue or it doesn't. Either way,
nothing matters. Nothing has since Tibesti—not even his arm.
The only one who could possibly stop him is the *singer*—the one
who makes people feel what he *wants* them to feel, and whose gift
has grown. *He's a helper,* the general (who was once a colonel)
once told them. *He helps people feel what he wants them to
feel. . . .*

But none of this matters. None of it matters at all.

We see the rounds from the new Israeli Tamirins, carried by
the soldiers in the square, remove chips from the great laminated
television screen. We see the weapons mounted on the jeeps—the
chemical lasers with alloy shields—pivot and fire, and the
campesinos and students who have come to hear the *singer* die.

We see these things because he sees them, Major, but they do
not matter.

The world turns blue.

I know what's it like, Mary, Steve says.

Yes, Steve, you do.

We see the stocky man move. His eyes are closed, but he's running. *I remember,* Steve says, *what it's like to run when your body isn't yours anymore, when something grabs you and carries you through a blue blue world.*

The stocky man takes a deep breath, makes the sound an animal would make and begins to run between the blue tracers of the rifles, the blue blue light of the *lasers,* and the screams—

There's another dream, or memory, without feeling. The boy is in his father's house. He's older now. "I don't understand," his father is saying. *I know him,* I say. *I know those shoulders--though they're thinner. I know those eyes, those eyelashes.*

We all do, Mary.

"What has he done to you?" his father is saying to him. The boy looks up. He has his father's eyes, his uncle's arms and chest. The boy, contempt rising like bile in his throat, says: "He hasn't done a thing. He's just told me the truth—why you quit . . . what you are." "And what *am* I?" his father asks. "What does he say I *am?*" "A coward," the boy answers. "Isn't that why she left?"

His father, thinner now, the bathrobe faded, hits him. Time stops. His father's face twists, crying. "I'm sorry," he says. "You don't understand what it was like. Ask Bucannon. *He* was there." But the boy is gone, back to the base, to the compound where he lives with the other children, back to the man who's old enough to be his father, or grandfather, though he isn't. Away from his father, who drinks now. When he understands years later what the general did to him, he remembers this moment as the last: *his father, in the bathrobe, crying.*

We feel nothing. We feel nothing even though we should.

We watch the stocky man run across the plaza with the students, who are doing their best to stay alive. When a girl is cut in half by a beam of light—her head and chest pinwheeling past him like some doll's—we feel nothing. Her blood is on his chest, but we feel nothing. The beam wasn't meant for him. The world hasn't turned blue.

The closest jeep slides to a stop twenty meters away. The weapon pivots.

It'll be now, Steve says.

The stocky man feels the calm move through him like a drug. The plaza flashes blue—and holds. The jeep doesn't move, rear wheels up on the curb. The shadows of the jacaranda leaves are *blue*. The face of the young gunner in the jeep is *blue*. The face of its driver is *blue*.

To the stocky man's left—to our left, too—a student veers to the right, shoes pounding the pavement, and the gunner takes his legs off with a hiss of blue light. Another student, running beside the stocky man, pulls a pipe from somewhere, tosses it. The pipe and his head disappear in a bright blue haze, under a sky that's even bluer.

He stops running. He looks at the gunner in the little jeep. The gunner looks back. The *seventy-kilo Dupont laser—tubes, ignition system, alloy shield*—turns toward him at last. The jeep inches forward. The gunner grins, nodding, teasing. *Now!* Steve says, and he's right.

The stocky man leaves his body. We leave ours, too.

Steve—or the voice that once was Steve—is crying. It can't stop. It knows who the stocky man is. *We both do*.

He's built like Jerry, the way Damico men are built. But he's got his father's eyes.

In this dream or memory there is a familiar room on a military base somewhere. The seven children—five boys and two girls—are almost grown now and he, the stocky kid, doesn't lead them anymore. The man who was a colonel—is now a general—once told him he'd always lead, the very best talent they had, his *blue* gift special even among so many gifts like these. The man who was a colonel—is now a general—took him under his wing like a father would, made him team leader, told him he would always be.

The other boy—the one with the wiry body, skin and hair the color of brass, oriental eyes—wasn't *anything* at first. His gift was barely there. His father had been good, sure—a telerec who could bridge others—but the son could barely hear someone thinking. "You'll *always* be their leader," the colonel told him. "You're just too damn good."

Everyone liked the Amerasian boy whose father was a telerec, who'd become it in the cells of a Southeast Asian prison, whose mother had been a bar-girl in Chu Lai. So the colonel kept him, and gradually the boy's talent changed.

In this dream or memory the boy with the Amerasian face— eyes like his mother's—is their leader, because the colonel wishes it now, because everyone does, because everyone likes the boy with oriental eyes whose talent, it turns out, is *helping*—helping others *feel* what he wants them to feel.

There were feelings to this dream once—*jealousy* or *rage*— but they are gone now. The stocky man doesn't feel them.

Neither do we.

Time slows. Everything in the plaza moves as slow as syrup. The rockets are like big blue fish, the rounds from the rifles like little fish. Even the blue light from the jeeps is no faster than fast eels. The legs of the students who are still running barely move at all. The stocky man is floating.

When he stops at last, we stop with him—a yard over the gunner's head, or not much more. We see how short the gunner's hair is cut—the rows of ornamental scars, like satin ribbons in it. We see how narrow the boy's shoulders are, how foreshortened his body looks from here.

We turn and look back at the stocky man's body, where it hasn't moved on the cobble street, legs apart, perfectly still, the eyes not on the gunner at all, but on *us*, where we're floating. The mouth in that face is softer than we thought, under those scars and stud. The eyes and the eyelashes aren't as cold. There should be feelings there.

We look down at the young gunner's hands, so close, and we see the trigger begin—so slowly—to move.

We look back at the stocky man's body, the eyes, looking at

us, and we know what will happen next. *He'll kill them*, Steve says, *like he always has—like you always have to do.*

The stocky man's body takes a long slow step to the right, toward the jeep, and the laser makes a sound like a moan, the blue light passing a few inches to the right of his head.

We look at the gunner's hand again. We watch the finger touch the button and the canlike barrel start to swivel, all of it so slowly that it might not be moving at all, Major.

We look at the stocky man's eyes again. We tell it what we have seen. The body takes another slow step, to the left this time, then five slow steps ahead, then jumps up, up, up in the air—into the jeep—the air like a blue fog now—the gunner's fingers and neck blue, too—the beam of blue light just missing the stocky man's head again.

And now he's back in his body, the world all noise and speed again, and he, half falling, half scrambling into the jeep before the driver or gunner can pull a sidearm out. The gunner swings the barrel around, tries to pin him against the shield, catches the prosthesis instead—a hundred kilos of manflesh with it—but the stocky man has the barrel, is swinging it into the gunner's crotch, and the gunner is screaming, scream lost in the concussions of the weapons firing everywhere.

We watch the stocky man. Someone is crying. We watch the stocky man kill the boy with his elbow, separating the mandible at the ear and sending the shock of it to his brain. We watch the stocky man kill the driver, too, with the steering wheel of the jeep, jamming the thin bone of the nose up into the first lobe of the cerebrum.

The movie goes on for a long, long time, Major. Many things happen. It's a day, a whole day—every second of it—a day we won't be there to see. So we watch it now, this way. We don't look away.

We watch the stocky man go to a train station in the city. We watch him use the key at a locker, where he finds a gun—a small electronic thing we've never seen before. He hides it under his jacket—against the skin of his back.

We watch him take the train to the hills outside the city, where the face on the screen is waiting, he knows.

We watch him get off the train at a village, where a woman, a little drunk, dances in the street, where most of the people have already left for the stadium—at the heart of the city.

We watch him walk through the rainy night, through the jungle of the hills, waiting for the *blue* that always keeps him alive.

We watch him find the adobe in the moonlight. We watch him kill two men and three special dogs—voiceless, heavy chests, flat skulls—outside the crumbling courtyard walls. We watch him stop, waiting for the *blue* to come again. We hear him tell himself again: *It's a contract, nothing more.*

We watch him go inside, calmly—where the *singer* is waiting, where one of the two girls—*the oldest girl, Willie*—waits with him, as she always has, waiting for the stocky man to come.

Of the seven children, a voice says suddenly, *only four are left, and here, Mary—on this very night, in this house—two of those four will die. This is where it leads. This is where it leads if you* let *it.*

We watch the stocky man face the *singer*. We know them both. We know all of the children. We watch the stocky man begin to feel something he's forgotten—a memory, a dream, something his parents knew—but the feeling goes away.

The movie ends.

We watch it again, Major. We don't say a word.

One of those two girls, Willie says suddenly, *was my daughter.*

Yes, Willie, we say. *Yes, she was.*

That's why I went back, Major. To make sure what we'd done was enough, that he wouldn't have our children, too.

Chapter 50

I took a .45 from the bunker. It was the only thing I could find.

I didn't tell the others. I didn't have to. They *knew*. We weren't the thing we'd once been, Major, but they *knew*.

There weren't any guards at the flap and there wasn't much light inside either. A single bulb hung on a wire over the table where Bucannon sat. His suit was dirty. In the yellow light of the bulb that swayed a little over his table, it looked *very* dirty.

He sat there, not moving, like someone thinking.

I walk toward him, Major, and his face is shadowed by the bulb swaying a little just above his head. He hears me, I'm sure, but he doesn't bother to turn. I keep walking.

I'm close enough to touch him. The barrel of the .45 is heavy, pulling.

When he turns around, it's slow. He looks up slowly. Even in the shadows—even in this bad light—I can see his face.

I can see his *eyes*.

They're burning. That's the only way I know to say it.

They're *burning*, Major.

I'd never seen eyes like those. Like the *burning* of the bodies Willie had seen, as he watched them walk toward death. Like us even, floating above the dike, making a whole *sky* burn that way.

They were burning with all the things they'd seen.

"You'll do it to them, too, won't you?" I say. He knows what I mean. He's seen it, too, because we've shown him.

"You'll take them just like you took us, Father, and do it to them, too."

He sees the gun. He wonders why he didn't see it before. He looks at it. He looks back up at my face. It's difficult, very difficult, for him to think, I know. With all the things he's seen—the things he never even imagined—it's difficult for him to *think*. He needs a little time, so I give him some.

When he's finished, when he finally understands why I might be here tonight, he doesn't say, "Mary, *please*. I'm not the person I was once." He doesn't say, "I gave *you* another chance. Won't you give me the same?" He doesn't say: "Oh my God. If I'd only *known*. . . ."

Instead, he says:

"*Do it, please.*"

I don't understand it. I tell myself: *He knows you. He knows you too well. He knows you'll stand here with a gun in your hand thinking you can do it when you really can't. You're a nurse, you're a daughter, and you can't. He wants you to admit it—to stop lying to yourself—that's why he said it. He knows us all so well. . . .*

"*Do it,*" he says again.

And I see how wrong I am.

The voice is pleading. It's saying: *Put the barrel in my mouth, Mary. Send the bullet to me. Do it now.*

It is saying:

Let me go. Please.

The toothpaste smell is gone. There's another now—a smell like an old man's breath. The hair is dirty. The hands are shaking. He's waiting.

I don't have to do it, I tell myself. He'll be like this forever, I know. He'll never have our children now.

You don't have to kill him.

I know.

I've turned to leave. The barrel of the .45 is aimed at the earth, the earth is pulling, and I've turned around to go.

I remember a dream.

It wasn't a lie, I realize. I thought it was when I told it to him, the night I tried, but it wasn't. It wasn't a lie. It was a dream like all the others.

The holes in his chest as they rush him to Saigon. The suction pump. The IV that won't do any good. Holes a little bigger than a 9-millimeter.

The nice white suit, dirty now. The man kneeling on the earth of his tent, asking for something. Pieces of his skull.

You didn't know, Mary.

We never do.

Is it life or is it death that shows us best what it means to be living, Lieutenant? Bach would say to me now. *Is it the dream of a park, or is it the bullets that take that dream away?*

Is it the light, Lieutenant, or is it the darkness where the light shines brightest that lets us really see our God?

Is it the ones we save or the ones we kill, Lieutenant, who tell us whether we are worth saving?

I look at the eyes, how they burn, and I remember a boy. I remember seeing him in all the other things we saw as we floated over a river, and later, over a long black wall.

His room in his parents' house in Wisconsin in the winter. The things he did there by himself. The things he loved. The curiosity in his eyes. The woman who loved him and let him be— *because that was all right.* The order he needed to be happy— *which was all right, too, wasn't it?*

"We forget," I tell him. "We forget where it began, Colonel."

I can *feel* what that woman felt for him. I can *feel* what other women felt later. I can *feel:*

It isn't really his fault.

I can feel for a moment the feelings they felt.

So I go ahead.

I stop the *burning.*

I put the barrel to his mouth. I make his skull come apart.

Chapter 51

They could've killed me. They could have killed the chief. They could've gotten one or two of us, I know. The thing we'd become at Dong Noi was gone. When I killed him, Major, it could end. I know that now. We could stop being what we'd become.

Bucannon would have understood. "There is no talent that does not operate out of the psychological needs of the individual," he would say. "You dreamed of death in the hope of stopping it, Mary. We both knew that. When you killed a man to save him, it could end, the dreams could stop, your gift could return to the darkness where it lay for a million years—so unneeded in civilization, in times of peace, in the humdrum existence of teenagers in Long Beach, California, where fathers believed their daughters to be whores or lesbians if they went to war to keep others safe. What you became could sleep again. Am I right?"

They could have given me a frontal and put me in a military hospital like the man in '46, who had evidence that Roosevelt knew about Pearl Harbor before it happened. They could have sent word down to have me pushed from a chopper on the way back to Saigon, or given me an overdose, or assigned me to a black op I'd never come back from. But they didn't.

They didn't because of what Steve and the chief and the captain and others at the camp said. They said: "You'll have to kill *us* if you kill her." They said: "You can't put her in jail. You can't hide her and throw away the key. You can't fuck with her head. If you do any of these things, there will be stories in the press and court trials and a bigger mess than My Lai ever was. That's a real promise."

Seventy-five talents were saying this, so the agency listened.

But I said: "It's okay." I said I really wanted to get away, to think about things, to get some rest and do some thinking, and that if they needed *someone* to put away for a while, that was okay.

I kept telling Steve this and finally he said, "Okay, Mary . . . okay." Then he said: "You can put her in *a hospital*—but only as long as she wants to be there. You can do this only because *she* wants it, because she's been through a lot, because she wants to think about things. If you hurt her, if you allow her to be hurt by others—drugs or instruments of any kind—we will *know* it. You *know* we will. And we'll do more to hurt you than you've ever dreamed."

I'm here for a year, that's all. There are ten other women in this wing. We get along fine—it's like a club. We talk a lot, sure. We tell each other what we're going to do when we get out—in the Big PX again.

Steve comes to see me. He's married now—to the one in Merced. They've got a baby, but he spends the money to fly down here, and he says she doesn't mind. He says the world hasn't turned blue since he got back, except maybe twice, real fast, on freeways in central California. He says he hasn't floated out of his body again—except once—when Kathy was having the baby and it started to come out wrong. *It's fading now,* he says. He says it with a laugh—with those big eyelashes and those great shoulders of his.

No. That isn't true, Major. He married her in another world, one where we never did the things we did.

The others come, too—to make sure I'm okay. Most of them left as soon as they could. They send me packages now. They bring me things. We talk about the mess this country is in. We talk about getting together, right after I get out. I don't know if they mean it. I don't know if we should. I tell Steve it's over, that we're back in the Big PX now, that we don't *need* it anymore—and even if we did, Steve, how could we ever find it again? Bucannon was right, I tell him. It's sleeping. We shouldn't get together at all.

He shakes his head. He gives me a look and I give him a look and we both know we should have used the room that night in Cam Ranh Bay, too.

"You never know," he says, grinning—those eyelashes, those shoulders. "You never know when the baby might wake up."

That's the way he talks these days, now that he's a father.

It isn't true, Major.

He married her in another world. I know he did. One where I did kill Bucannon with a needle, because the captain wasn't there, because he died at Ap Lao his second year. One where we never went to Vientiane, or saw the lights of the boulevard there, never bought ponies or walked beside them in the rain, and never saw the eyes of children watching us through holes in woven walls.

In *this* world, Major, Steve's waiting for me. I know he is.

He comes to see me. We sit for hours in my room.

We never say, "It's sleeping, Mary." Or "Do you think, Steve, it will ever wake?"

We don't say a thing, Major.

We don't use words at all.

Chapter 52

Collateral Intelligence, HUMINT, Operation Orangutan EVAL
(Cleared for Intra-Agency Use)

*SFC Frederik Hogan, 905347850, 8th Army Security Agency,
Tape 1 Transcript*

The year after I left the Nam I spent as a fire fighter in Detroit. What you're asking me about didn't start happening until then. I saw more action in one week in the Motor City than I did the entire year at Cam Ranh Bay. I'd wake up two or three minutes before the bell rang. It probably doesn't sound that impressive, but when it happens to you enough times, it gets your attention. A lot of injuries occur before you even get to a fire—when you're half asleep. I'd be ready a couple of minutes before the bell went off, so I avoided some injuries that way. I didn't fall off the pole. I didn't fall off the truck, the way some guys do. There was never a false alarm. I mean, I never got that *feeling* unless there really was a fire. I reenlisted. I guess I already said that. I didn't do it to get back to war. I did it to get out of Detroit—to get back to Cam Ranh Bay. Those beaches, that incredible blue South China Sea. It wasn't like a war at all.

*PFC Dennis McAvoy, 259547069, 2d Battalion, 12th Cavalry
(Airmobile), Tape 2 Transcript*

I didn't work for a while after Nam. I didn't do much of anything. I came back to Taft, where my mother lived, where I'd grown up, and that was probably the wrong thing to do. I couldn't talk to anyone. I'd try to. I'd find some old friends and we'd start talking and they'd say, "How many guys did you kill?" I'd start to tell them and they'd just look away. They didn't care. I'd be drunk and I'd drive home to get one of the guns in the house and my mother would have to stop me. She'd stand in the doorway and start crying. I didn't want to do that to her but I was angry. I thought a lot about going back to Nam, how I'd be happier there, but that seemed a little crazy, too.

I didn't have any more of those experiences you want to know about *after* I left the service. I didn't have any more of them after I got home. I didn't think about them either. They were part of the war, and that was over.

One day I'm watching television in the house. I had a job with a nursery, but I wasn't going to it—I was hanging around the house all day. It's a *Twilight Zone* show—you know, that kind. It's about a soldier in World War II or Korea—I don't remember which—who knows when his friends are going to die. My mother comes in for something, the way she does, and it doesn't even register that she's standing there by the sofa, that she hasn't gone out again. I'm stoned—I've had a couple of beers—and I don't even know she's been standing there the whole time.

I look up and I say "Hi." I don't know what else to do. I ask her if she wants to sit down with me. It's real lame, but I really don't know what else to do. We haven't talked in a long, long time. She just stands there looking at the television set.

When the show's over, she sits down on the sofa right beside me. Suddenly she's telling me about my father, how it was the same for him in World War II as it was for the guy on television. How my father *knew* where the safe places were to step, and some-times even who was going to die. It was the Big Red One, I know. It was Sicily, Italy and North Africa and he always tried to get people to listen, but no one would, she said.

She's crying. I get up and give her a hug. I don't know why she's crying and I don't even know why I'm giving her a hug. I haven't hugged her in a long time, I know. I really want to tell her what Nam was like, the experiences I had there, but I don't know how to do it. I haven't been a very good son, I know. I want to tell her that, too.

A few weeks later we're at the dinner table, just the two of us, and I go ahead. I just stand up and tell her. I tell her everything.

1st Lt. Deborah Frey, 118303529, Army Nurse Corps, Tape 4 Transcript

When I got back to The World, I left the Army but I stayed in nursing. I didn't know what else to do. I was having problems and was seeing a counselor, but he didn't understand it any better than I did. I remember trying a veteran's group a few times, but they didn't know what to do with me either. [Laughs] Some of the guys were well-meaning, but some were so angry they'd come up to you and say, "You couldn't possibly understand. You're a *woman*." Or "You have *absolutely* no idea what we're feeling, ma'am." I went two or three times and then stopped. I didn't know there were other women out there who were feeling the same thing.

I got the training I needed for infant ICU—something I'd always wanted to do. I'd done a little work at that orphanage outside Da Nang, but other than that I'd really never had a chance to work with children. I knew I didn't want to work with adult patients anymore. I did know that.

One of my first ICU patients was this very ill baby who was dying of herpes. She was being given all kinds of experimental drugs. They had her on a Sechrist ventilator—which means very high pressures, very high rates, and of course oxygen. What I felt for this little girl was special, I knew. She'd been so beautiful when they first brought her in, but during the course of this disease she'd lost all of her beauty. That was something I could understand. She was very contagious, too, and no one really wanted to be with her.

I was on my way to lunch that day—that was two floors down from the ICU nursery—when this scream, this baby's scream, went through me. It was only in my mind, but I could see which baby it was—I could see the little girl clearly. I could see the ventilator recycling to maximum and staying there, and no one knowing it. I could see her lungs expanding like a balloon, and then, like a balloon, exploding. I ran as hard as I could to the ward and broke isolation and managed to grab her from the machine. At that moment the Sechrist did it—did what I'd seen. It cycled to maximum, stayed there and began to alarm. Like it had in my little daydream. While I hand-bagged her someone else brought a new machine. She never got the breath from the machine that would have killed her. That's what I'm trying to say.

Later I told everyone I'd heard the machine make a funny noise—that that was why I'd run in. But it wasn't true. It was Long Binh—the flashes, the daydreams—all over again. It was going to happen here, too, I knew.

That little girl recovered and went home and is living a normal life now. I think of her a lot. I think of her as my "dream baby"—the one I was able to save with a dream.

Letter of transmittal, Charles S. Narda, M.D. (Colonel, USAR), to the Office of the DDP

On the basis of investigations conducted by this team from March to November of this year, *Operation Orangutan EVAL* recommends against continuation of *Operation Orangutan*. Our several reasons are detailed in the attached report. Qualifications of a replacement for the director, it should be noted, are not at issue, and the team are unanimous in their recommendation. If further documents in support of our conclusions would be helpful, do not hesitate to let us know.

(in pen)
Bill—
Majors Carlyle and Streiber have done an outstanding job on the interviews. Let's make sure Innes hears.
C.N.

Epilogue

Letter 2/12/68, to President Le Duan, Democratic Republic of Vietnam, Hanoi, care of Michel Planchat, Moderator, Paris Peace Talks

The White House
Washington
February 12, 1968

The Honorable Le Duan
The Democratic Republic of Vietnam
Hanoi

Dear Mr. Duan:

I was pleased to learn from Mr. Hollander that you have held useful and constructive discussions with him in Vinh in preparation for his meeting with your representatives in Paris. We join the rest of the world in hoping that the recovery of Hanoi and of the Song Hong Ha Delta from the tragic dike failure near Dong Noi and subsequent catastrophic flooding will be a speedy one.

I understand from Mr. Hollander and from your own letter of January 29 that your principal remaining concern with respect to the draft treaty is economic aid during and after recovery. Let me assure you that we are looking forward, once agreement on the new treaty is reached, to thorough discussions of how the United

States might help in the North's recovery and, just as importantly, in the general effort of reunification of your proud country.

Sincerely,

John F. Kennedy

Copy: His Excellency Nguyen Van Thieu
     President of the Republic of Vietnam
     Saigon